THE
SHADOW OUT OF
TIME

First published 2013
by SelfMadeHero
5 Upper Wimpole Street
London W1G 6BP
www.selfmadehero.com

Illustrator and Adaptor: I.N.J. Culbard
Cover Designer: I.N.J. Culbard
Editorial & Production Manager: Lizzie Kaye
Sales & Marketing Manager: Sam Humphrey
Publishing Director: Emma Hayley
With thanks to: Dan Lockwood, Nick de Somogyi and Jane Laporte

Dedication
For Katy, Joseph and Benjamin
— I. N. J. Culbard

A CIP record for this book is available from the British Library

ISBN: 978-1-906838-68-3

10 9 8 7 6 5 4 3 2 1

Printed and bound in China

THE SHADOW OUT OF TIME

ADAPTED FROM THE ORIGINAL NOVEL BY
H.P. LOVECRAFT
TEXT ADAPTED AND ILLUSTRATED BY
I.N.J. CULBARD

SELF MADE HERO

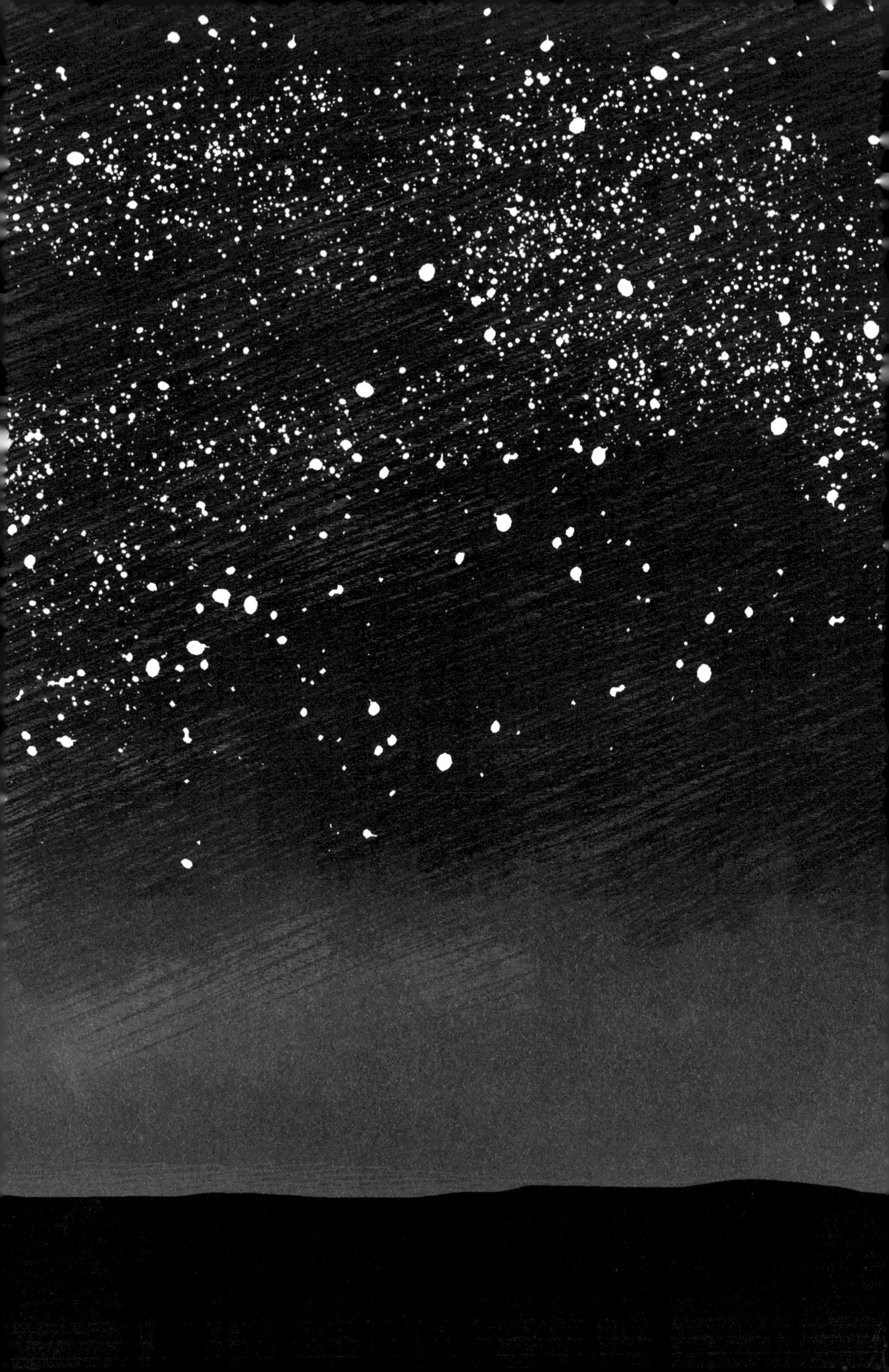

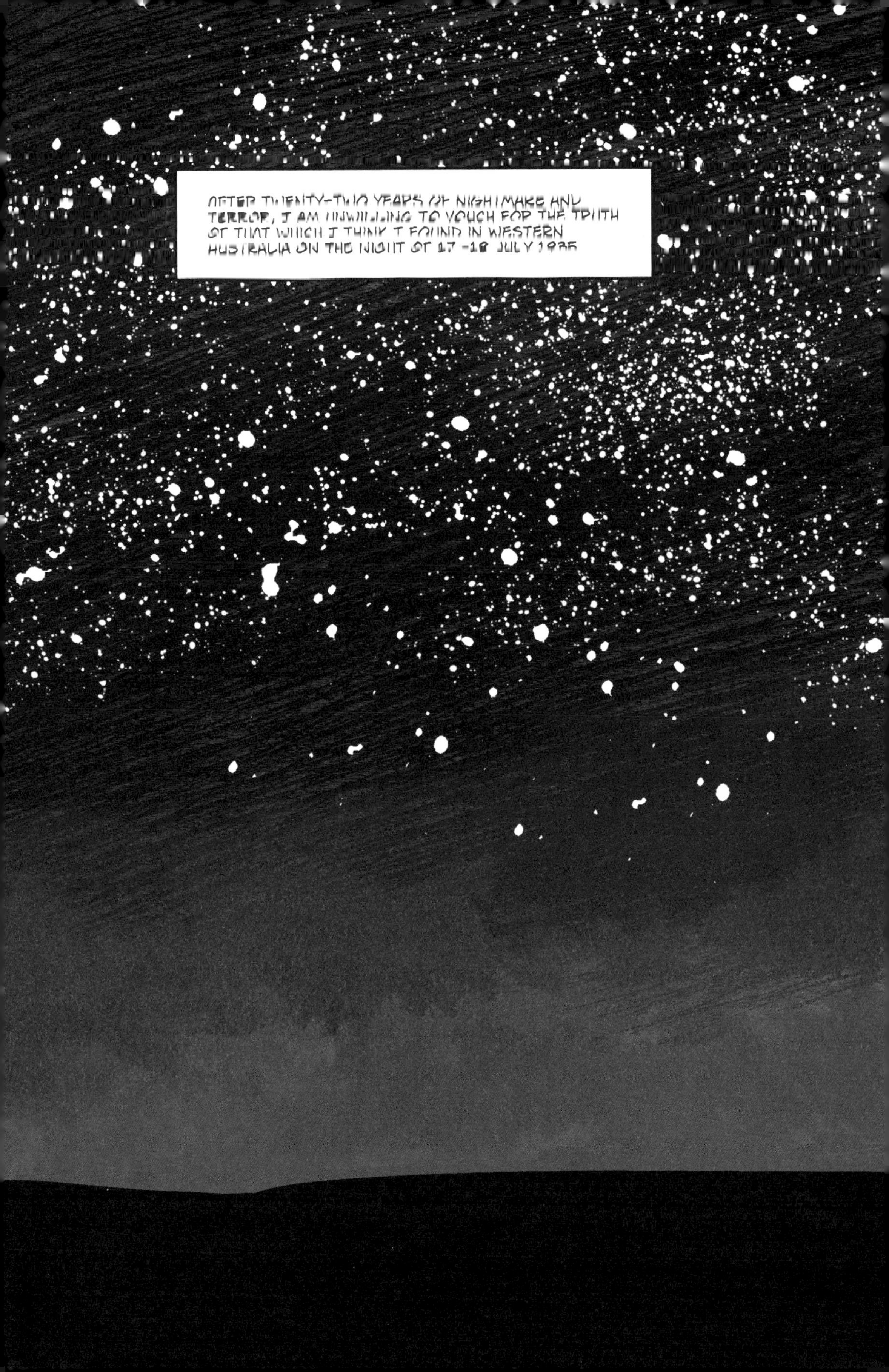
AFTER TWENTY-TWO YEARS OF NIGHTMARE AND TERROR, I AM UNWILLING TO VOUCH FOR THE TRUTH OF THAT WHICH I THINK I FOUND IN WESTERN AUSTRALIA ON THE NIGHT OF 17 -18 JULY 1935

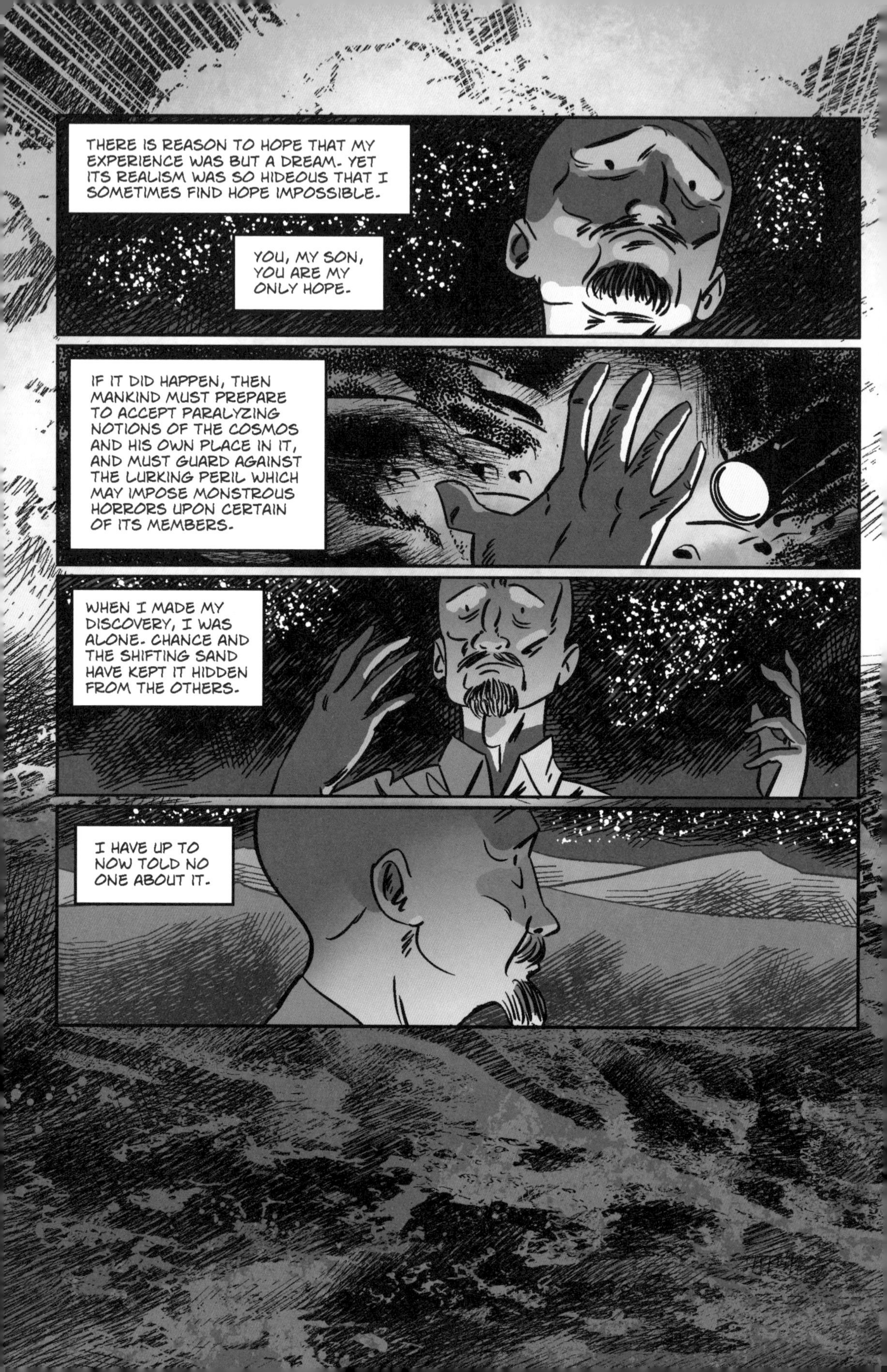
THERE IS REASON TO HOPE THAT MY EXPERIENCE WAS BUT A DREAM. YET ITS REALISM WAS SO HIDEOUS THAT I SOMETIMES FIND HOPE IMPOSSIBLE.
YOU, MY SON, YOU ARE MY ONLY HOPE.
IF IT DID HAPPEN, THEN MANKIND MUST PREPARE TO ACCEPT PARALYZING NOTIONS OF THE COSMOS AND HIS OWN PLACE IN IT, AND MUST GUARD AGAINST THE LURKING PERIL WHICH MAY IMPOSE MONSTROUS HORRORS UPON CERTAIN OF ITS MEMBERS.
WHEN I MADE MY DISCOVERY, I WAS ALONE. CHANCE AND THE SHIFTING SAND HAVE KEPT IT HIDDEN FROM THE OTHERS.
I HAVE UP TO NOW TOLD NO ONE ABOUT IT.

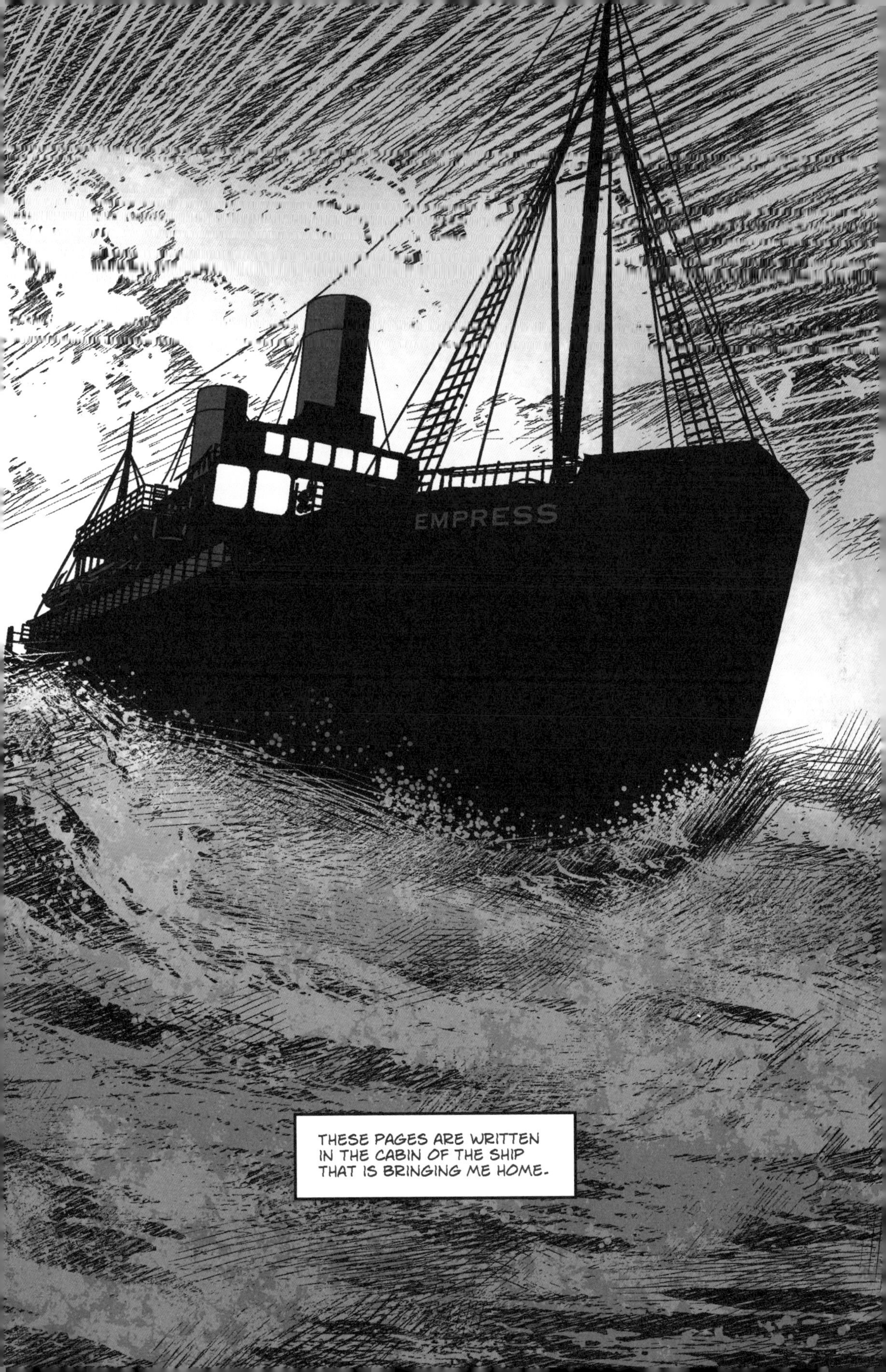
EMPRESS
THESE PAGES ARE WRITTEN IN THE CABIN OF THE SHIP THAT IS BRINGING ME HOME.

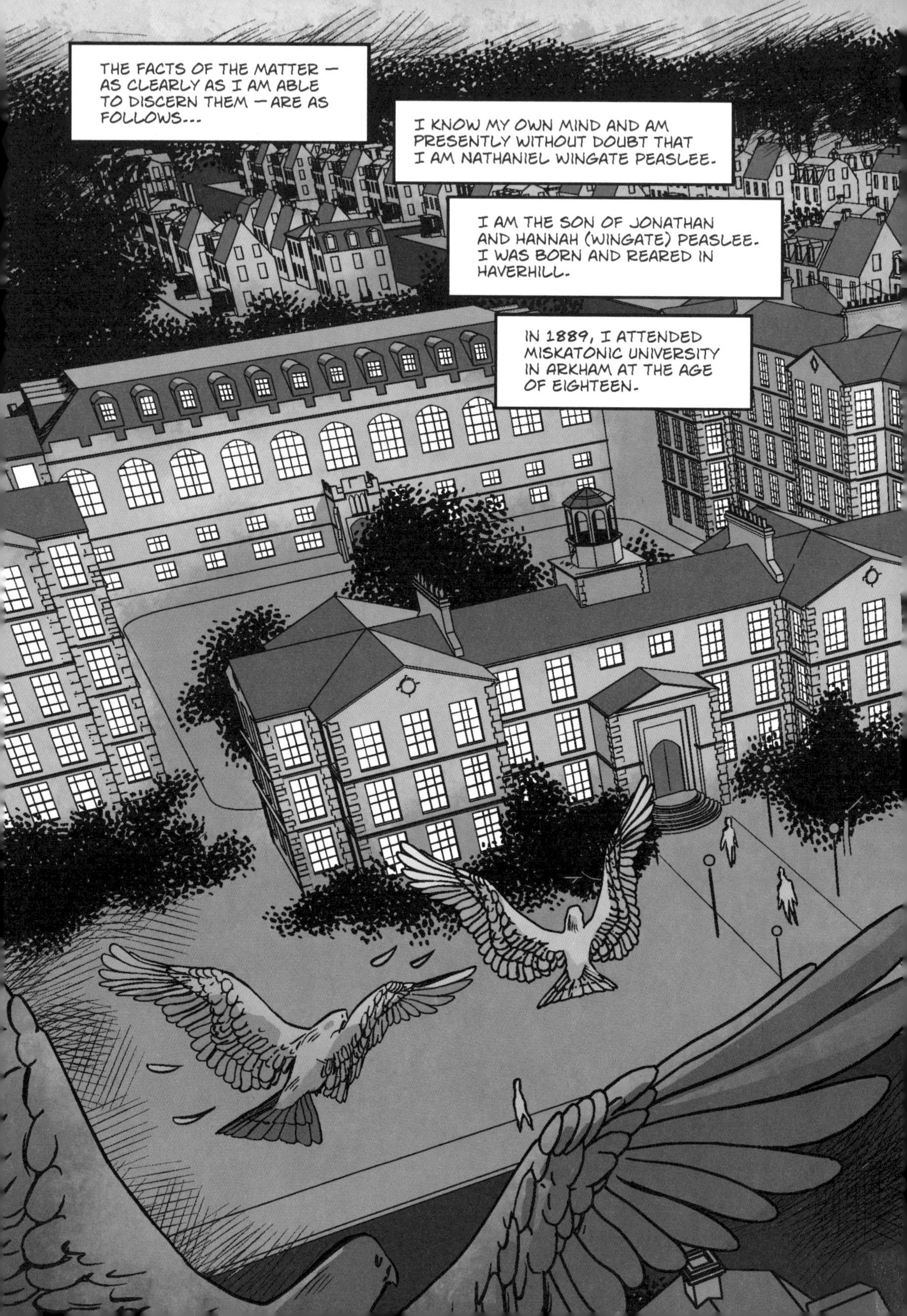
THE FACTS OF THE MATTER — AS CLEARLY AS I AM ABLE TO DISCERN THEM — ARE AS FOLLOWS...
I KNOW MY OWN MIND AND AM PRESENTLY WITHOUT DOUBT THAT I AM NATHANIEL WINGATE PEASLEE.
I AM THE SON OF JONATHAN AND HANNAH (WINGATE) PEASLEE. I WAS BORN AND REARED IN HAVERHILL.
IN 1889, I ATTENDED MISKATONIC UNIVERSITY IN ARKHAM AT THE AGE OF EIGHTEEN.

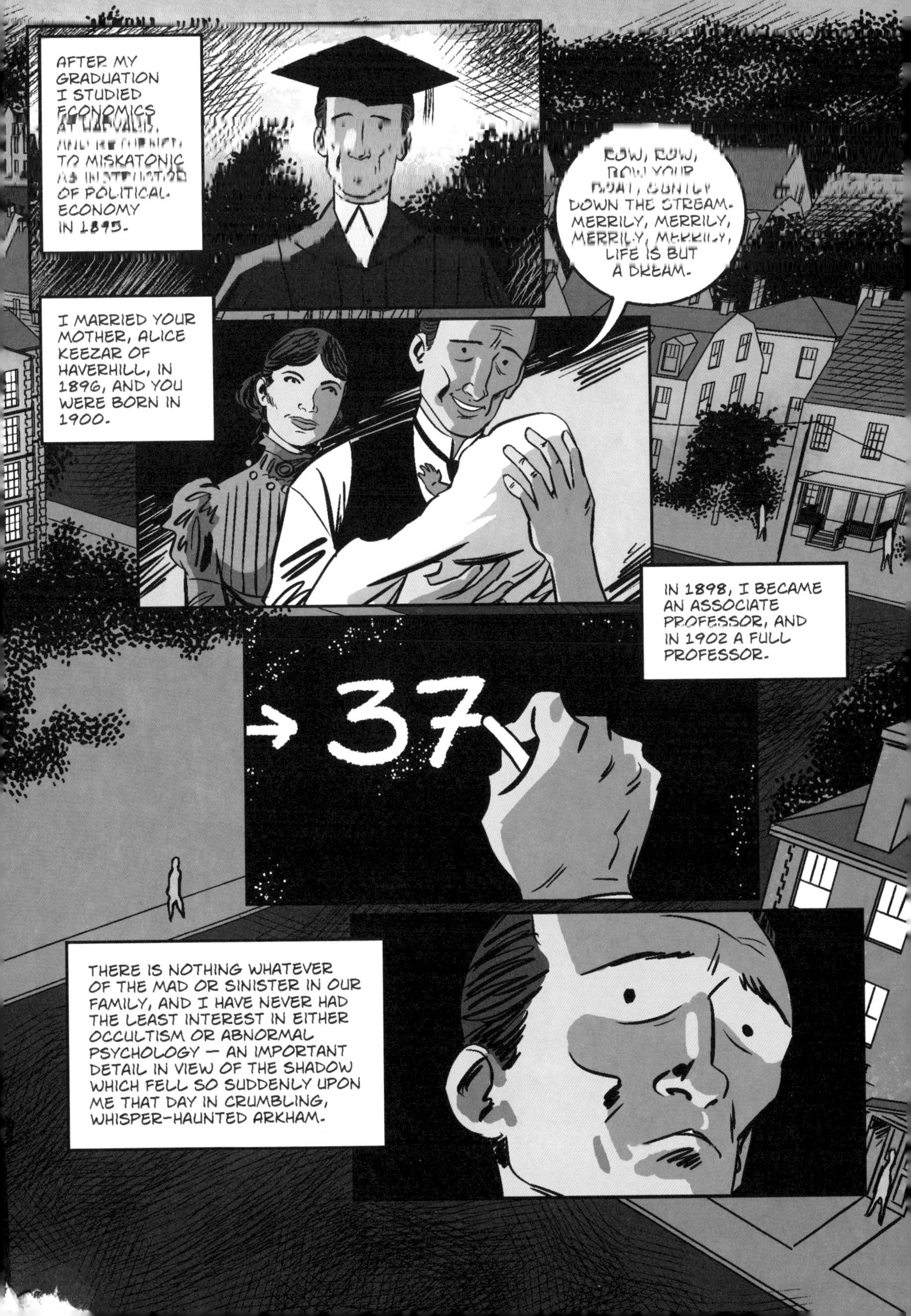
AFTER MY GRADUATION I STUDIED ECONOMICS
TO MISKATONIC
OF POLITICAL ECONOMY IN 1895.
ROW, ROW, ROW YOUR
DOWN THE STREAM. MERRILY, MERRILY, MERRILY, MERRILY, LIFE IS BUT A DREAM.
I MARRIED YOUR MOTHER, ALICE KEEZAR OF HAVERHILL, IN 1896, AND YOU WERE BORN IN 1900.
IN 1898, I BECAME AN ASSOCIATE PROFESSOR, AND IN 1902 A FULL PROFESSOR.
→ 37
THERE IS NOTHING WHATEVER OF THE MAD OR SINISTER IN OUR FAMILY, AND I HAVE NEVER HAD THE LEAST INTEREST IN EITHER OCCULTISM OR ABNORMAL PSYCHOLOGY — AN IMPORTANT DETAIL IN VIEW OF THE SHADOW WHICH FELL SO SUDDENLY UPON ME THAT DAY IN CRUMBLING, WHISPER-HAUNTED ARKHAM.

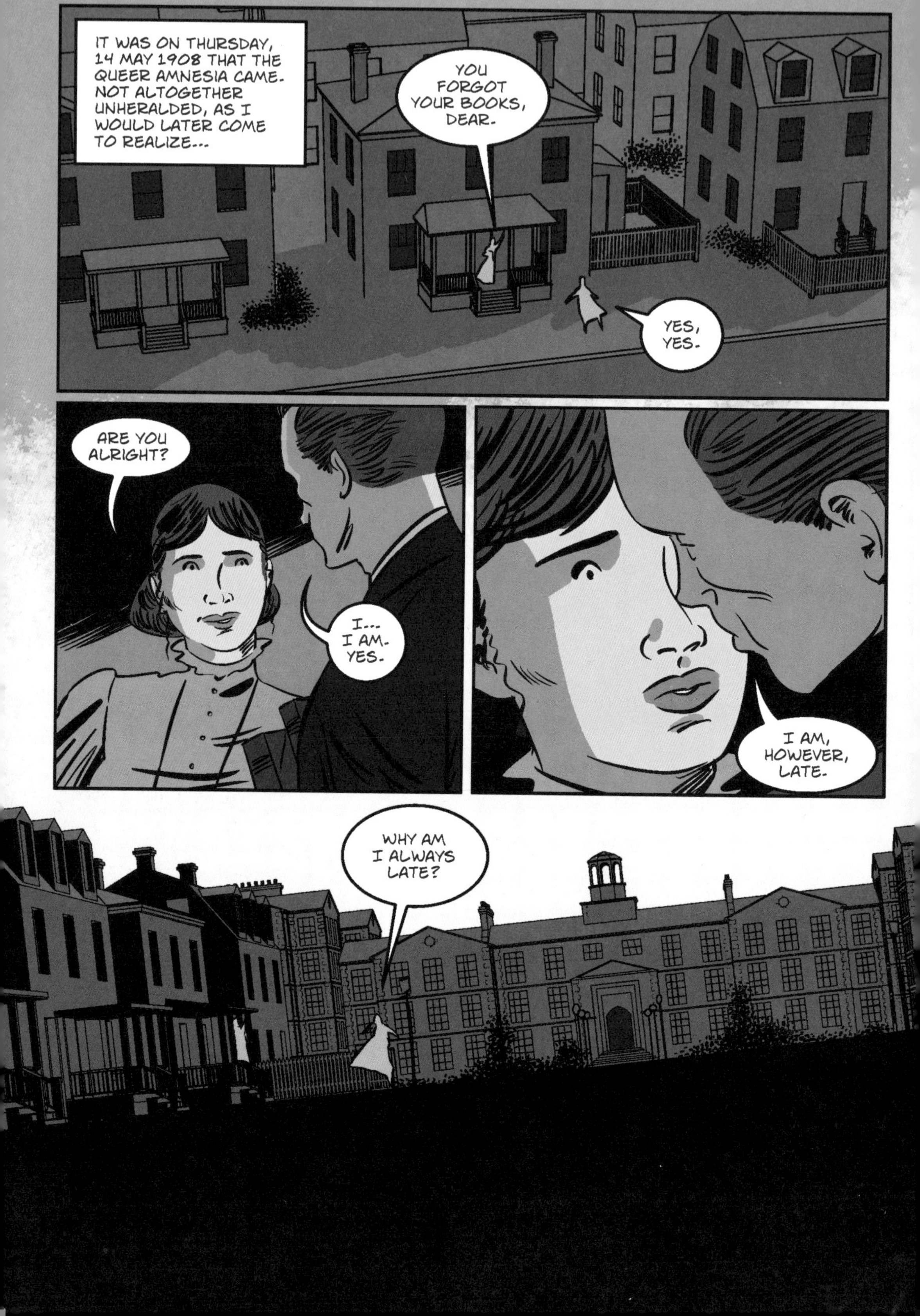
IT WAS ON THURSDAY, 14 MAY 1908 THAT THE QUEER AMNESIA CAME. NOT ALTOGETHER UNHERALDED, AS I WOULD LATER COME TO REALIZE...
YOU FORGOT YOUR BOOKS, DEAR.
YES, YES.
ARE YOU ALRIGHT?
I... I AM. YES.
I AM, HOWEVER, LATE.
WHY AM I ALWAYS LATE?

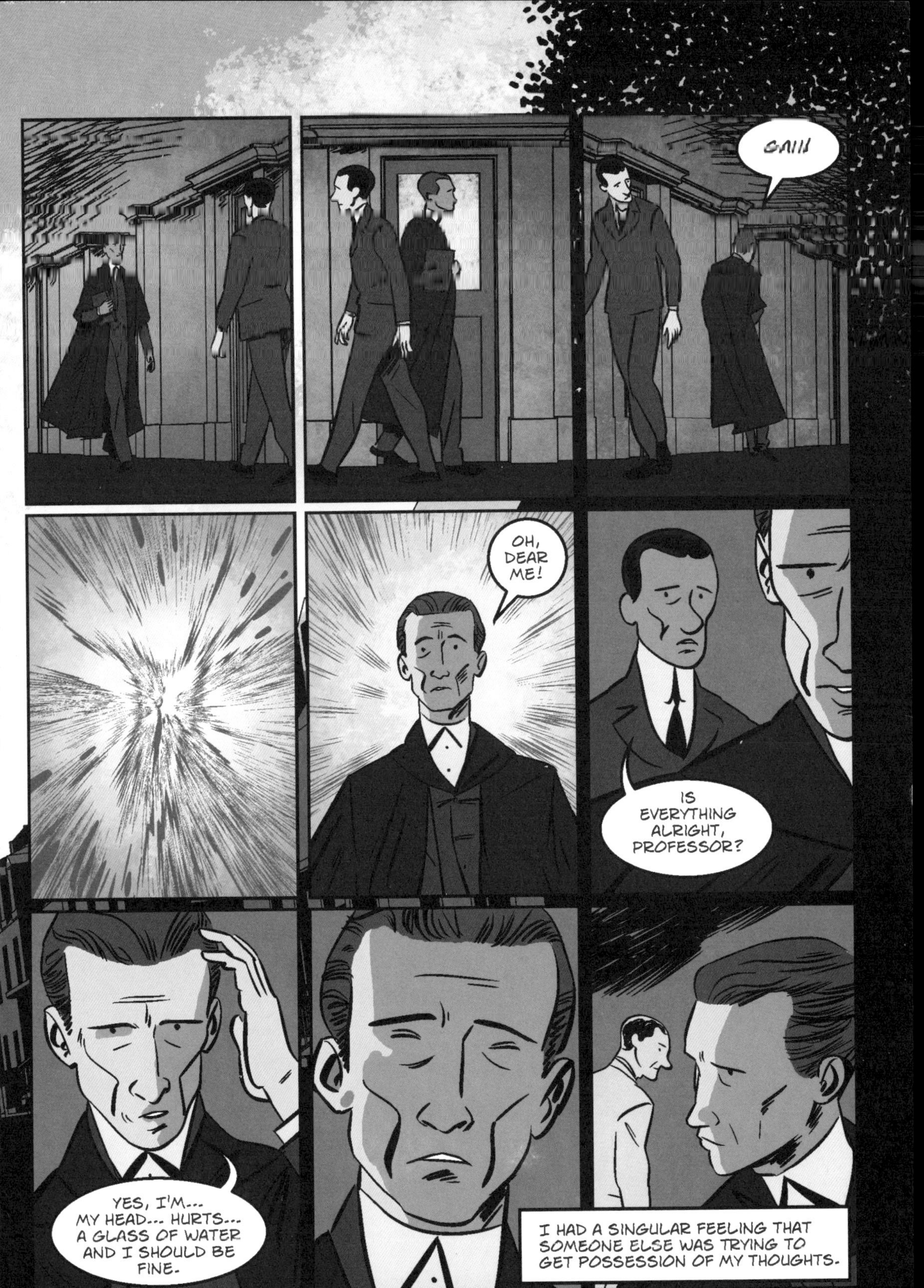
OH, DEAR ME!
IS EVERYTHING ALRIGHT, PROFESSOR?
YES, I'M... MY HEAD... HURTS... A GLASS OF WATER AND I SHOULD BE FINE.
I HAD A SINGULAR FEELING THAT SOMEONE ELSE WAS TRYING TO GET POSSESSION OF MY THOUGHTS.

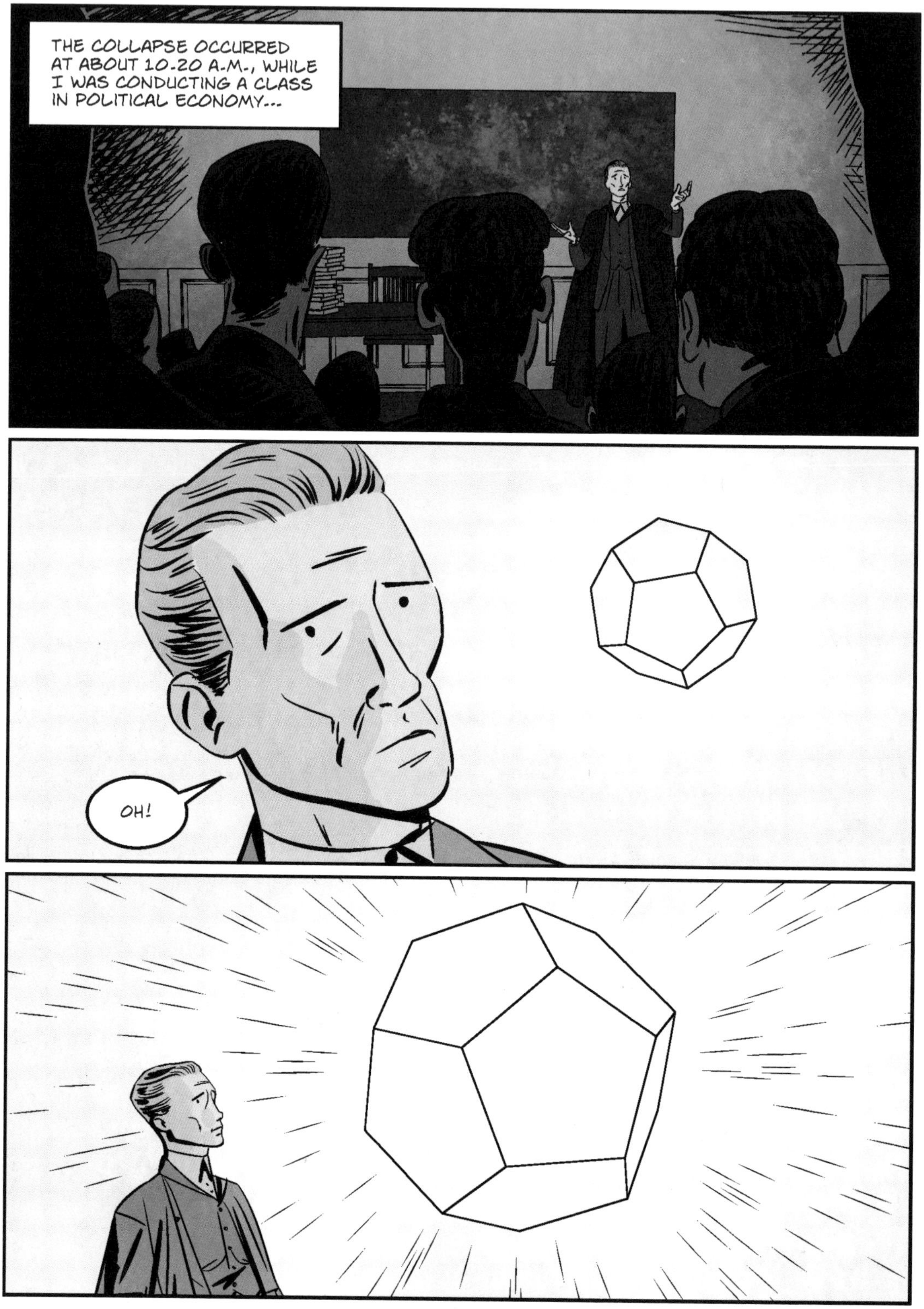
THE COLLAPSE OCCURRED AT ABOUT 10.20 A.M., WHILE I WAS CONDUCTING A CLASS IN POLITICAL ECONOMY...
OH!

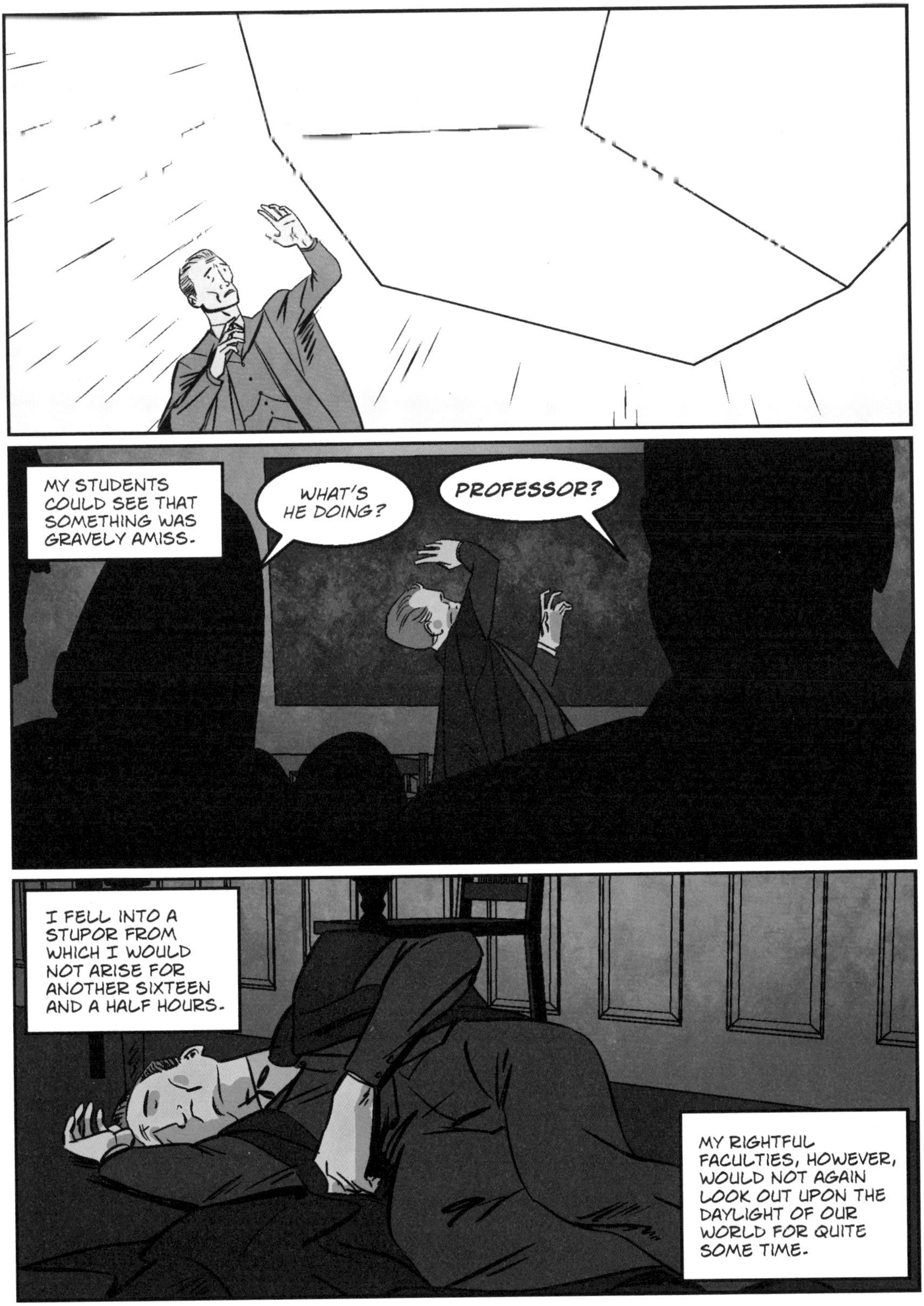
MY STUDENTS COULD SEE THAT SOMETHING WAS GRAVELY AMISS.
WHAT'S HE DOING?
PROFESSOR?
I FELL INTO A STUPOR FROM WHICH I WOULD NOT ARISE FOR ANOTHER SIXTEEN AND A HALF HOURS.
MY RIGHTFUL FACULTIES, HOWEVER, WOULD NOT AGAIN LOOK OUT UPON THE DAYLIGHT OF OUR WORLD FOR QUITE SOME TIME.

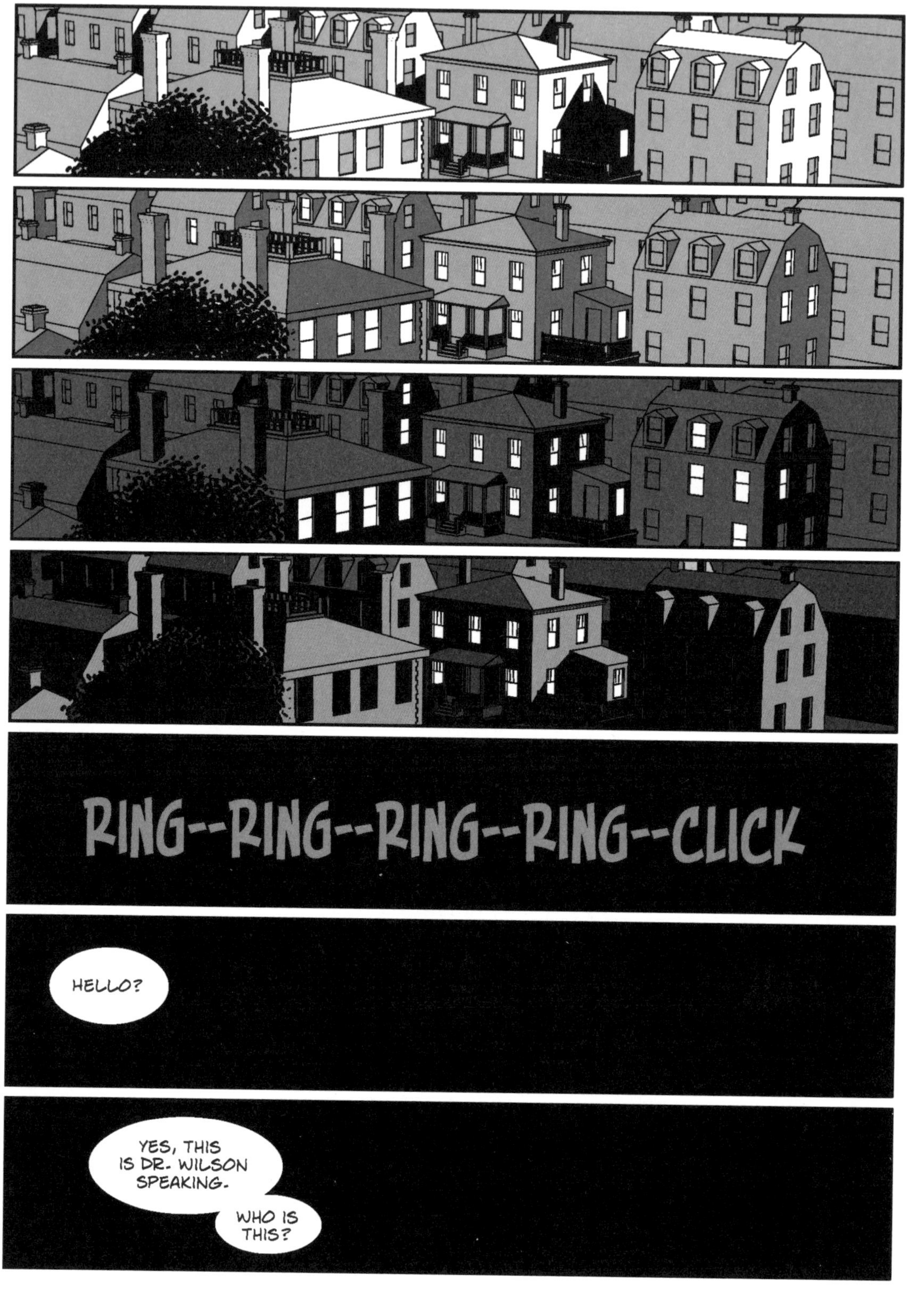
RING--RING--RING--RING--CLICK
HELLO?
YES, THIS IS DR. WILSON SPEAKING.
WHO IS THIS?

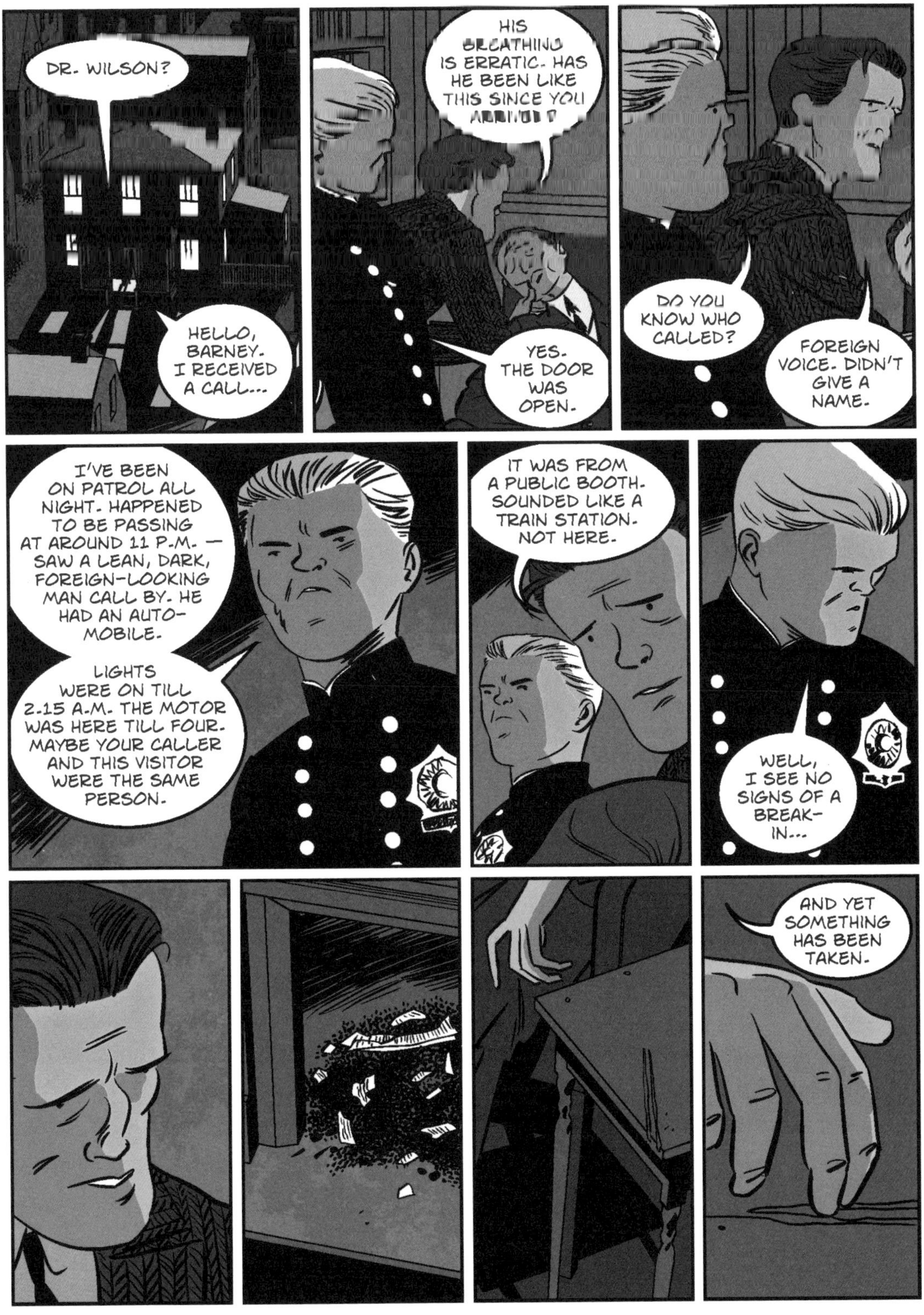
DR. WILSON?
HELLO, BARNEY. I RECEIVED A CALL...
HIS BREATHING IS ERRATIC. HAS HE BEEN LIKE THIS SINCE YOU
YES. THE DOOR WAS OPEN.
DO YOU KNOW WHO CALLED?
FOREIGN VOICE. DIDN'T GIVE A NAME.
I'VE BEEN ON PATROL ALL NIGHT. HAPPENED TO BE PASSING AT AROUND 11 P.M. — SAW A LEAN, DARK, FOREIGN-LOOKING MAN CALL BY. HE HAD AN AUTO-MOBILE.
LIGHTS WERE ON TILL 2.15 A.M. THE MOTOR WAS HERE TILL FOUR. MAYBE YOUR CALLER AND THIS VISITOR WERE THE SAME PERSON.
IT WAS FROM A PUBLIC BOOTH. SOUNDED LIKE A TRAIN STATION. NOT HERE.
WELL, I SEE NO SIGNS OF A BREAK-IN...
AND YET SOMETHING HAS BEEN TAKEN.

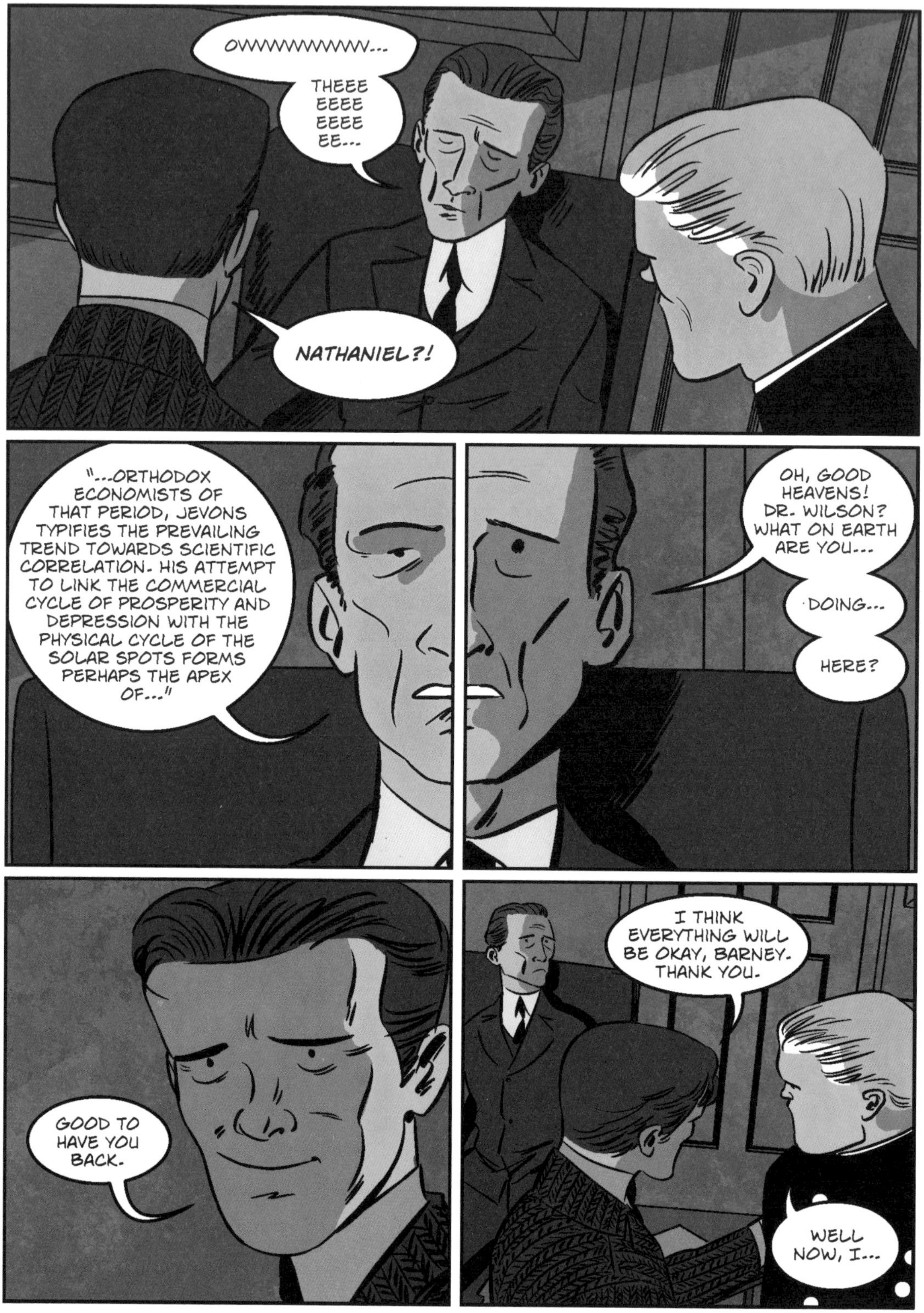
OWWWWWWWWWV...
THEEE EEEE EEEE EE...
NATHANIEL?!
"...ORTHODOX ECONOMISTS OF THAT PERIOD, JEVONS TYPIFIES THE PREVAILING TREND TOWARDS SCIENTIFIC CORRELATION. HIS ATTEMPT TO LINK THE COMMERCIAL CYCLE OF PROSPERITY AND DEPRESSION WITH THE PHYSICAL CYCLE OF THE SOLAR SPOTS FORMS PERHAPS THE APEX OF..."
OH, GOOD HEAVENS! DR. WILSON? WHAT ON EARTH ARE YOU...
DOING...
HERE?
GOOD TO HAVE YOU BACK.
I THINK EVERYTHING WILL BE OKAY, BARNEY. THANK YOU.
WELL NOW, I...

BE REASSURED, I WILL KEEP YOU INFORMED OF ANY DEVELOPMENTS. LIKE ALL OF PROFESSOR PEARSE'S IN MY PATIENTS...

VERY WELL, DOC.

THE LOSS OF FIVE YEARS CREATES MORE COMPLICATIONS THAN YOU CAN IMAGINE, AND IN YOUR CASE THERE ARE COUNTLESS MATTERS TO BE ADJUSTED...

F-FIVE YEARS? I DON'T UNDERSTAND...

NATHANIEL... YOU COLLAPSED IN YOUR ECONOMICS CLASS ON 14 MAY 1908...

IT'S THURSDAY.

IT WAS. IT IS NOW SATURDAY, 27 SEPTEMBER 1913.

WHAT ARE YOU TALKING ABOUT? WHY AM I HERE?

I'M AFRAID THERE'S NO EASY WAY TO TELL YOU THIS...

WHERE'S ALICE? WHERE'S WINGATE? WHAT HAPPENED?

LISTEN TO ME CAREFULLY, NATHANIEL. LISTEN TO ME VERY, VERY CAREFULLY.

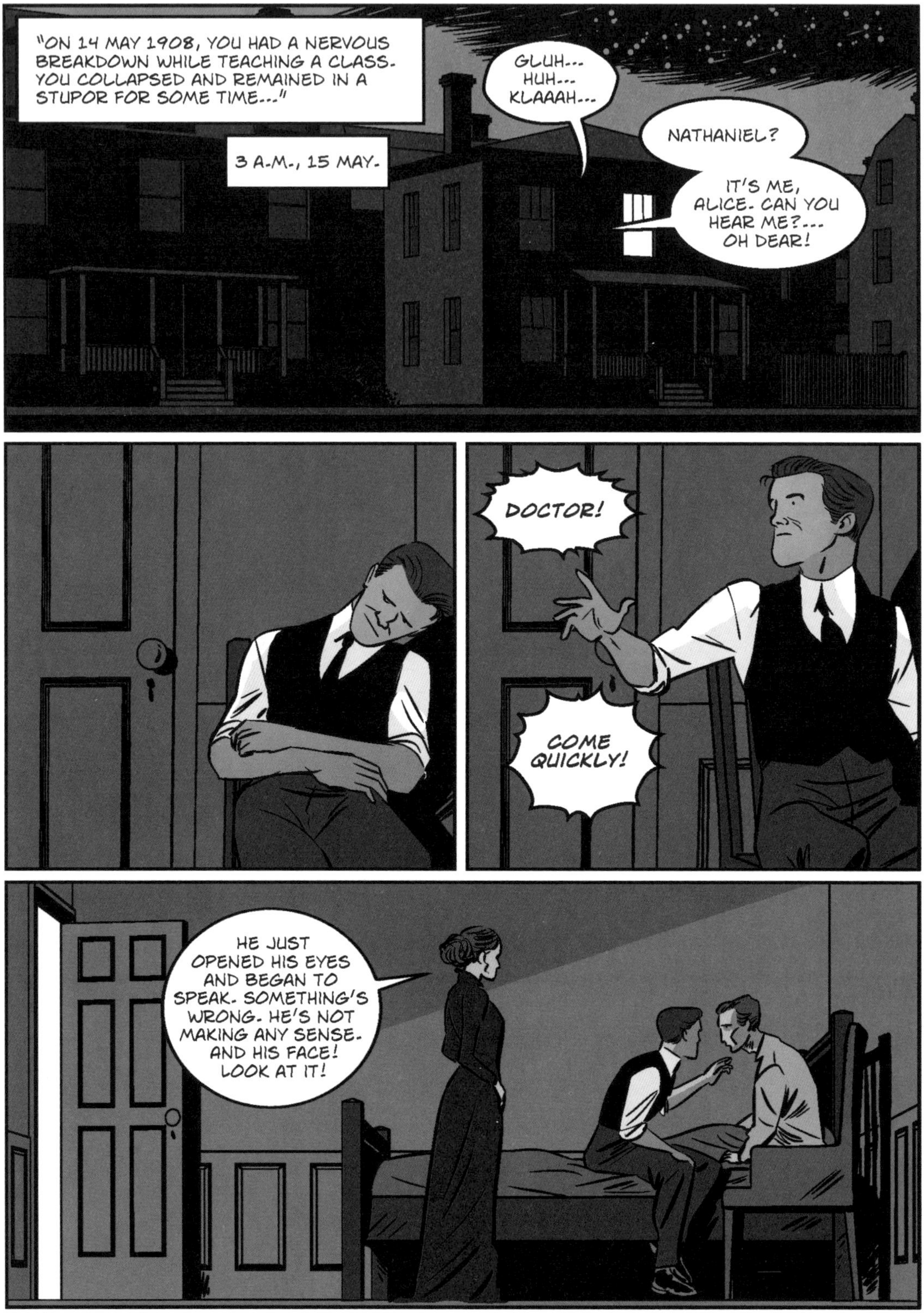
"ON 14 MAY 1908, YOU HAD A NERVOUS BREAKDOWN WHILE TEACHING A CLASS. YOU COLLAPSED AND REMAINED IN A STUPOR FOR SOME TIME..."
3 A.M., 15 MAY.
GLUH... HUH... KLAAAH...
NATHANIEL?
IT'S ME, ALICE. CAN YOU HEAR ME?... OH DEAR!
DOCTOR!
COME QUICKLY!
HE JUST OPENED HIS EYES AND BEGAN TO SPEAK. SOMETHING'S WRONG. HE'S NOT MAKING ANY SENSE. AND HIS FACE! LOOK AT IT!

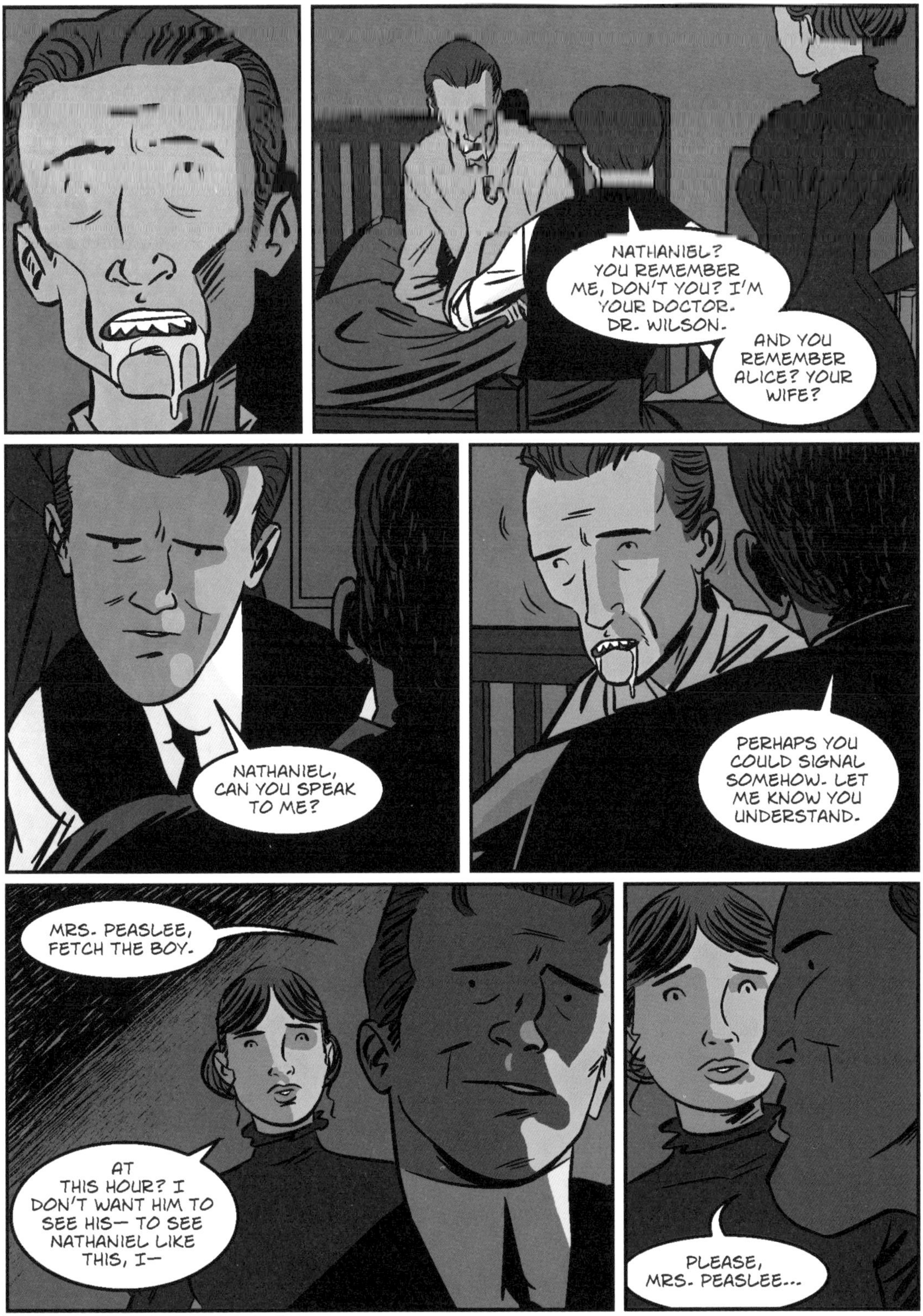
NATHANIEL? YOU REMEMBER ME, DON'T YOU? I'M YOUR DOCTOR. DR. WILSON.
AND YOU REMEMBER ALICE? YOUR WIFE?
NATHANIEL, CAN YOU SPEAK TO ME?
PERHAPS YOU COULD SIGNAL SOMEHOW. LET ME KNOW YOU UNDERSTAND.
MRS. PEASLEE, FETCH THE BOY.
AT THIS HOUR? I DON'T WANT HIM TO SEE HIS— TO SEE NATHANIEL LIKE THIS, I—
PLEASE, MRS. PEASLEE...

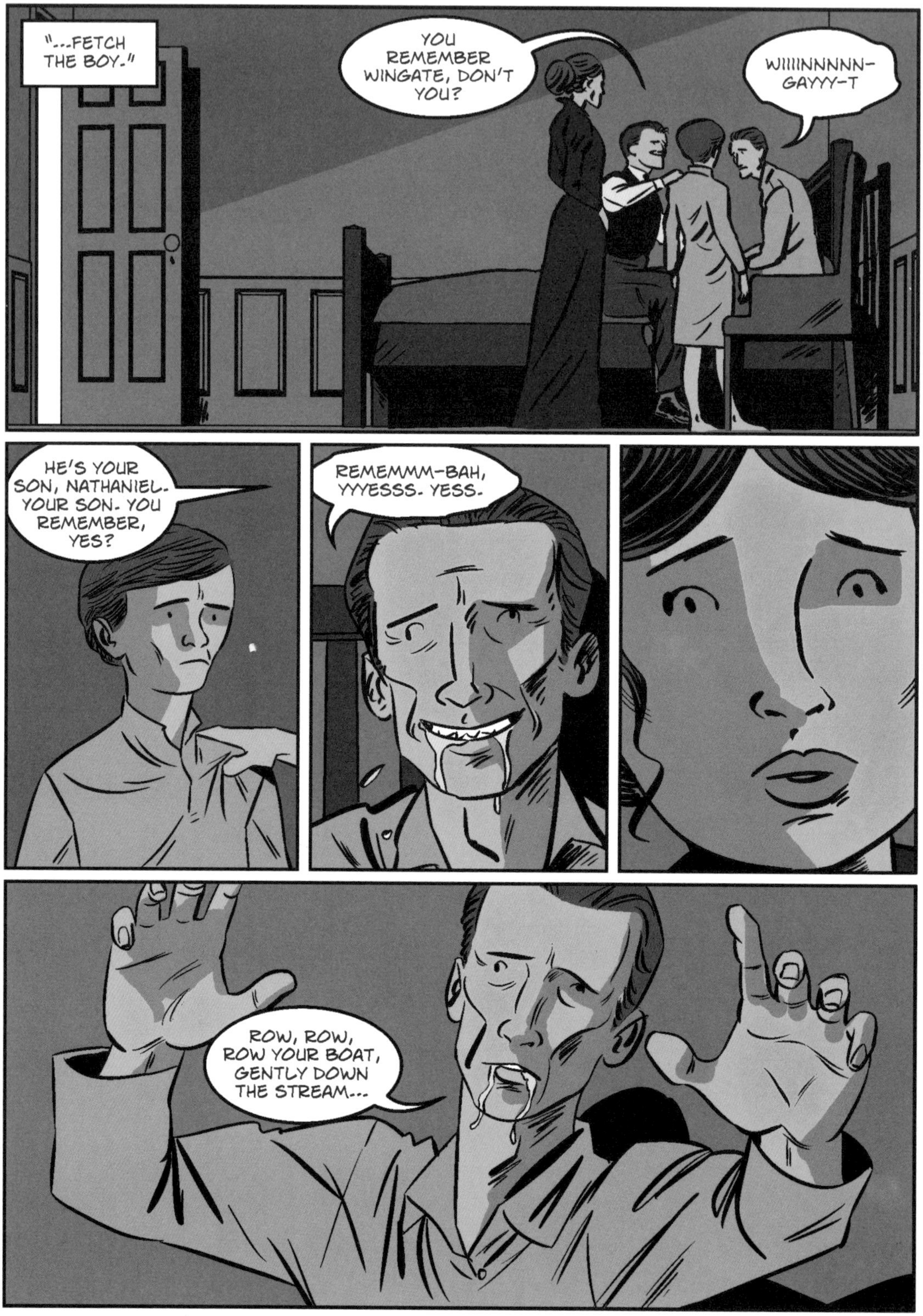
"...FETCH THE BOY."
YOU REMEMBER WINGATE, DON'T YOU?
WIIIINNNNN-GAYYY-T
HE'S YOUR SON, NATHANIEL. YOUR SON. YOU REMEMBER, YES?
REMEMMM-BAH, YYYESSS. YESS.
ROW, ROW, ROW YOUR BOAT, GENTLY DOWN THE STREAM...

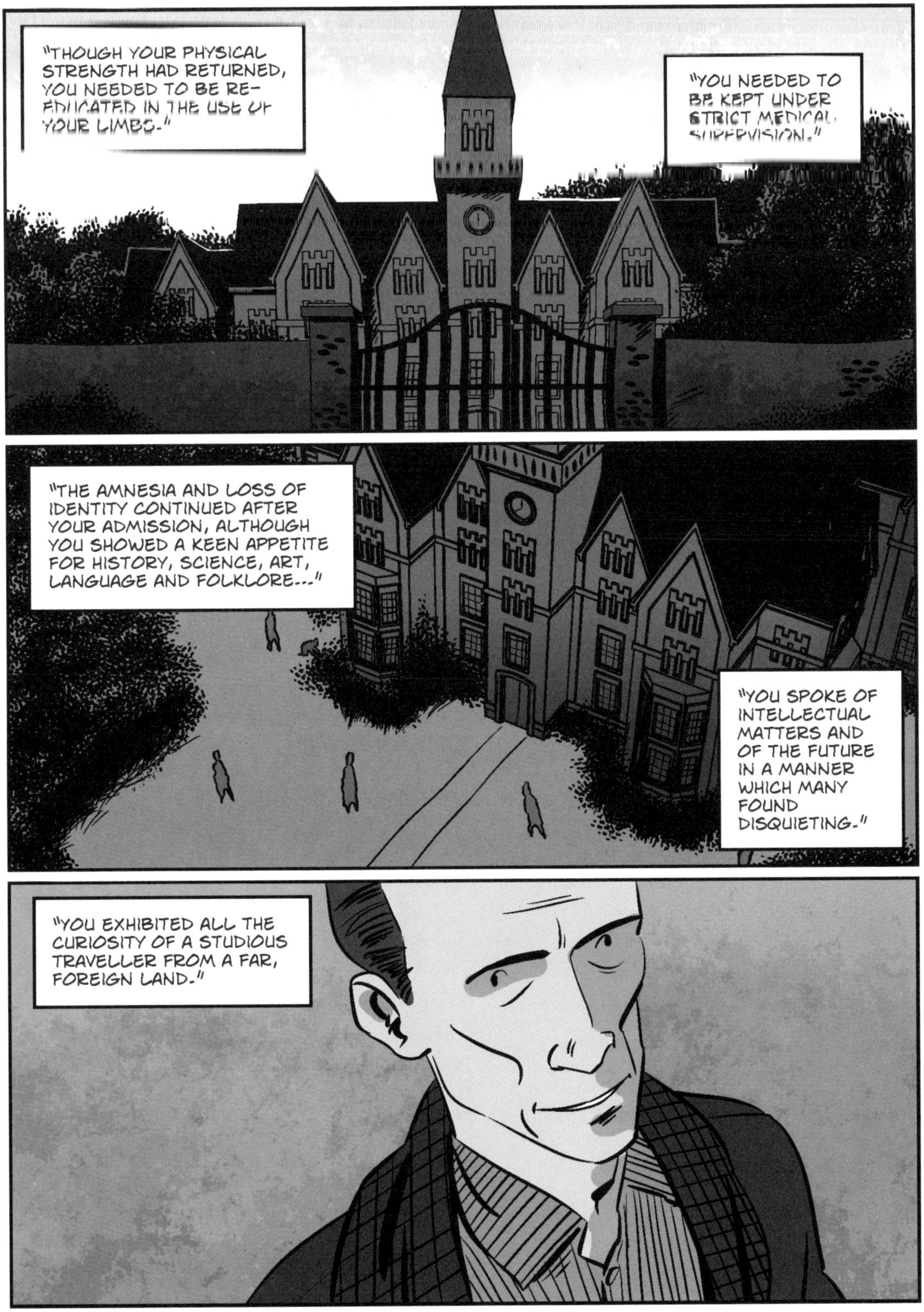
"THOUGH YOUR PHYSICAL STRENGTH HAD RETURNED, YOU NEEDED TO BE RE-EDUCATED IN THE USE OF YOUR LIMBS."
"YOU NEEDED TO BE KEPT UNDER STRICT MEDICAL SUPERVISION."
"THE AMNESIA AND LOSS OF IDENTITY CONTINUED AFTER YOUR ADMISSION, ALTHOUGH YOU SHOWED A KEEN APPETITE FOR HISTORY, SCIENCE, ART, LANGUAGE AND FOLKLORE..."
"YOU SPOKE OF INTELLECTUAL MATTERS AND OF THE FUTURE IN A MANNER WHICH MANY FOUND DISQUIETING."
"YOU EXHIBITED ALL THE CURIOSITY OF A STUDIOUS TRAVELLER FROM A FAR, FOREIGN LAND."

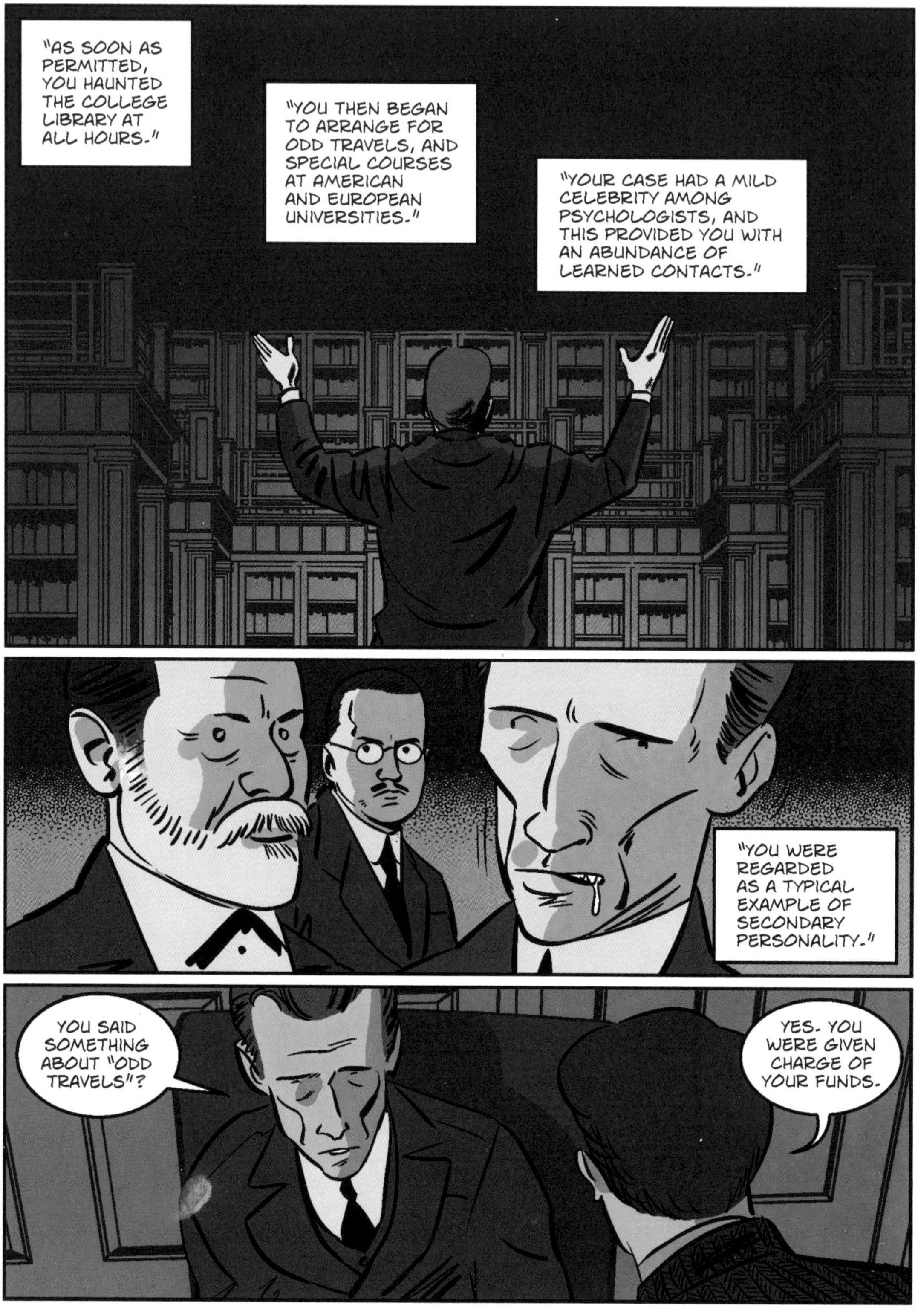
"AS SOON AS PERMITTED, YOU HAUNTED THE COLLEGE LIBRARY AT ALL HOURS."
"YOU THEN BEGAN TO ARRANGE FOR ODD TRAVELS, AND SPECIAL COURSES AT AMERICAN AND EUROPEAN UNIVERSITIES."
"YOUR CASE HAD A MILD CELEBRITY AMONG PSYCHOLOGISTS, AND THIS PROVIDED YOU WITH AN ABUNDANCE OF LEARNED CONTACTS."
"YOU WERE REGARDED AS A TYPICAL EXAMPLE OF SECONDARY PERSONALITY."
YOU SAID SOMETHING ABOUT "ODD TRAVELS"?
YES. YOU WERE GIVEN CHARGE OF YOUR FUNDS.

"IN 1909, YOU SPENT A MONTH IN THE HIMALAYAS."

"IN 1911, YOU TOOK A CAMEL TRIP INTO SOME UNKNOWN REGIONS OF THE ARABIAN DESERT."

"DURING THE SUMMER OF 1912, YOU CHARTERED A SHIP AND SAILED IN THE ARCTIC, NORTH OF SPITZBERGEN. YOU RETURNED QUITE DISAPPOINTED."

WHAT WAS THE PURPOSE OF THESE EXPEDITIONS?

I DON'T KNOW. YOU WERE CERTAINLY NOT FORTHCOMING WITH ANY ACCOUNT.

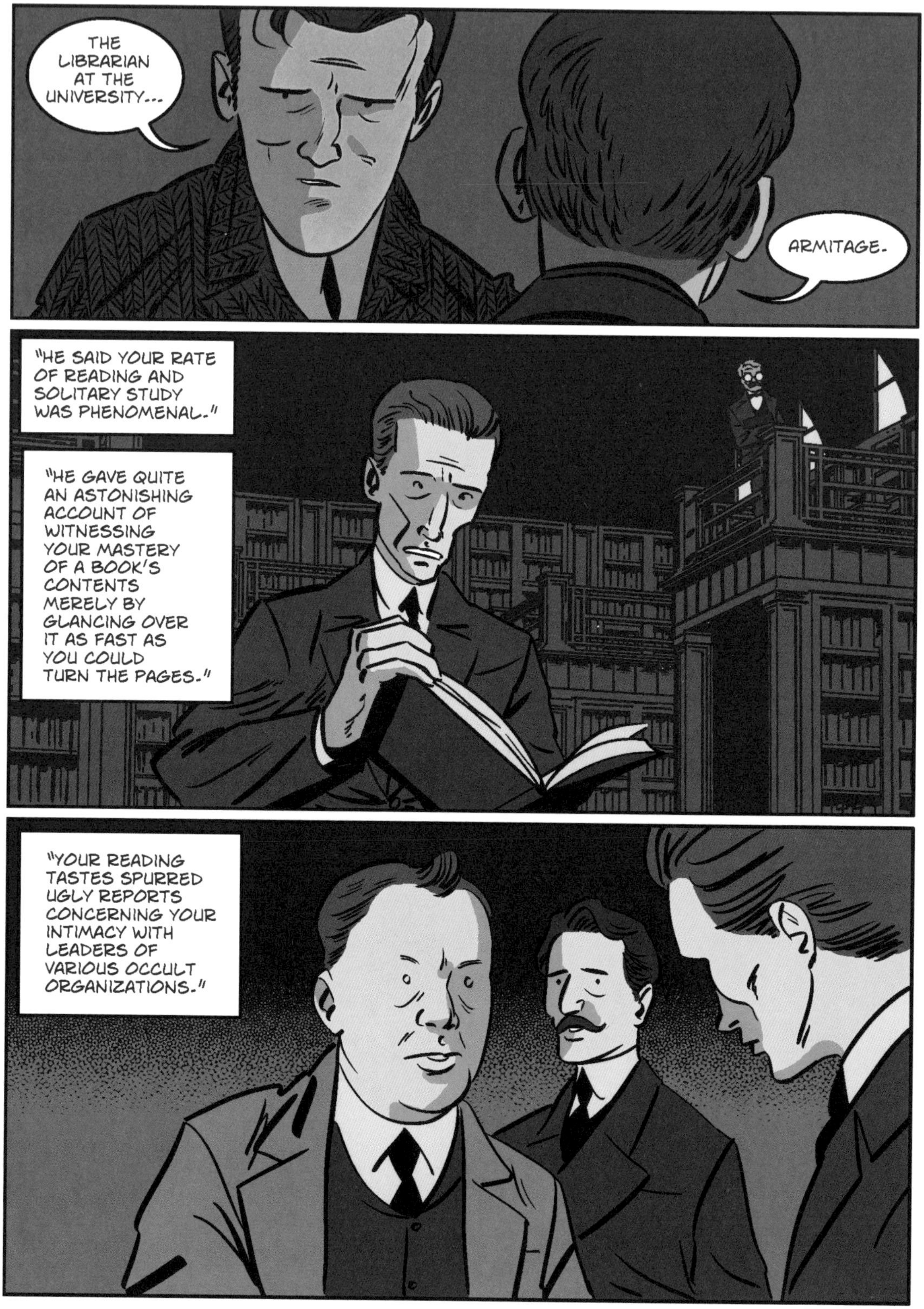
THE LIBRARIAN AT THE UNIVERSITY...
ARMITAGE.
"HE SAID YOUR RATE OF READING AND SOLITARY STUDY WAS PHENOMENAL."
"HE GAVE QUITE AN ASTONISHING ACCOUNT OF WITNESSING YOUR MASTERY OF A BOOK'S CONTENTS MERELY BY GLANCING OVER IT AS FAST AS YOU COULD TURN THE PAGES."
"YOUR READING TASTES SPURRED UGLY REPORTS CONCERNING YOUR INTIMACY WITH LEADERS OF VARIOUS OCCULT ORGANIZATIONS."

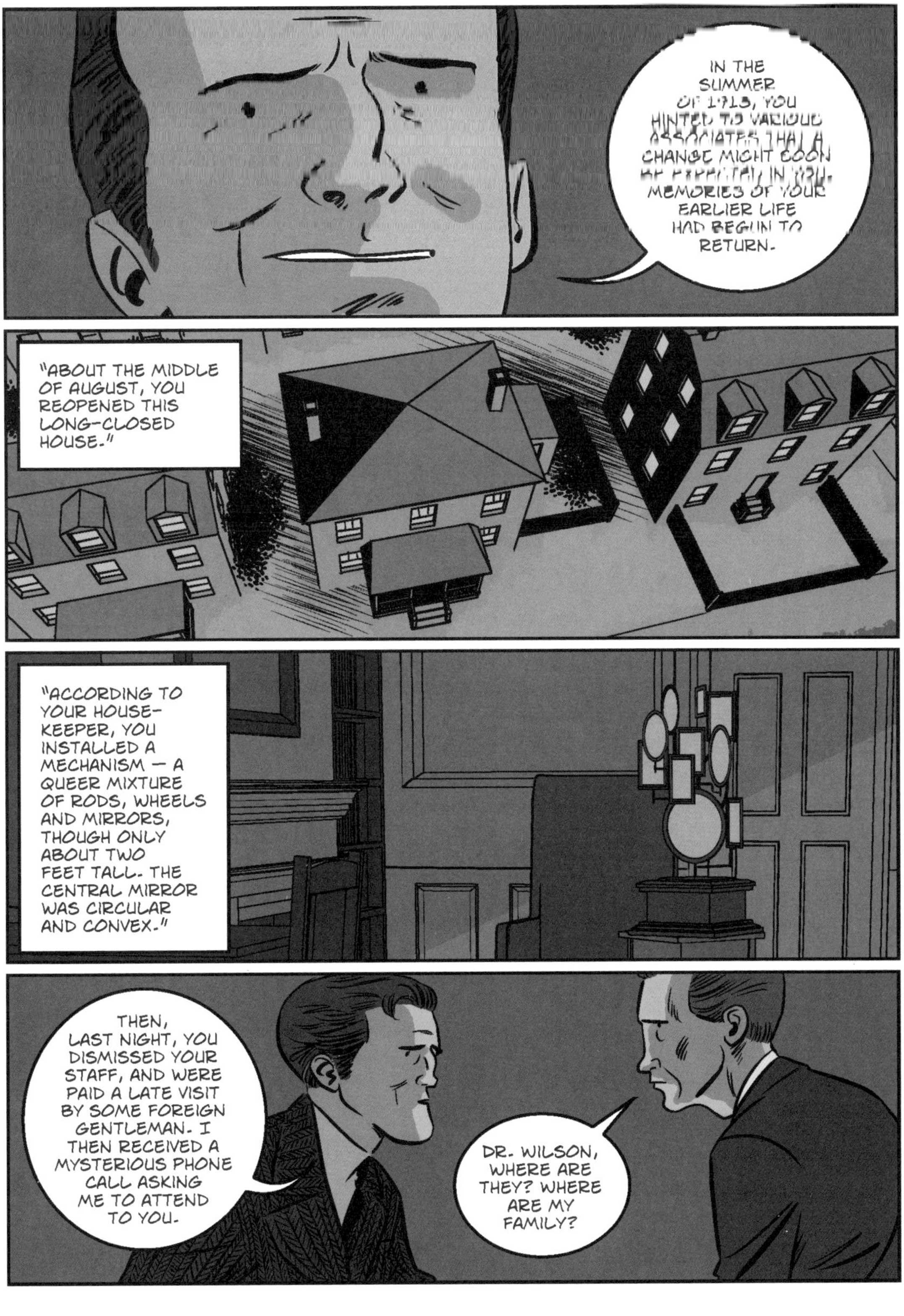
IN THE SUMMER OF 1913, YOU HINTED TO VARIOUS ASSOCIATES THAT A CHANGE MIGHT SOON BE EXPECTED IN YOU. MEMORIES OF YOUR EARLIER LIFE HAD BEGUN TO RETURN.
"ABOUT THE MIDDLE OF AUGUST, YOU REOPENED THIS LONG-CLOSED HOUSE."
"ACCORDING TO YOUR HOUSE-KEEPER, YOU INSTALLED A MECHANISM — A QUEER MIXTURE OF RODS, WHEELS AND MIRRORS, THOUGH ONLY ABOUT TWO FEET TALL. THE CENTRAL MIRROR WAS CIRCULAR AND CONVEX."
THEN, LAST NIGHT, YOU DISMISSED YOUR STAFF, AND WERE PAID A LATE VISIT BY SOME FOREIGN GENTLEMAN. I THEN RECEIVED A MYSTERIOUS PHONE CALL ASKING ME TO ATTEND TO YOU.
DR. WILSON, WHERE ARE THEY? WHERE ARE MY FAMILY?

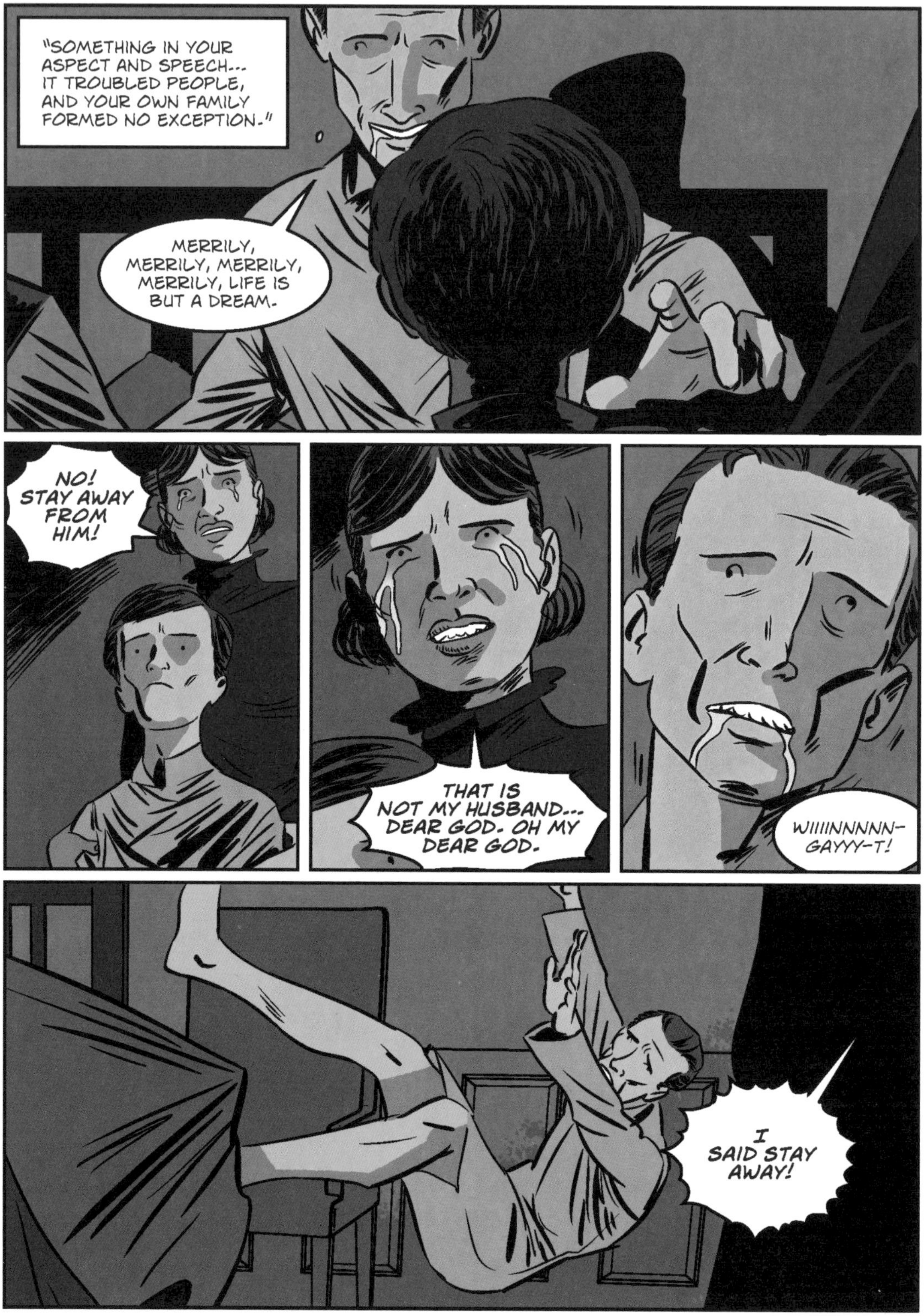
"SOMETHING IN YOUR ASPECT AND SPEECH... IT TROUBLED PEOPLE, AND YOUR OWN FAMILY FORMED NO EXCEPTION."
MERRILY, MERRILY, MERRILY, MERRILY, LIFE IS BUT A DREAM.
NO! STAY AWAY FROM HIM!
THAT IS NOT MY HUSBAND... DEAR GOD. OH MY DEAR GOD.
WIIIINNNNN-GAYYY-T!
I SAID STAY AWAY!

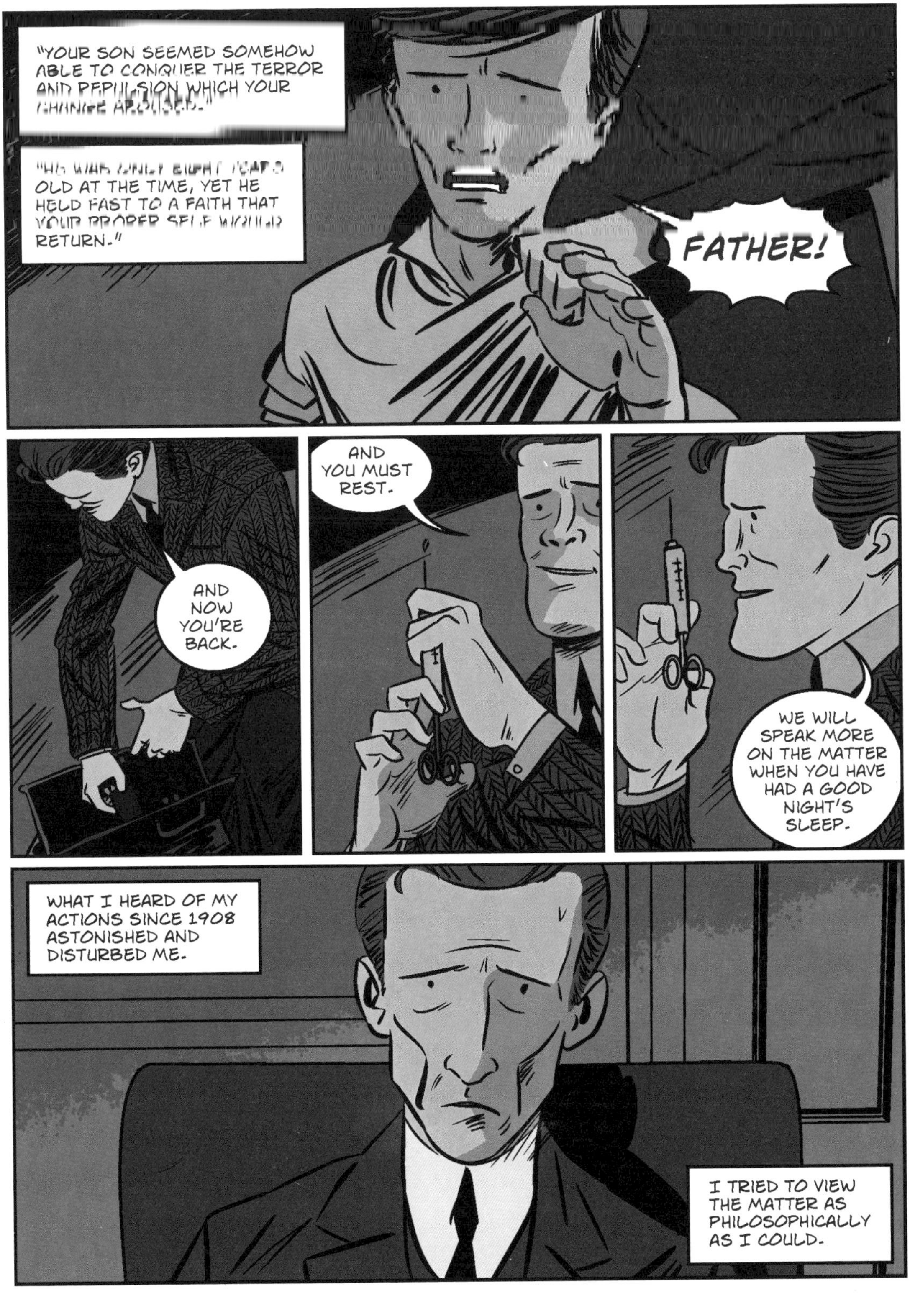
"YOUR SON SEEMED SOMEHOW ABLE TO CONQUER THE TERROR AND REPULSION WHICH YOUR CHANGE AROUSED."
"HE WAS ONLY EIGHT YEARS OLD AT THE TIME, YET HE HELD FAST TO A FAITH THAT YOUR PROPER SELF WOULD RETURN."
FATHER!
AND NOW YOU'RE BACK.
AND YOU MUST REST.
WE WILL SPEAK MORE ON THE MATTER WHEN YOU HAVE HAD A GOOD NIGHT'S SLEEP.
WHAT I HEARD OF MY ACTIONS SINCE 1908 ASTONISHED AND DISTURBED ME.
I TRIED TO VIEW THE MATTER AS PHILOSOPHICALLY AS I COULD.

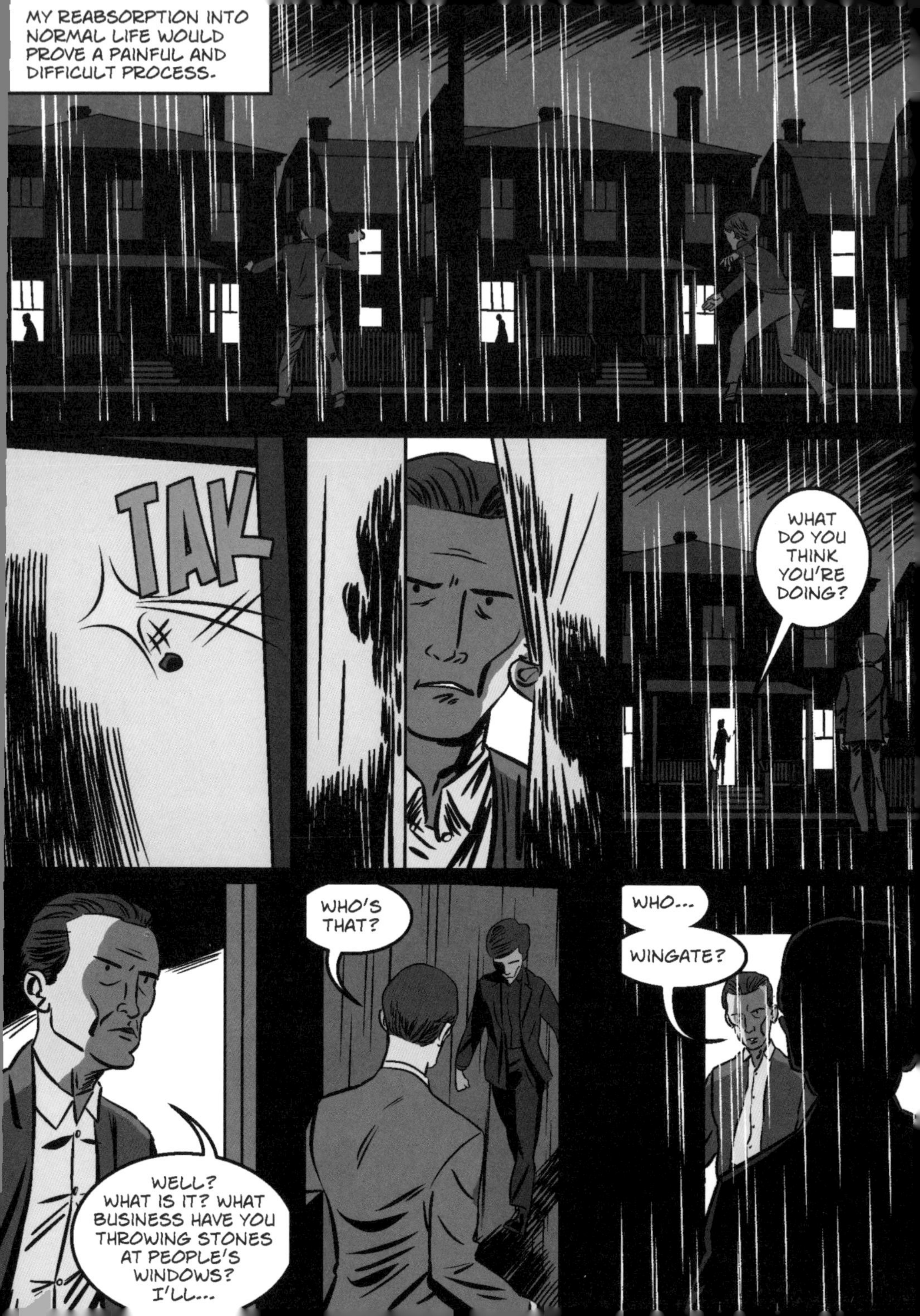
MY REABSORPTION INTO NORMAL LIFE WOULD PROVE A PAINFUL AND DIFFICULT PROCESS.
TAK
WHAT DO YOU THINK YOU'RE DOING?
WELL? WHAT IS IT? WHAT BUSINESS HAVE YOU THROWING STONES AT PEOPLE'S WINDOWS? I'LL...
WHO'S THAT?
WHO...
WINGATE?

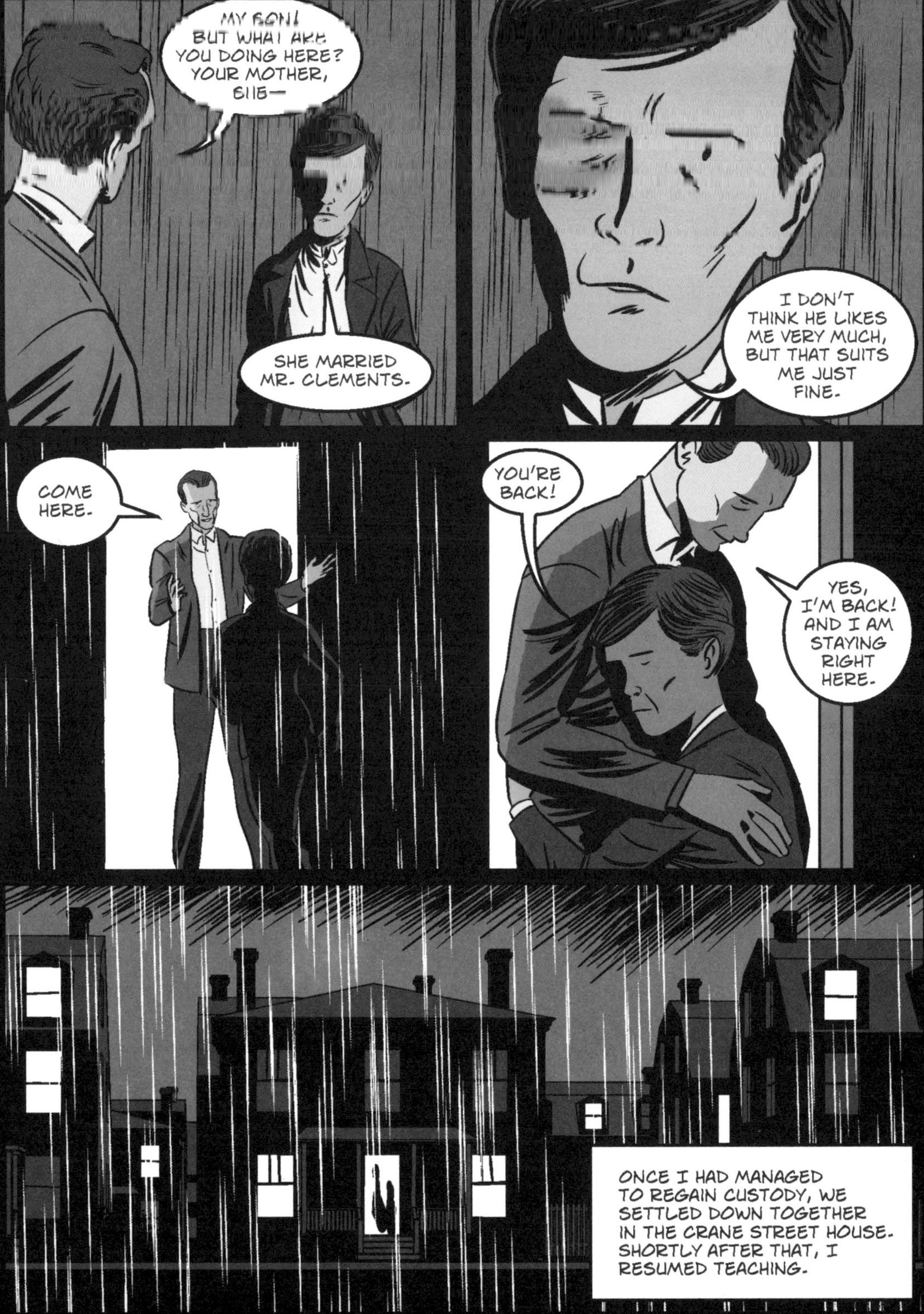
MY SON! BUT WHAT ARE YOU DOING HERE? YOUR MOTHER, SHE—
SHE MARRIED MR. CLEMENTS.
I DON'T THINK HE LIKES ME VERY MUCH, BUT THAT SUITS ME JUST FINE.
COME HERE.
YOU'RE BACK!
YES, I'M BACK! AND I AM STAYING RIGHT HERE.
ONCE I HAD MANAGED TO REGAIN CUSTODY, WE SETTLED DOWN TOGETHER IN THE CRANE STREET HOUSE. SHORTLY AFTER THAT, I RESUMED TEACHING.

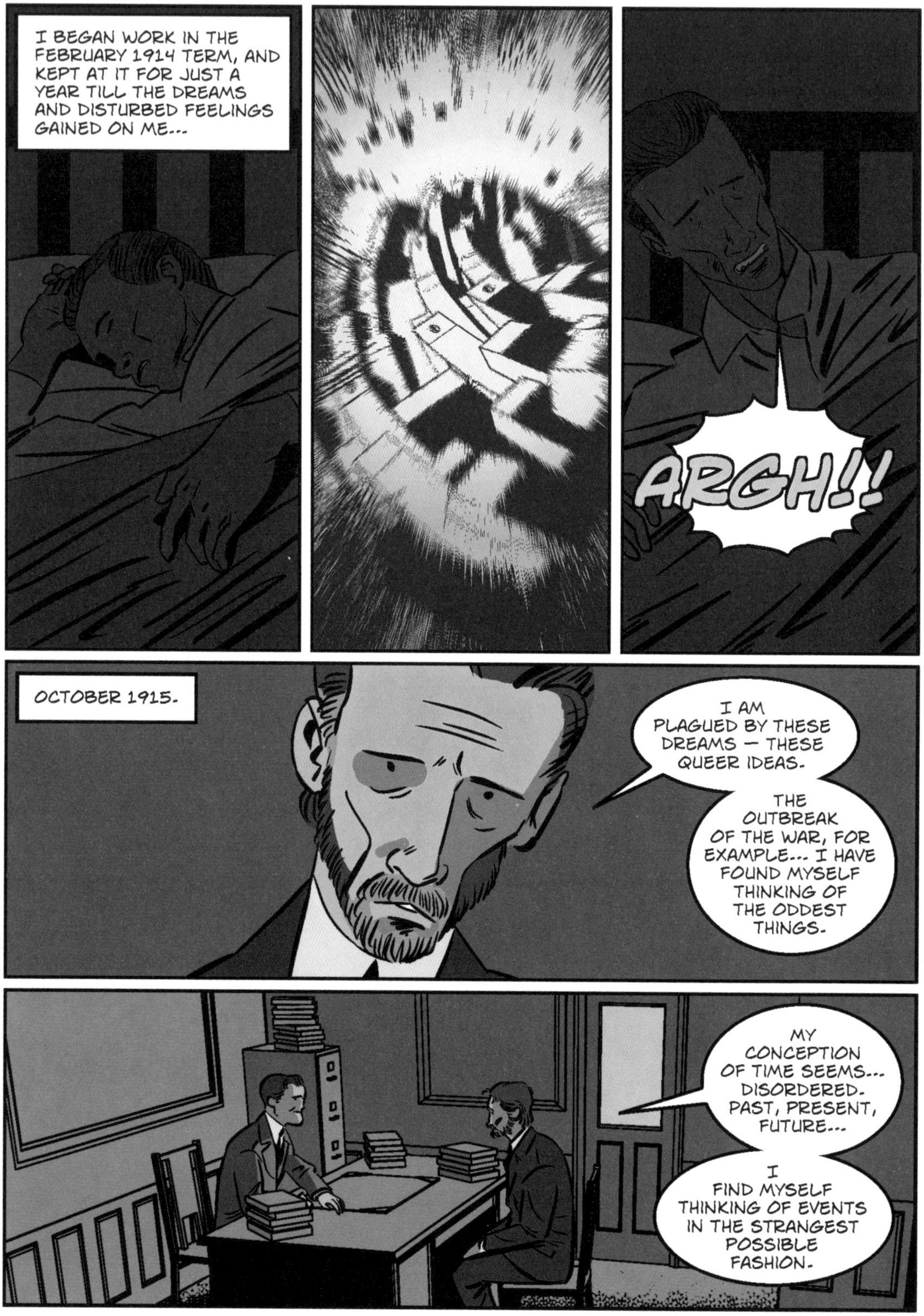
I BEGAN WORK IN THE FEBRUARY 1914 TERM, AND KEPT AT IT FOR JUST A YEAR TILL THE DREAMS AND DISTURBED FEELINGS GAINED ON ME...
ARGH!!
OCTOBER 1915.
I AM PLAGUED BY THESE DREAMS — THESE QUEER IDEAS.
THE OUTBREAK OF THE WAR, FOR EXAMPLE... I HAVE FOUND MYSELF THINKING OF THE ODDEST THINGS.
MY CONCEPTION OF TIME SEEMS... DISORDERED. PAST, PRESENT, FUTURE...
I FIND MYSELF THINKING OF EVENTS IN THE STRANGEST POSSIBLE FASHION.

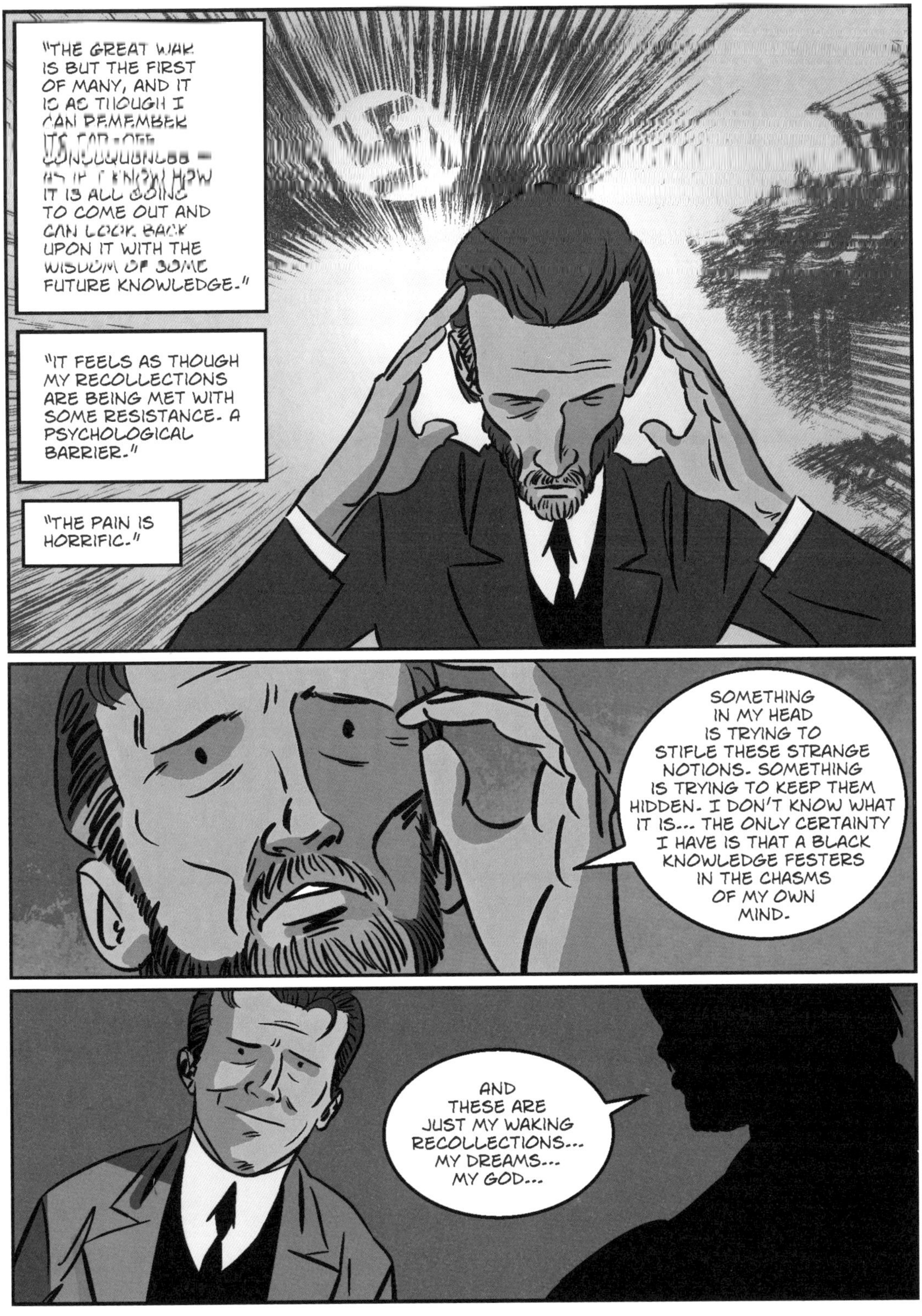
"THE GREAT WAR IS BUT THE FIRST OF MANY, AND IT IS AS THOUGH I CAN REMEMBER ITS FAR-OFF CONSEQUENCES — AS IF I KNOW HOW IT IS ALL GOING TO COME OUT AND CAN LOOK BACK UPON IT WITH THE WISDOM OF SOME FUTURE KNOWLEDGE."
"IT FEELS AS THOUGH MY RECOLLECTIONS ARE BEING MET WITH SOME RESISTANCE. A PSYCHOLOGICAL BARRIER."
"THE PAIN IS HORRIFIC."
SOMETHING IN MY HEAD IS TRYING TO STIFLE THESE STRANGE NOTIONS. SOMETHING IS TRYING TO KEEP THEM HIDDEN. I DON'T KNOW WHAT IT IS... THE ONLY CERTAINTY I HAVE IS THAT A BLACK KNOWLEDGE FESTERS IN THE CHASMS OF MY OWN MIND.
AND THESE ARE JUST MY WAKING RECOLLECTIONS... MY DREAMS... MY GOD...

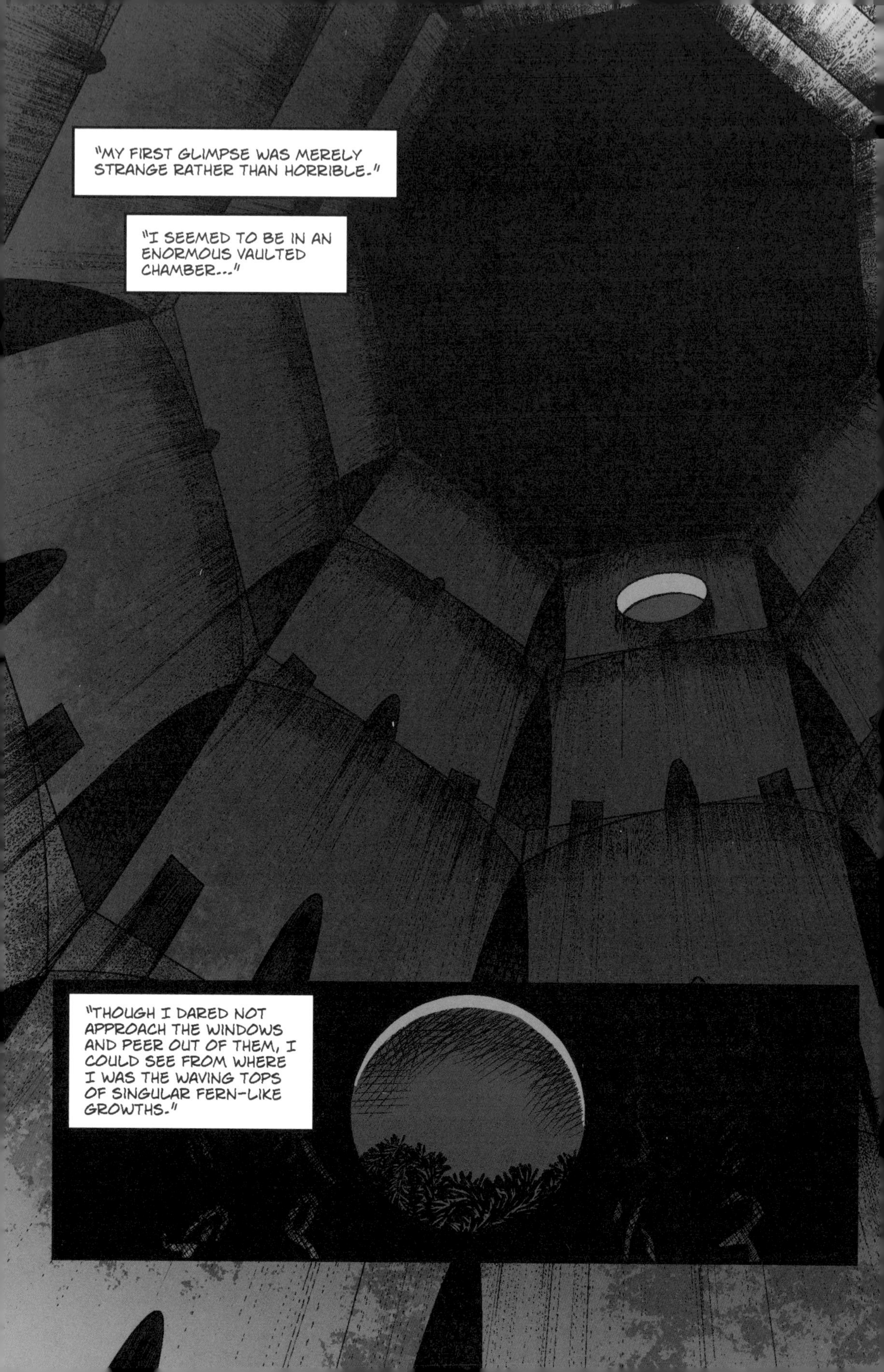
"MY FIRST GLIMPSE WAS MERELY STRANGE RATHER THAN HORRIBLE."
"I SEEMED TO BE IN AN ENORMOUS VAULTED CHAMBER..."
"THOUGH I DARED NOT APPROACH THE WINDOWS AND PEER OUT OF THEM, I COULD SEE FROM WHERE I WAS THE WAVING TOPS OF SINGULAR FERN-LIKE GROWTHS."

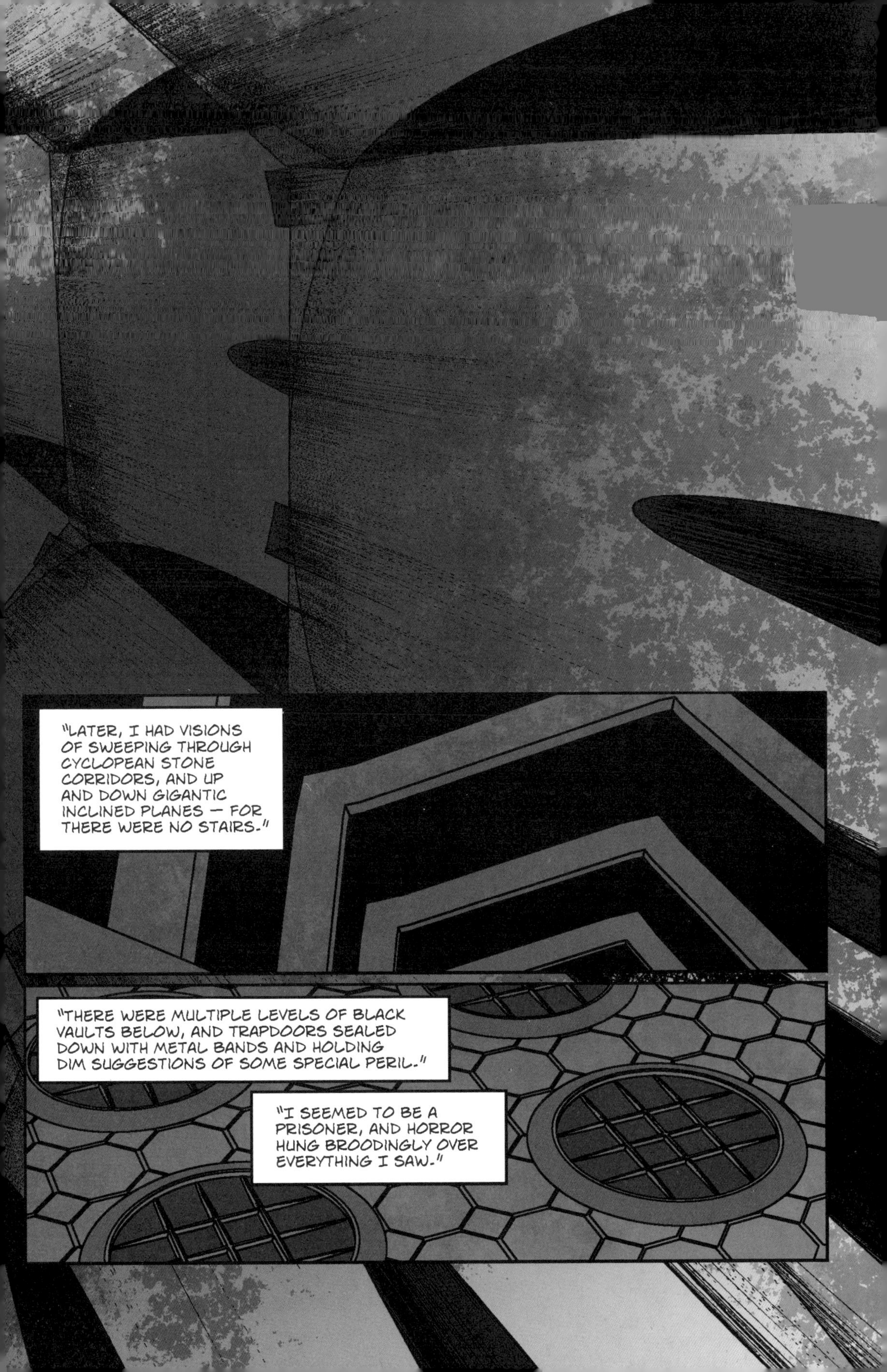
"LATER, I HAD VISIONS OF SWEEPING THROUGH CYCLOPEAN STONE CORRIDORS, AND UP AND DOWN GIGANTIC INCLINED PLANES — FOR THERE WERE NO STAIRS."
"THERE WERE MULTIPLE LEVELS OF BLACK VAULTS BELOW, AND TRAPDOORS SEALED DOWN WITH METAL BANDS AND HOLDING DIM SUGGESTIONS OF SOME SPECIAL PERIL."
"I SEEMED TO BE A PRISONER, AND HORROR HUNG BROODINGLY OVER EVERYTHING I SAW."

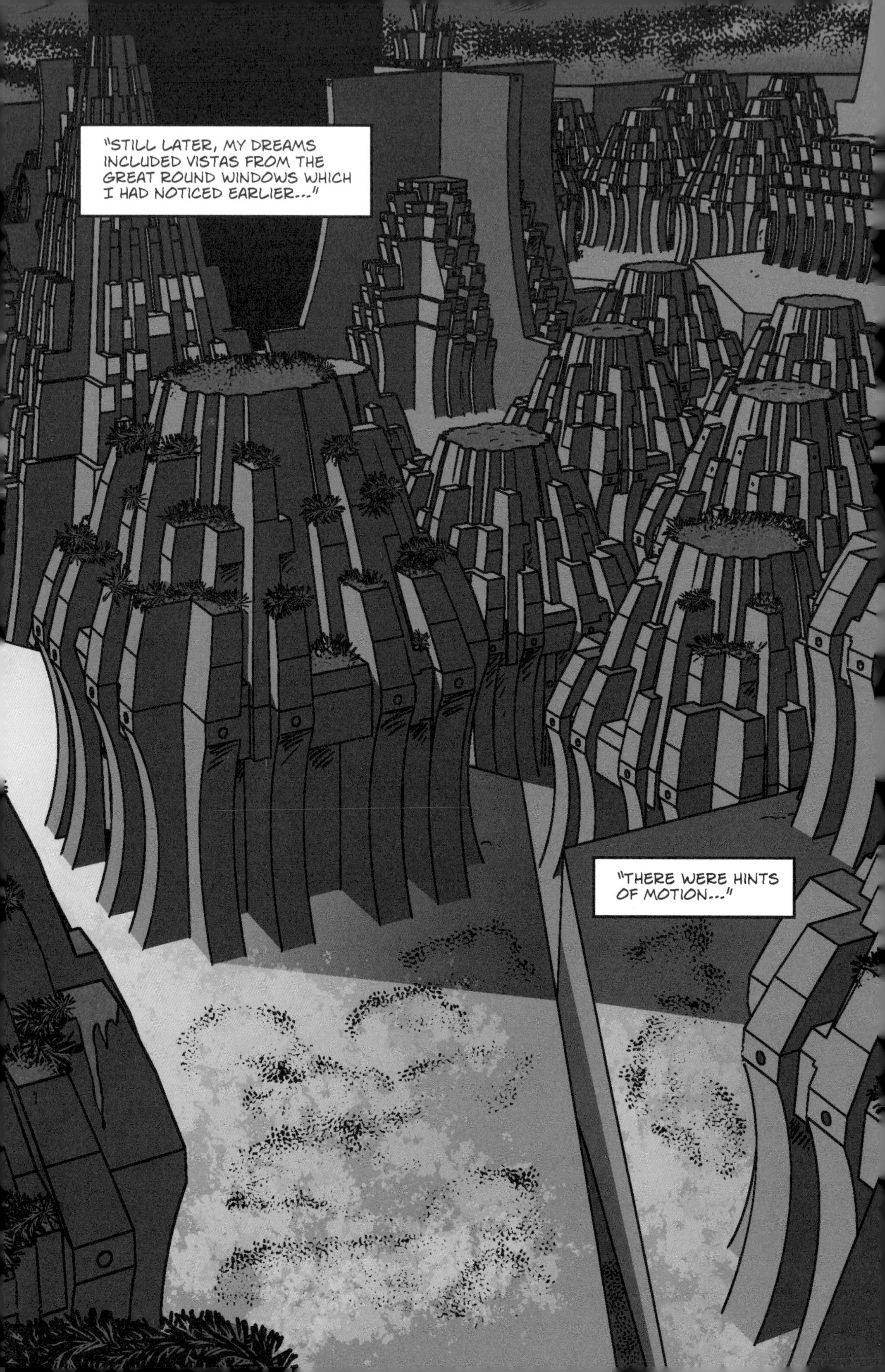
"STILL LATER, MY DREAMS INCLUDED VISTAS FROM THE GREAT ROUND WINDOWS WHICH I HAD NOTICED EARLIER..."
"THERE WERE HINTS OF MOTION..."

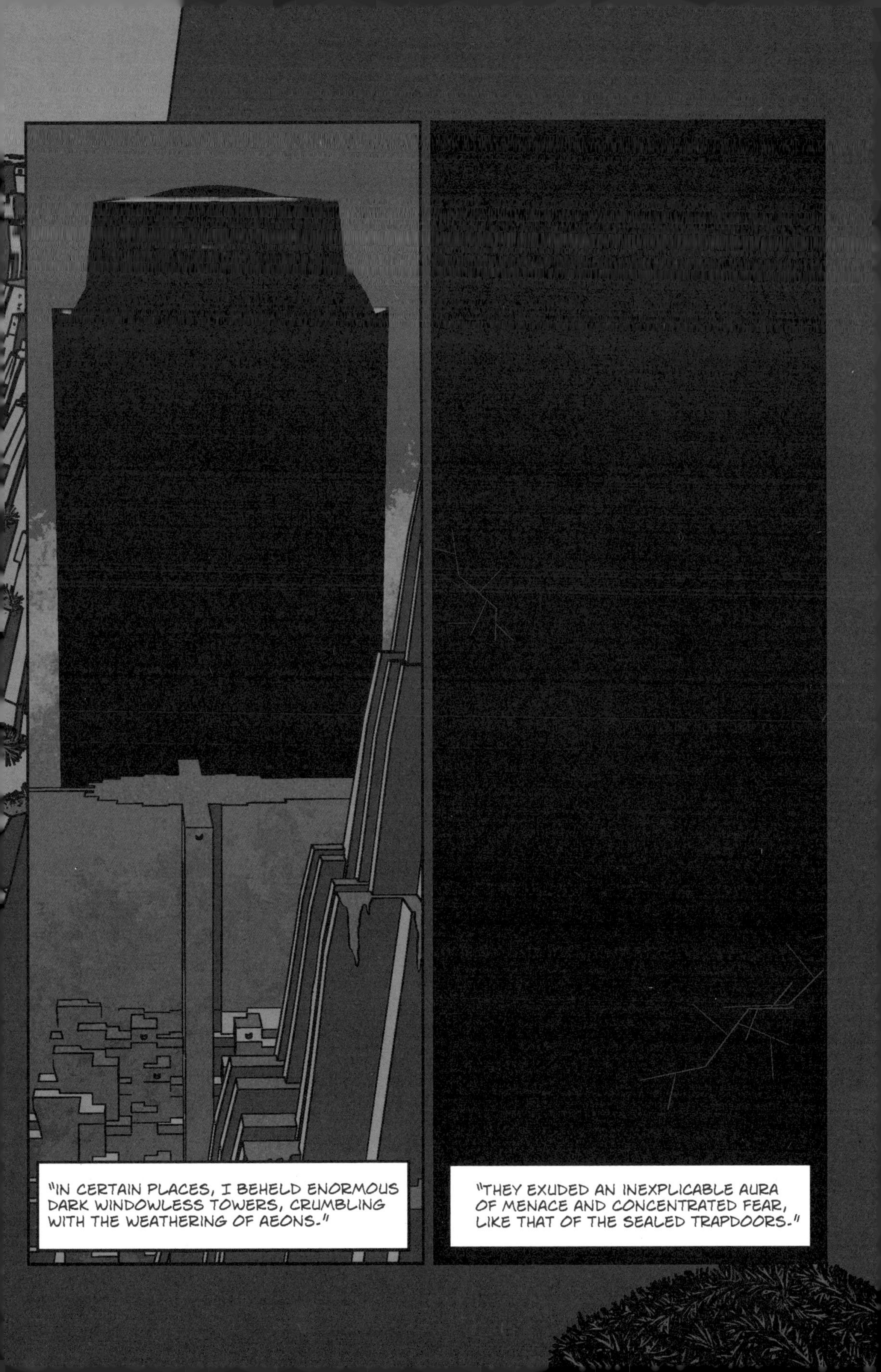
"IN CERTAIN PLACES, I BEHELD ENORMOUS DARK WINDOWLESS TOWERS, CRUMBLING WITH THE WEATHERING OF AEONS."
"THEY EXUDED AN INEXPLICABLE AURA OF MENACE AND CONCENTRATED FEAR, LIKE THAT OF THE SEALED TRAPDOORS."

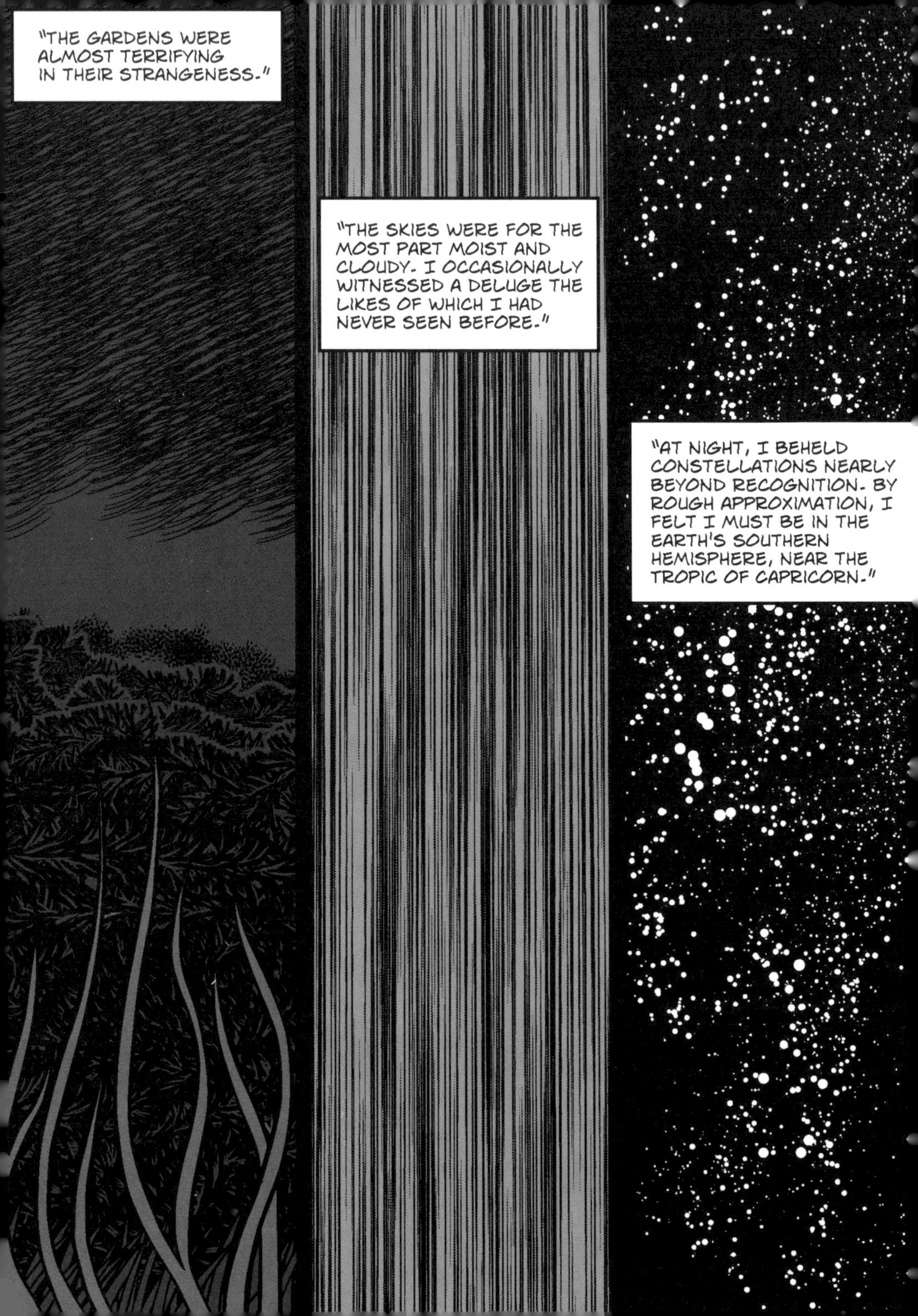
"THE GARDENS WERE ALMOST TERRIFYING IN THEIR STRANGENESS."
"THE SKIES WERE FOR THE MOST PART MOIST AND CLOUDY. I OCCASIONALLY WITNESSED A DELUGE THE LIKES OF WHICH I HAD NEVER SEEN BEFORE."
"AT NIGHT, I BEHELD CONSTELLATIONS NEARLY BEYOND RECOGNITION. BY ROUGH APPROXIMATION, I FELT I MUST BE IN THE EARTH'S SOUTHERN HEMISPHERE, NEAR THE TROPIC OF CAPRICORN."

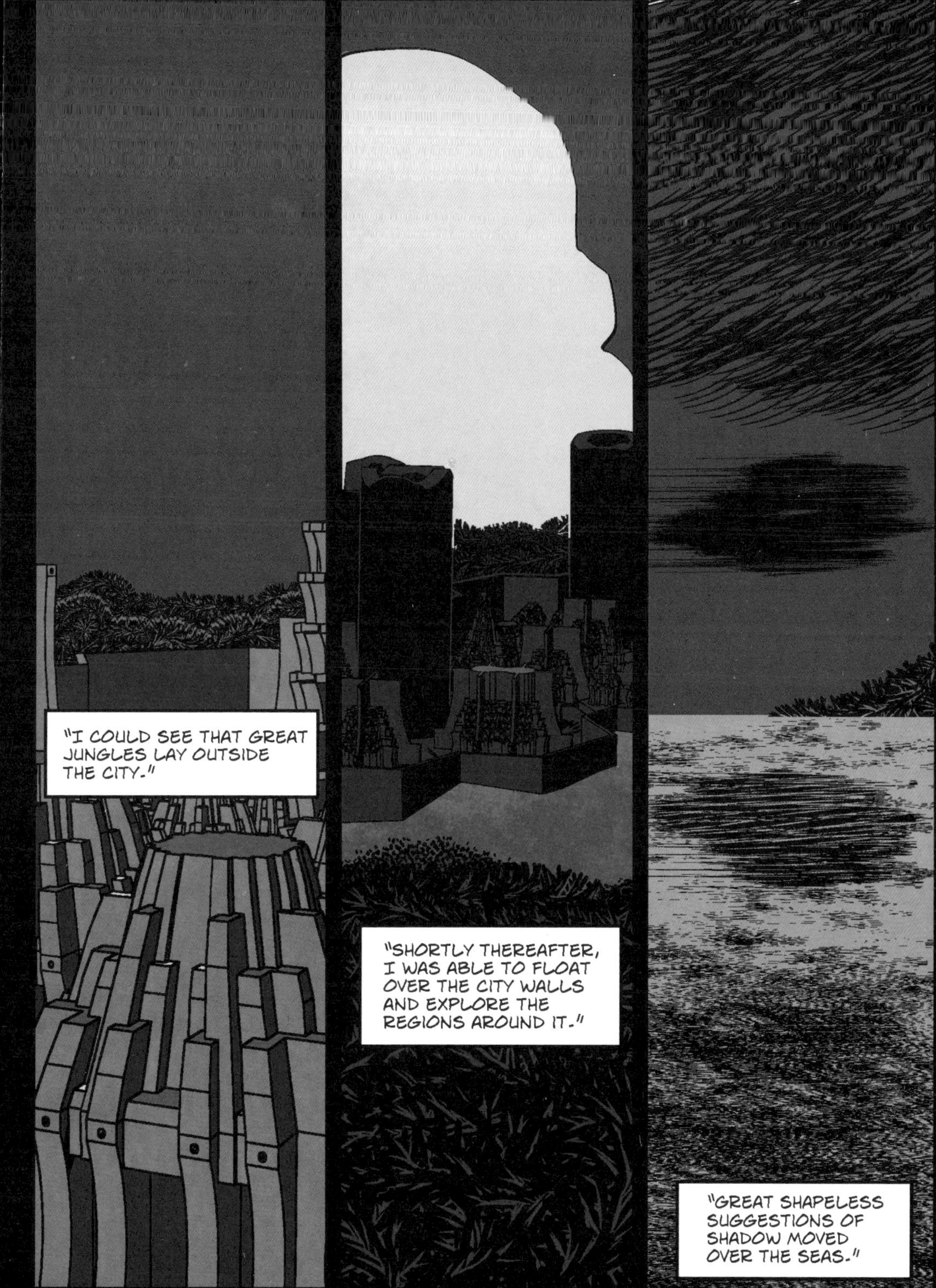
"I COULD SEE THAT GREAT JUNGLES LAY OUTSIDE THE CITY."
"SHORTLY THEREAFTER, I WAS ABLE TO FLOAT OVER THE CITY WALLS AND EXPLORE THE REGIONS AROUND IT."
"GREAT SHAPELESS SUGGESTIONS OF SHADOW MOVED OVER THE SEAS."

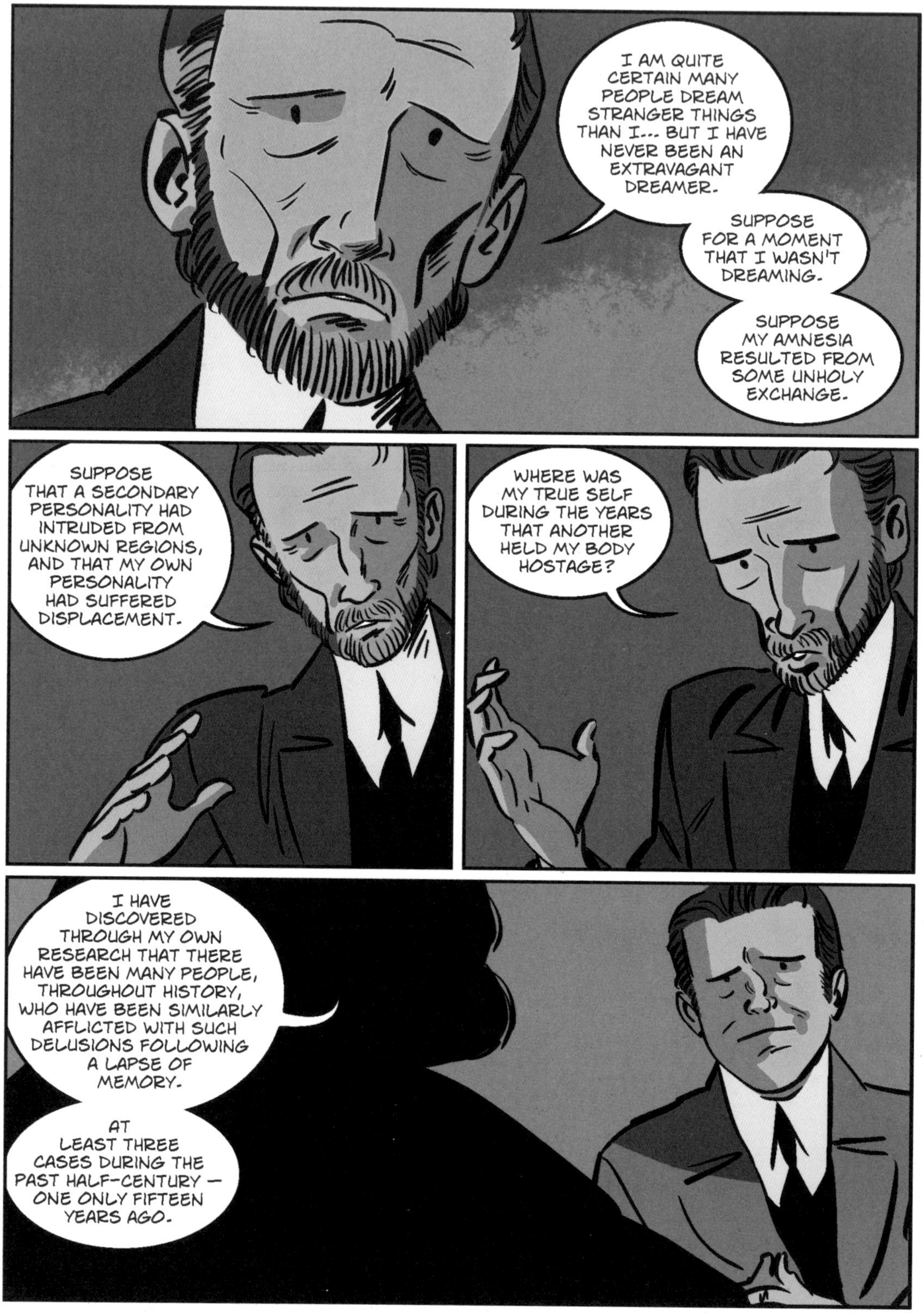
I AM QUITE CERTAIN MANY PEOPLE DREAM STRANGER THINGS THAN I... BUT I HAVE NEVER BEEN AN EXTRAVAGANT DREAMER.
SUPPOSE FOR A MOMENT THAT I WASN'T DREAMING.
SUPPOSE MY AMNESIA RESULTED FROM SOME UNHOLY EXCHANGE.
SUPPOSE THAT A SECONDARY PERSONALITY HAD INTRUDED FROM UNKNOWN REGIONS, AND THAT MY OWN PERSONALITY HAD SUFFERED DISPLACEMENT.
WHERE WAS MY TRUE SELF DURING THE YEARS THAT ANOTHER HELD MY BODY HOSTAGE?
I HAVE DISCOVERED THROUGH MY OWN RESEARCH THAT THERE HAVE BEEN MANY PEOPLE, THROUGHOUT HISTORY, WHO HAVE BEEN SIMILARLY AFFLICTED WITH SUCH DELUSIONS FOLLOWING A LAPSE OF MEMORY.
AT LEAST THREE CASES DURING THE PAST HALF-CENTURY — ONE ONLY FIFTEEN YEARS AGO.

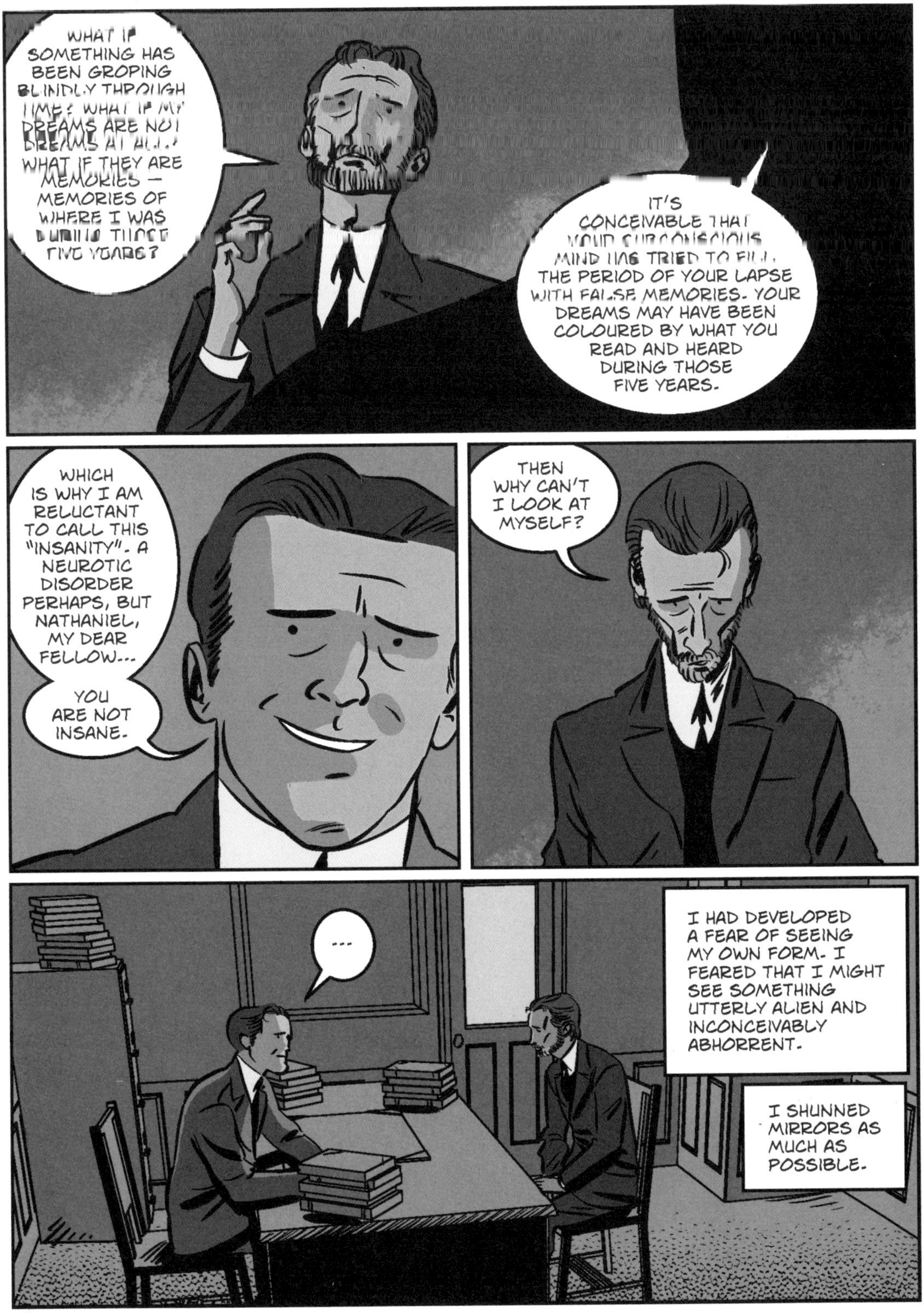
WHAT IF SOMETHING HAS BEEN GROPING BLINDLY THROUGH TIME? WHAT IF MY DREAMS ARE NOT DREAMS AT ALL? WHAT IF THEY ARE MEMORIES — MEMORIES OF WHERE I WAS DURING THOSE FIVE YEARS?
IT'S CONCEIVABLE THAT YOUR SUBCONSCIOUS MIND HAS TRIED TO FILL THE PERIOD OF YOUR LAPSE WITH FALSE MEMORIES. YOUR DREAMS MAY HAVE BEEN COLOURED BY WHAT YOU READ AND HEARD DURING THOSE FIVE YEARS.
WHICH IS WHY I AM RELUCTANT TO CALL THIS "INSANITY". A NEUROTIC DISORDER PERHAPS, BUT NATHANIEL, MY DEAR FELLOW...
YOU ARE NOT INSANE.
THEN WHY CAN'T I LOOK AT MYSELF?
...
I HAD DEVELOPED A FEAR OF SEEING MY OWN FORM. I FEARED THAT I MIGHT SEE SOMETHING UTTERLY ALIEN AND INCONCEIVABLY ABHORRENT.
I SHUNNED MIRRORS AS MUCH AS POSSIBLE.

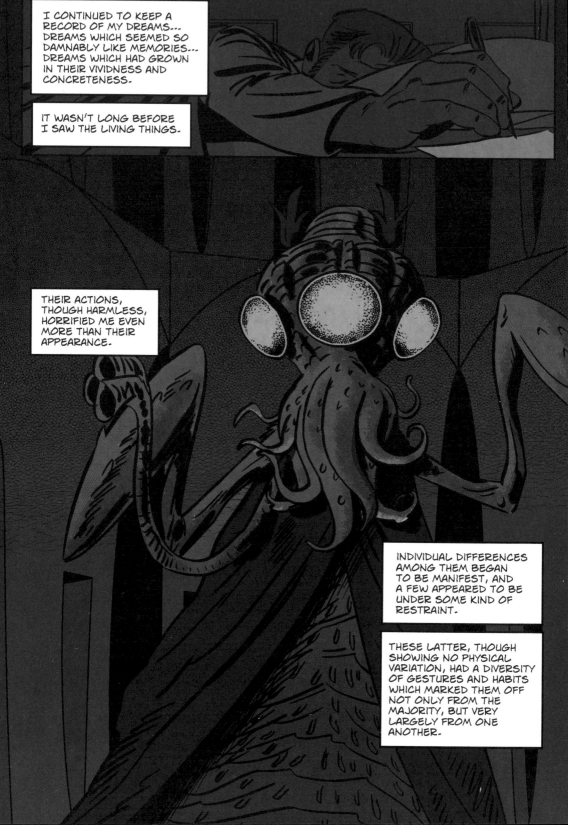

I CONTINUED TO KEEP A RECORD OF MY DREAMS... DREAMS WHICH SEEMED SO DAMNABLY LIKE MEMORIES... DREAMS WHICH HAD GROWN IN THEIR VIVIDNESS AND CONCRETENESS.

IT WASN'T LONG BEFORE I SAW THE LIVING THINGS.

THEIR ACTIONS, THOUGH HARMLESS, HORRIFIED ME EVEN MORE THAN THEIR APPEARANCE.

INDIVIDUAL DIFFERENCES AMONG THEM BEGAN TO BE MANIFEST, AND A FEW APPEARED TO BE UNDER SOME KIND OF RESTRAINT.

THESE LATTER, THOUGH SHOWING NO PHYSICAL VARIATION, HAD A DIVERSITY OF GESTURES AND HABITS WHICH MARKED THEM OFF NOT ONLY FROM THE MAJORITY, BUT VERY LARGELY FROM ONE ANOTHER.

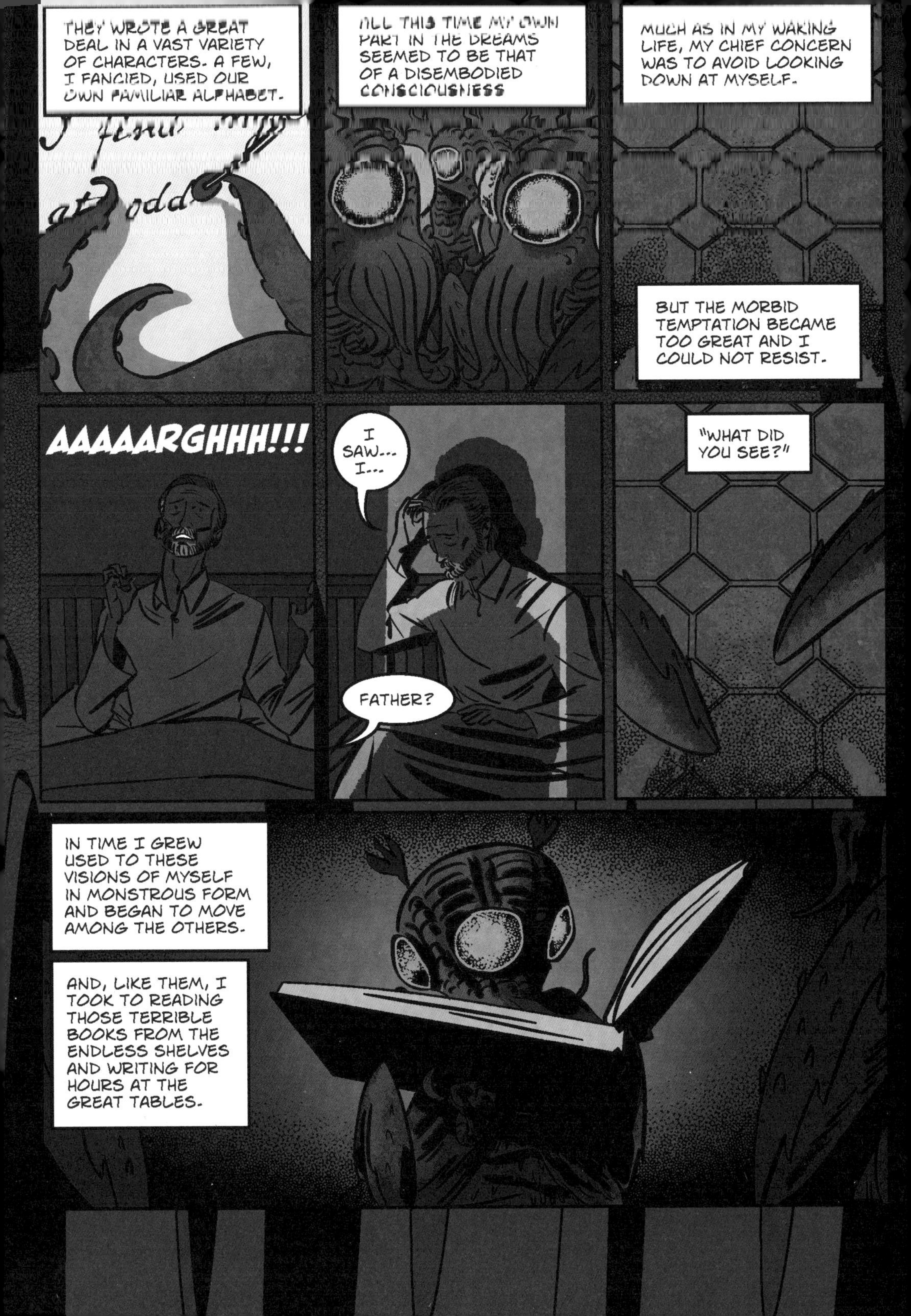
THEY WROTE A GREAT DEAL IN A VAST VARIETY OF CHARACTERS. A FEW, I FANCIED, USED OUR OWN FAMILIAR ALPHABET.
ALL THIS TIME MY OWN PART IN THE DREAMS SEEMED TO BE THAT OF A DISEMBODIED CONSCIOUSNESS
MUCH AS IN MY WAKING LIFE, MY CHIEF CONCERN WAS TO AVOID LOOKING DOWN AT MYSELF.
BUT THE MORBID TEMPTATION BECAME TOO GREAT AND I COULD NOT RESIST.
AAAAARGHHH!!!
I SAW... I...
FATHER?
"WHAT DID YOU SEE?"
IN TIME I GREW USED TO THESE VISIONS OF MYSELF IN MONSTROUS FORM AND BEGAN TO MOVE AMONG THE OTHERS.
AND, LIKE THEM, I TOOK TO READING THOSE TERRIBLE BOOKS FROM THE ENDLESS SHELVES AND WRITING FOR HOURS AT THE GREAT TABLES.

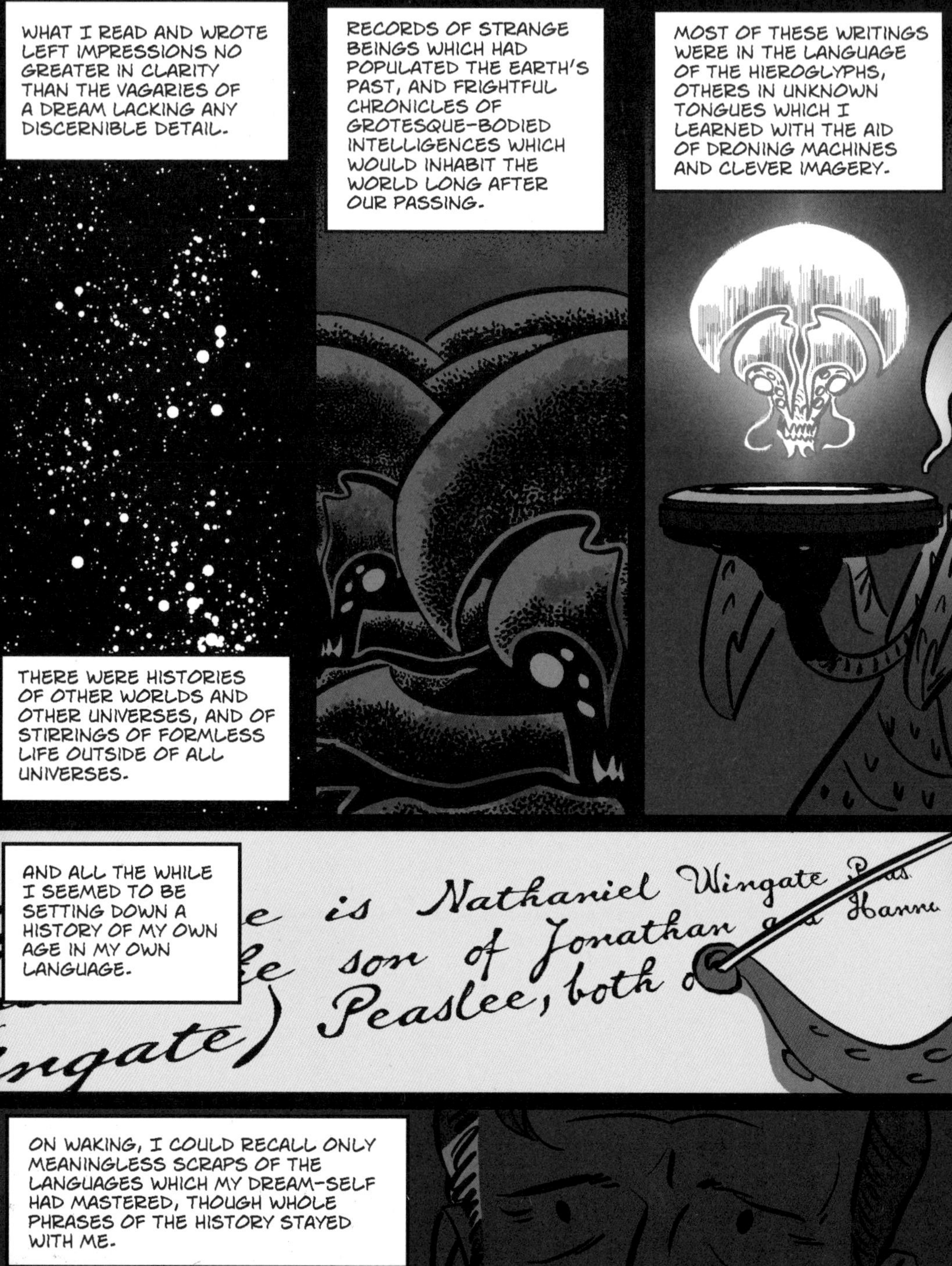
WHAT I READ AND WROTE LEFT IMPRESSIONS NO GREATER IN CLARITY THAN THE VAGARIES OF A DREAM LACKING ANY DISCERNIBLE DETAIL.
RECORDS OF STRANGE BEINGS WHICH HAD POPULATED THE EARTH'S PAST, AND FRIGHTFUL CHRONICLES OF GROTESQUE-BODIED INTELLIGENCES WHICH WOULD INHABIT THE WORLD LONG AFTER OUR PASSING.
MOST OF THESE WRITINGS WERE IN THE LANGUAGE OF THE HIEROGLYPHS, OTHERS IN UNKNOWN TONGUES WHICH I LEARNED WITH THE AID OF DRONING MACHINES AND CLEVER IMAGERY.
THERE WERE HISTORIES OF OTHER WORLDS AND OTHER UNIVERSES, AND OF STIRRINGS OF FORMLESS LIFE OUTSIDE OF ALL UNIVERSES.
AND ALL THE WHILE I SEEMED TO BE SETTING DOWN A HISTORY OF MY OWN AGE IN MY OWN LANGUAGE.
is Nathaniel Wingate
son of Jonathan
Peaslee, both
ON WAKING, I COULD RECALL ONLY MEANINGLESS SCRAPS OF THE LANGUAGES WHICH MY DREAM-SELF HAD MASTERED, THOUGH WHOLE PHRASES OF THE HISTORY STAYED WITH ME.

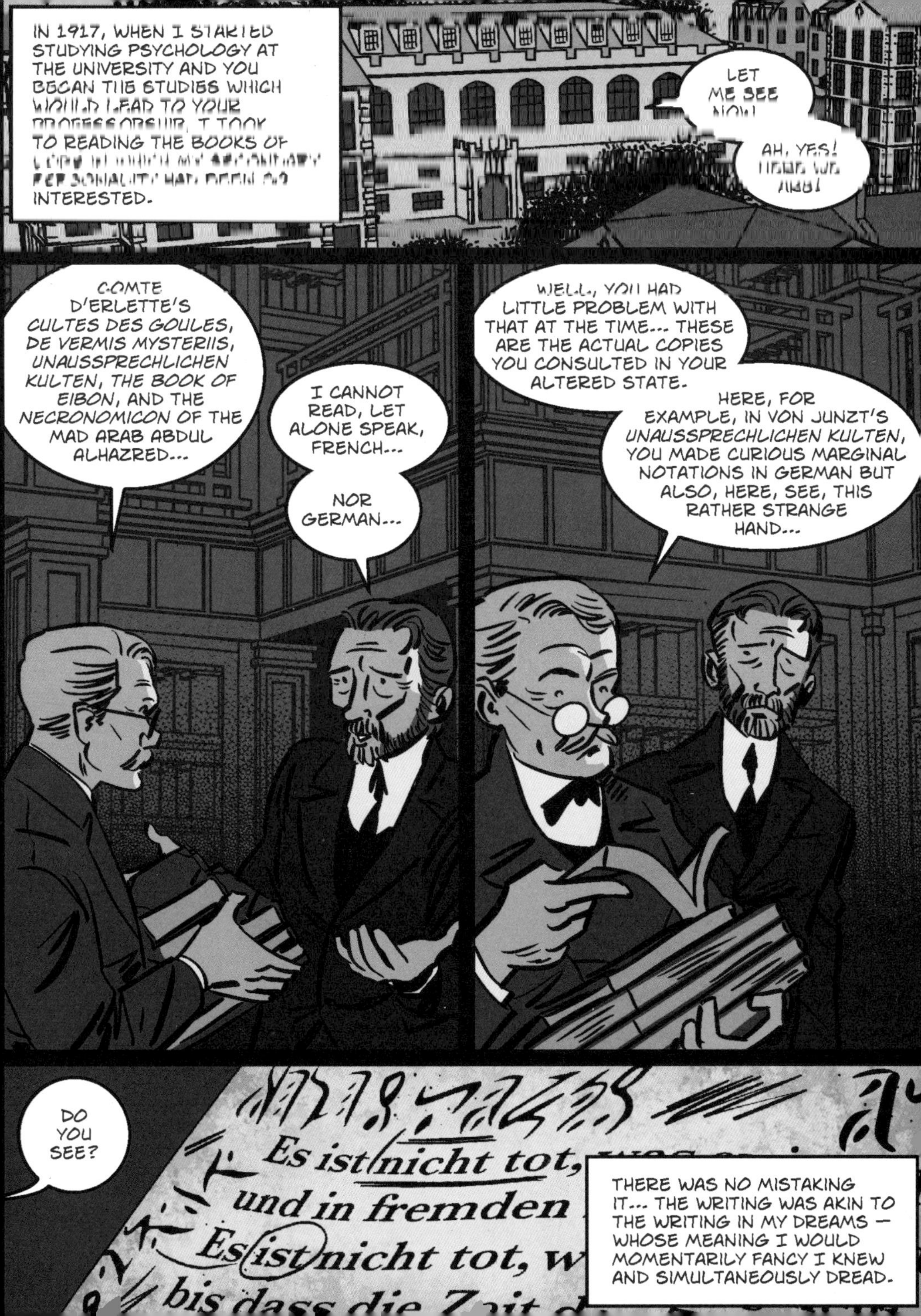
IN 1917, WHEN I STARTED STUDYING PSYCHOLOGY AT THE UNIVERSITY AND YOU BEGAN THE STUDIES WHICH WOULD LEAD TO YOUR PROFESSORSHIP, I TOOK TO READING THE BOOKS OF
INTERESTED.
LET ME SEE NOW.
AH, YES!
COMTE D'ERLETTE'S CULTES DES GOULES, DE VERMIS MYSTERIIS, UNAUSSPRECHLICHEN KULTEN, THE BOOK OF EIBON, AND THE NECRONOMICON OF THE MAD ARAB ABDUL ALHAZRED...
I CANNOT READ, LET ALONE SPEAK, FRENCH...
NOR GERMAN...
WELL, YOU HAD LITTLE PROBLEM WITH THAT AT THE TIME... THESE ARE THE ACTUAL COPIES YOU CONSULTED IN YOUR ALTERED STATE.
HERE, FOR EXAMPLE, IN VON JUNZT'S UNAUSSPRECHLICHEN KULTEN, YOU MADE CURIOUS MARGINAL NOTATIONS IN GERMAN BUT ALSO, HERE, SEE, THIS RATHER STRANGE HAND...
DO YOU SEE?
Es ist nicht tot,
und in fremden
Es ist nicht tot,
bis dass die
THERE WAS NO MISTAKING IT... THE WRITING WAS AKIN TO THE WRITING IN MY DREAMS — WHOSE MEANING I WOULD MOMENTARILY FANCY I KNEW AND SIMULTANEOUSLY DREAD.

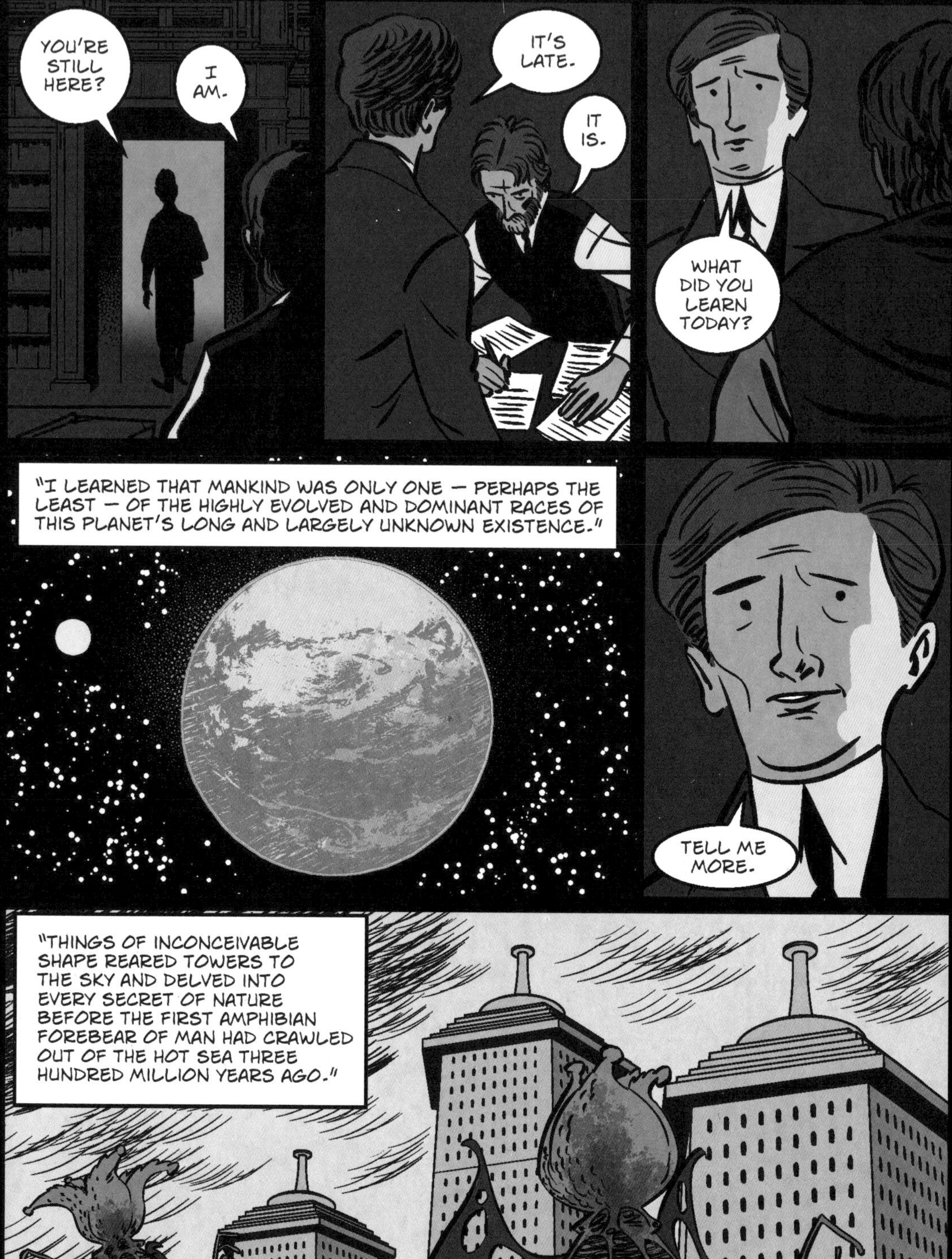
YOU'RE STILL HERE?
I AM.
IT'S LATE.
IT IS.
WHAT DID YOU LEARN TODAY?
"I LEARNED THAT MANKIND WAS ONLY ONE — PERHAPS THE LEAST — OF THE HIGHLY EVOLVED AND DOMINANT RACES OF THIS PLANET'S LONG AND LARGELY UNKNOWN EXISTENCE."
TELL ME MORE.
"THINGS OF INCONCEIVABLE SHAPE REARED TOWERS TO THE SKY AND DELVED INTO EVERY SECRET OF NATURE BEFORE THE FIRST AMPHIBIAN FOREBEAR OF MAN HAD CRAWLED OUT OF THE HOT SEA THREE HUNDRED MILLION YEARS AGO."

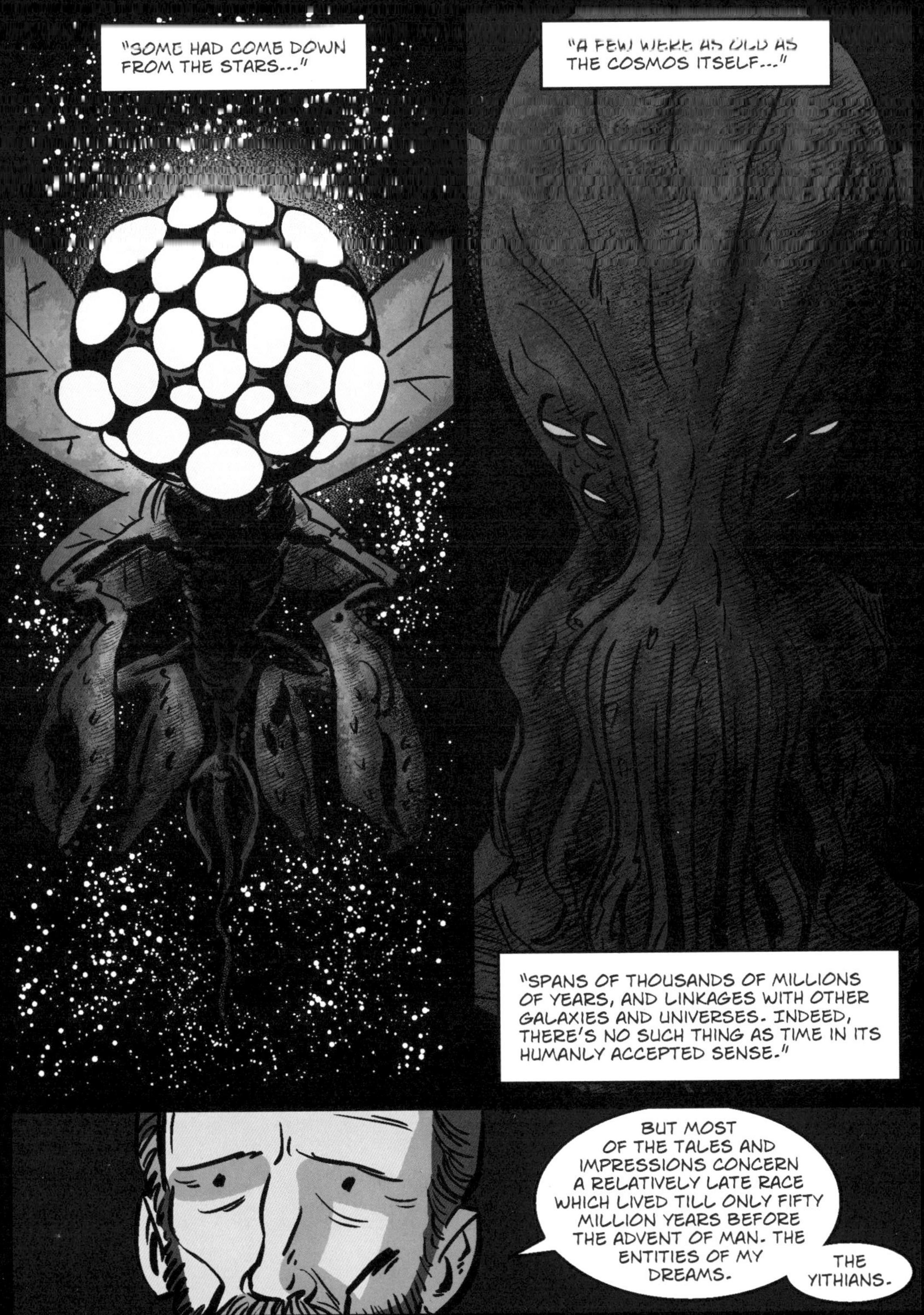
"SOME HAD COME DOWN FROM THE STARS..."
"A FEW WERE AS OLD AS THE COSMOS ITSELF..."
"SPANS OF THOUSANDS OF MILLIONS OF YEARS, AND LINKAGES WITH OTHER GALAXIES AND UNIVERSES. INDEED, THERE'S NO SUCH THING AS TIME IN ITS HUMANLY ACCEPTED SENSE."
BUT MOST OF THE TALES AND IMPRESSIONS CONCERN A RELATIVELY LATE RACE WHICH LIVED TILL ONLY FIFTY MILLION YEARS BEFORE THE ADVENT OF MAN. THE ENTITIES OF MY DREAMS.
THE YITHIANS.

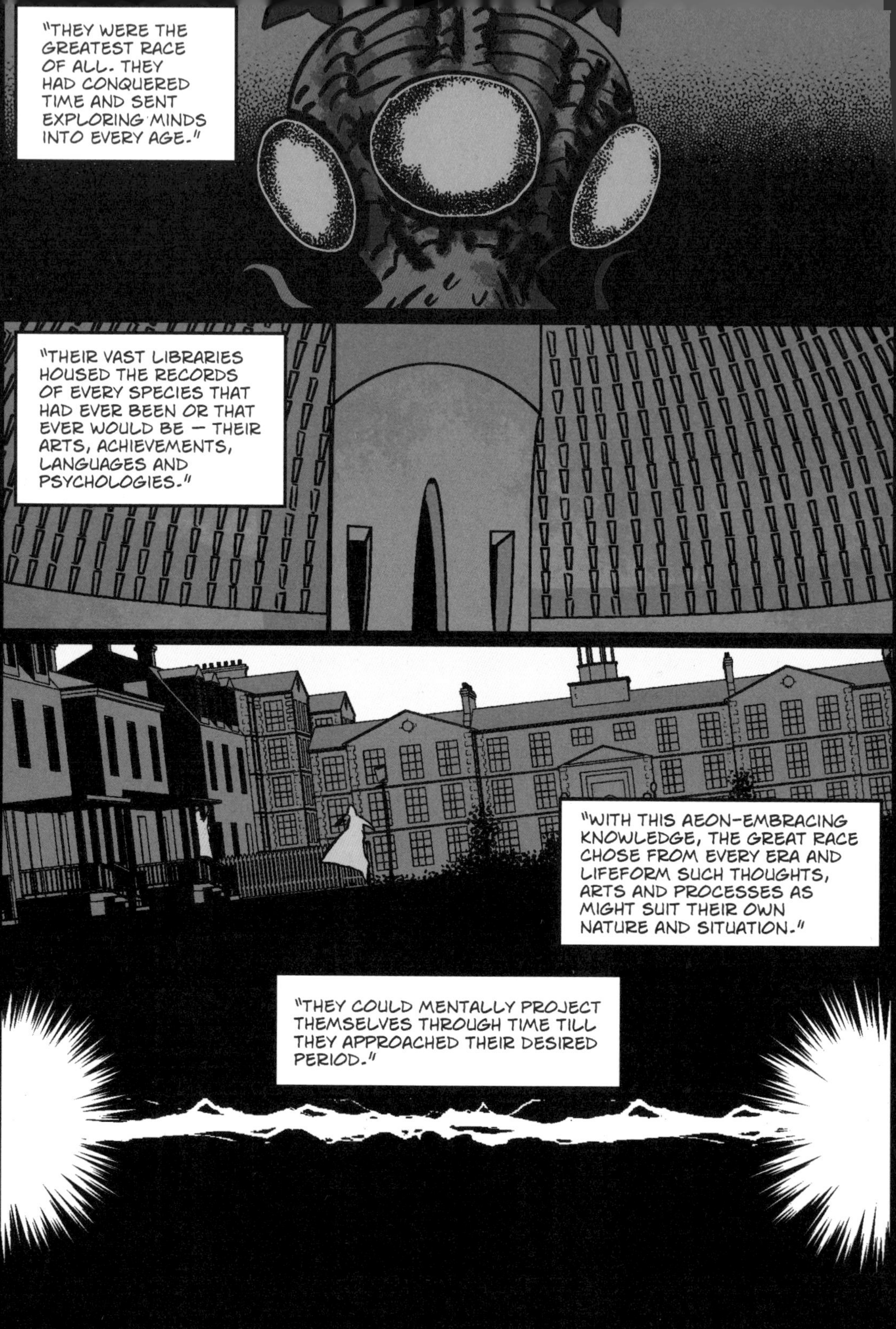
"THEY WERE THE GREATEST RACE OF ALL. THEY HAD CONQUERED TIME AND SENT EXPLORING MINDS INTO EVERY AGE."
"THEIR VAST LIBRARIES HOUSED THE RECORDS OF EVERY SPECIES THAT HAD EVER BEEN OR THAT EVER WOULD BE — THEIR ARTS, ACHIEVEMENTS, LANGUAGES AND PSYCHOLOGIES."
"WITH THIS AEON-EMBRACING KNOWLEDGE, THE GREAT RACE CHOSE FROM EVERY ERA AND LIFEFORM SUCH THOUGHTS, ARTS AND PROCESSES AS MIGHT SUIT THEIR OWN NATURE AND SITUATION."
"THEY COULD MENTALLY PROJECT THEMSELVES THROUGH TIME TILL THEY APPROACHED THEIR DESIRED PERIOD."

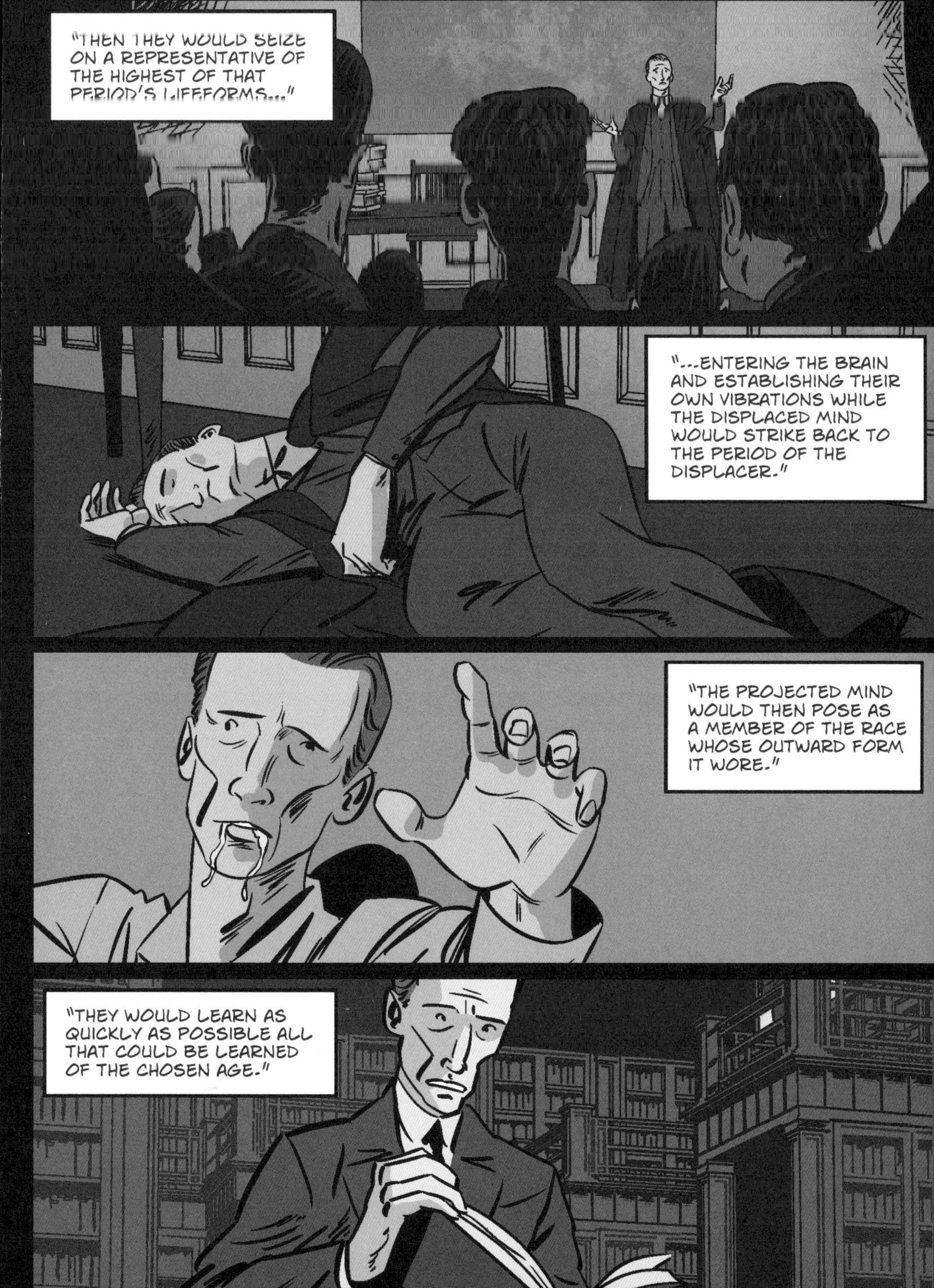
"THEN THEY WOULD SEIZE ON A REPRESENTATIVE OF THE HIGHEST OF THAT PERIOD'S LIFEFORMS..."
"...ENTERING THE BRAIN AND ESTABLISHING THEIR OWN VIBRATIONS WHILE THE DISPLACED MIND WOULD STRIKE BACK TO THE PERIOD OF THE DISPLACER."
"THE PROJECTED MIND WOULD THEN POSE AS A MEMBER OF THE RACE WHOSE OUTWARD FORM IT WORE."
"THEY WOULD LEARN AS QUICKLY AS POSSIBLE ALL THAT COULD BE LEARNED OF THE CHOSEN AGE."

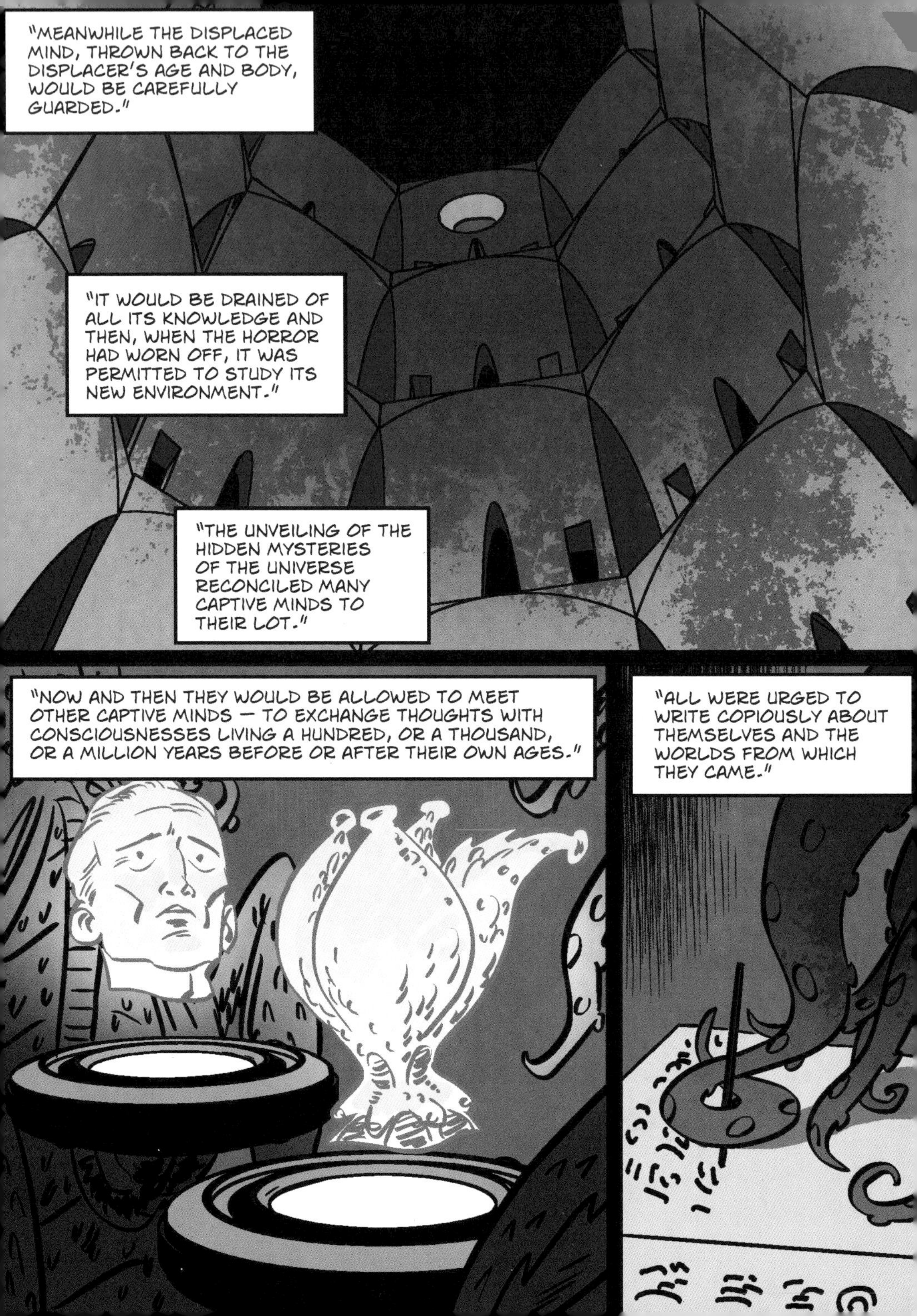
"MEANWHILE THE DISPLACED MIND, THROWN BACK TO THE DISPLACER'S AGE AND BODY, WOULD BE CAREFULLY GUARDED."
"IT WOULD BE DRAINED OF ALL ITS KNOWLEDGE AND THEN, WHEN THE HORROR HAD WORN OFF, IT WAS PERMITTED TO STUDY ITS NEW ENVIRONMENT."
"THE UNVEILING OF THE HIDDEN MYSTERIES OF THE UNIVERSE RECONCILED MANY CAPTIVE MINDS TO THEIR LOT."
"NOW AND THEN THEY WOULD BE ALLOWED TO MEET OTHER CAPTIVE MINDS — TO EXCHANGE THOUGHTS WITH CONSCIOUSNESSES LIVING A HUNDRED, OR A THOUSAND, OR A MILLION YEARS BEFORE OR AFTER THEIR OWN AGES."
"ALL WERE URGED TO WRITE COPIOUSLY ABOUT THEMSELVES AND THE WORLDS FROM WHICH THEY CAME."

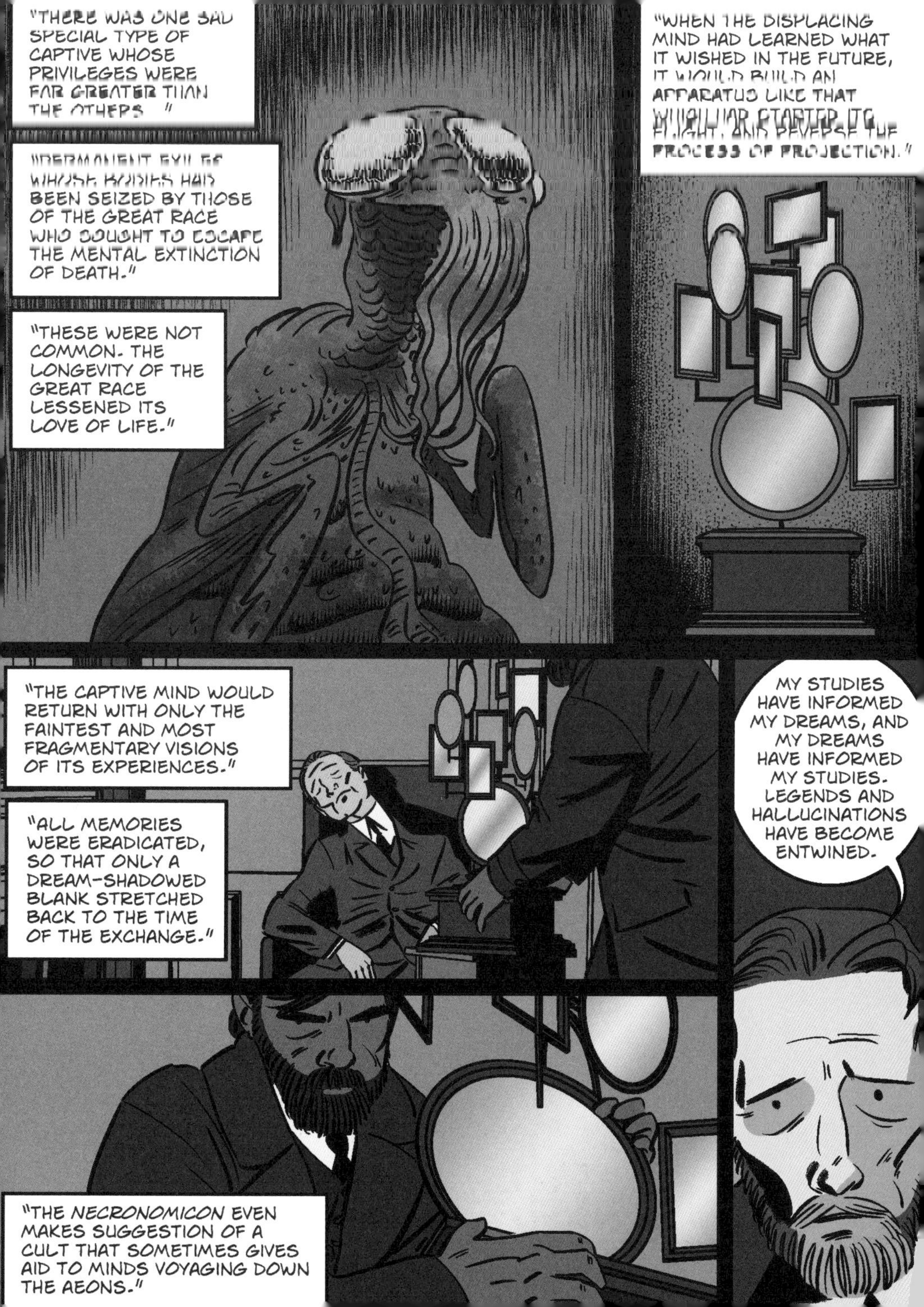
"THERE WAS ONE SAD SPECIAL TYPE OF CAPTIVE WHOSE PRIVILEGES WERE FAR GREATER THAN THE OTHERS."
"PERMANENT EXILES WHOSE BODIES HAD BEEN SEIZED BY THOSE OF THE GREAT RACE WHO SOUGHT TO ESCAPE THE MENTAL EXTINCTION OF DEATH."
"THESE WERE NOT COMMON. THE LONGEVITY OF THE GREAT RACE LESSENED ITS LOVE OF LIFE."
"WHEN THE DISPLACING MIND HAD LEARNED WHAT IT WISHED IN THE FUTURE, IT WOULD BUILD AN APPARATUS LIKE THAT WHICH HAD STARTED ITS FLIGHT, AND REVERSE THE PROCESS OF PROJECTION."
"THE CAPTIVE MIND WOULD RETURN WITH ONLY THE FAINTEST AND MOST FRAGMENTARY VISIONS OF ITS EXPERIENCES."
"ALL MEMORIES WERE ERADICATED, SO THAT ONLY A DREAM-SHADOWED BLANK STRETCHED BACK TO THE TIME OF THE EXCHANGE."
MY STUDIES HAVE INFORMED MY DREAMS, AND MY DREAMS HAVE INFORMED MY STUDIES. LEGENDS AND HALLUCINATIONS HAVE BECOME ENTWINED.
"THE *NECRONOMICON* EVEN MAKES SUGGESTION OF A CULT THAT SOMETIMES GIVES AID TO MINDS VOYAGING DOWN THE AEONS."

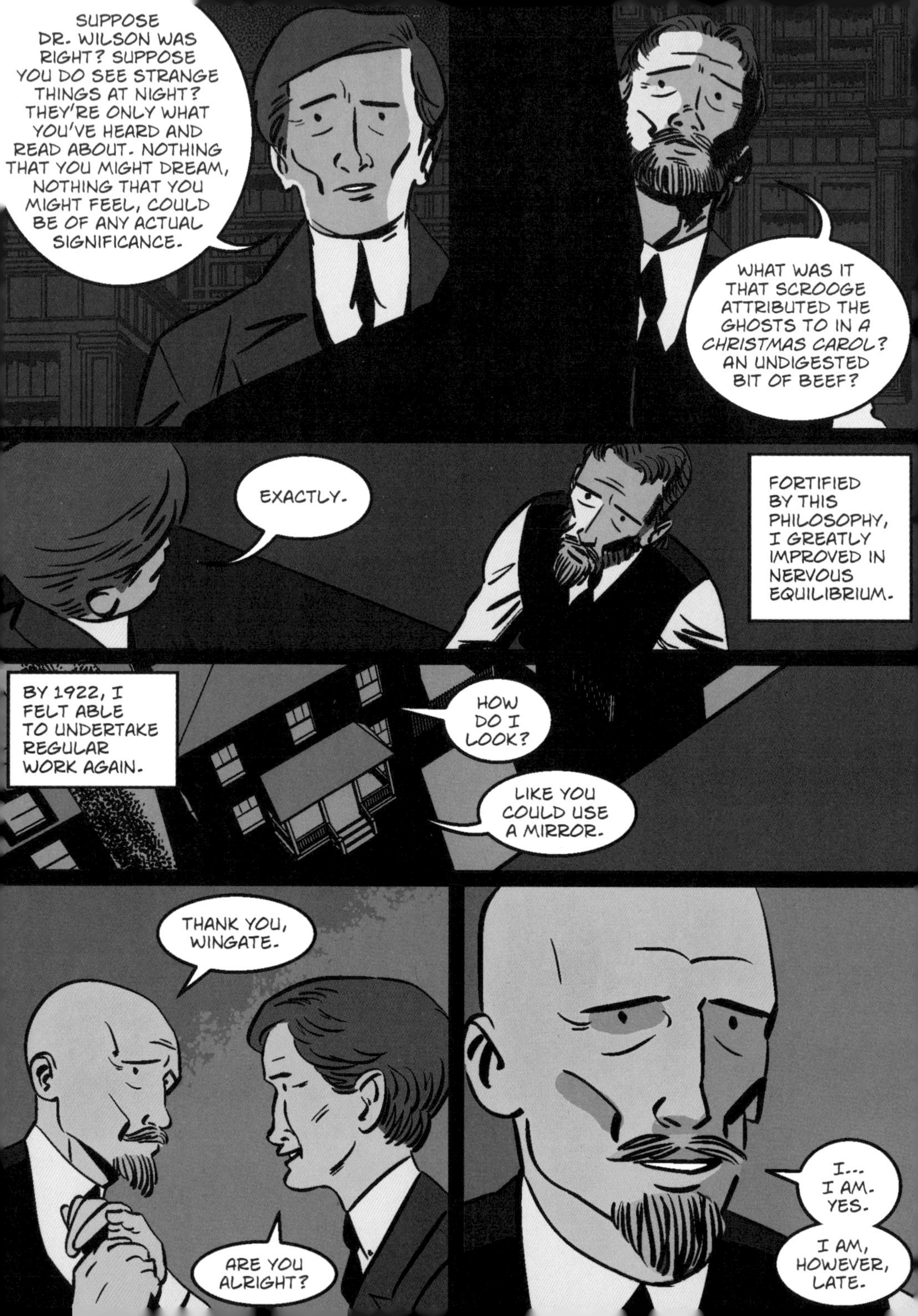
SUPPOSE DR. WILSON WAS RIGHT? SUPPOSE YOU DO SEE STRANGE THINGS AT NIGHT? THEY'RE ONLY WHAT YOU'VE HEARD AND READ ABOUT. NOTHING THAT YOU MIGHT DREAM, NOTHING THAT YOU MIGHT FEEL, COULD BE OF ANY ACTUAL SIGNIFICANCE.
WHAT WAS IT THAT SCROOGE ATTRIBUTED THE GHOSTS TO IN A *CHRISTMAS CAROL*? AN UNDIGESTED BIT OF BEEF?
EXACTLY.
FORTIFIED BY THIS PHILOSOPHY, I GREATLY IMPROVED IN NERVOUS EQUILIBRIUM.
BY 1922, I FELT ABLE TO UNDERTAKE REGULAR WORK AGAIN.
HOW DO I LOOK?
LIKE YOU COULD USE A MIRROR.
THANK YOU, WINGATE.
ARE YOU ALRIGHT?
I... I AM. YES.
I AM, HOWEVER, LATE.

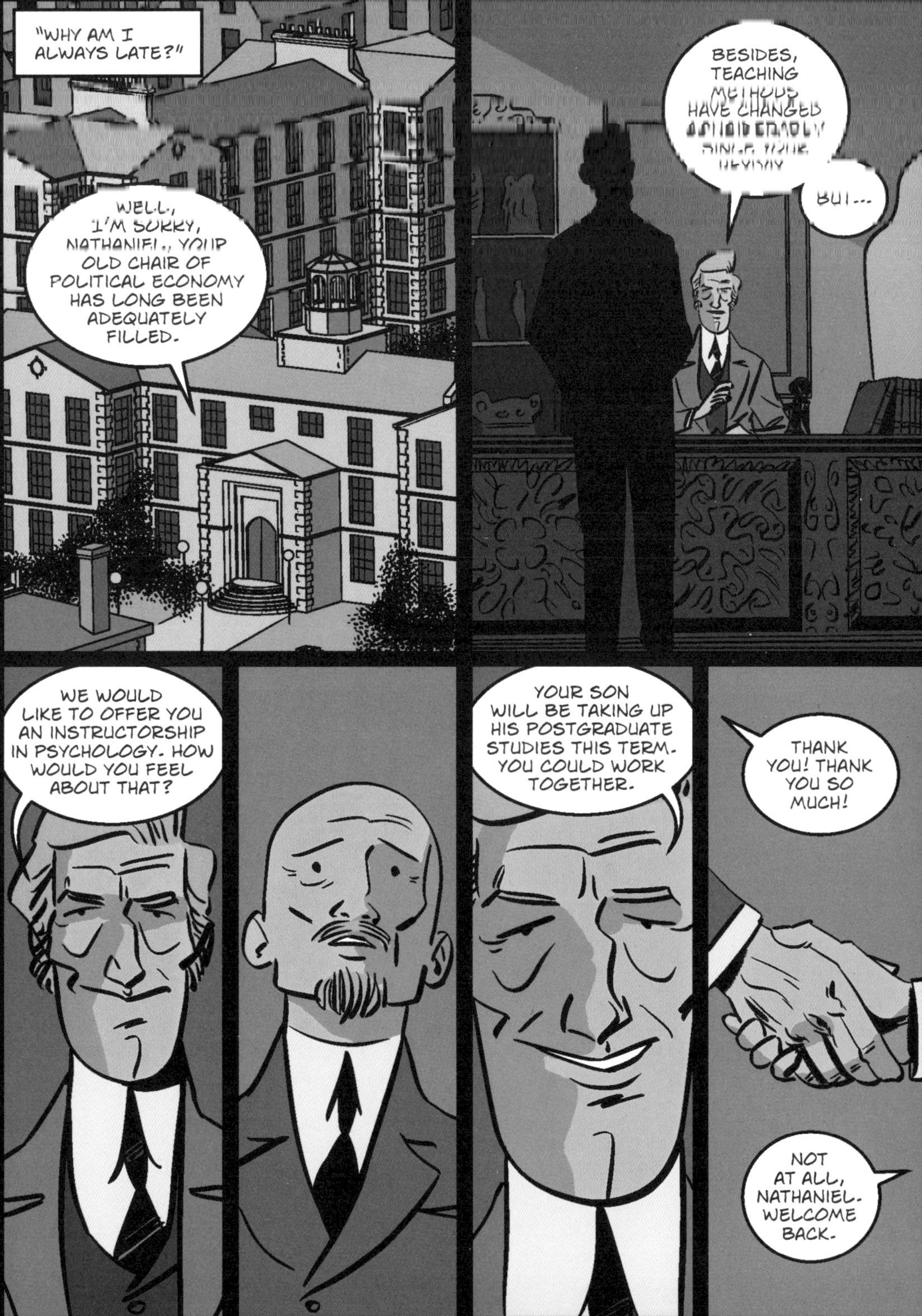
"WHY AM I ALWAYS LATE?"
WELL, I'M SORRY, NATHANIEL, YOUR OLD CHAIR OF POLITICAL ECONOMY HAS LONG BEEN ADEQUATELY FILLED.
BESIDES, TEACHING METHODS HAVE CHANGED
BUT...
WE WOULD LIKE TO OFFER YOU AN INSTRUCTORSHIP IN PSYCHOLOGY. HOW WOULD YOU FEEL ABOUT THAT?
YOUR SON WILL BE TAKING UP HIS POSTGRADUATE STUDIES THIS TERM. YOU COULD WORK TOGETHER.
THANK YOU! THANK YOU SO MUCH!
NOT AT ALL, NATHANIEL. WELCOME BACK.

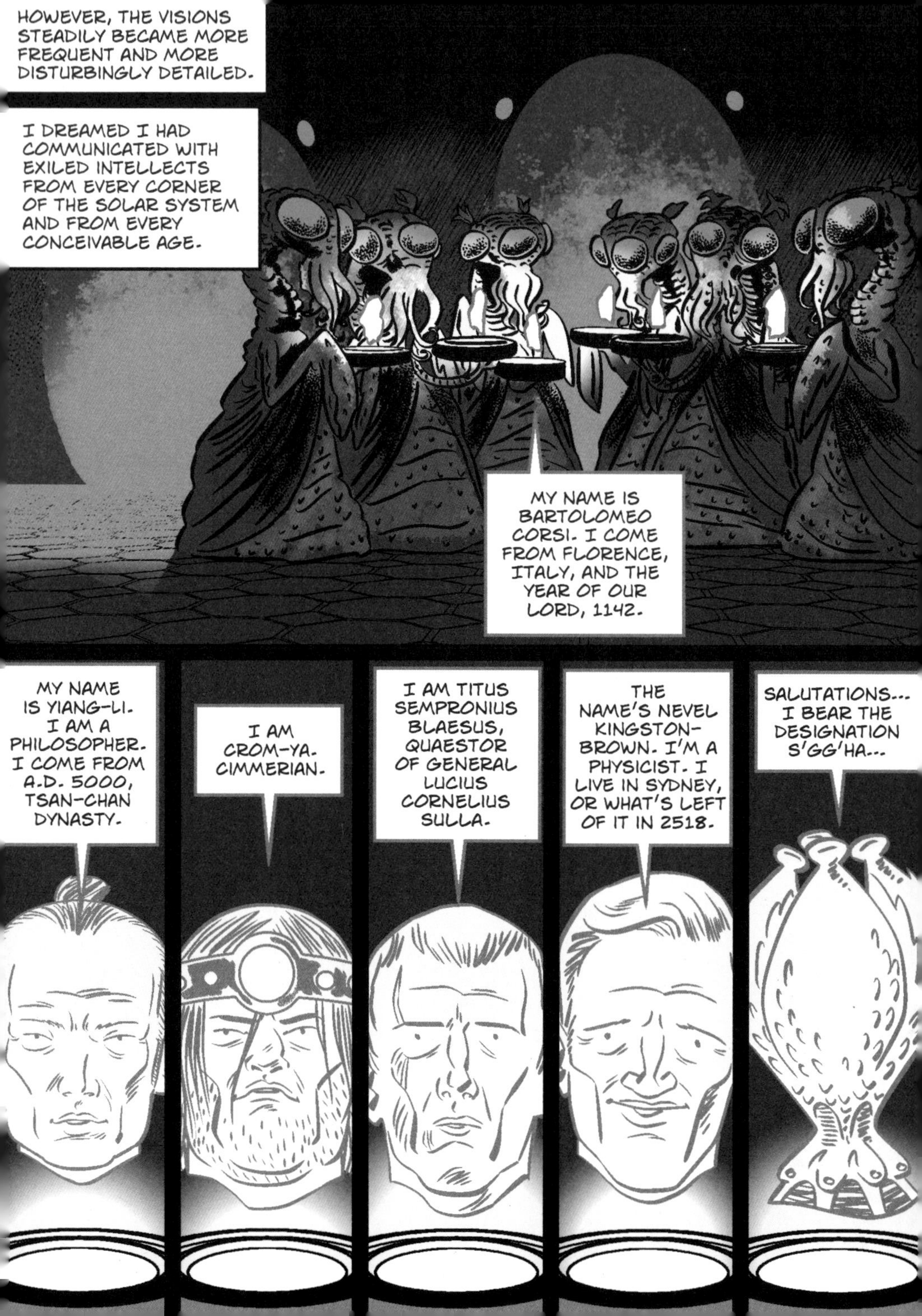
HOWEVER, THE VISIONS STEADILY BECAME MORE FREQUENT AND MORE DISTURBINGLY DETAILED.
I DREAMED I HAD COMMUNICATED WITH EXILED INTELLECTS FROM EVERY CORNER OF THE SOLAR SYSTEM AND FROM EVERY CONCEIVABLE AGE.
MY NAME IS BARTOLOMEO CORSI. I COME FROM FLORENCE, ITALY, AND THE YEAR OF OUR LORD, 1142.
MY NAME IS YIANG-LI. I AM A PHILOSOPHER. I COME FROM A.D. 5000, TSAN-CHAN DYNASTY.
I AM CROM-YA. CIMMERIAN.
I AM TITUS SEMPRONIUS BLAESUS, QUAESTOR OF GENERAL LUCIUS CORNELIUS SULLA.
THE NAME'S NEVEL KINGSTON-BROWN. I'M A PHYSICIST. I LIVE IN SYDNEY, OR WHAT'S LEFT OF IT IN 2518.
SALUTATIONS... I BEAR THE DESIGNATION S'GG'HA...

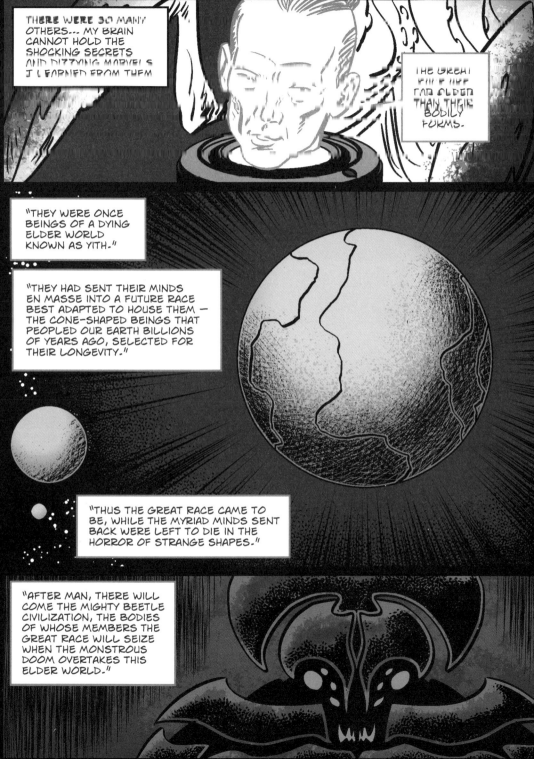

THERE WERE SO MANY OTHERS... MY BRAIN CANNOT HOLD THE SHOCKING SECRETS AND DIZZYING MARVELS I LEARNED FROM THEM.

THE GREAT RACE ARE FAR OLDER THAN THEIR BODILY FORMS.

"THEY WERE ONCE BEINGS OF A DYING ELDER WORLD KNOWN AS YITH."

"THEY HAD SENT THEIR MINDS EN MASSE INTO A FUTURE RACE BEST ADAPTED TO HOUSE THEM — THE CONE-SHAPED BEINGS THAT PEOPLED OUR EARTH BILLIONS OF YEARS AGO, SELECTED FOR THEIR LONGEVITY."

"THUS THE GREAT RACE CAME TO BE, WHILE THE MYRIAD MINDS SENT BACK WERE LEFT TO DIE IN THE HORROR OF STRANGE SHAPES."

"AFTER MAN, THERE WILL COME THE MIGHTY BEETLE CIVILIZATION, THE BODIES OF WHOSE MEMBERS THE GREAT RACE WILL SEIZE WHEN THE MONSTROUS DOOM OVERTAKES THIS ELDER WORLD."

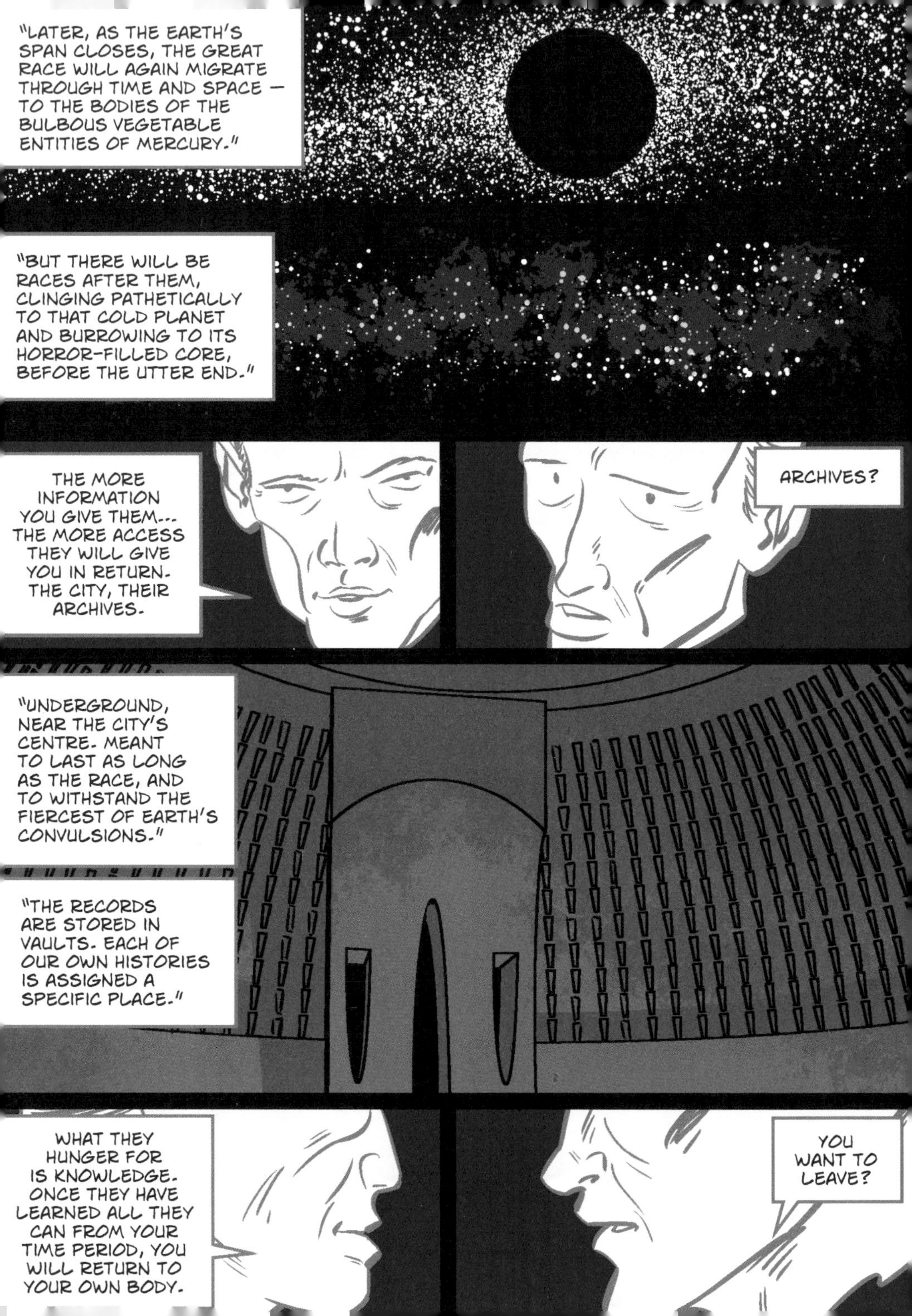
"LATER, AS THE EARTH'S SPAN CLOSES, THE GREAT RACE WILL AGAIN MIGRATE THROUGH TIME AND SPACE — TO THE BODIES OF THE BULBOUS VEGETABLE ENTITIES OF MERCURY."
"BUT THERE WILL BE RACES AFTER THEM, CLINGING PATHETICALLY TO THAT COLD PLANET AND BURROWING TO ITS HORROR-FILLED CORE, BEFORE THE UTTER END."
THE MORE INFORMATION YOU GIVE THEM... THE MORE ACCESS THEY WILL GIVE YOU IN RETURN. THE CITY, THEIR ARCHIVES.
ARCHIVES?
"UNDERGROUND, NEAR THE CITY'S CENTRE. MEANT TO LAST AS LONG AS THE RACE, AND TO WITHSTAND THE FIERCEST OF EARTH'S CONVULSIONS."
"THE RECORDS ARE STORED IN VAULTS. EACH OF OUR OWN HISTORIES IS ASSIGNED A SPECIFIC PLACE."
WHAT THEY HUNGER FOR IS KNOWLEDGE. ONCE THEY HAVE LEARNED ALL THEY CAN FROM YOUR TIME PERIOD, YOU WILL RETURN TO YOUR OWN BODY.
YOU WANT TO LEAVE?

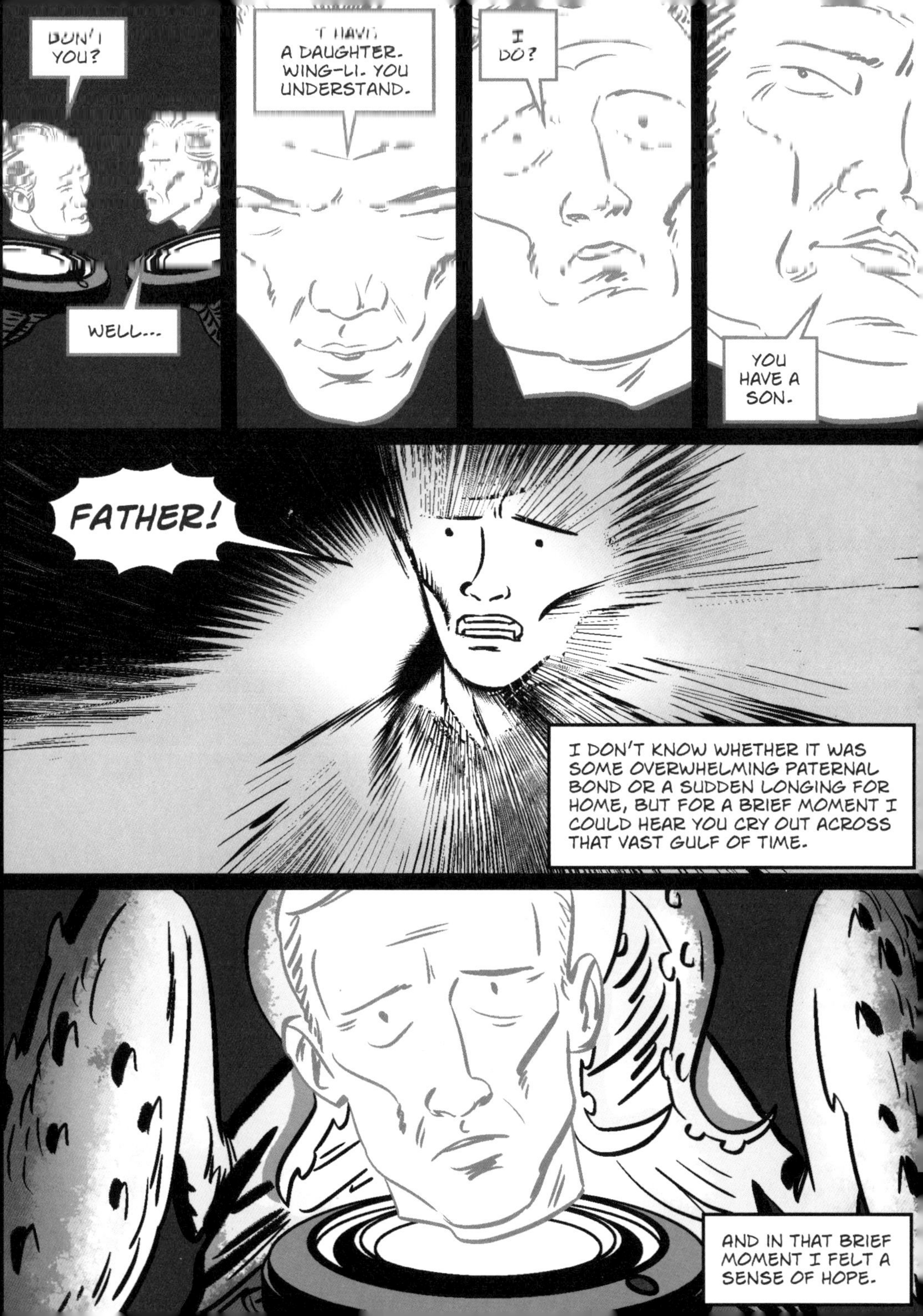
DON'T YOU?
WELL...
I HAVE A DAUGHTER. WING-LI. YOU UNDERSTAND.
I DO?
YOU HAVE A SON.
FATHER!
I DON'T KNOW WHETHER IT WAS SOME OVERWHELMING PATERNAL BOND OR A SUDDEN LONGING FOR HOME, BUT FOR A BRIEF MOMENT I COULD HEAR YOU CRY OUT ACROSS THAT VAST GULF OF TIME.
AND IN THAT BRIEF MOMENT I FELT A SENSE OF HOPE.

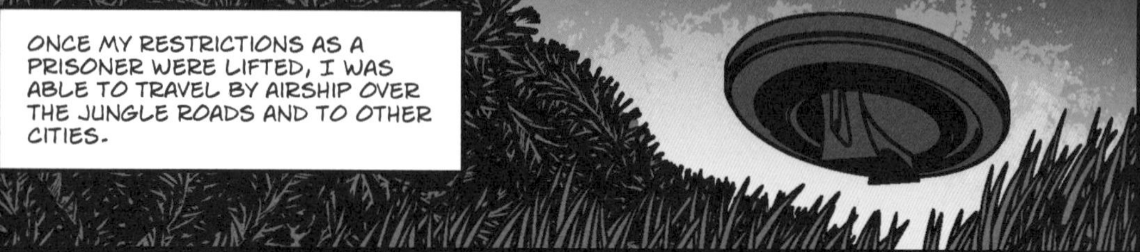
ONCE MY RESTRICTIONS AS A PRISONER WERE LIFTED, I WAS ABLE TO TRAVEL BY AIRSHIP OVER THE JUNGLE ROADS AND TO OTHER CITIES.

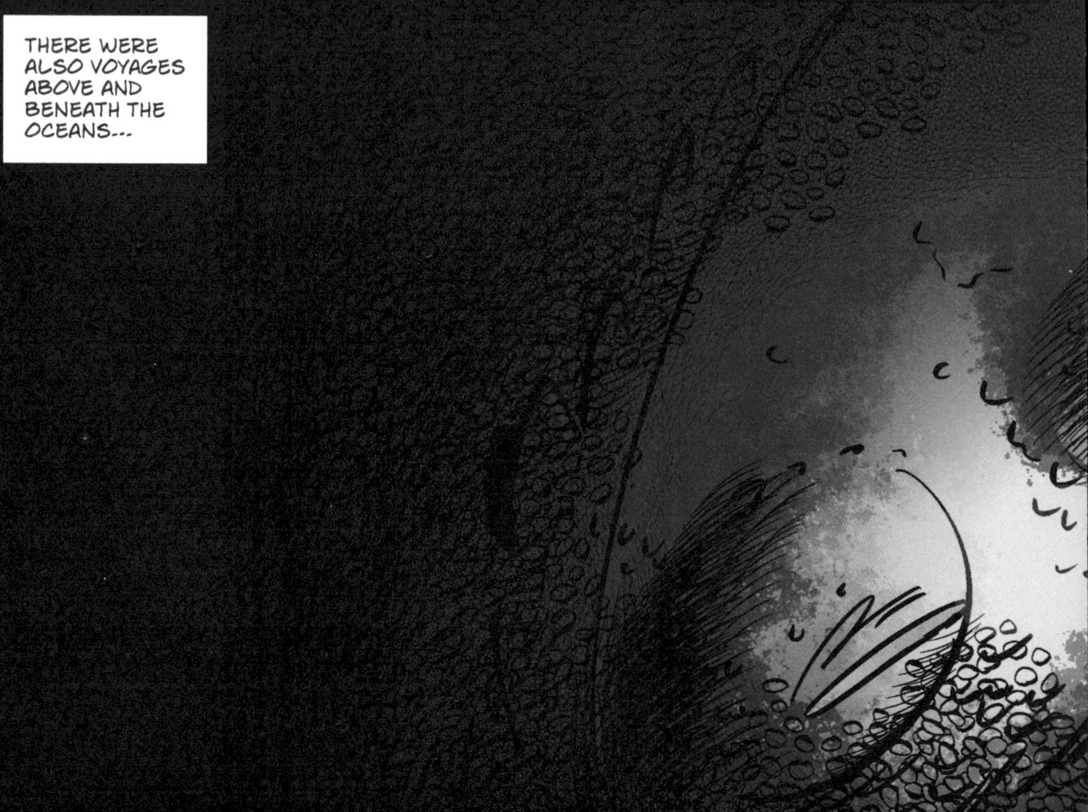
THERE WERE ALSO VOYAGES ABOVE AND BENEATH THE OCEANS...

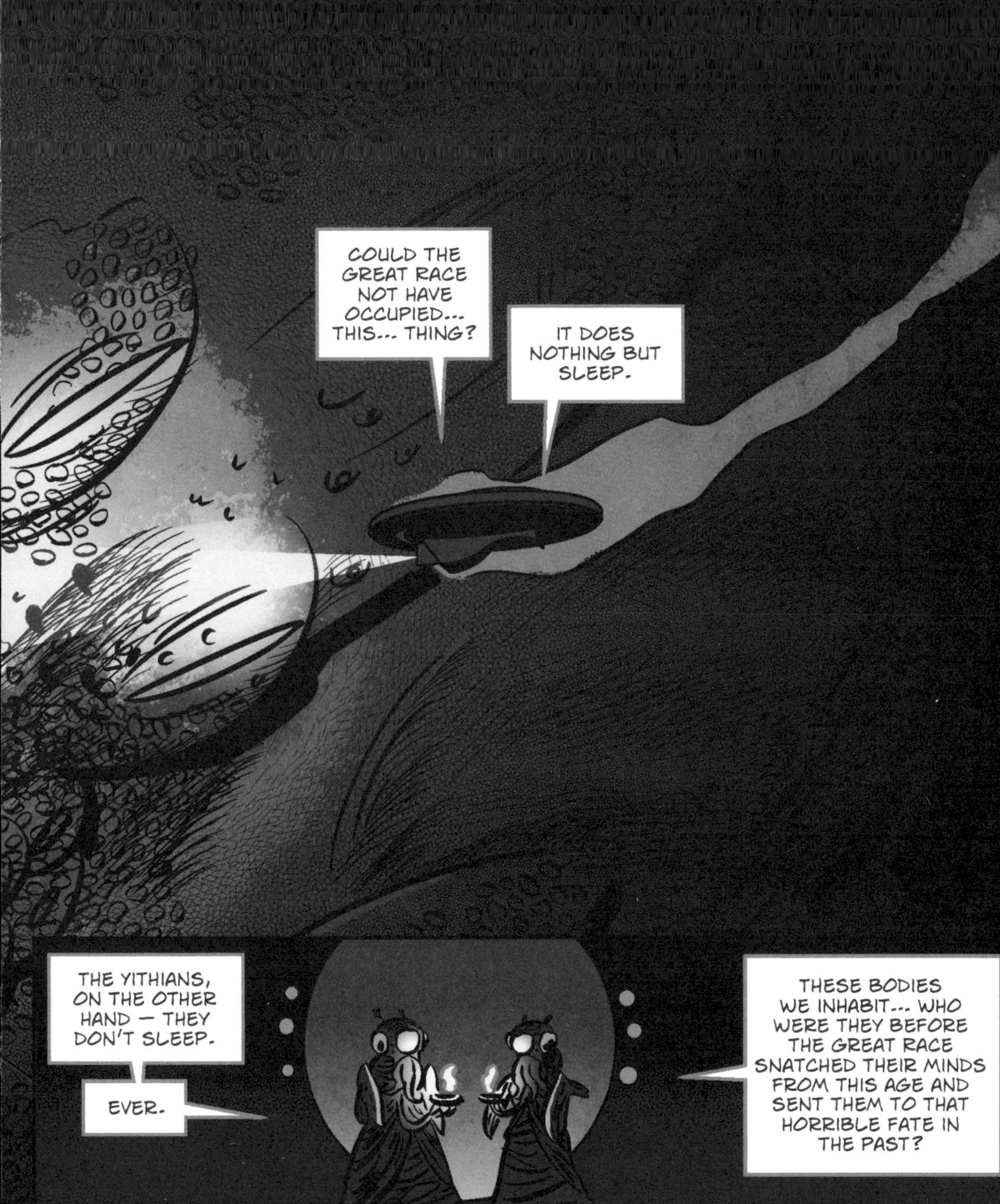
COULD THE GREAT RACE NOT HAVE OCCUPIED... THIS... THING?
IT DOES NOTHING BUT SLEEP.
THE YITHIANS, ON THE OTHER HAND — THEY DON'T SLEEP.
EVER.
THESE BODIES WE INHABIT... WHO WERE THEY BEFORE THE GREAT RACE SNATCHED THEIR MINDS FROM THIS AGE AND SENT THEM TO THAT HORRIBLE FATE IN THE PAST?

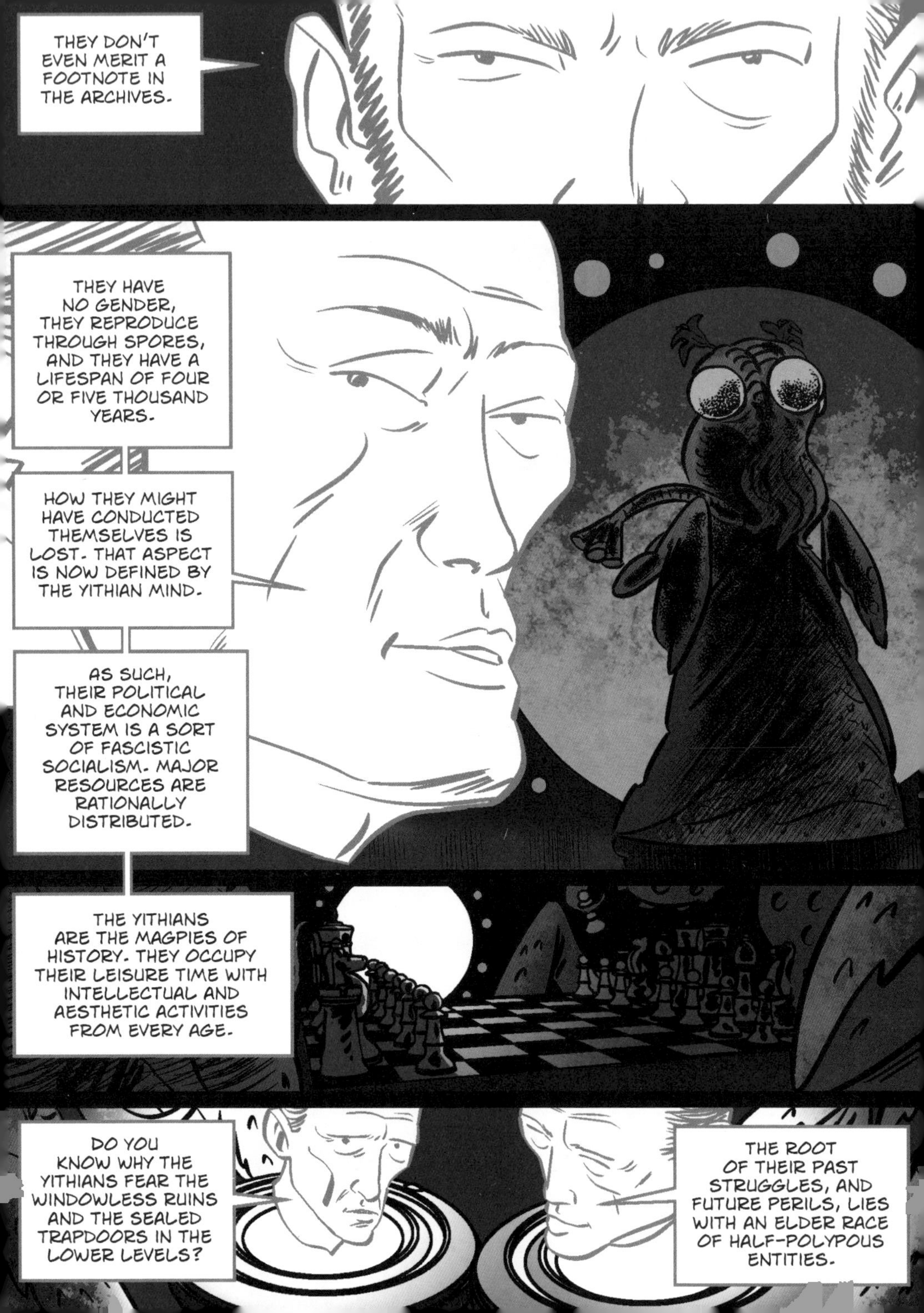
THEY DON'T EVEN MERIT A FOOTNOTE IN THE ARCHIVES.
THEY HAVE NO GENDER, THEY REPRODUCE THROUGH SPORES, AND THEY HAVE A LIFESPAN OF FOUR OR FIVE THOUSAND YEARS.
HOW THEY MIGHT HAVE CONDUCTED THEMSELVES IS LOST. THAT ASPECT IS NOW DEFINED BY THE YITHIAN MIND.
AS SUCH, THEIR POLITICAL AND ECONOMIC SYSTEM IS A SORT OF FASCISTIC SOCIALISM. MAJOR RESOURCES ARE RATIONALLY DISTRIBUTED.
THE YITHIANS ARE THE MAGPIES OF HISTORY. THEY OCCUPY THEIR LEISURE TIME WITH INTELLECTUAL AND AESTHETIC ACTIVITIES FROM EVERY AGE.
DO YOU KNOW WHY THE YITHIANS FEAR THE WINDOWLESS RUINS AND THE SEALED TRAPDOORS IN THE LOWER LEVELS?
THE ROOT OF THEIR PAST STRUGGLES, AND FUTURE PERILS, LIES WITH AN ELDER RACE OF HALF-POLYPOUS ENTITIES.

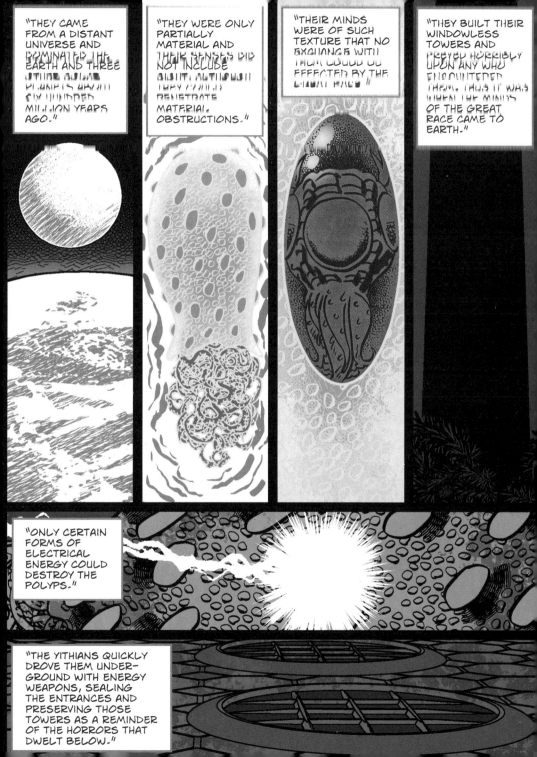

"THEY CAME FROM A DISTANT UNIVERSE AND DOMINATED THE EARTH AND THREE OTHER SOLAR PLANETS ABOUT SIX HUNDRED MILLION YEARS AGO."

"THEY WERE ONLY PARTIALLY MATERIAL AND THEIR SENSES DID NOT INCLUDE SIGHT, ALTHOUGH THEY WOULD PENETRATE MATERIAL OBSTRUCTIONS."

"THEIR MINDS WERE OF SUCH TEXTURE THAT NO EXCHANGE WITH THEM COULD BE EFFECTED BY THE GREAT RACE."

"THEY BUILT THEIR WINDOWLESS TOWERS AND PREYED HORRIBLY UPON ANY WHO ENCOUNTERED THEM. THUS IT WAS WHEN THE MINDS OF THE GREAT RACE CAME TO EARTH."

"ONLY CERTAIN FORMS OF ELECTRICAL ENERGY COULD DESTROY THE POLYPS."

"THE YITHIANS QUICKLY DROVE THEM UNDER-GROUND WITH ENERGY WEAPONS, SEALING THE ENTRANCES AND PRESERVING THOSE TOWERS AS A REMINDER OF THE HORRORS THAT DWELT BELOW."

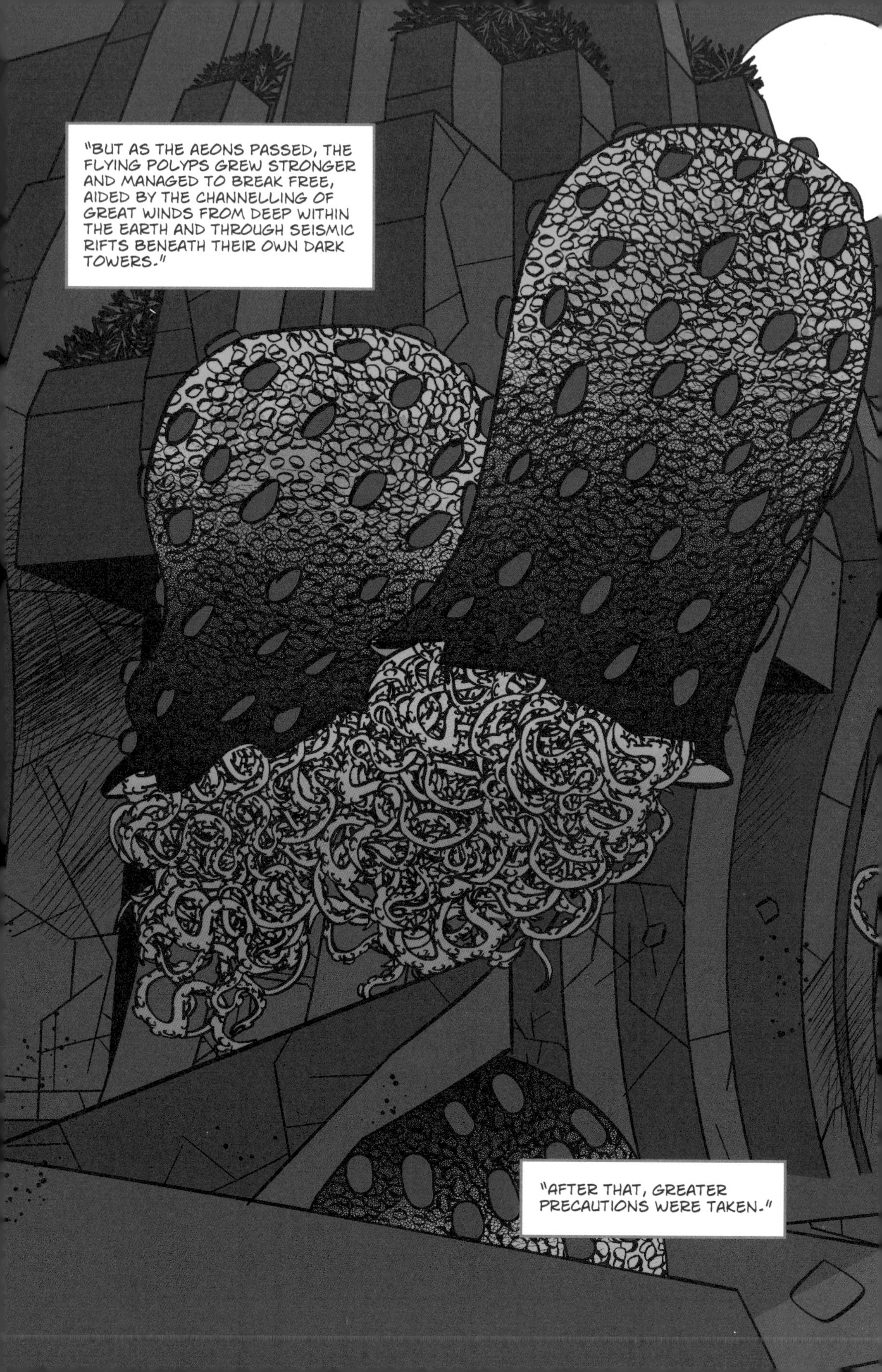
"BUT AS THE AEONS PASSED, THE FLYING POLYPS GREW STRONGER AND MANAGED TO BREAK FREE, AIDED BY THE CHANNELLING OF GREAT WINDS FROM DEEP WITHIN THE EARTH AND THROUGH SEISMIC RIFTS BENEATH THEIR OWN DARK TOWERS."
"AFTER THAT, GREATER PRECAUTIONS WERE TAKEN."

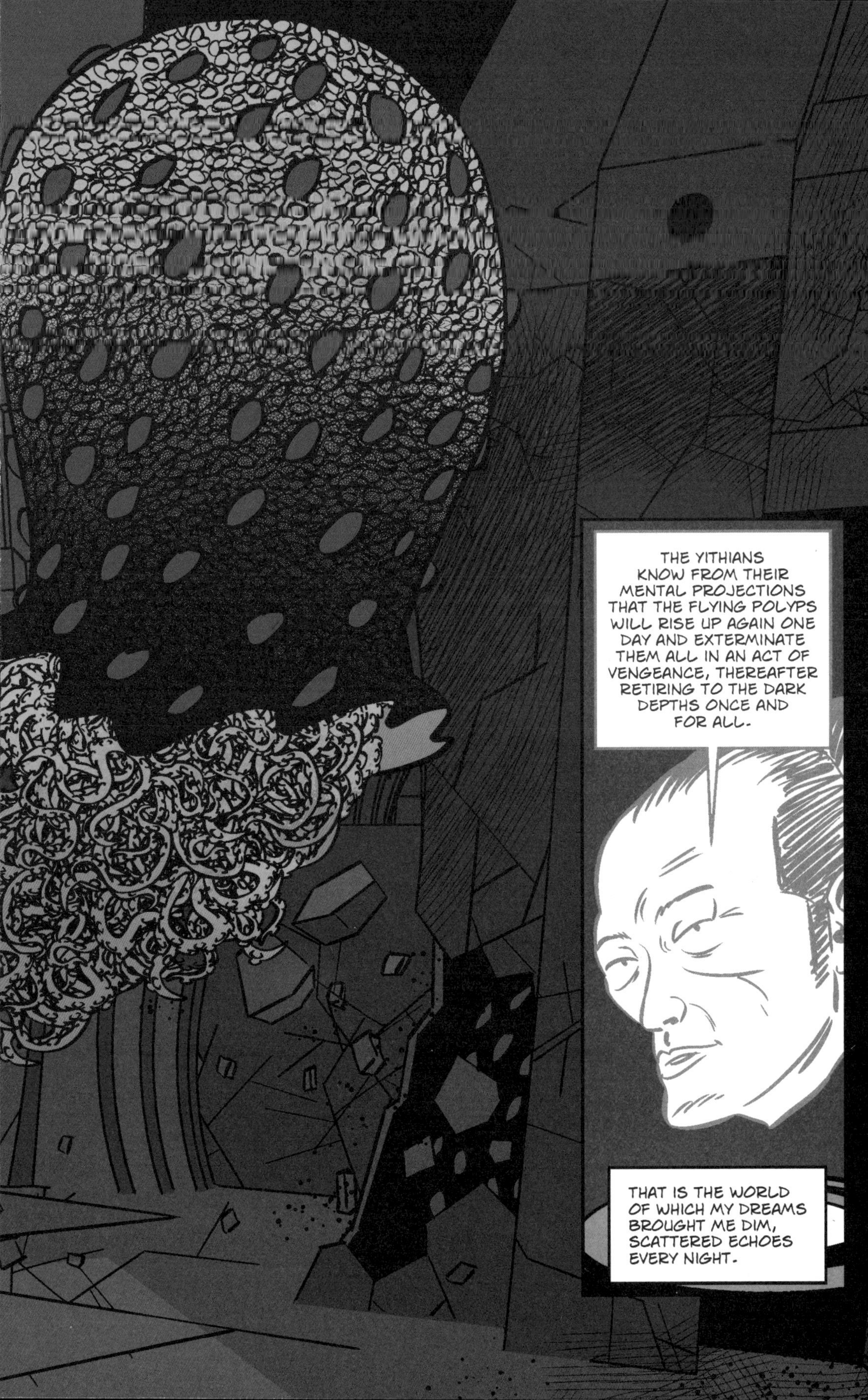
THE YITHIANS KNOW FROM THEIR MENTAL PROJECTIONS THAT THE FLYING POLYPS WILL RISE UP AGAIN ONE DAY AND EXTERMINATE THEM ALL IN AN ACT OF VENGEANCE, THEREAFTER RETIRING TO THE DARK DEPTHS ONCE AND FOR ALL.
THAT IS THE WORLD OF WHICH MY DREAMS BROUGHT ME DIM, SCATTERED ECHOES EVERY NIGHT.

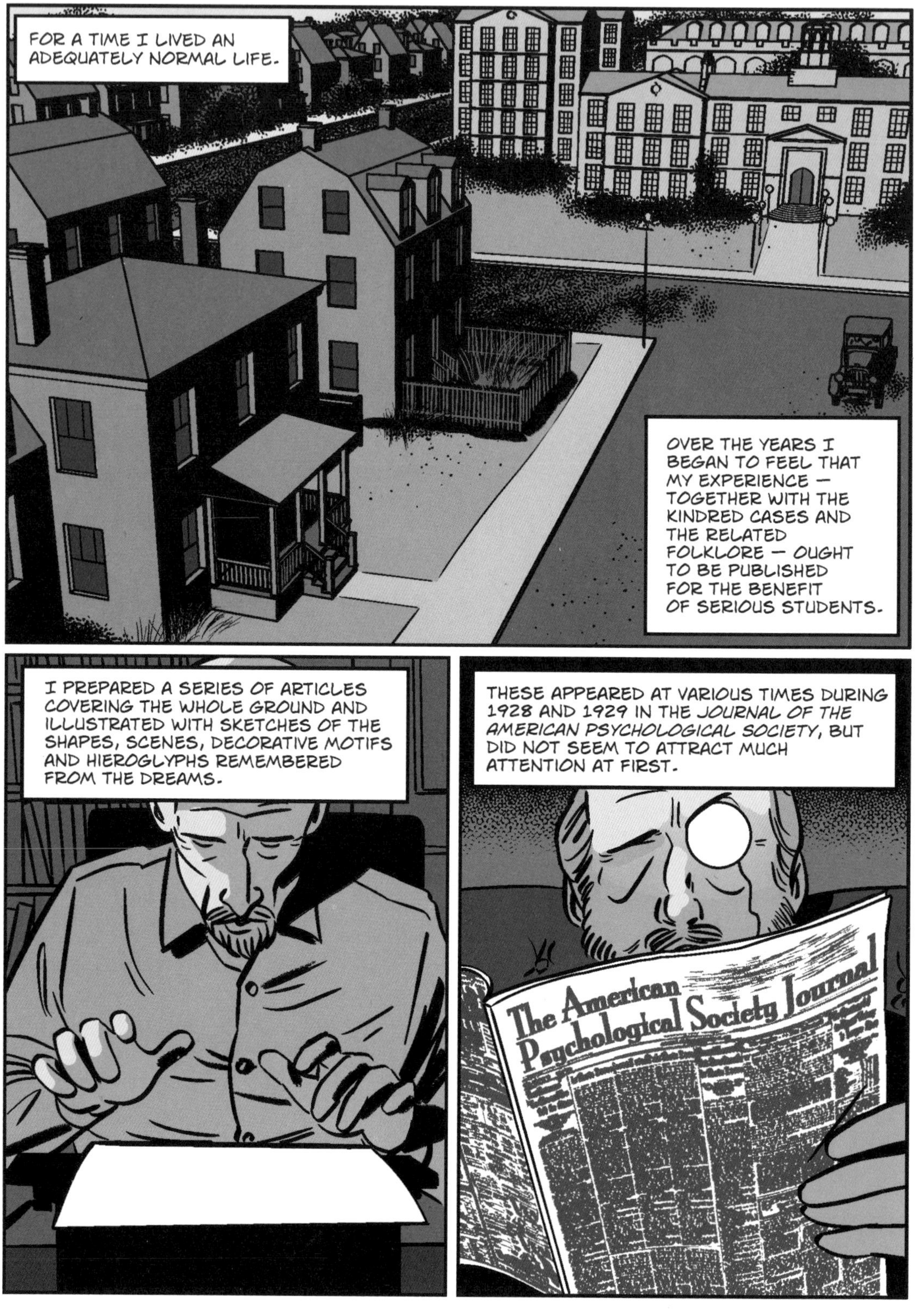
FOR A TIME I LIVED AN ADEQUATELY NORMAL LIFE.
OVER THE YEARS I BEGAN TO FEEL THAT MY EXPERIENCE — TOGETHER WITH THE KINDRED CASES AND THE RELATED FOLKLORE — OUGHT TO BE PUBLISHED FOR THE BENEFIT OF SERIOUS STUDENTS.
I PREPARED A SERIES OF ARTICLES COVERING THE WHOLE GROUND AND ILLUSTRATED WITH SKETCHES OF THE SHAPES, SCENES, DECORATIVE MOTIFS AND HIEROGLYPHS REMEMBERED FROM THE DREAMS.
THESE APPEARED AT VARIOUS TIMES DURING 1928 AND 1929 IN THE *JOURNAL OF THE AMERICAN PSYCHOLOGICAL SOCIETY*, BUT DID NOT SEEM TO ATTRACT MUCH ATTENTION AT FIRST.
The American Psychological Society Journal

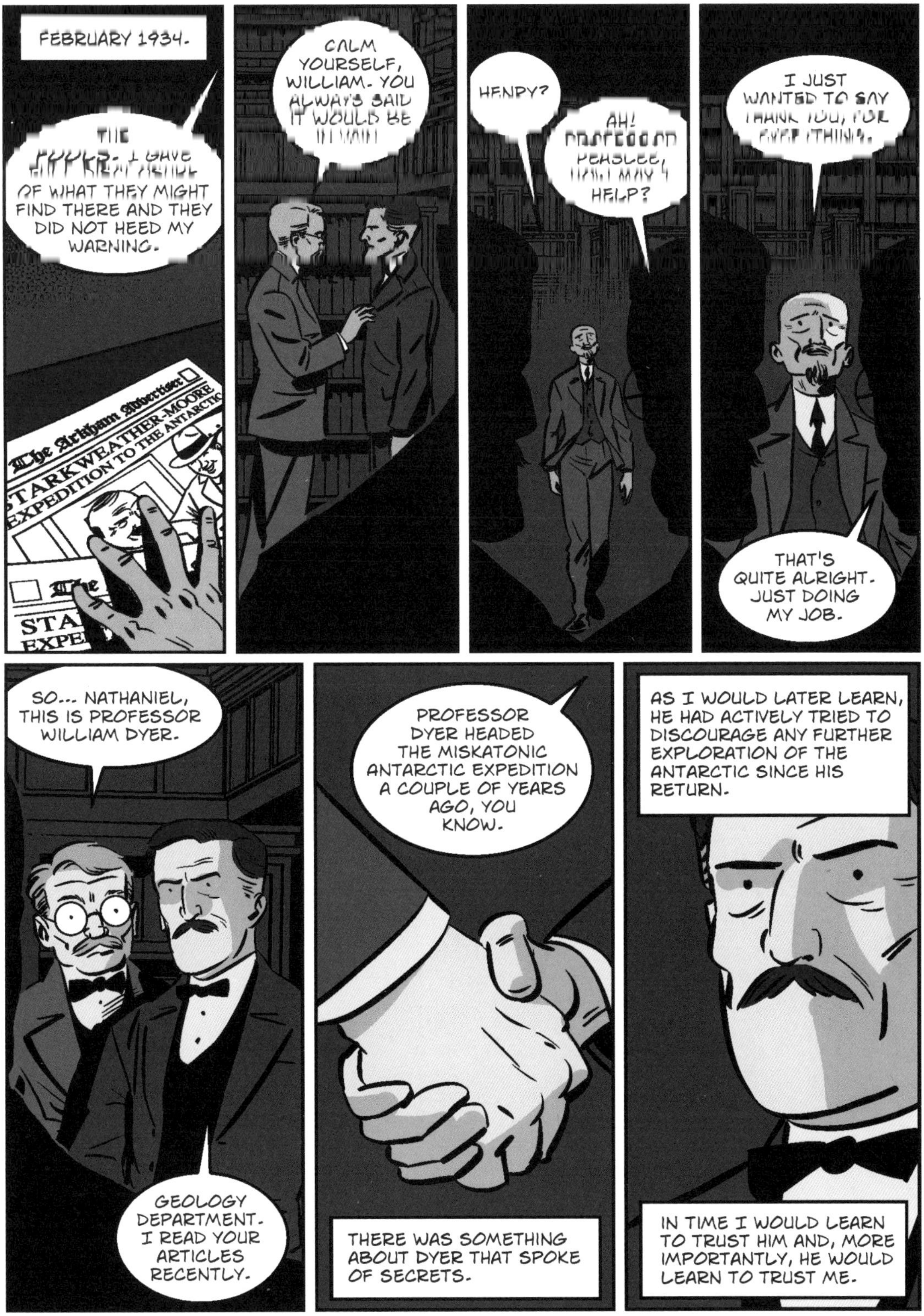
FEBRUARY 1934.
THE
OF WHAT THEY MIGHT FIND THERE AND THEY DID NOT HEED MY WARNING.
The Arkham Advertiser
STARKWEATHER-MOORE EXPEDITION TO THE ANTARCTIC
CALM YOURSELF, WILLIAM. YOU ALWAYS SAID IT WOULD BE
AH!
HELP?
I JUST WANTED TO SAY
THAT'S QUITE ALRIGHT. JUST DOING MY JOB.
SO... NATHANIEL, THIS IS PROFESSOR WILLIAM DYER.
GEOLOGY DEPARTMENT. I READ YOUR ARTICLES RECENTLY.
PROFESSOR DYER HEADED THE MISKATONIC ANTARCTIC EXPEDITION A COUPLE OF YEARS AGO, YOU KNOW.
THERE WAS SOMETHING ABOUT DYER THAT SPOKE OF SECRETS.
AS I WOULD LATER LEARN, HE HAD ACTIVELY TRIED TO DISCOURAGE ANY FURTHER EXPLORATION OF THE ANTARCTIC SINCE HIS RETURN.
IN TIME I WOULD LEARN TO TRUST HIM AND, MORE IMPORTANTLY, HE WOULD LEARN TO TRUST ME.

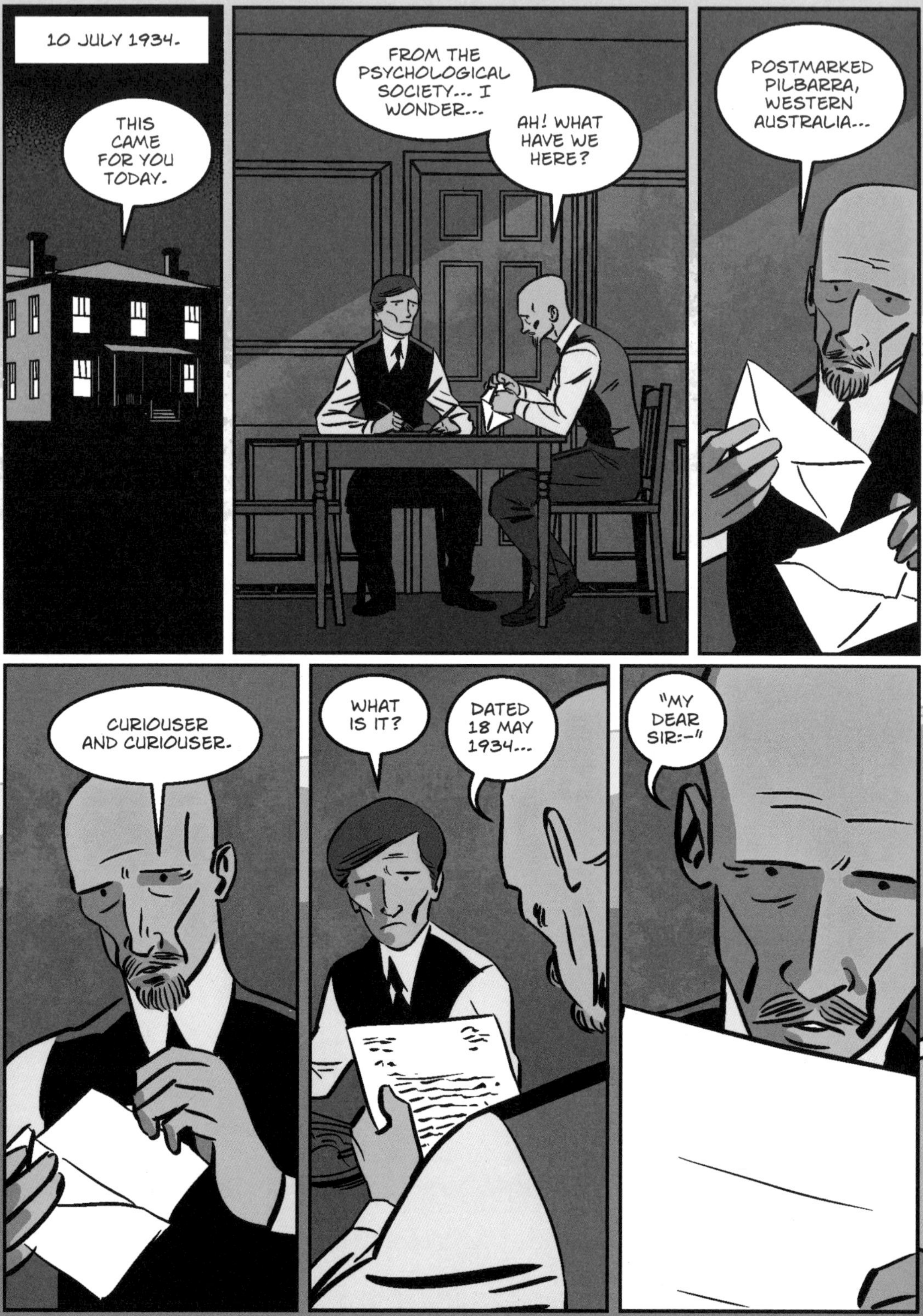
10 JULY 1934.
THIS CAME FOR YOU TODAY.
FROM THE PSYCHOLOGICAL SOCIETY... I WONDER...
AH! WHAT HAVE WE HERE?
POSTMARKED PILBARRA, WESTERN AUSTRALIA...
CURIOUSER AND CURIOUSER.
WHAT IS IT?
DATED 18 MAY 1934...
"MY DEAR SIR:-"

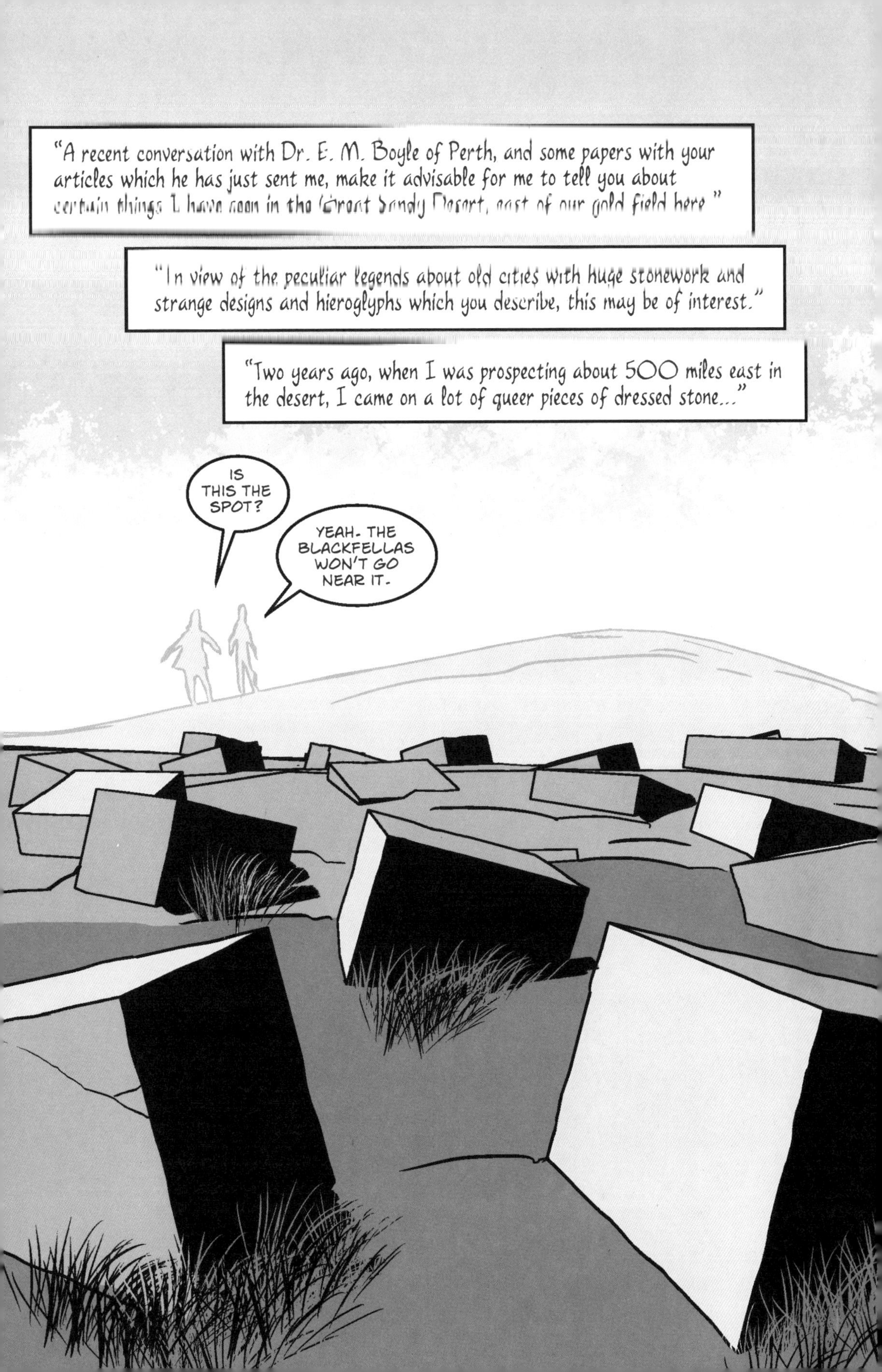
"A recent conversation with Dr. E. M. Boyle of Perth, and some papers with your articles which he has just sent me, make it advisable for me to tell you about certain things I have seen in the Great Sandy Desert, east of our gold field here."
"In view of the peculiar legends about old cities with huge stonework and strange designs and hieroglyphs which you describe, this may be of interest."
"Two years ago, when I was prospecting about 500 miles east in the desert, I came on a lot of queer pieces of dressed stone..."
IS THIS THE SPOT?
YEAH. THE BLACKFELLAS WON'T GO NEAR IT.

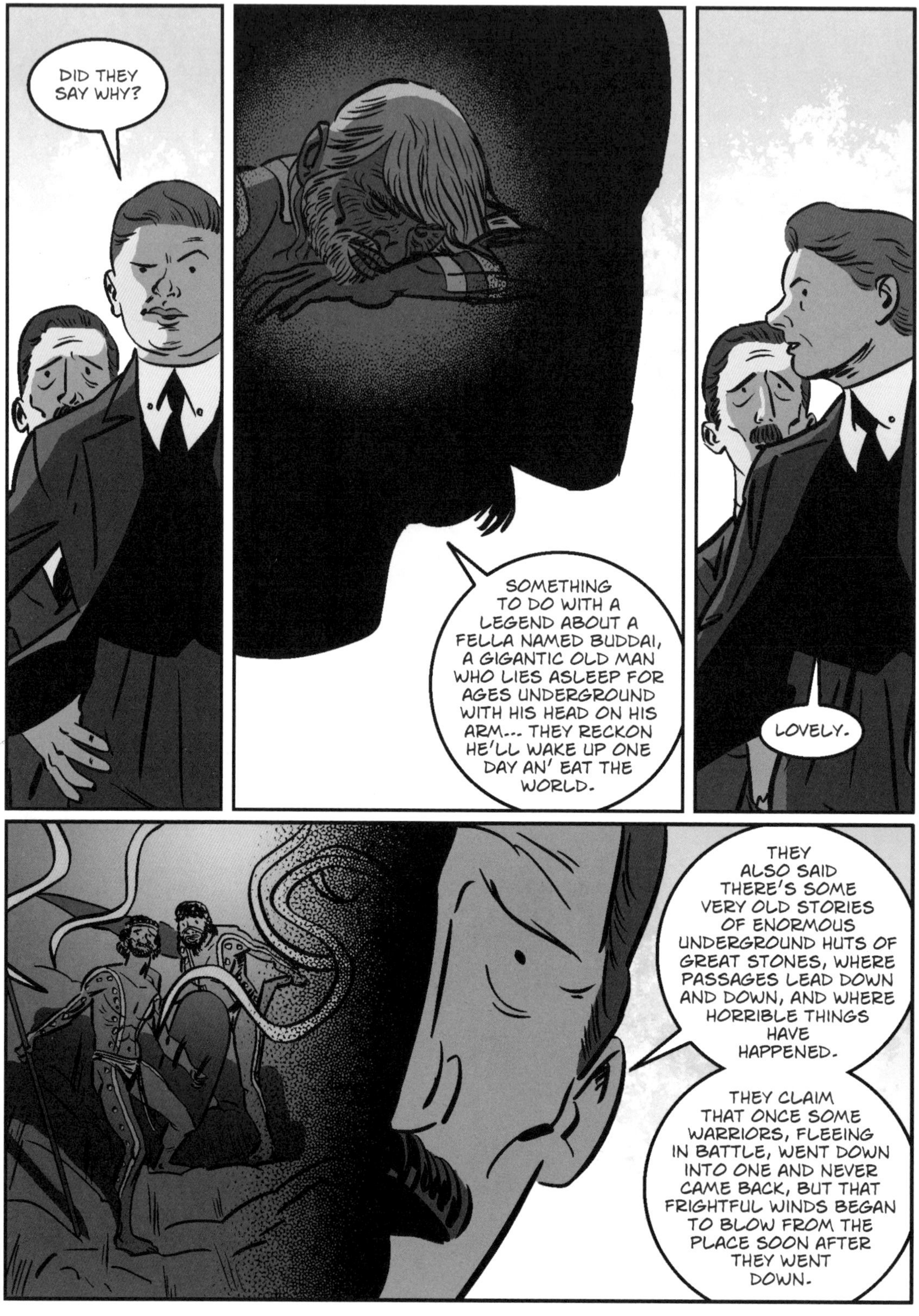
DID THEY SAY WHY?
SOMETHING TO DO WITH A LEGEND ABOUT A FELLA NAMED BUDDAI, A GIGANTIC OLD MAN WHO LIES ASLEEP FOR AGES UNDERGROUND WITH HIS HEAD ON HIS ARM... THEY RECKON HE'LL WAKE UP ONE DAY AN' EAT THE WORLD.
LOVELY.
THEY ALSO SAID THERE'S SOME VERY OLD STORIES OF ENORMOUS UNDERGROUND HUTS OF GREAT STONES, WHERE PASSAGES LEAD DOWN AND DOWN, AND WHERE HORRIBLE THINGS HAVE HAPPENED.
THEY CLAIM THAT ONCE SOME WARRIORS, FLEEING IN BATTLE, WENT DOWN INTO ONE AND NEVER CAME BACK, BUT THAT FRIGHTFUL WINDS BEGAN TO BLOW FROM THE PLACE SOON AFTER THEY WENT DOWN.

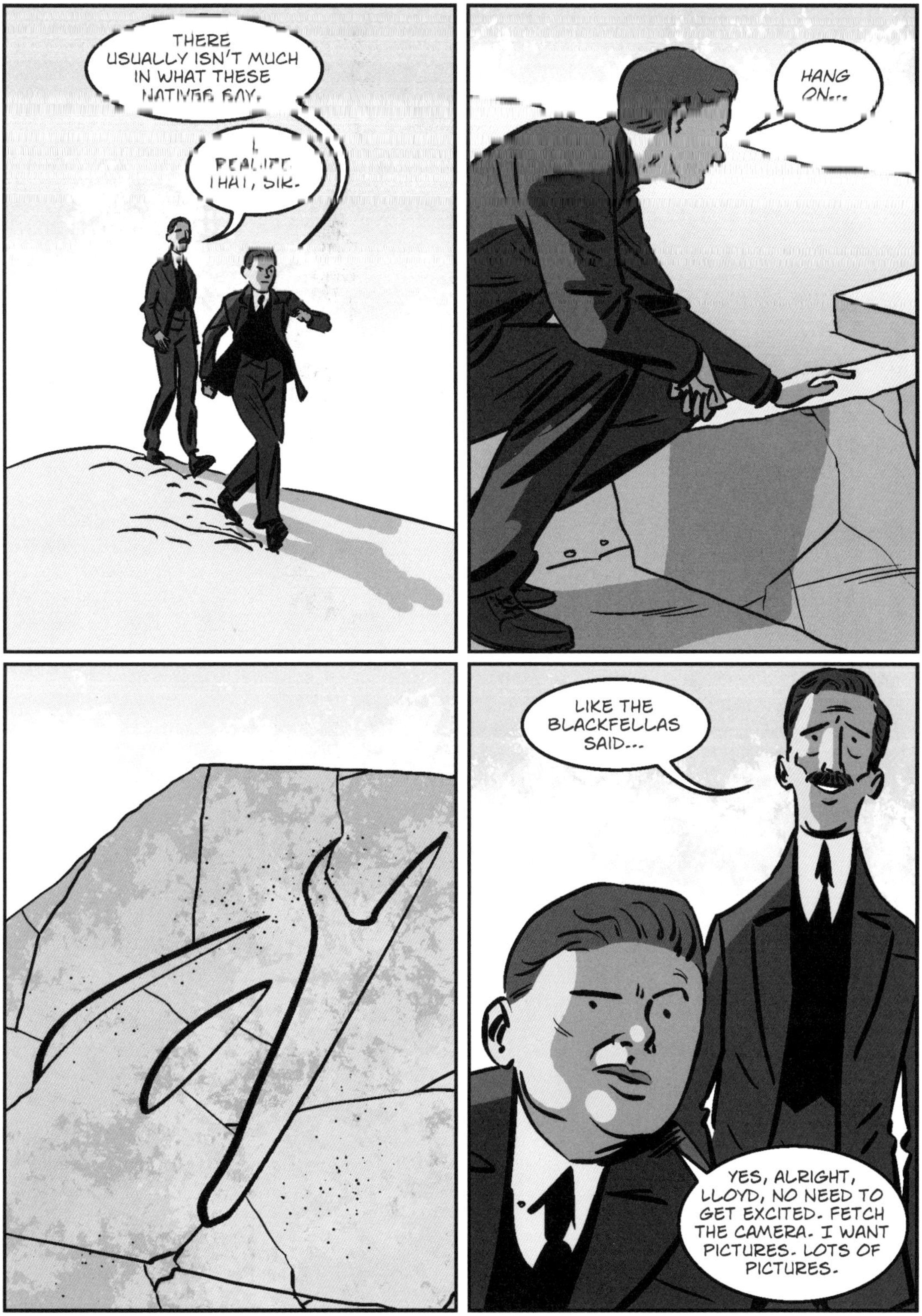
THERE USUALLY ISN'T MUCH IN WHAT THESE NATIVES SAY.
I THAT, SIR.
HANG ON...
LIKE THE BLACKFELLAS SAID...
YES, ALRIGHT, LLOYD, NO NEED TO GET EXCITED. FETCH THE CAMERA. I WANT PICTURES. LOTS OF PICTURES.

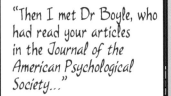

"Then I met Dr Boyle, who had read your articles in the *Journal of the American Psychological Society...*"

I DID. THEY WANTED NOTHING TO DO WITH THEM.

VERY INTERESTING, MR. MACKENZIE, VERY INTERESTING INDEED.

THE MARKINGS ARE JUST AS DESCRIBED.

AND YOU SAY YOU HANDED THESE OVER TO THE GOVERNMENT AT PERTH?

YOU SAY YOU'RE A MINING ENGINEER. YOU HAVE SOME KNOWLEDGE OF GEOLOGY?

THAT'S RIGHT. THEY'RE MOSTLY SANDSTONE AND GRANITE, THOUGH ONE IS ALMOST CERTAINLY MADE OF A QUEER SORT OF CEMENT OR CONCRETE.

THERE'S EVIDENCE FROM THESE BLOCKS THAT THIS PART OF THE WORLD WAS UNDERWATER AT SOME POINT. WE'RE TALKING A MATTER OF HUNDREDS OF THOUSANDS OF YEARS — OR HEAVEN KNOWS HOW MUCH MORE.

THESE BLOCKS ARE SO ANCIENT THEY FRIGHTEN ME.

WITHOUT QUESTION, MR. MACKENZIE, WE ARE FACED WITH THE PROBLEM OF AN UNKNOWN CIVILIZATION OLDER THAN ANY DREAMED OF BEFORE.

"In view of your previous diligent work, you will no doubt want to lead an expedition to the desert and make some archaeological excavations."

Dr. Boyle and I are prepared to cooperate in such work if you – or organizations known to you – can furnish the funds.

I shall welcome further correspondence upon this subject, and am keenly eager to assist in any plan you may devise.

Hoping profoundly for an early message,

Most faithfully yours,
Robert B. F. Mackenzie.

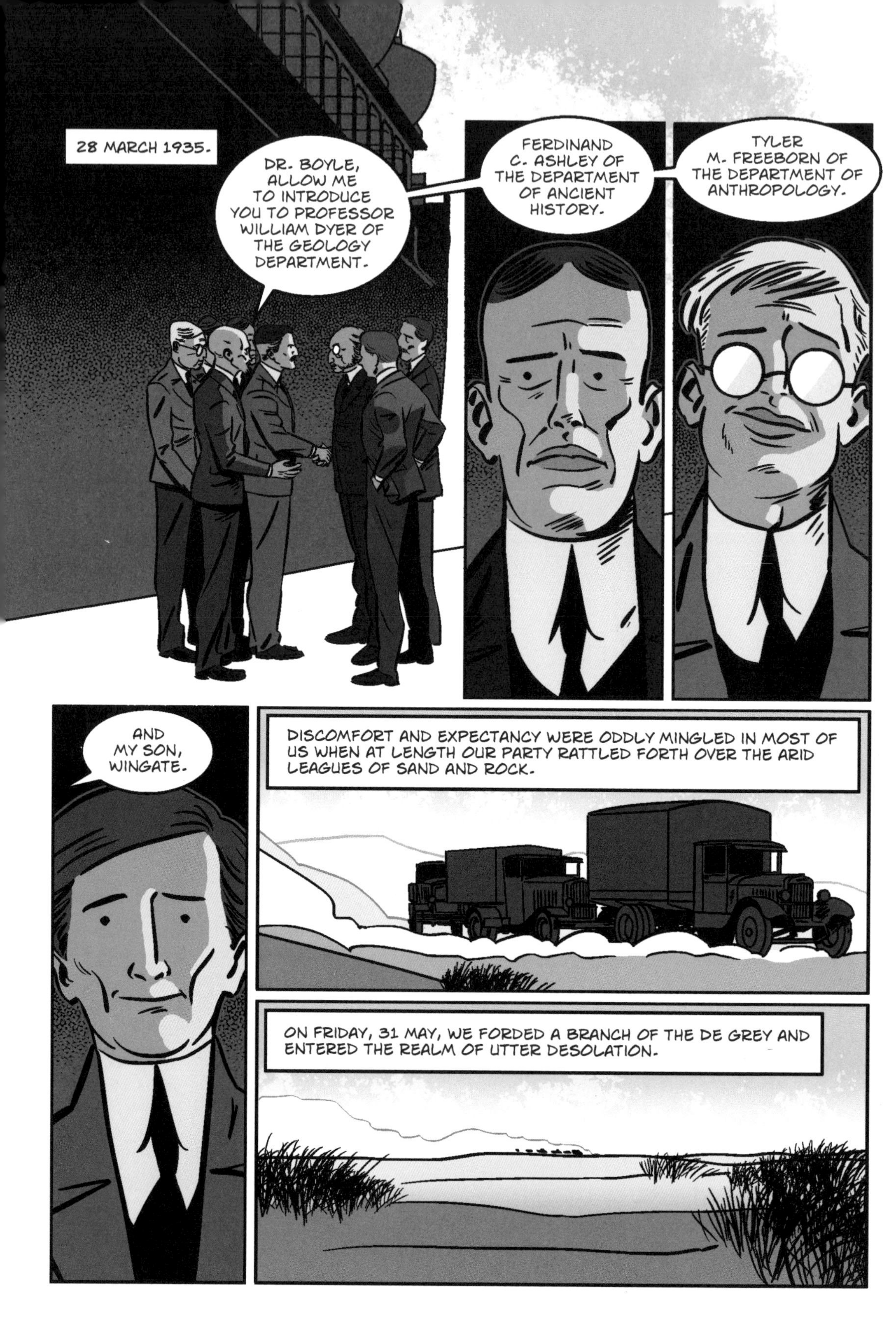
28 MARCH 1935.
DR. BOYLE, ALLOW ME TO INTRODUCE YOU TO PROFESSOR WILLIAM DYER OF THE GEOLOGY DEPARTMENT.
FERDINAND C. ASHLEY OF THE DEPARTMENT OF ANCIENT HISTORY.
TYLER M. FREEBORN OF THE DEPARTMENT OF ANTHROPOLOGY.
AND MY SON, WINGATE.
DISCOMFORT AND EXPECTANCY WERE ODDLY MINGLED IN MOST OF US WHEN AT LENGTH OUR PARTY RATTLED FORTH OVER THE ARID LEAGUES OF SAND AND ROCK.
ON FRIDAY, 31 MAY, WE FORDED A BRANCH OF THE DE GREY AND ENTERED THE REALM OF UTTER DESOLATION.

THEN ON MONDAY, 3 JUNE, WE SAW THE FIRST OF THE HALF-BURIED BLOCKS...

THIS IS IT!

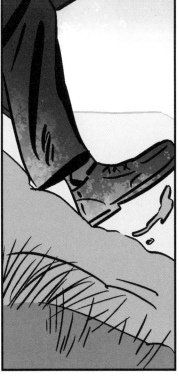

I CANNOT DESCRIBE THE EMOTIONS WITH WHICH I ACTUALLY TOUCHED — IN OBJECTIVE REALITY — A FRAGMENT OF CYCLOPEAN MASONRY IN EVERY RESPECT LIKE THE BLOCKS IN THE WALLS OF MY DREAM-BUILDINGS.

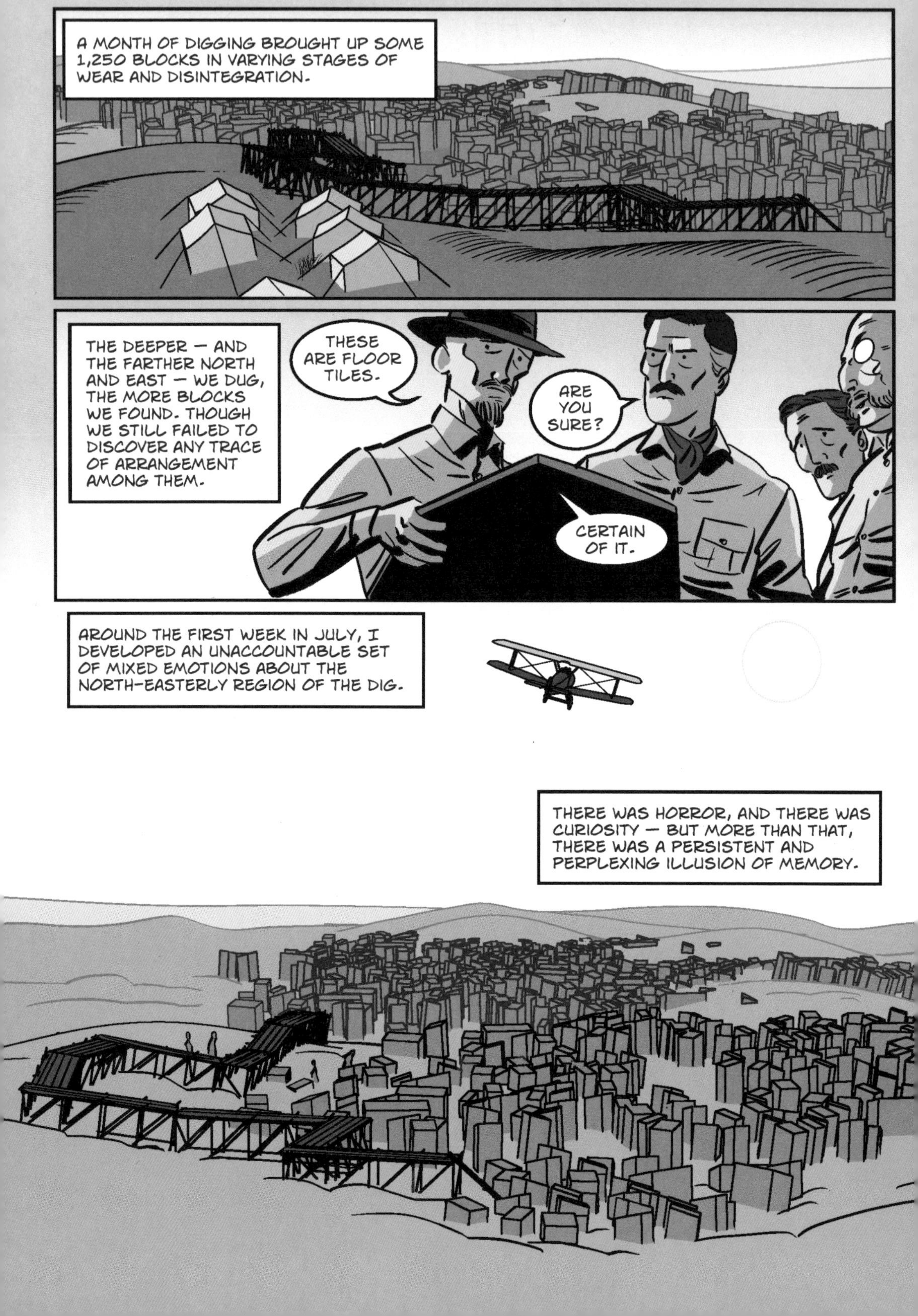
A MONTH OF DIGGING BROUGHT UP SOME 1,250 BLOCKS IN VARYING STAGES OF WEAR AND DISINTEGRATION.
THE DEEPER — AND THE FARTHER NORTH AND EAST — WE DUG, THE MORE BLOCKS WE FOUND. THOUGH WE STILL FAILED TO DISCOVER ANY TRACE OF ARRANGEMENT AMONG THEM.
THESE ARE FLOOR TILES.
ARE YOU SURE?
CERTAIN OF IT.
AROUND THE FIRST WEEK IN JULY, I DEVELOPED AN UNACCOUNTABLE SET OF MIXED EMOTIONS ABOUT THE NORTH-EASTERLY REGION OF THE DIG.
THERE WAS HORROR, AND THERE WAS CURIOSITY — BUT MORE THAN THAT, THERE WAS A PERSISTENT AND PERPLEXING ILLUSION OF MEMORY.

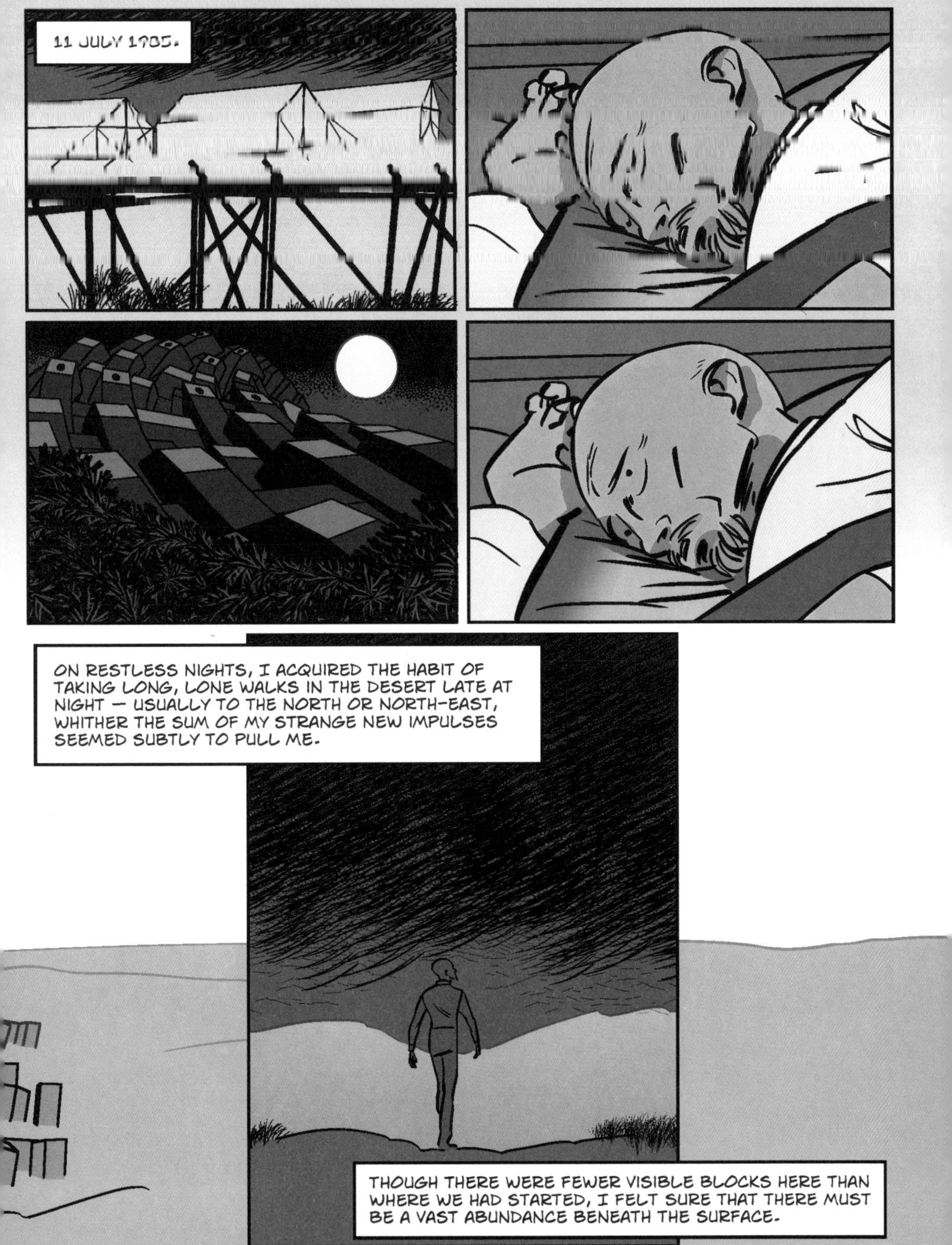
11 JULY 1985.
ON RESTLESS NIGHTS, I ACQUIRED THE HABIT OF TAKING LONG, LONE WALKS IN THE DESERT LATE AT NIGHT — USUALLY TO THE NORTH OR NORTH-EAST, WHITHER THE SUM OF MY STRANGE NEW IMPULSES SEEMED SUBTLY TO PULL ME.
THOUGH THERE WERE FEWER VISIBLE BLOCKS HERE THAN WHERE WE HAD STARTED, I FELT SURE THAT THERE MUST BE A VAST ABUNDANCE BENEATH THE SURFACE.

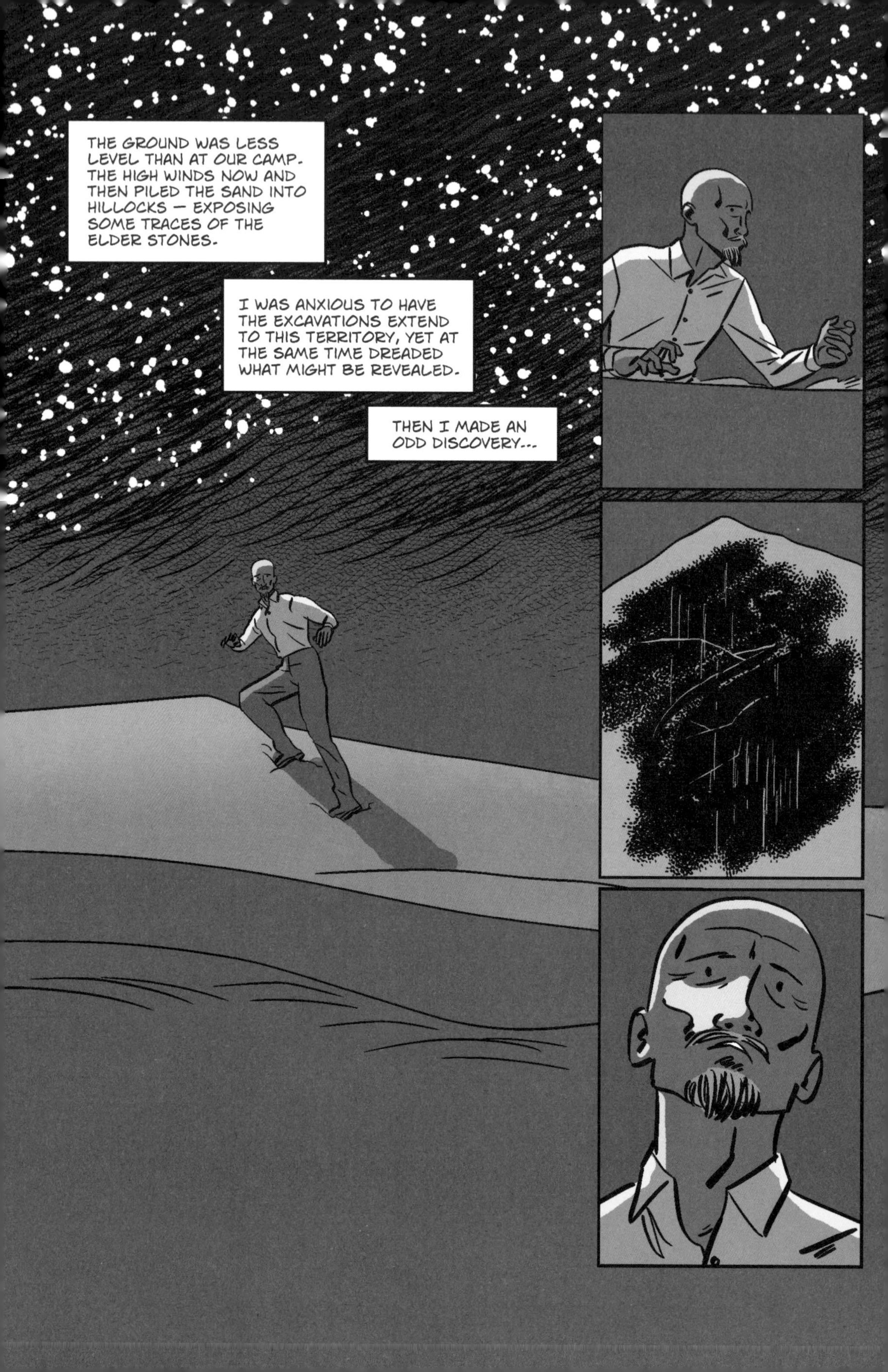
THE GROUND WAS LESS LEVEL THAN AT OUR CAMP. THE HIGH WINDS NOW AND THEN PILED THE SAND INTO HILLOCKS — EXPOSING SOME TRACES OF THE ELDER STONES.
I WAS ANXIOUS TO HAVE THE EXCAVATIONS EXTEND TO THIS TERRITORY, YET AT THE SAME TIME DREADED WHAT MIGHT BE REVEALED.
THEN I MADE AN ODD DISCOVERY...

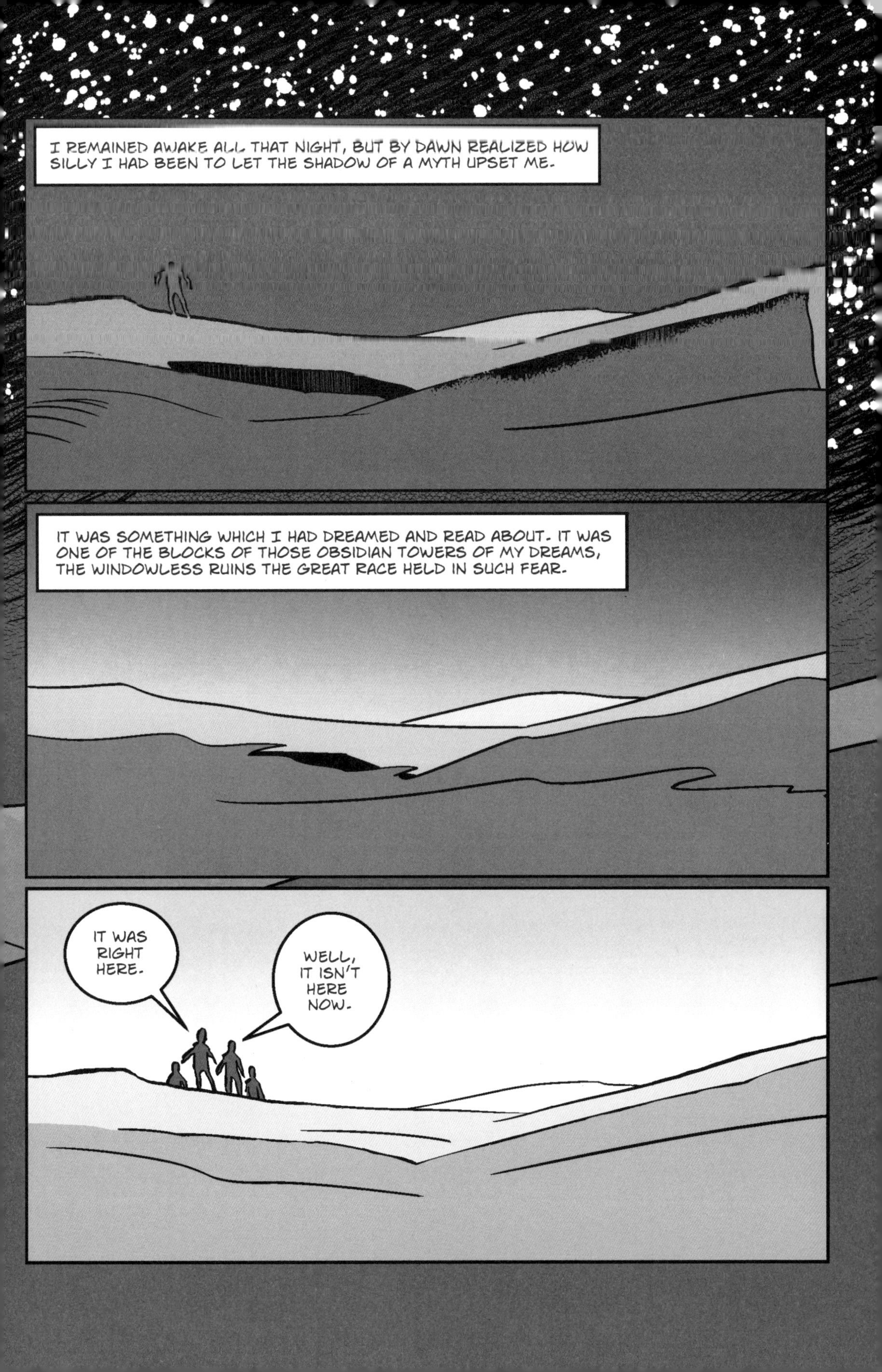
I REMAINED AWAKE ALL THAT NIGHT, BUT BY DAWN REALIZED HOW SILLY I HAD BEEN TO LET THE SHADOW OF A MYTH UPSET ME.
IT WAS SOMETHING WHICH I HAD DREAMED AND READ ABOUT. IT WAS ONE OF THE BLOCKS OF THOSE OBSIDIAN TOWERS OF MY DREAMS, THE WINDOWLESS RUINS THE GREAT RACE HELD IN SUCH FEAR.
IT WAS RIGHT HERE.
WELL, IT ISN'T HERE NOW.

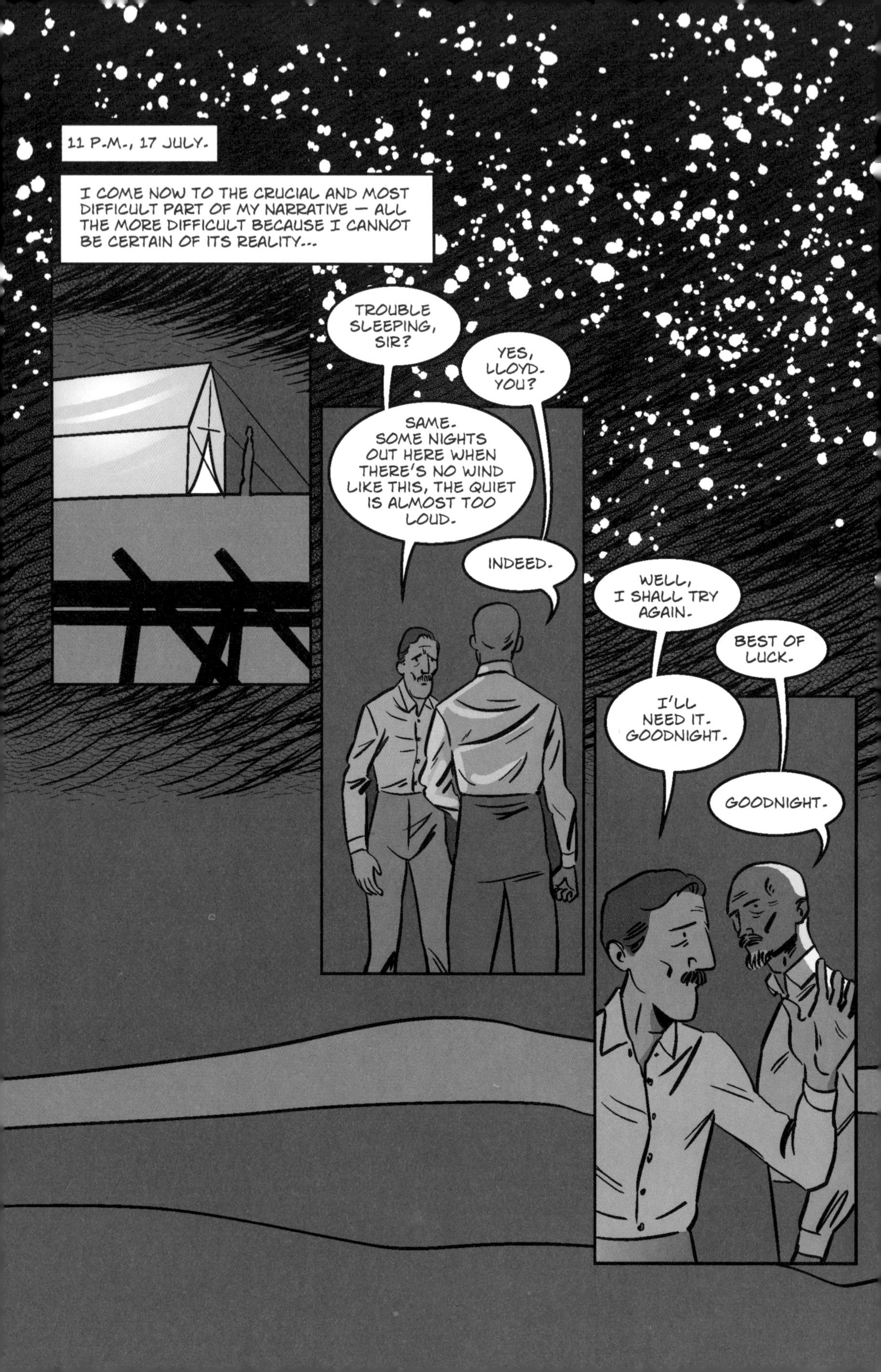
11 P.M., 17 JULY.
I COME NOW TO THE CRUCIAL AND MOST DIFFICULT PART OF MY NARRATIVE — ALL THE MORE DIFFICULT BECAUSE I CANNOT BE CERTAIN OF ITS REALITY...
TROUBLE SLEEPING, SIR?
YES, LLOYD. YOU?
SAME. SOME NIGHTS OUT HERE WHEN THERE'S NO WIND LIKE THIS, THE QUIET IS ALMOST TOO LOUD.
INDEED.
WELL, I SHALL TRY AGAIN.
BEST OF LUCK.
I'LL NEED IT. GOODNIGHT.
GOODNIGHT.

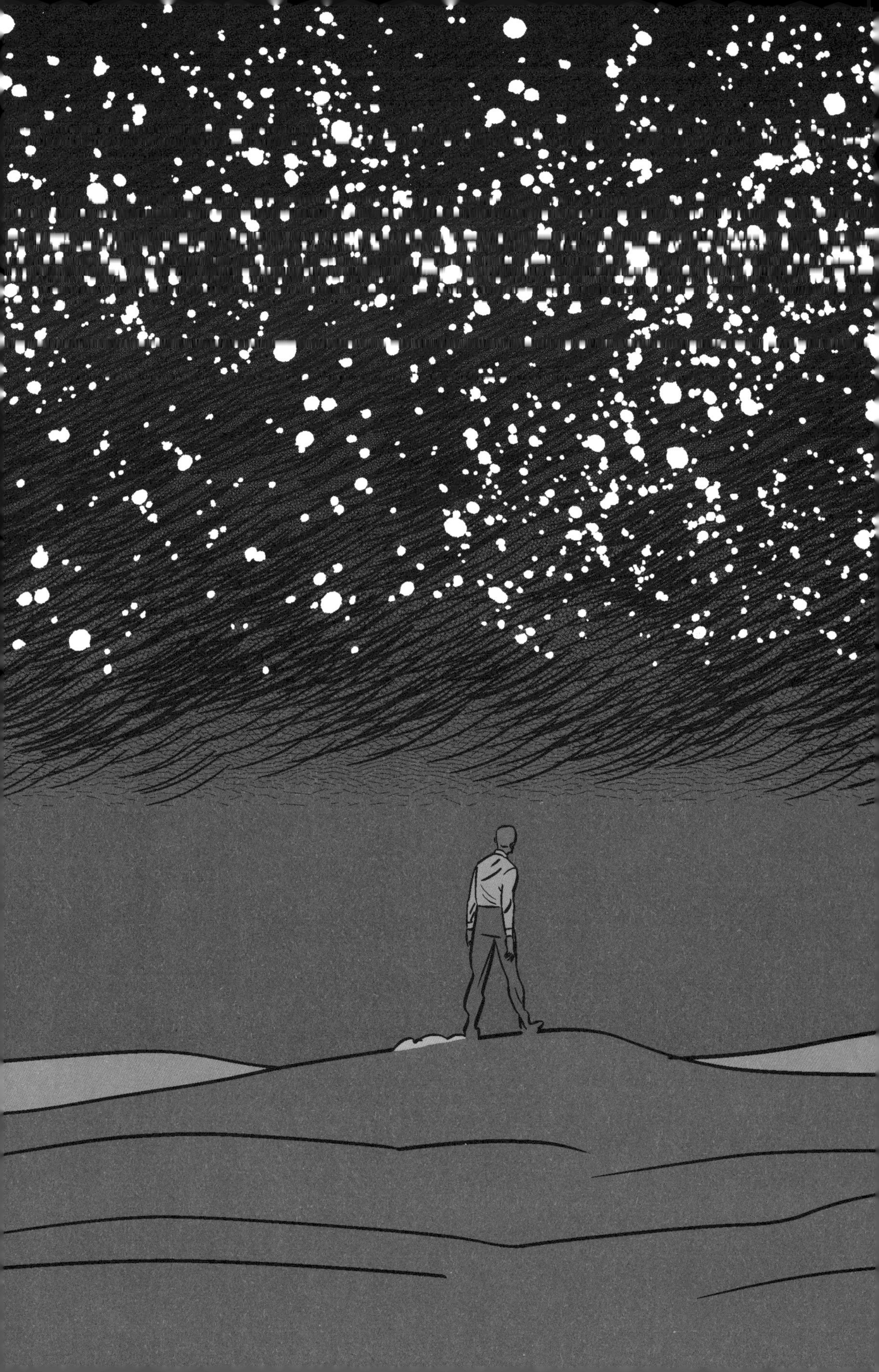

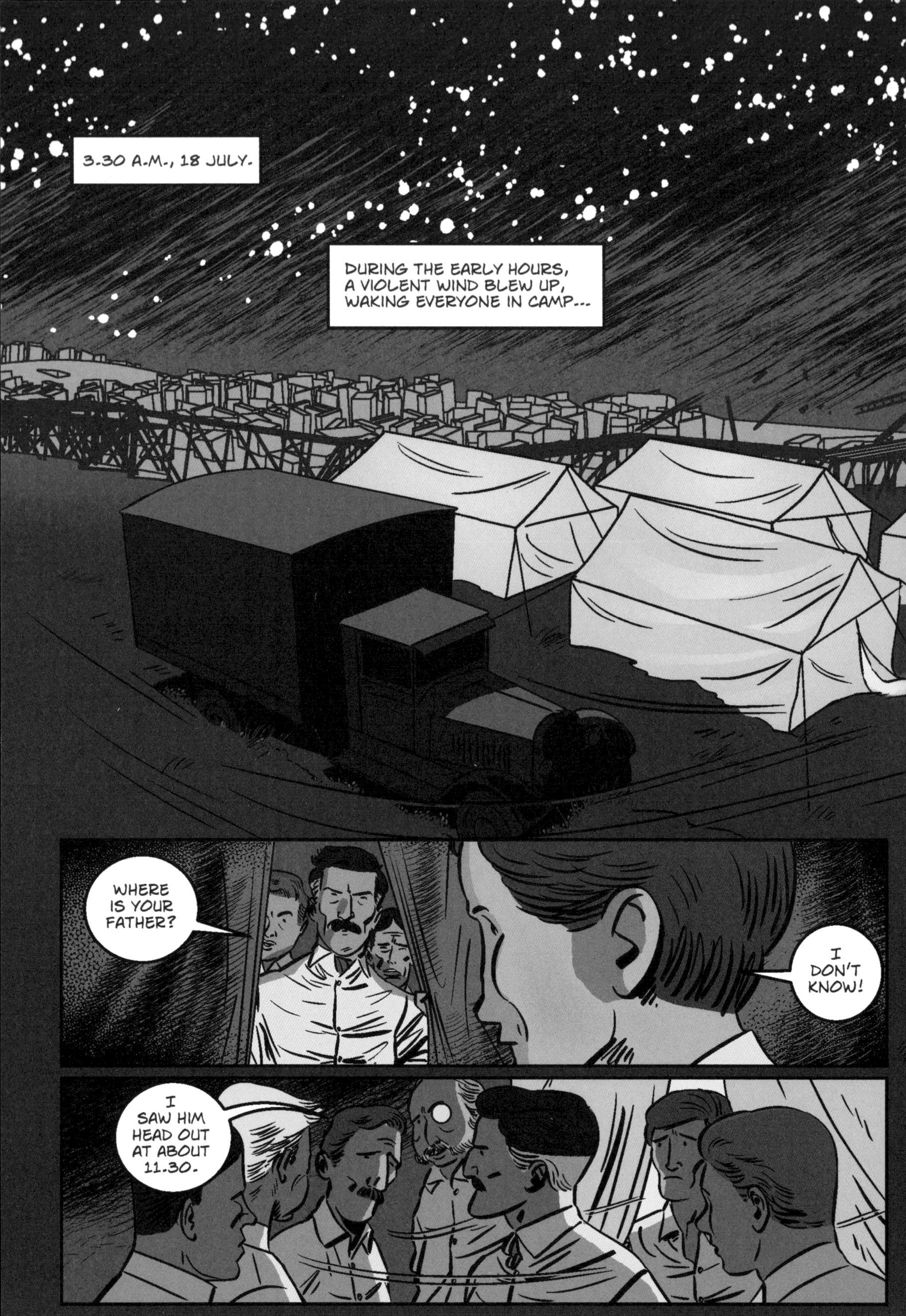
3.30 A.M., 18 JULY.
DURING THE EARLY HOURS, A VIOLENT WIND BLEW UP, WAKING EVERYONE IN CAMP...
WHERE IS YOUR FATHER?
I DON'T KNOW!
I SAW HIM HEAD OUT AT ABOUT 11.30.

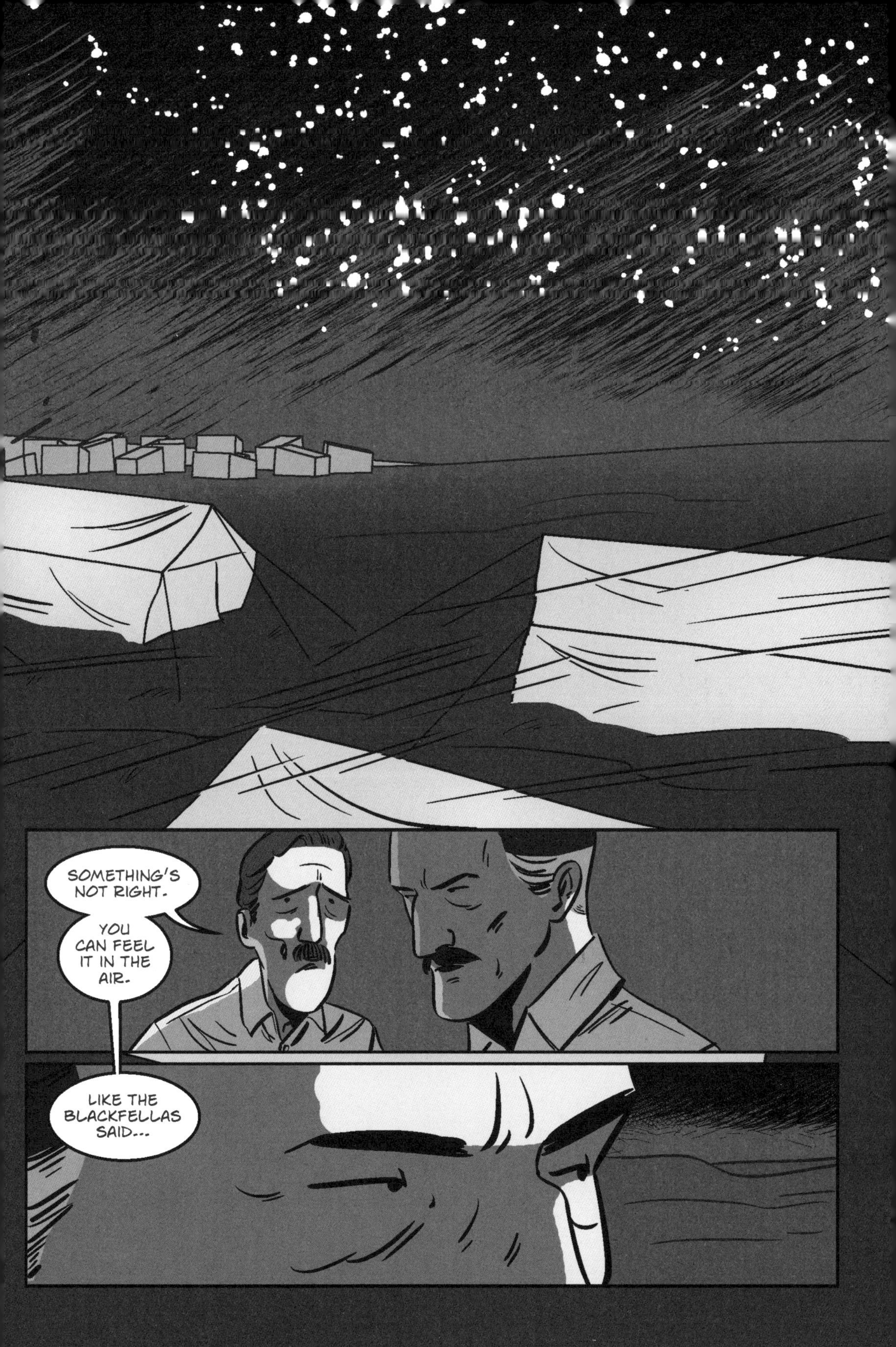
SOMETHING'S NOT RIGHT.
YOU CAN FEEL IT IN THE AIR.
LIKE THE BLACKFELLAS SAID...

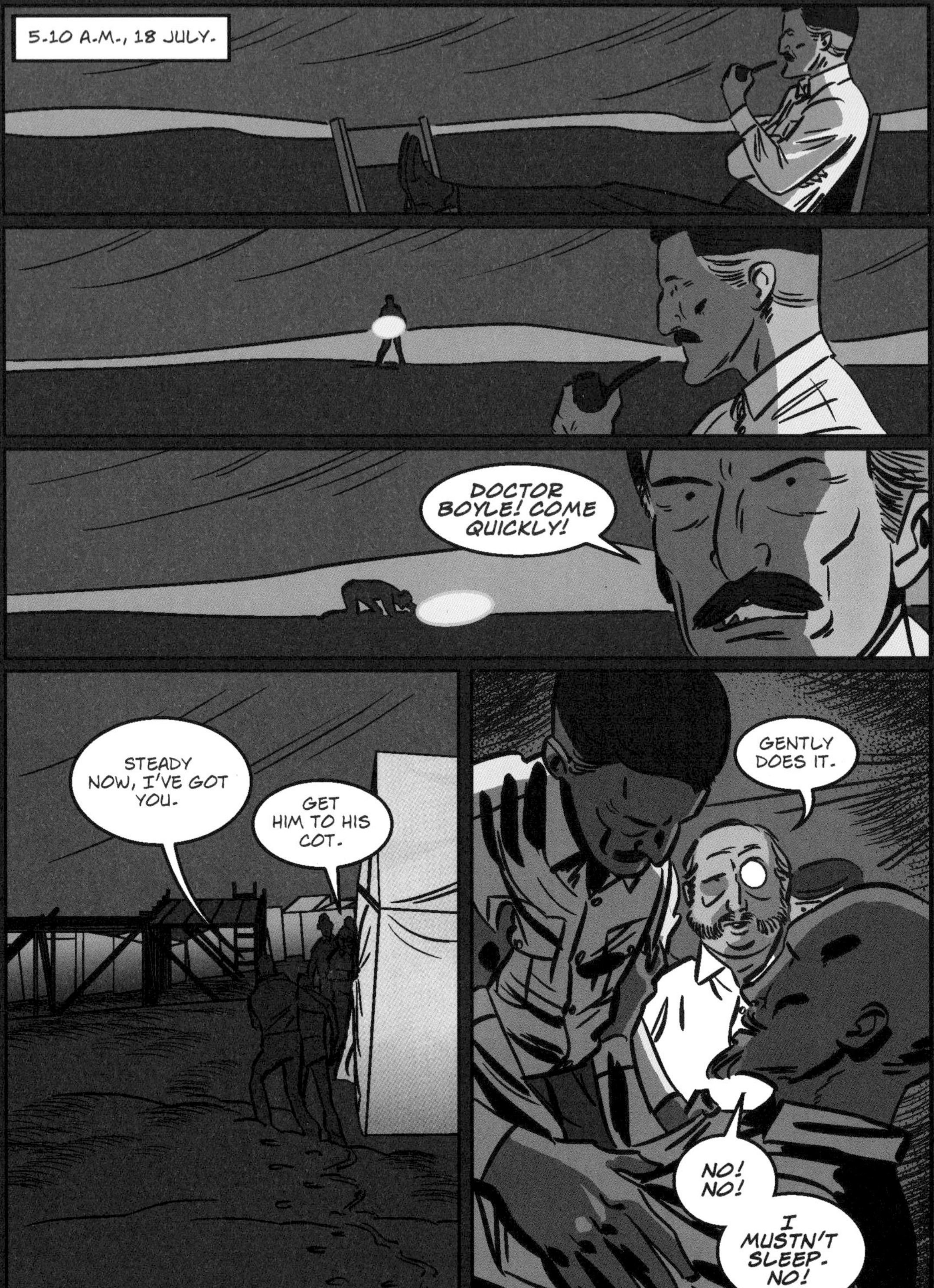
5.10 A.M., 18 JULY.
DOCTOR BOYLE! COME QUICKLY!
STEADY NOW, I'VE GOT YOU.
GET HIM TO HIS COT.
GENTLY DOES IT.
NO! NO!
I MUSTN'T SLEEP. NO!

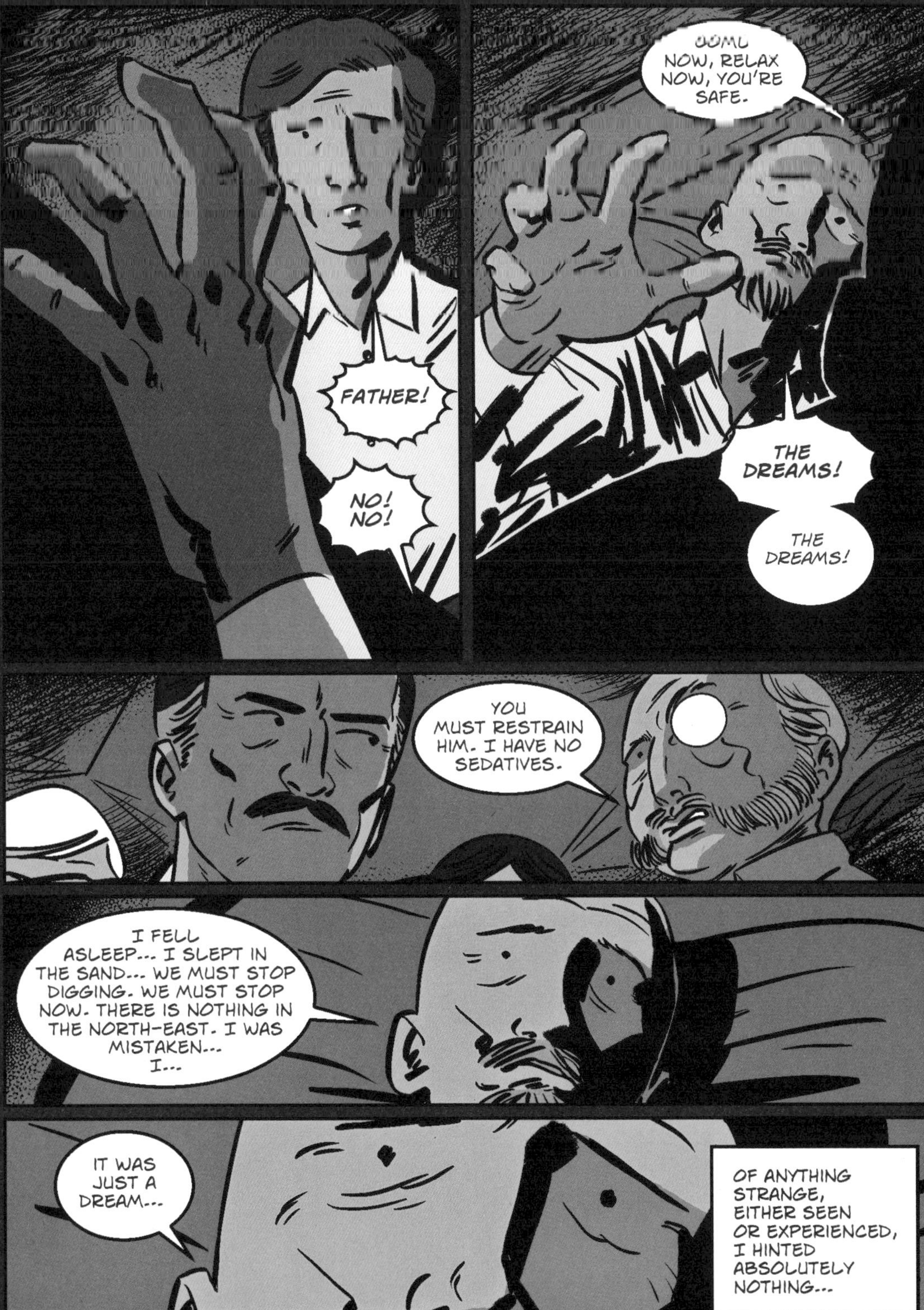
FATHER!
NO! NO!
NOW, RELAX NOW, YOU'RE SAFE.
THE DREAMS!
THE DREAMS!
YOU MUST RESTRAIN HIM. I HAVE NO SEDATIVES.
I FELL ASLEEP... I SLEPT IN THE SAND... WE MUST STOP DIGGING. WE MUST STOP NOW. THERE IS NOTHING IN THE NORTH-EAST. I WAS MISTAKEN... I...
IT WAS JUST A DREAM...
OF ANYTHING STRANGE, EITHER SEEN OR EXPERIENCED, I HINTED ABSOLUTELY NOTHING...

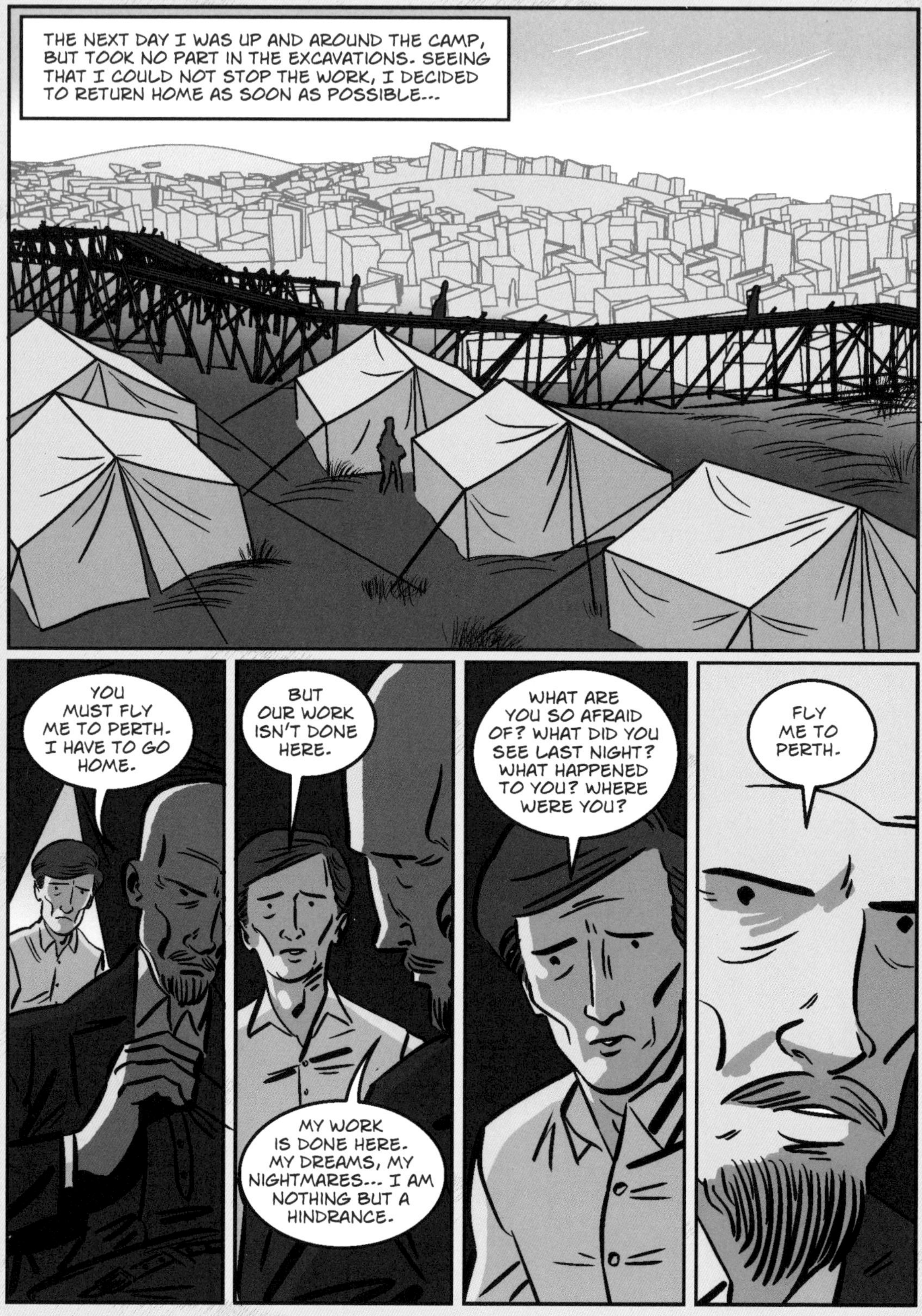
THE NEXT DAY I WAS UP AND AROUND THE CAMP, BUT TOOK NO PART IN THE EXCAVATIONS. SEEING THAT I COULD NOT STOP THE WORK, I DECIDED TO RETURN HOME AS SOON AS POSSIBLE...
YOU MUST FLY ME TO PERTH. I HAVE TO GO HOME.
BUT OUR WORK ISN'T DONE HERE.
MY WORK IS DONE HERE. MY DREAMS, MY NIGHTMARES... I AM NOTHING BUT A HINDRANCE.
WHAT ARE YOU SO AFRAID OF? WHAT DID YOU SEE LAST NIGHT? WHAT HAPPENED TO YOU? WHERE WERE YOU?
FLY ME TO PERTH.

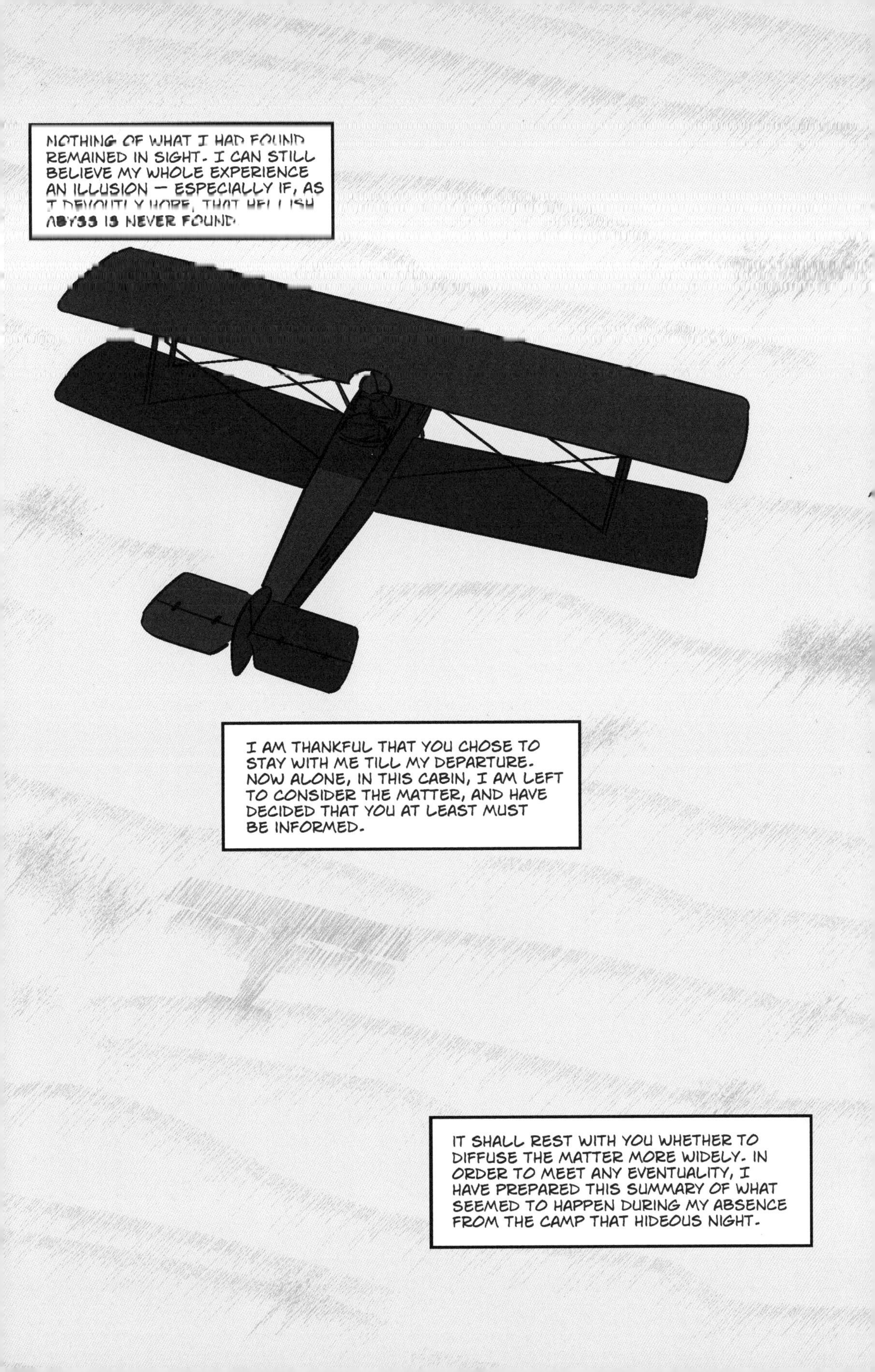
NOTHING OF WHAT I HAD FOUND REMAINED IN SIGHT. I CAN STILL BELIEVE MY WHOLE EXPERIENCE AN ILLUSION — ESPECIALLY IF, AS I DEVOUTLY HOPE, THAT HELLISH ABYSS IS NEVER FOUND.
I AM THANKFUL THAT YOU CHOSE TO STAY WITH ME TILL MY DEPARTURE. NOW ALONE, IN THIS CABIN, I AM LEFT TO CONSIDER THE MATTER, AND HAVE DECIDED THAT YOU AT LEAST MUST BE INFORMED.
IT SHALL REST WITH YOU WHETHER TO DIFFUSE THE MATTER MORE WIDELY. IN ORDER TO MEET ANY EVENTUALITY, I HAVE PREPARED THIS SUMMARY OF WHAT SEEMED TO HAPPEN DURING MY ABSENCE FROM THE CAMP THAT HIDEOUS NIGHT.

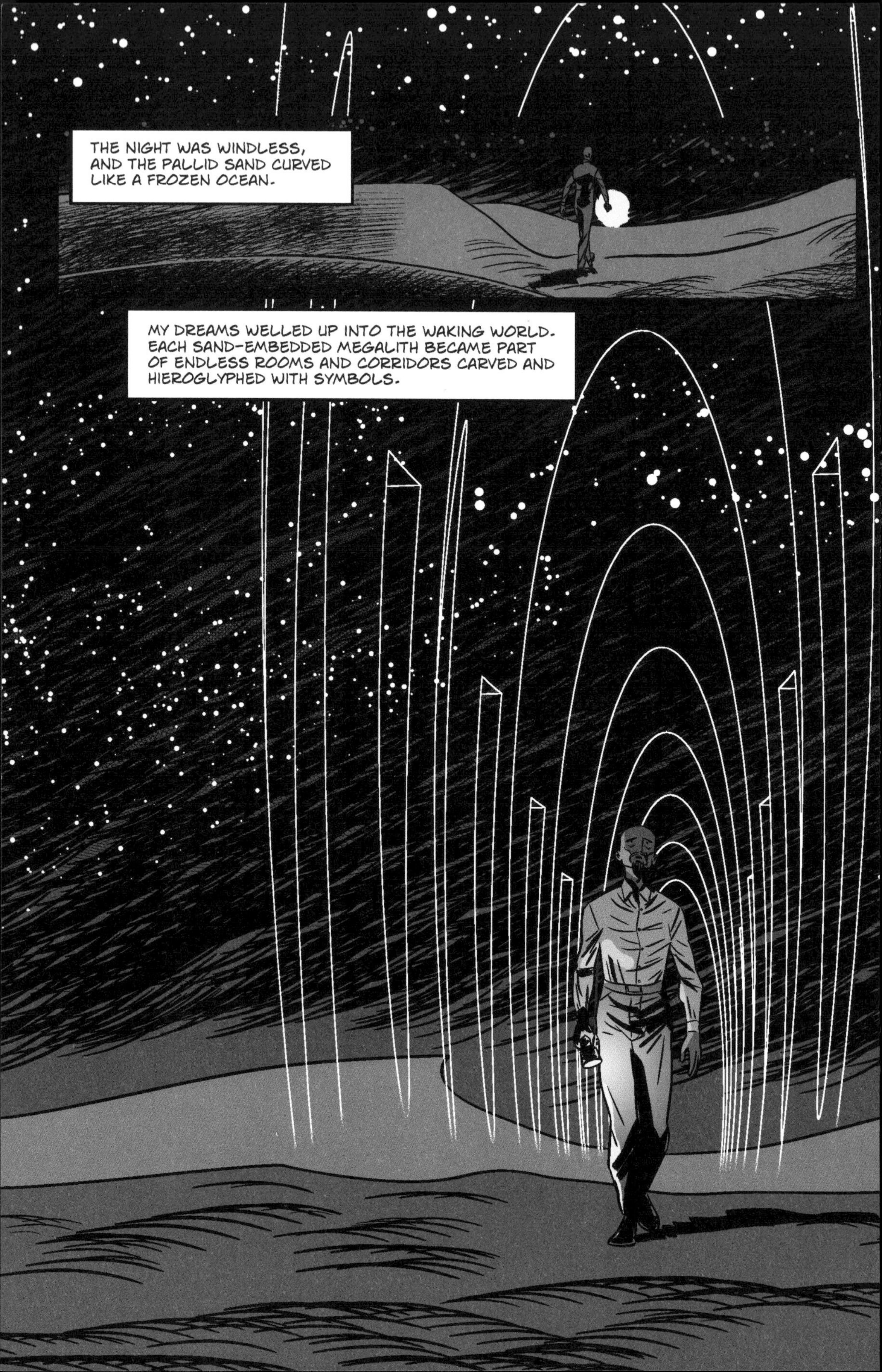
THE NIGHT WAS WINDLESS, AND THE PALLID SAND CURVED LIKE A FROZEN OCEAN.
MY DREAMS WELLED UP INTO THE WAKING WORLD. EACH SAND-EMBEDDED MEGALITH BECAME PART OF ENDLESS ROOMS AND CORRIDORS CARVED AND HIEROGLYPHED WITH SYMBOLS.

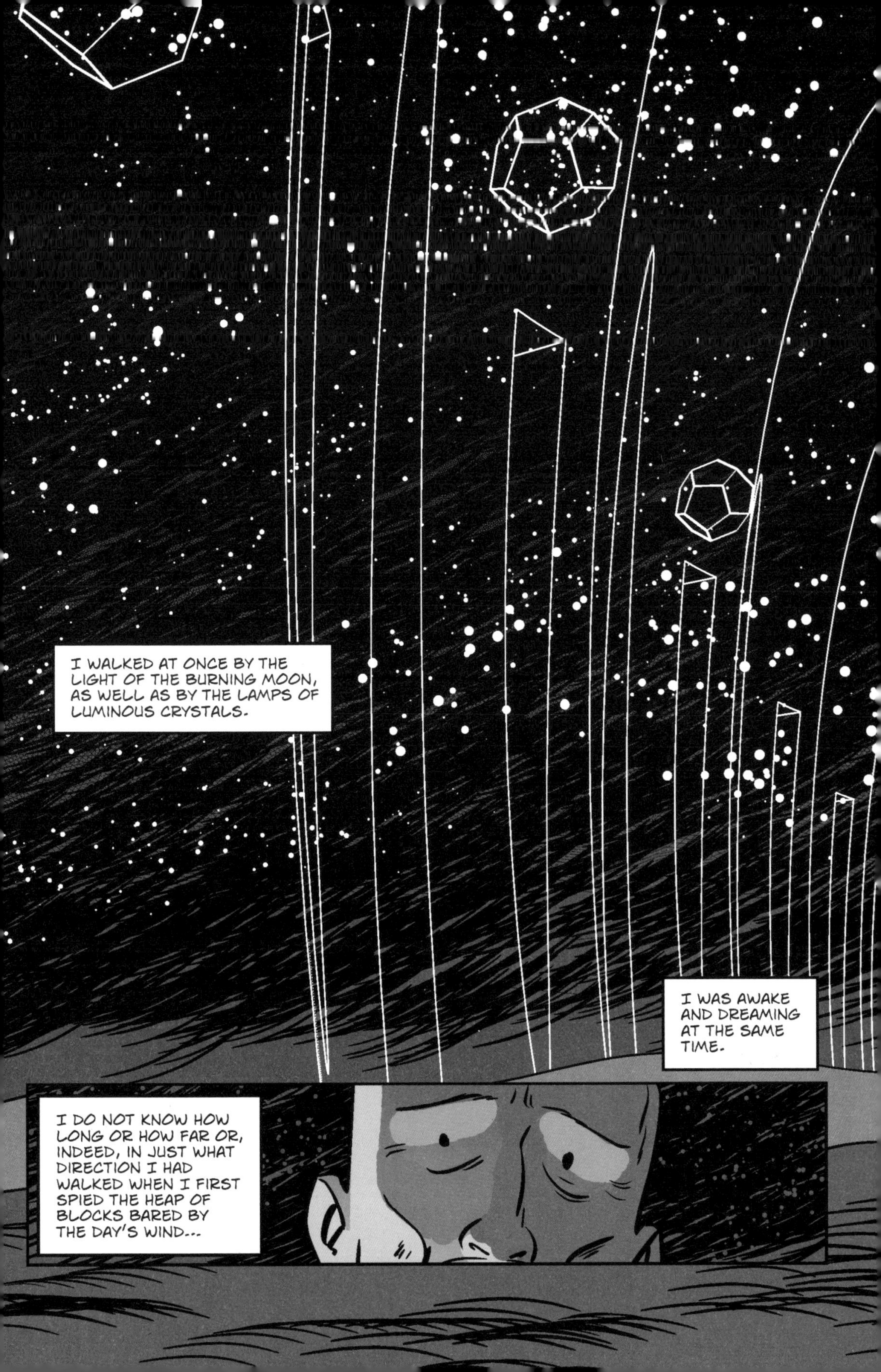
I WALKED AT ONCE BY THE LIGHT OF THE BURNING MOON, AS WELL AS BY THE LAMPS OF LUMINOUS CRYSTALS.
I WAS AWAKE AND DREAMING AT THE SAME TIME.
I DO NOT KNOW HOW LONG OR HOW FAR OR, INDEED, IN JUST WHAT DIRECTION I HAD WALKED WHEN I FIRST SPIED THE HEAP OF BLOCKS BARED BY THE DAY'S WIND...

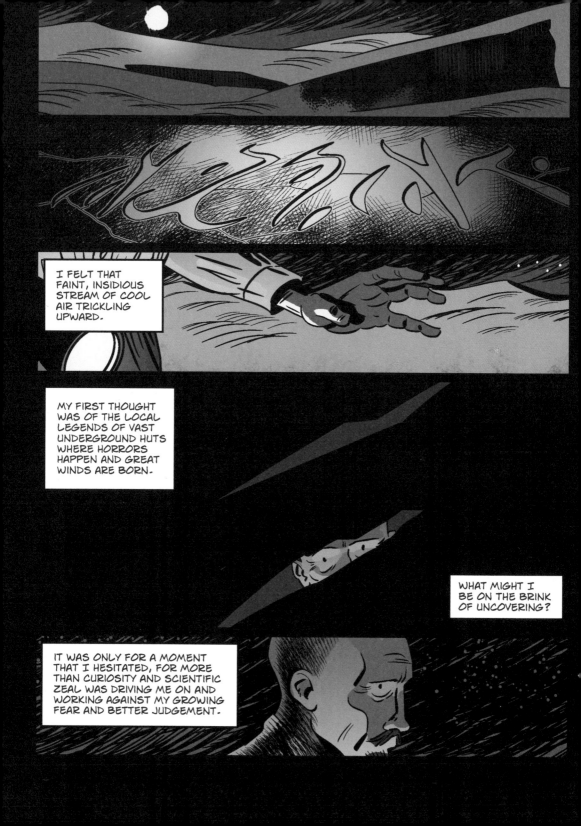

I FELT THAT FAINT, INSIDIOUS STREAM OF COOL AIR TRICKLING UPWARD.

MY FIRST THOUGHT WAS OF THE LOCAL LEGENDS OF VAST UNDERGROUND HUTS WHERE HORRORS HAPPEN AND GREAT WINDS ARE BORN.

WHAT MIGHT I BE ON THE BRINK OF UNCOVERING?

IT WAS ONLY FOR A MOMENT THAT I HESITATED, FOR MORE THAN CURIOSITY AND SCIENTIFIC ZEAL WAS DRIVING ME ON AND WORKING AGAINST MY GROWING FEAR AND BETTER JUDGEMENT.

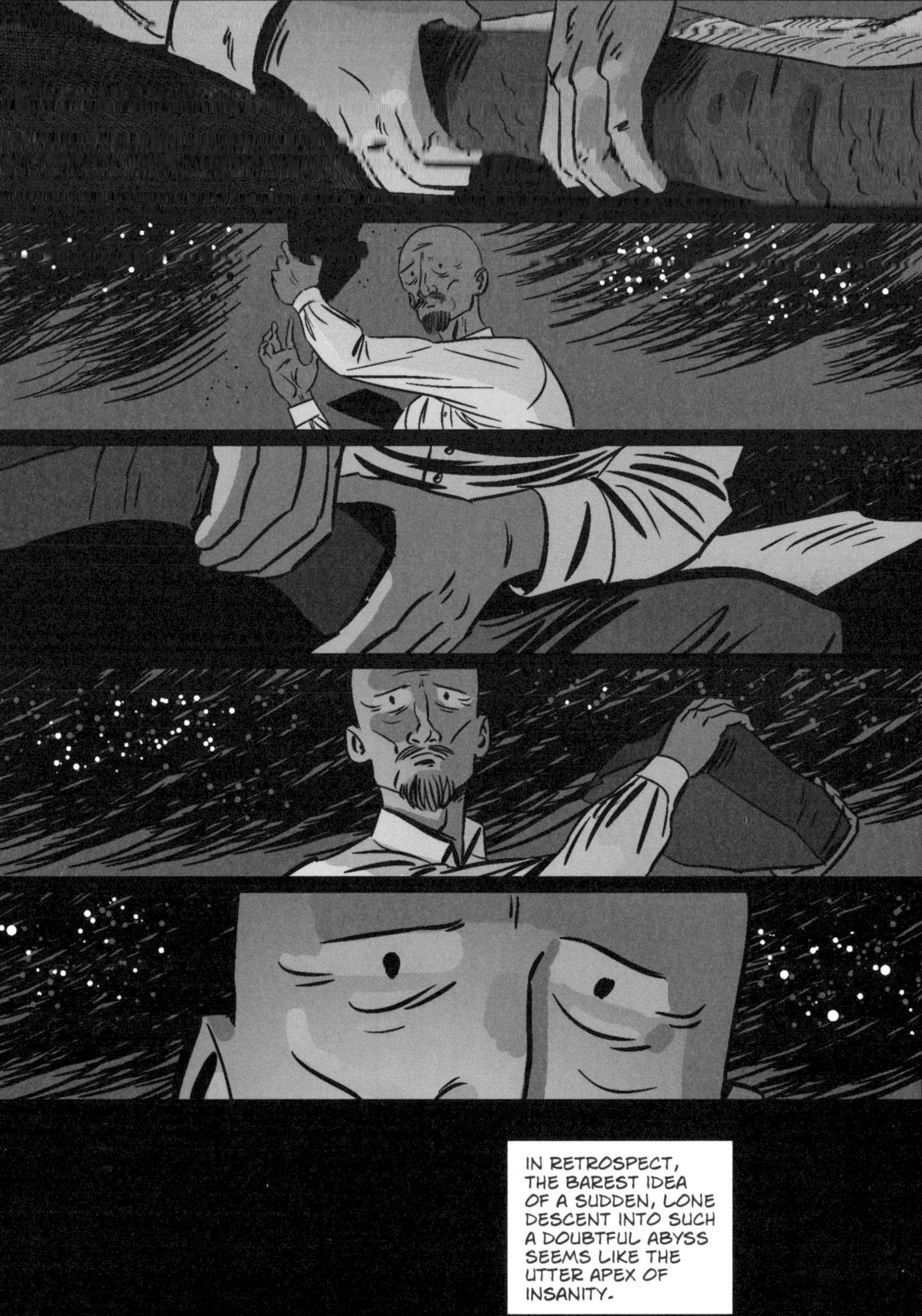

IN RETROSPECT, THE BAREST IDEA OF A SUDDEN, LONE DESCENT INTO SUCH A DOUBTFUL ABYSS SEEMS LIKE THE UTTER APEX OF INSANITY.

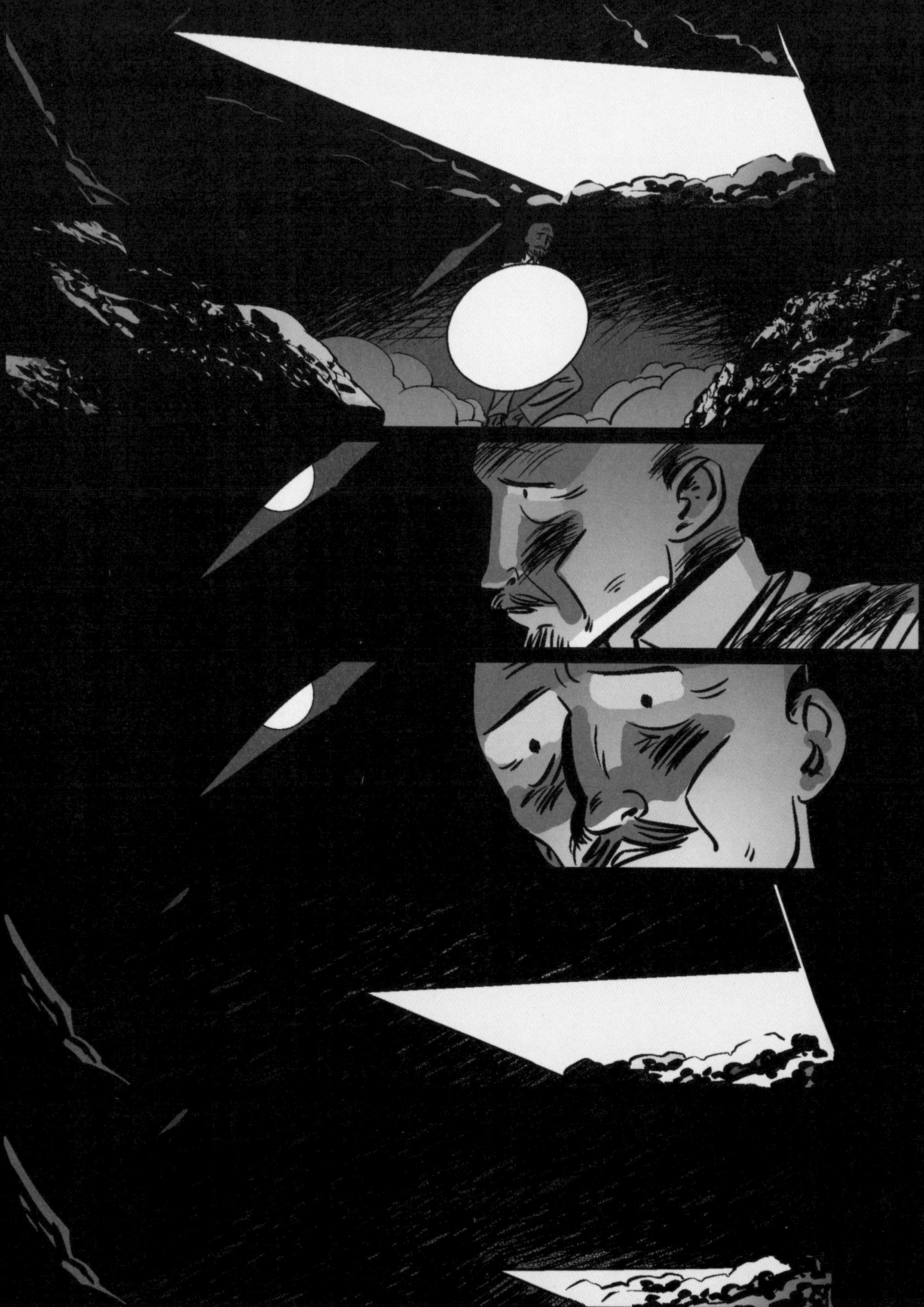

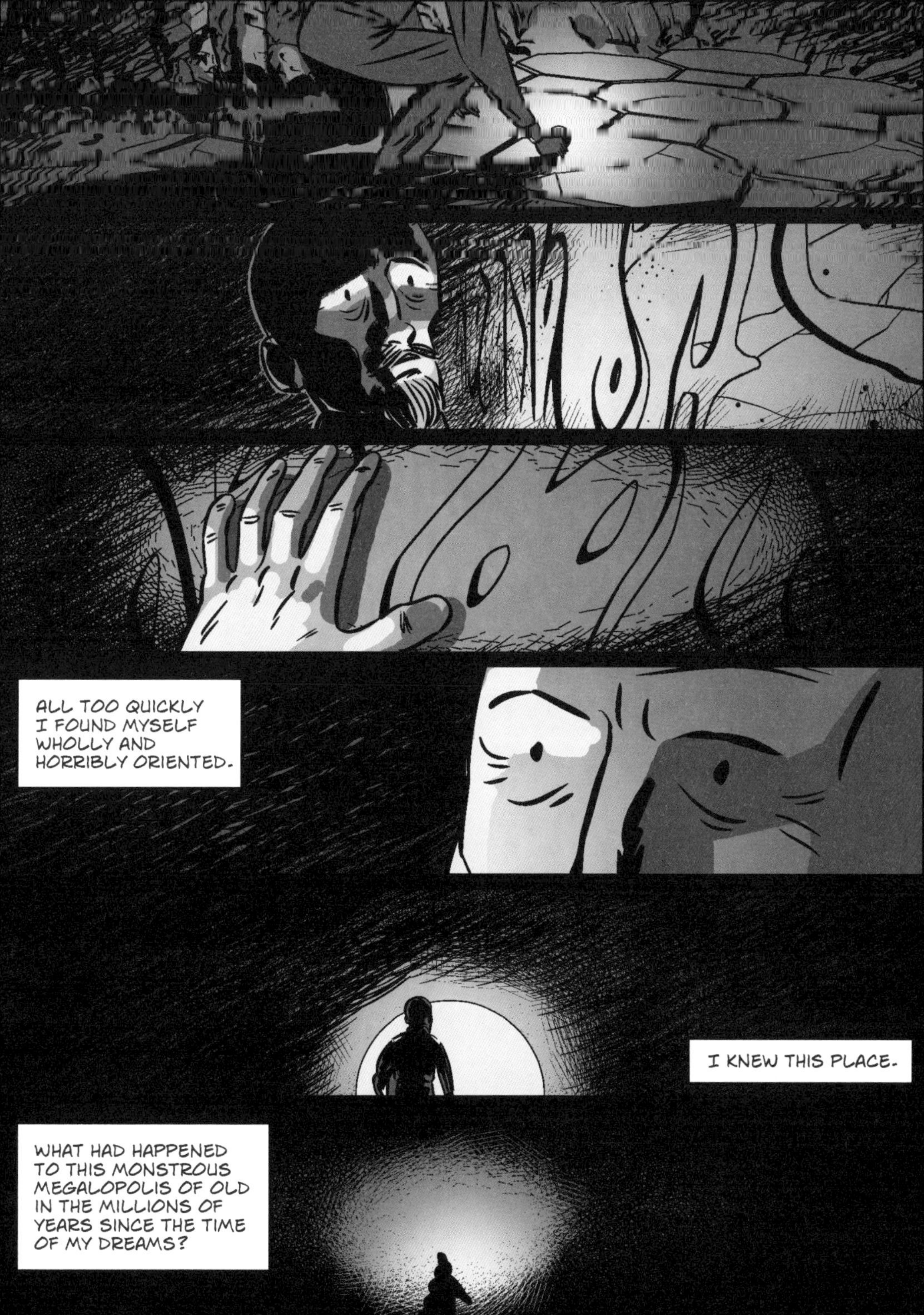
ALL TOO QUICKLY I FOUND MYSELF WHOLLY AND HORRIBLY ORIENTED.
I KNEW THIS PLACE.
WHAT HAD HAPPENED TO THIS MONSTROUS MEGALOPOLIS OF OLD IN THE MILLIONS OF YEARS SINCE THE TIME OF MY DREAMS?

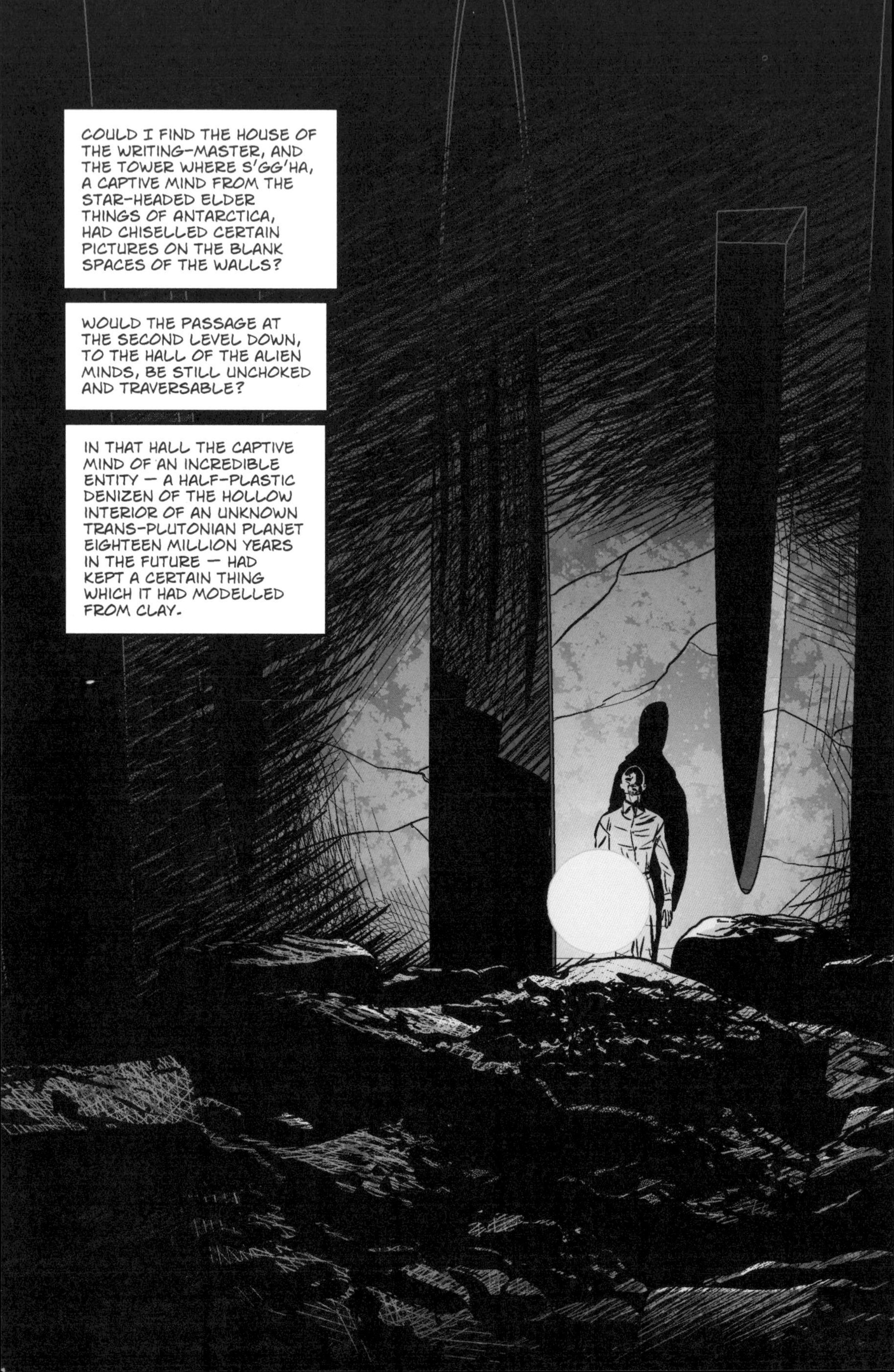
COULD I FIND THE HOUSE OF THE WRITING-MASTER, AND THE TOWER WHERE S'GG'HA, A CAPTIVE MIND FROM THE STAR-HEADED ELDER THINGS OF ANTARCTICA, HAD CHISELLED CERTAIN PICTURES ON THE BLANK SPACES OF THE WALLS?
WOULD THE PASSAGE AT THE SECOND LEVEL DOWN, TO THE HALL OF THE ALIEN MINDS, BE STILL UNCHOKED AND TRAVERSABLE?
IN THAT HALL THE CAPTIVE MIND OF AN INCREDIBLE ENTITY — A HALF-PLASTIC DENIZEN OF THE HOLLOW INTERIOR OF AN UNKNOWN TRANS-PLUTONIAN PLANET EIGHTEEN MILLION YEARS IN THE FUTURE — HAD KEPT A CERTAIN THING WHICH IT HAD MODELLED FROM CLAY.

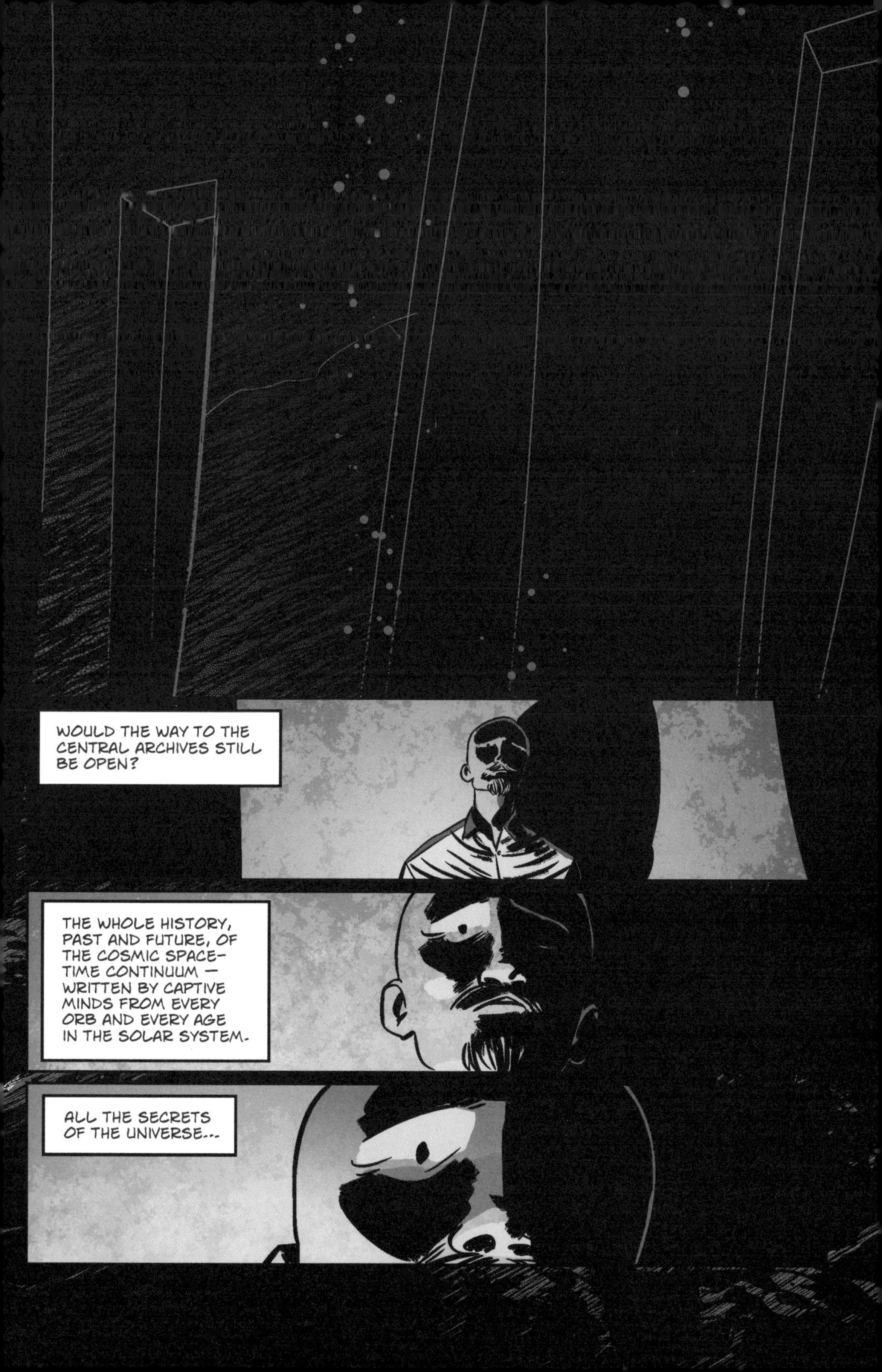
WOULD THE WAY TO THE CENTRAL ARCHIVES STILL BE OPEN?
THE WHOLE HISTORY, PAST AND FUTURE, OF THE COSMIC SPACE-TIME CONTINUUM — WRITTEN BY CAPTIVE MINDS FROM EVERY ORB AND EVERY AGE IN THE SOLAR SYSTEM.
ALL THE SECRETS OF THE UNIVERSE...

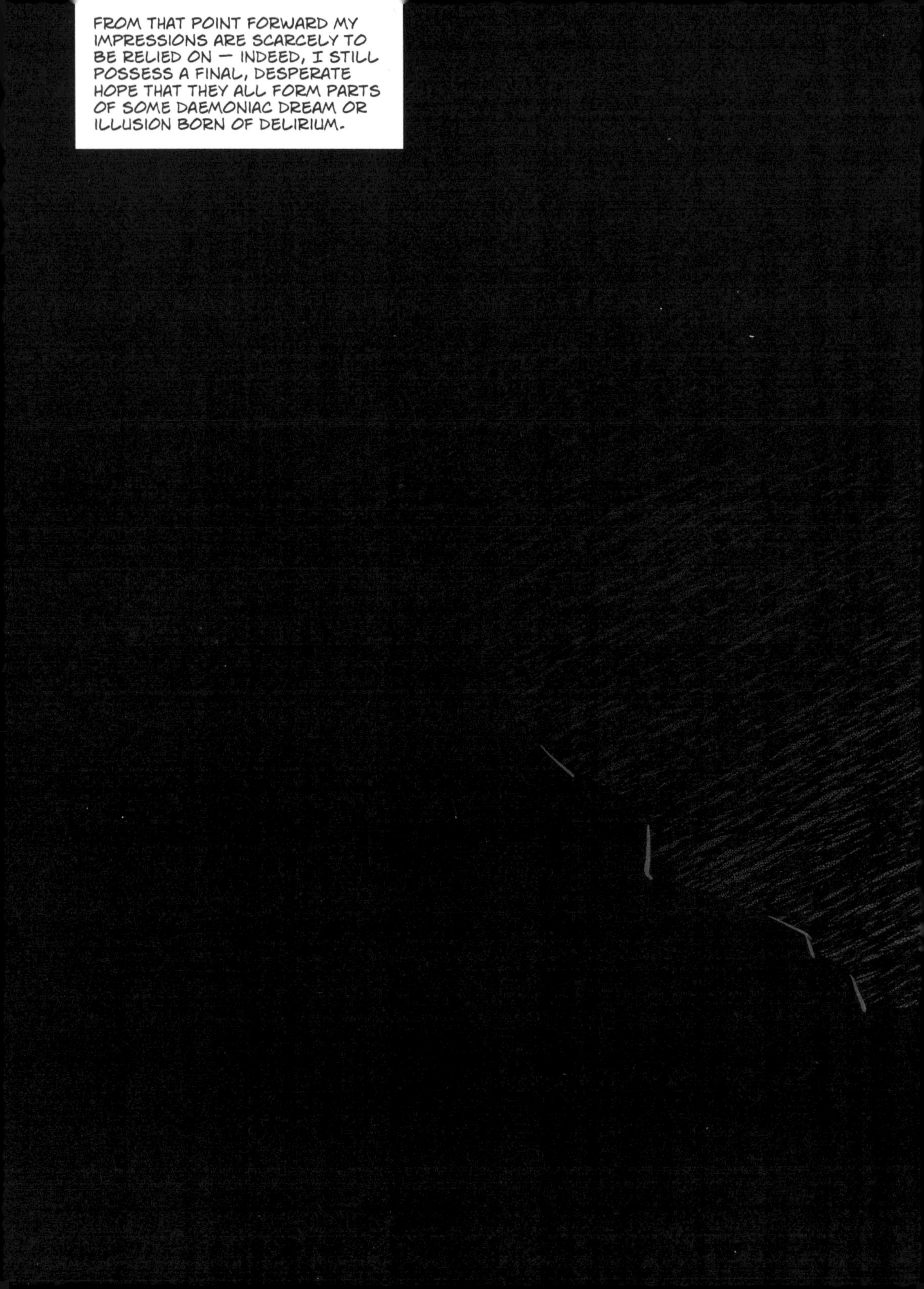
FROM THAT POINT FORWARD MY IMPRESSIONS ARE SCARCELY TO BE RELIED ON — INDEED, I STILL POSSESS A FINAL, DESPERATE HOPE THAT THEY ALL FORM PARTS OF SOME DAEMONIAC DREAM OR ILLUSION BORN OF DELIRIUM.

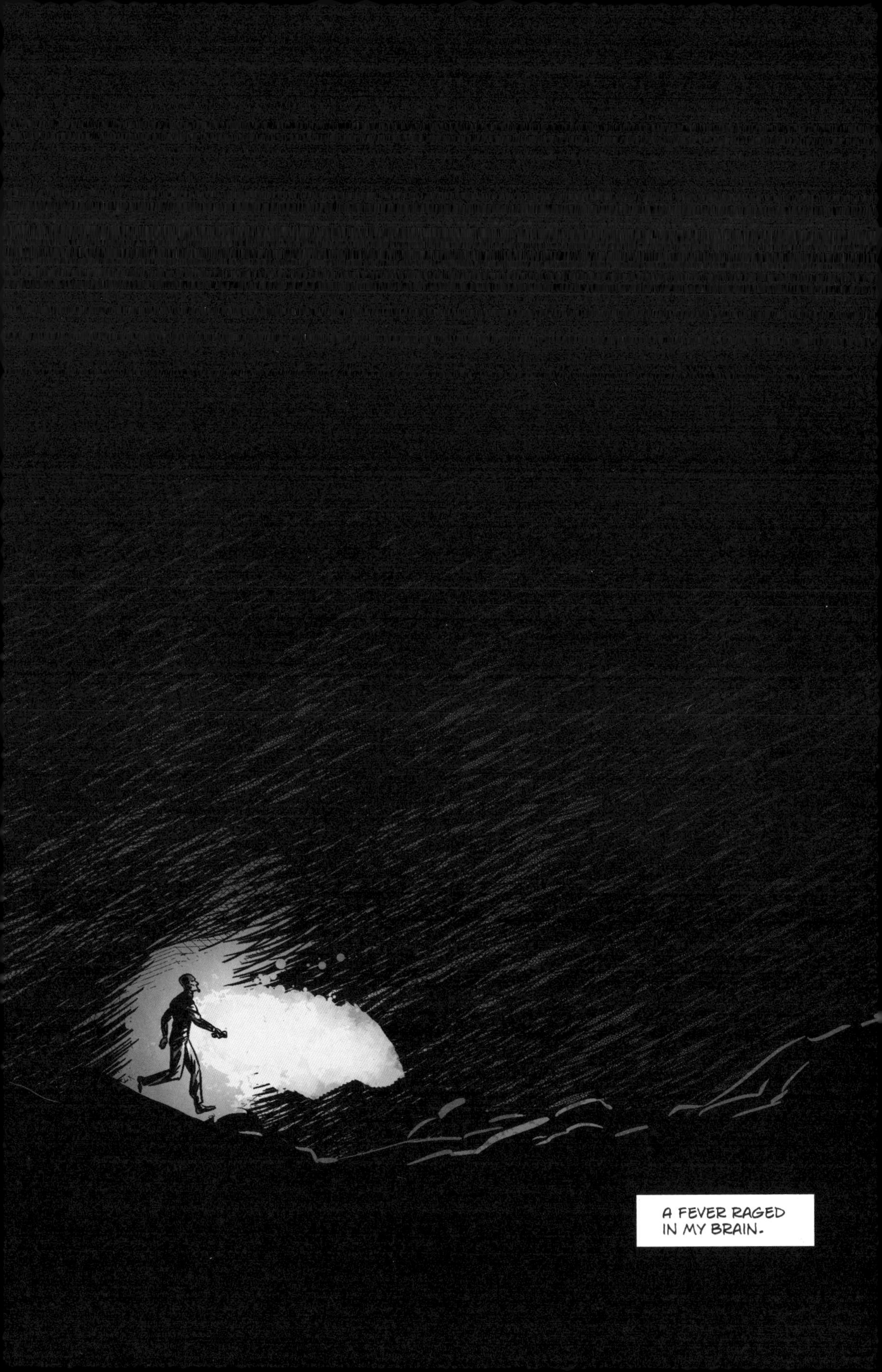
A FEVER RAGED IN MY BRAIN.

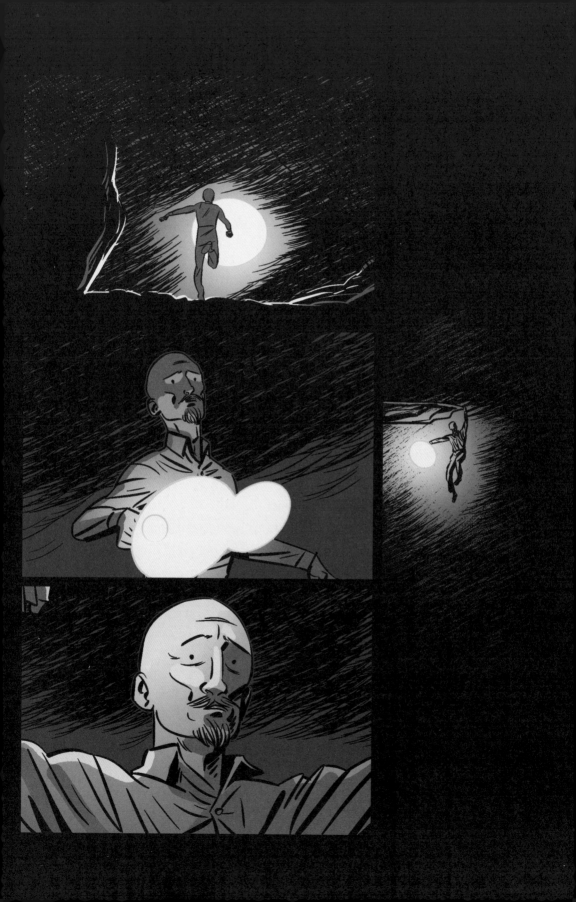

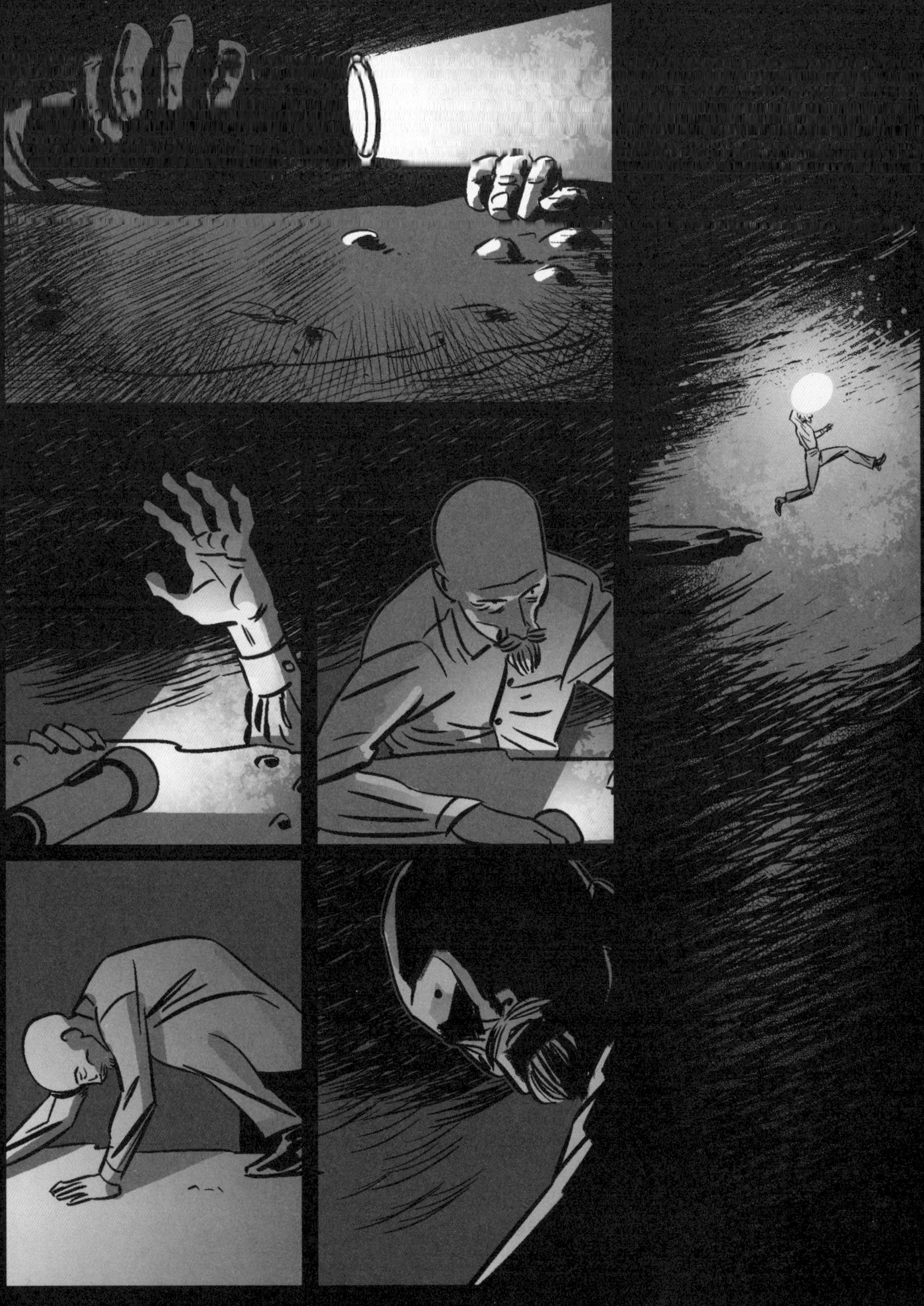

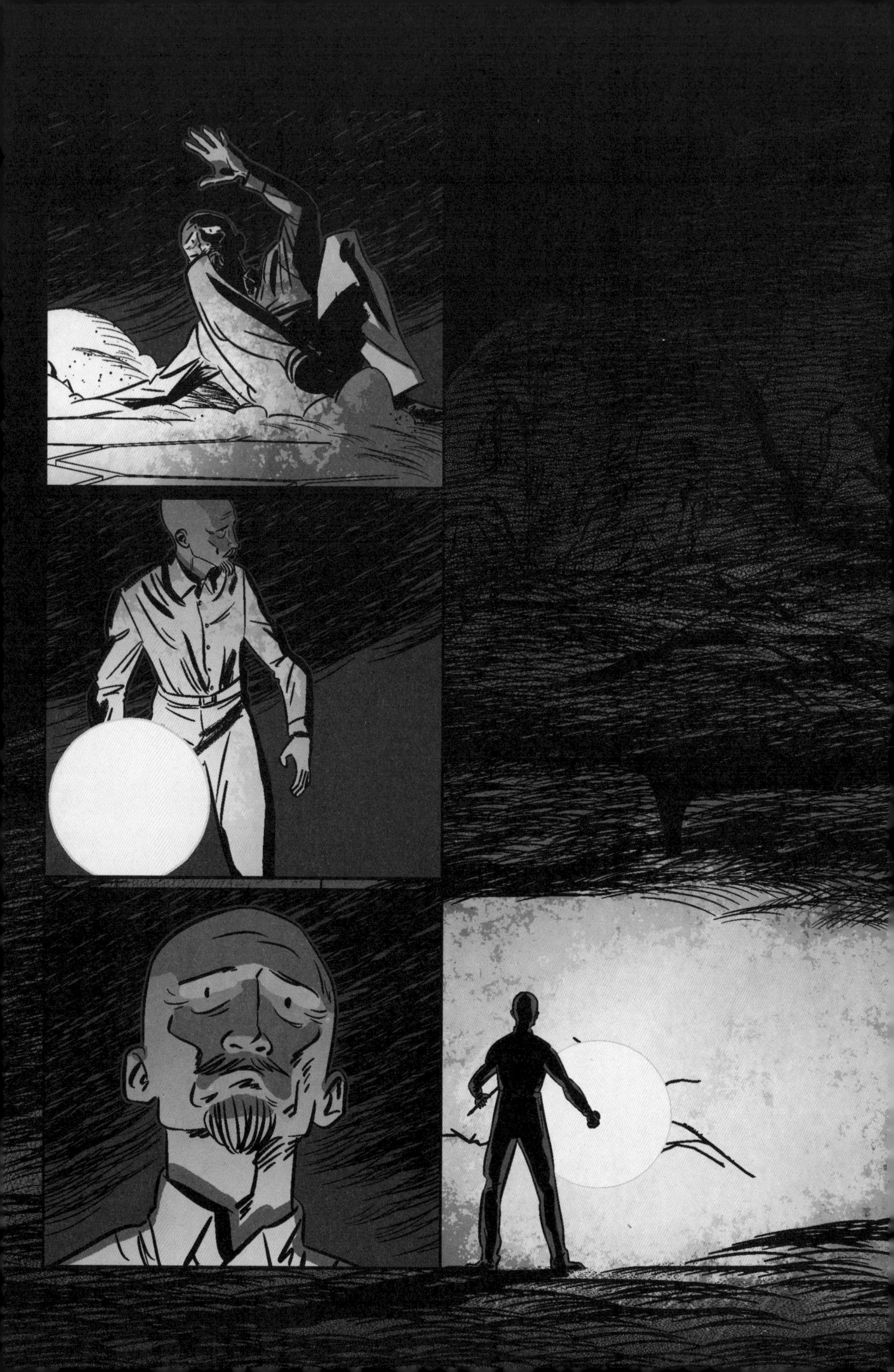

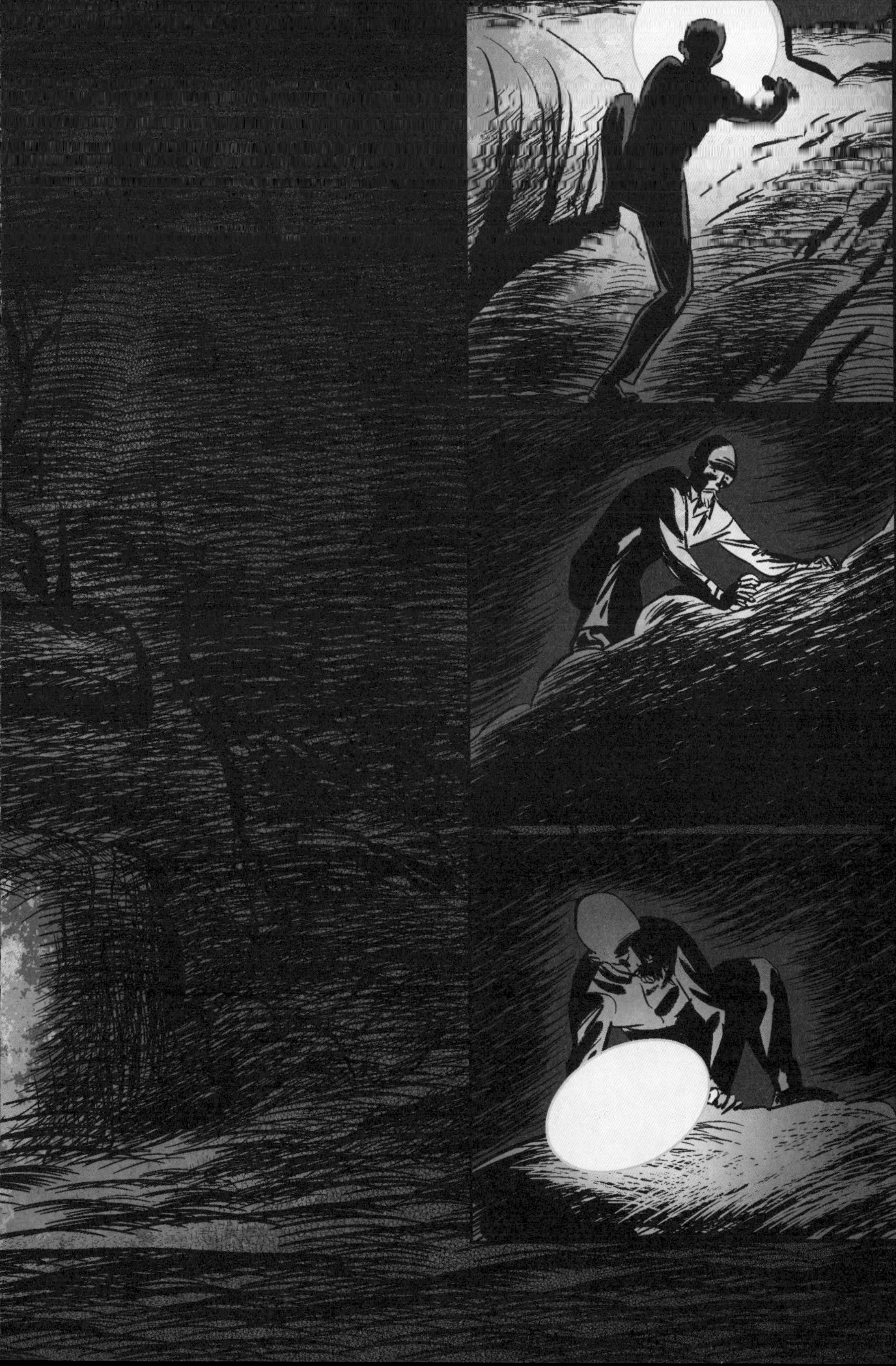

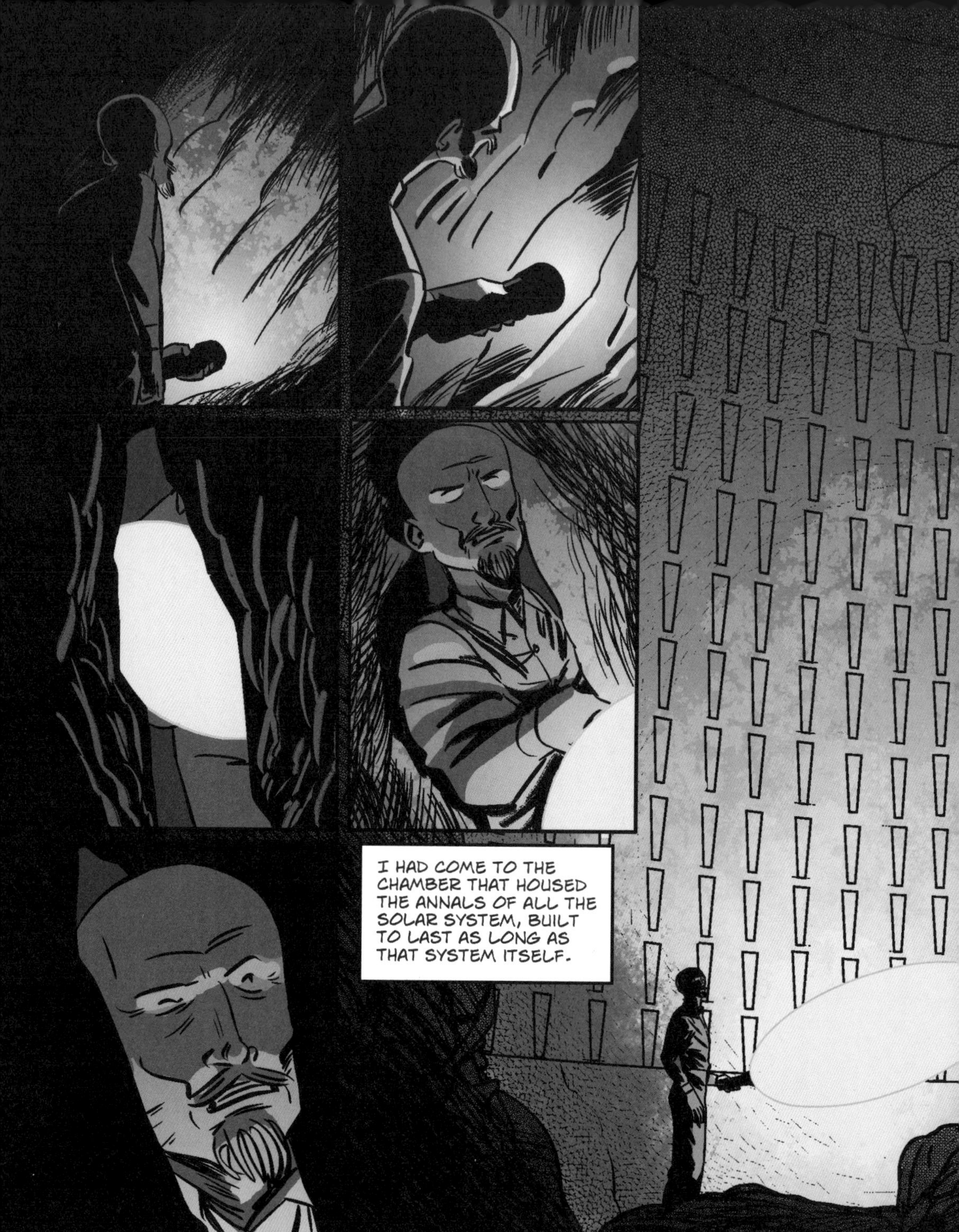
I HAD COME TO THE CHAMBER THAT HOUSED THE ANNALS OF ALL THE SOLAR SYSTEM, BUILT TO LAST AS LONG AS THAT SYSTEM ITSELF.

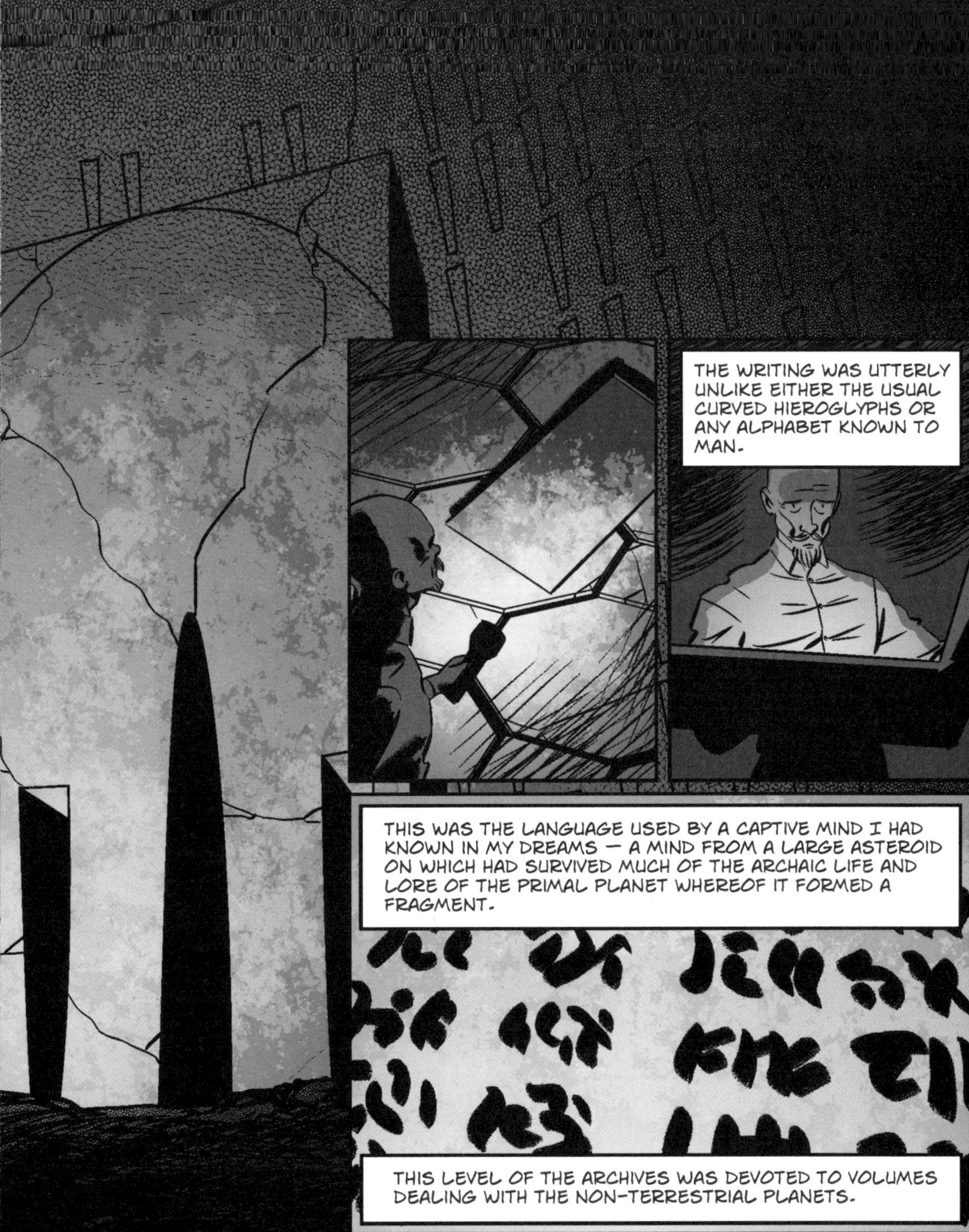
THE WRITING WAS UTTERLY UNLIKE EITHER THE USUAL CURVED HIEROGLYPHS OR ANY ALPHABET KNOWN TO MAN.
THIS WAS THE LANGUAGE USED BY A CAPTIVE MIND I HAD KNOWN IN MY DREAMS — A MIND FROM A LARGE ASTEROID ON WHICH HAD SURVIVED MUCH OF THE ARCHAIC LIFE AND LORE OF THE PRIMAL PLANET WHEREOF IT FORMED A FRAGMENT.
THIS LEVEL OF THE ARCHIVES WAS DEVOTED TO VOLUMES DEALING WITH THE NON-TERRESTRIAL PLANETS.

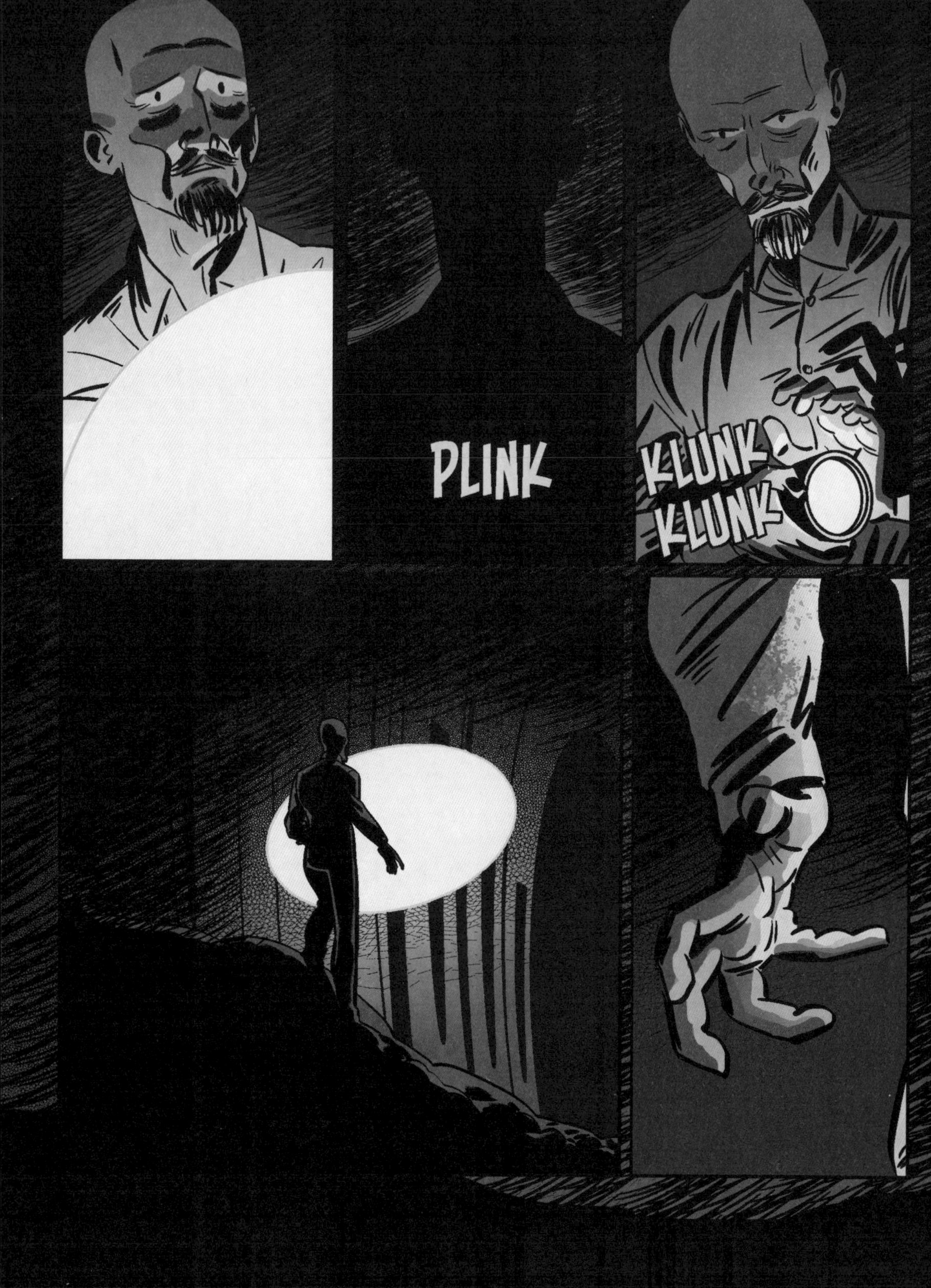
PLINK
KLUNK
KLUNK

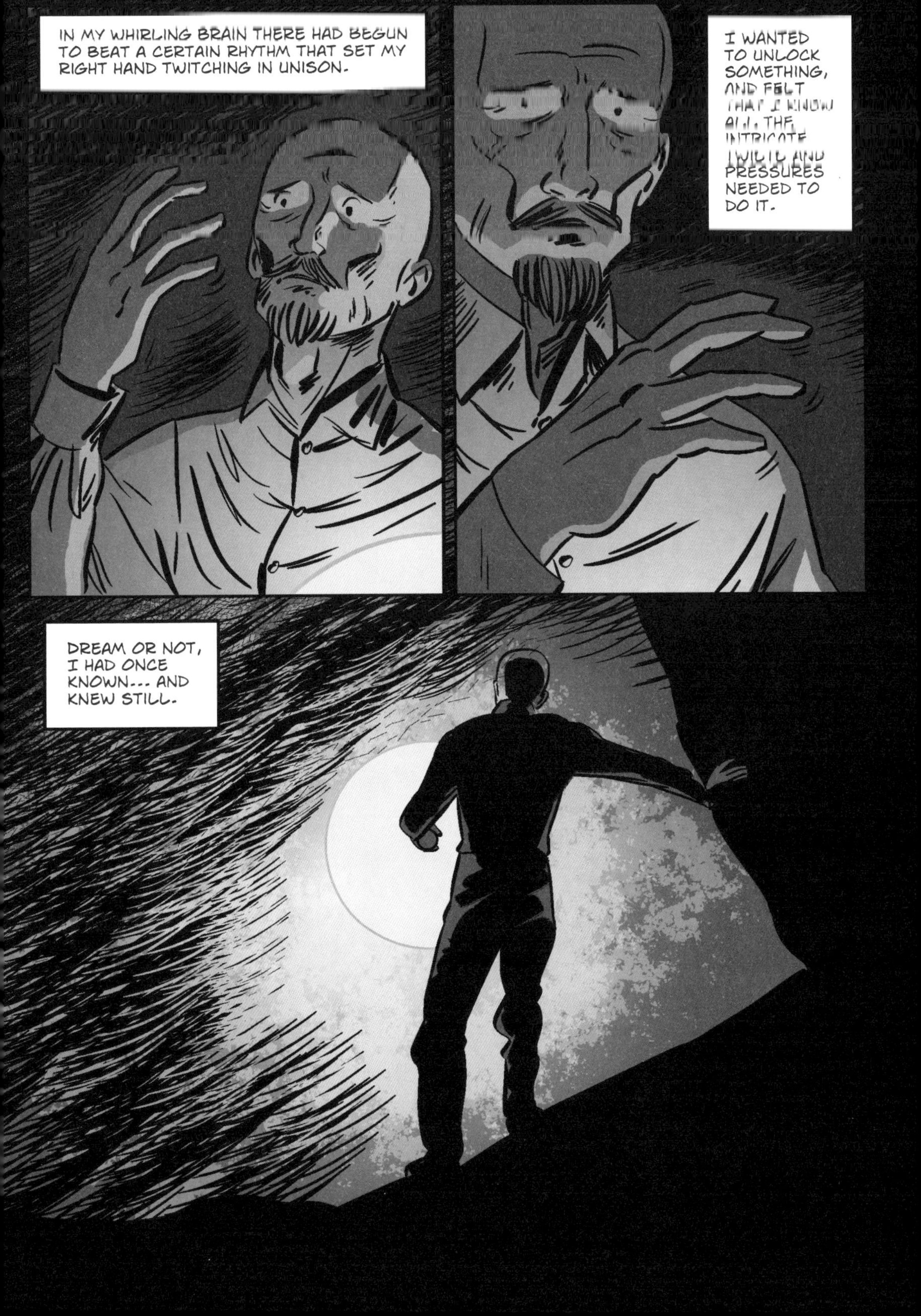
IN MY WHIRLING BRAIN THERE HAD BEGUN TO BEAT A CERTAIN RHYTHM THAT SET MY RIGHT HAND TWITCHING IN UNISON.
I WANTED TO UNLOCK SOMETHING, AND FELT
ALL THE INTRICATE
PRESSURES NEEDED TO DO IT.
DREAM OR NOT, I HAD ONCE KNOWN... AND KNEW STILL.

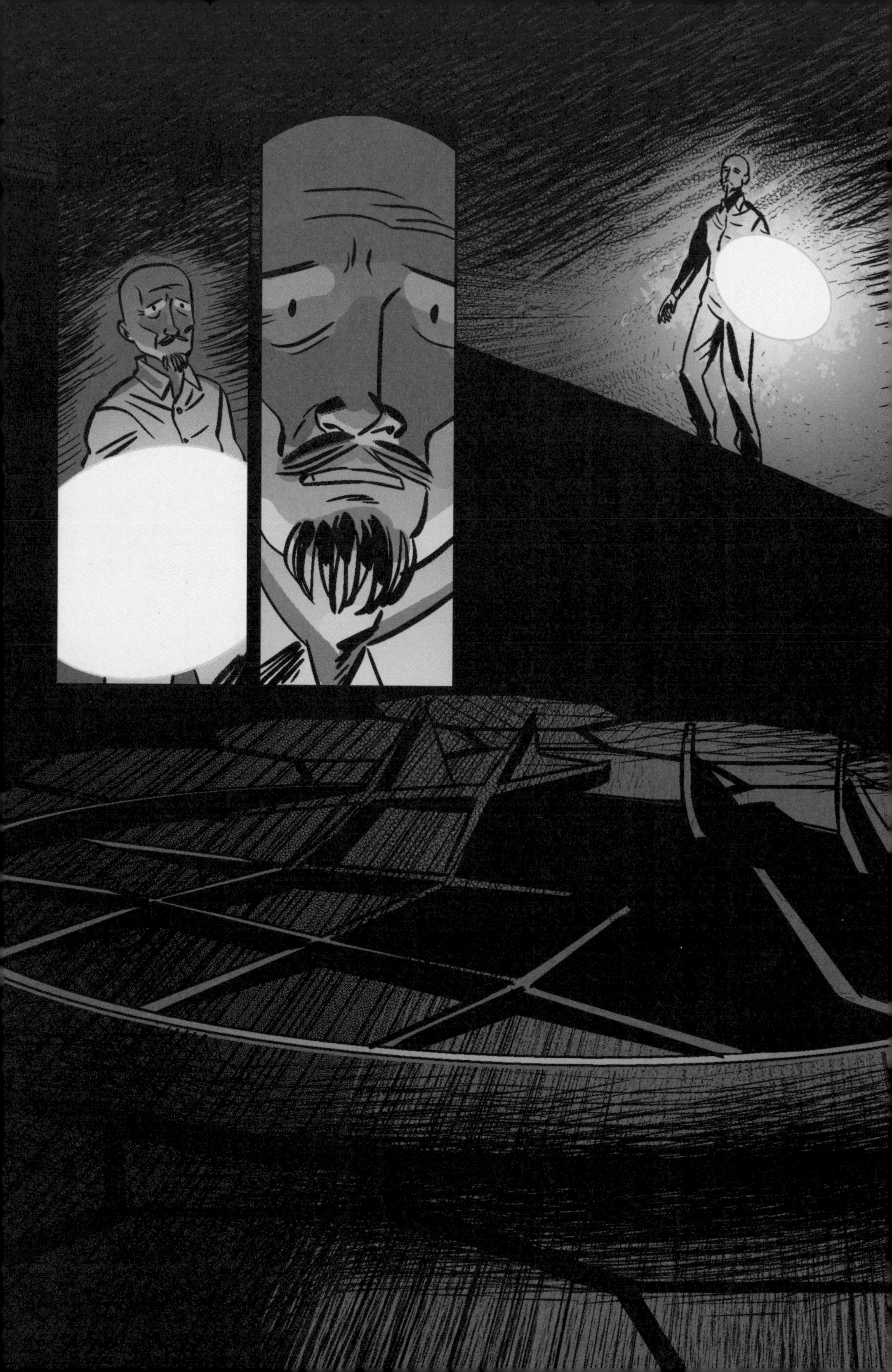

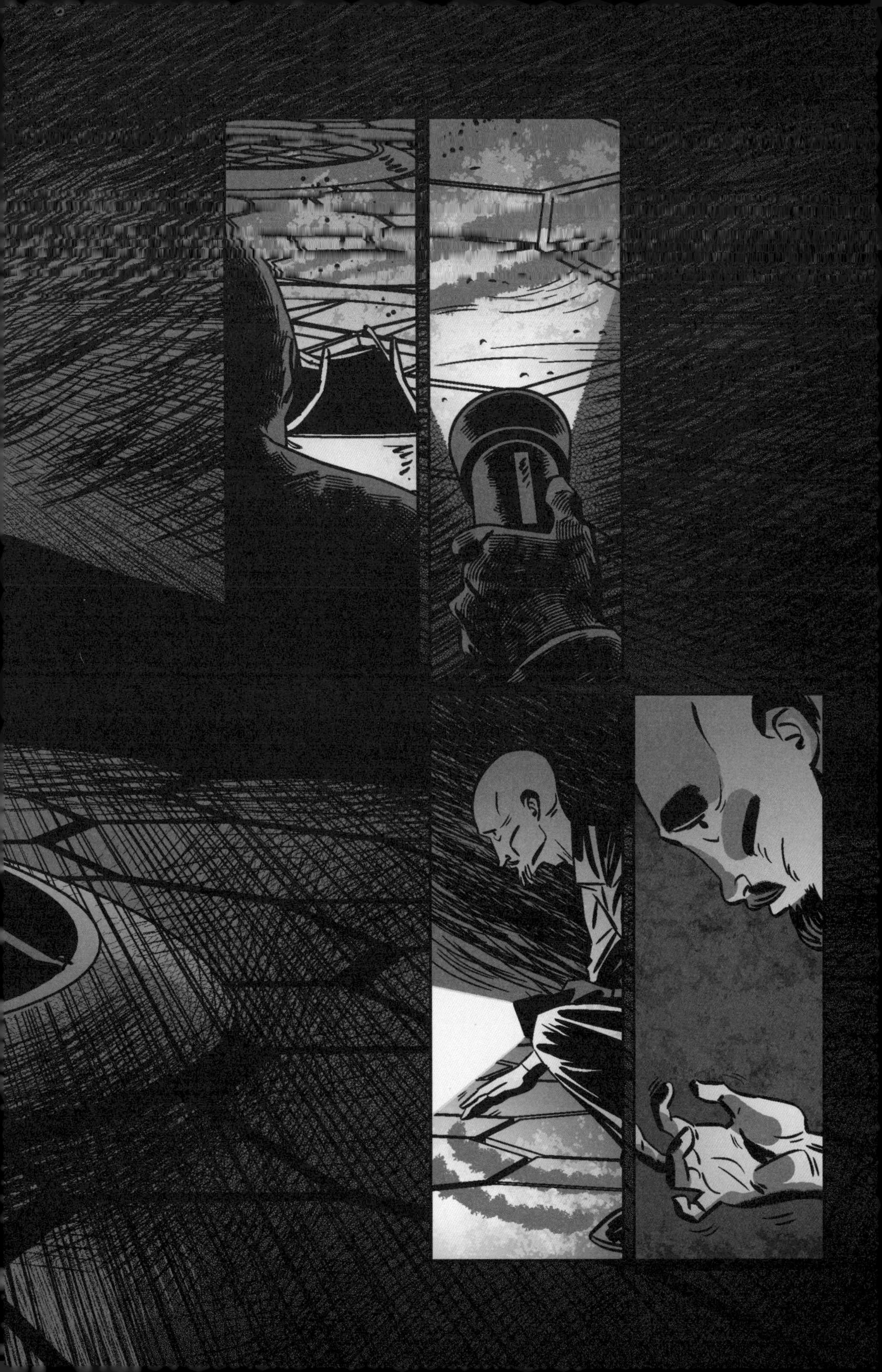

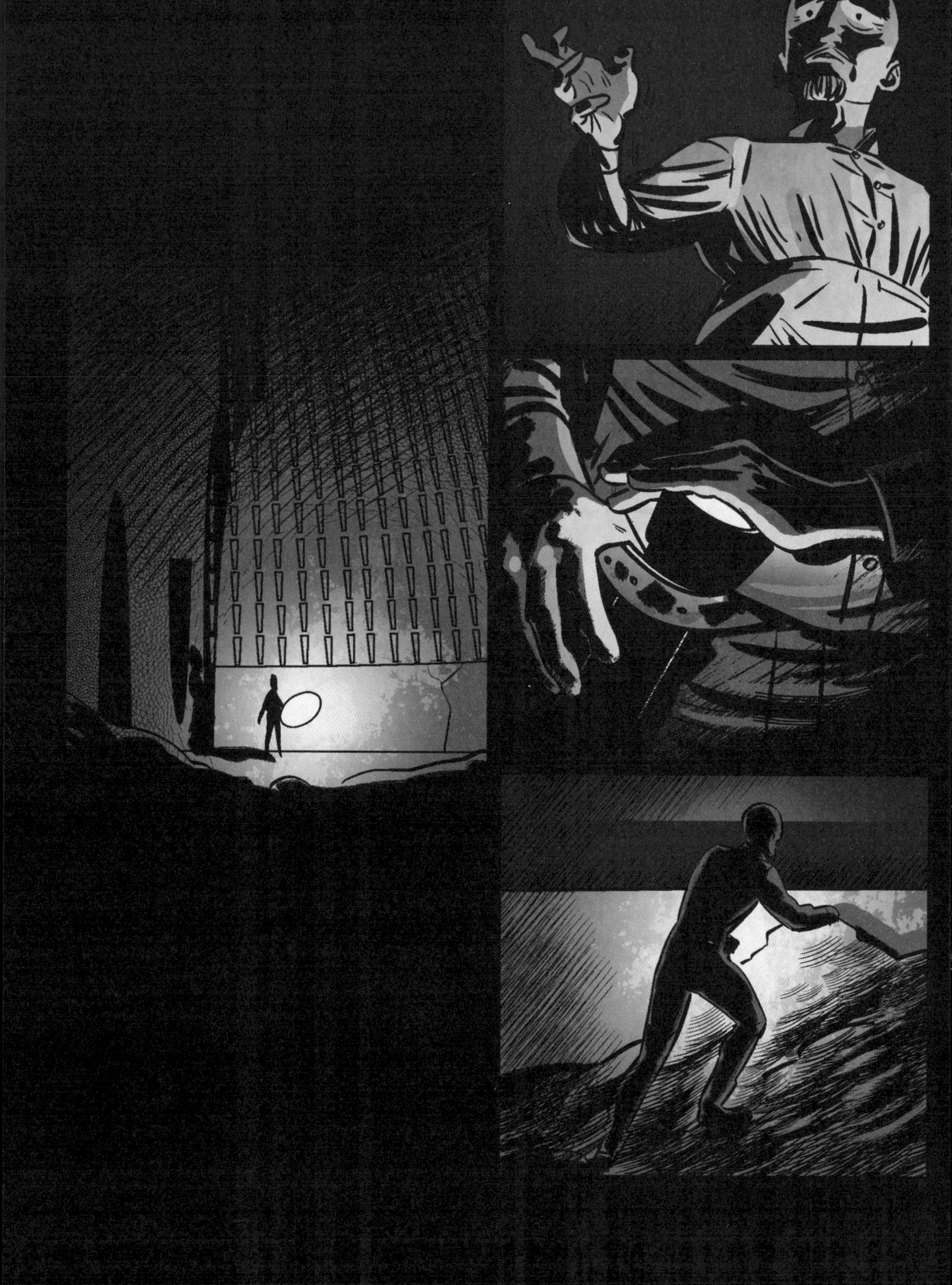

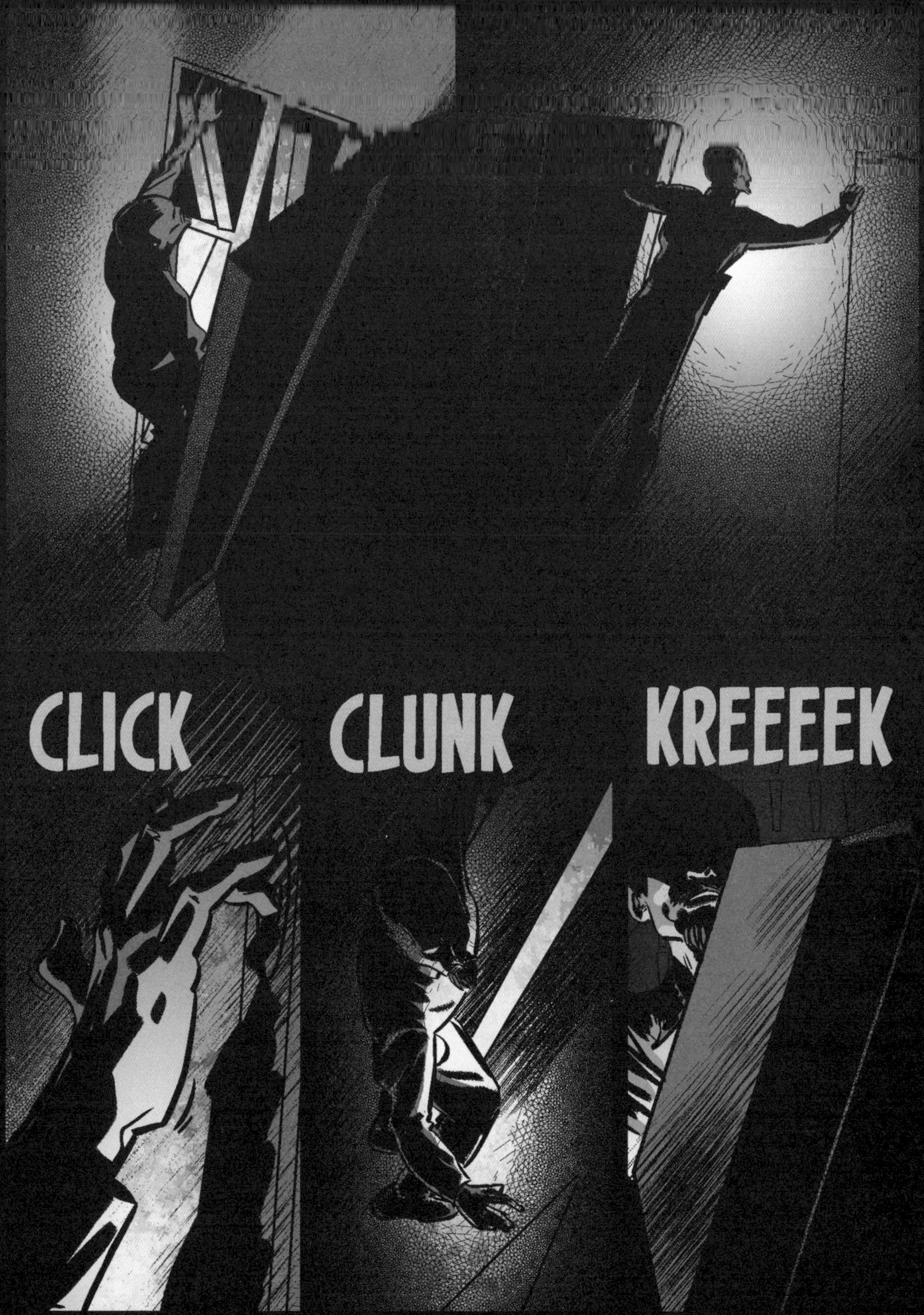
CLICK
CLUNK
KREEEEK

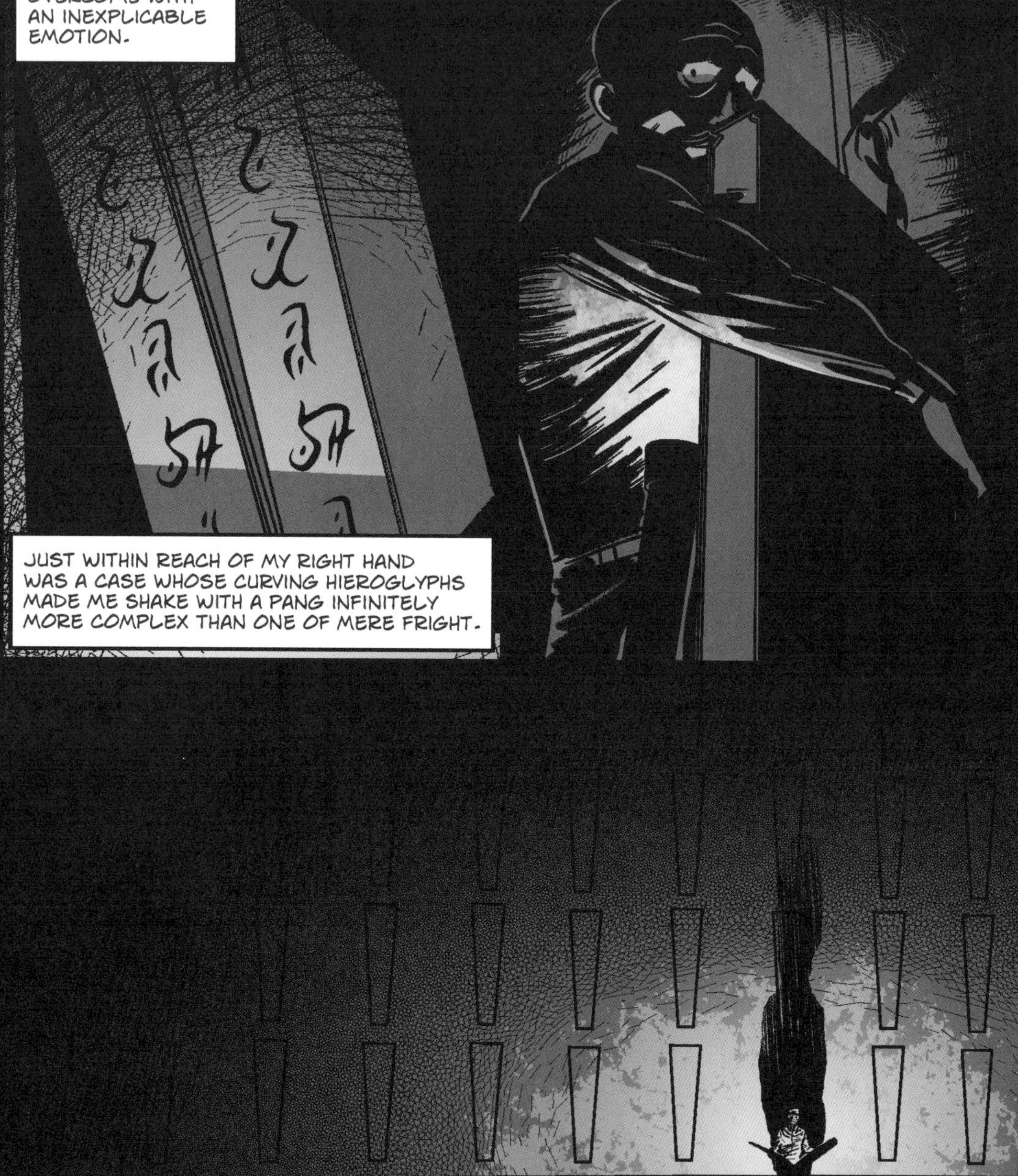
AN INEXPLICABLE EMOTION.
JUST WITHIN REACH OF MY RIGHT HAND WAS A CASE WHOSE CURVING HIEROGLYPHS MADE ME SHAKE WITH A PANG INFINITELY MORE COMPLEX THAN ONE OF MERE FRIGHT.

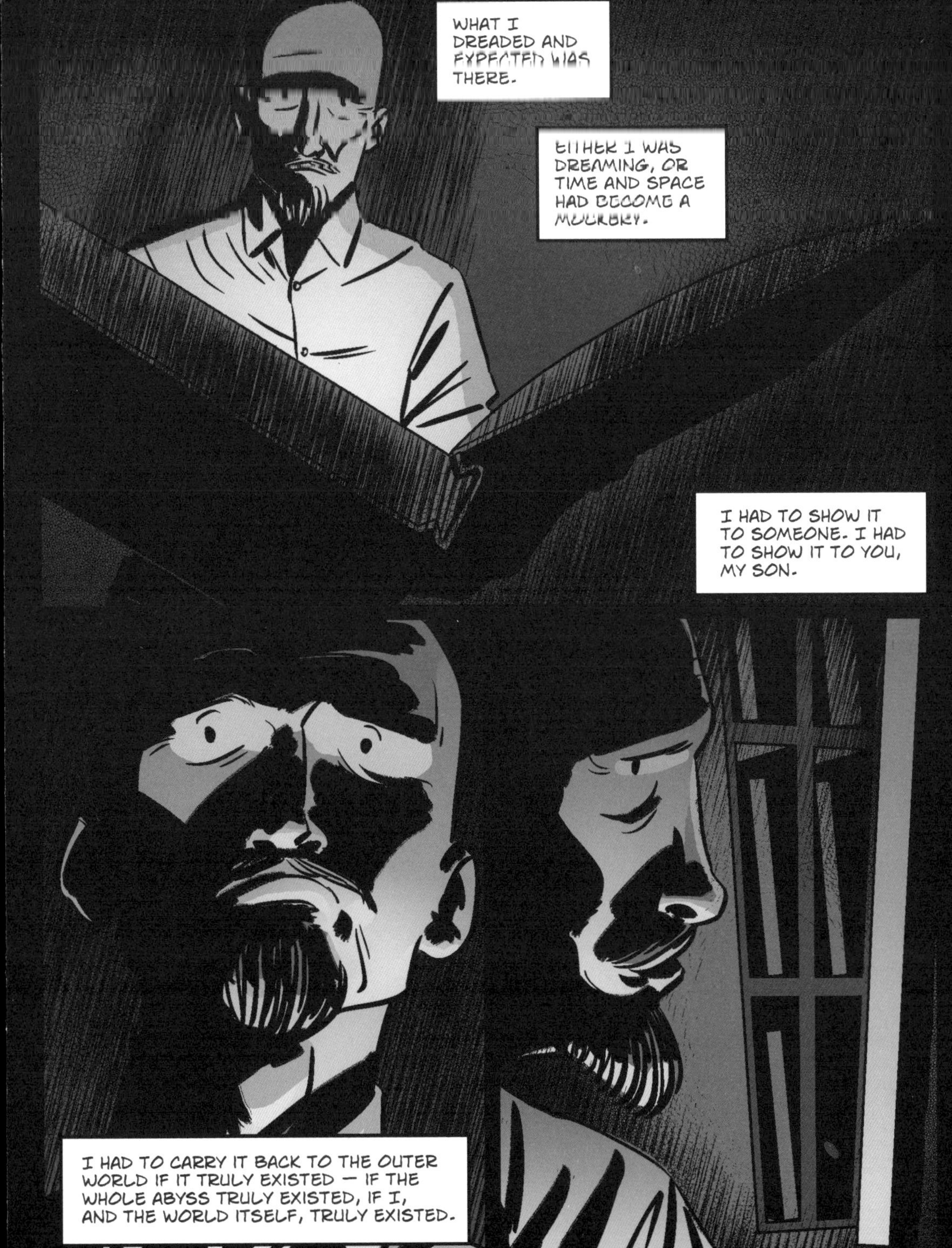
WHAT I DREADED AND EXPECTED WAS THERE.
EITHER I WAS DREAMING, OR TIME AND SPACE HAD BECOME A MOCKERY.
I HAD TO SHOW IT TO SOMEONE. I HAD TO SHOW IT TO YOU, MY SON.
I HAD TO CARRY IT BACK TO THE OUTER WORLD IF IT TRULY EXISTED — IF THE WHOLE ABYSS TRULY EXISTED, IF I, AND THE WORLD ITSELF, TRULY EXISTED.

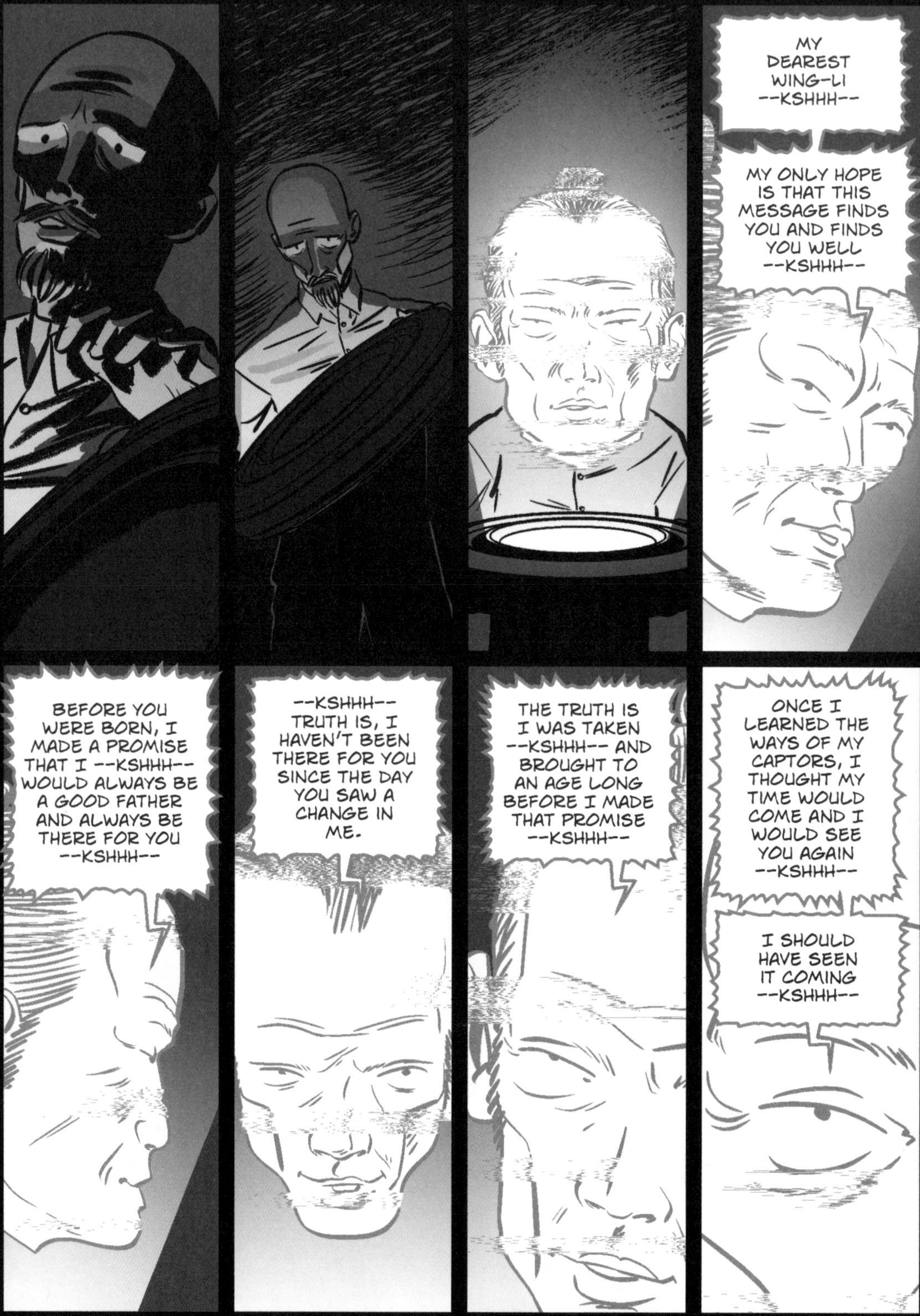
MY DEAREST WING-LI --KSHHH--
MY ONLY HOPE IS THAT THIS MESSAGE FINDS YOU AND FINDS YOU WELL --KSHHH--
BEFORE YOU WERE BORN, I MADE A PROMISE THAT I --KSHHH-- WOULD ALWAYS BE A GOOD FATHER AND ALWAYS BE THERE FOR YOU --KSHHH--
--KSHHH-- TRUTH IS, I HAVEN'T BEEN THERE FOR YOU SINCE THE DAY YOU SAW A CHANGE IN ME.
THE TRUTH IS I WAS TAKEN --KSHHH-- AND BROUGHT TO AN AGE LONG BEFORE I MADE THAT PROMISE --KSHHH--
ONCE I LEARNED THE WAYS OF MY CAPTORS, I THOUGHT MY TIME WOULD COME AND I WOULD SEE YOU AGAIN --KSHHH--
I SHOULD HAVE SEEN IT COMING --KSHHH--

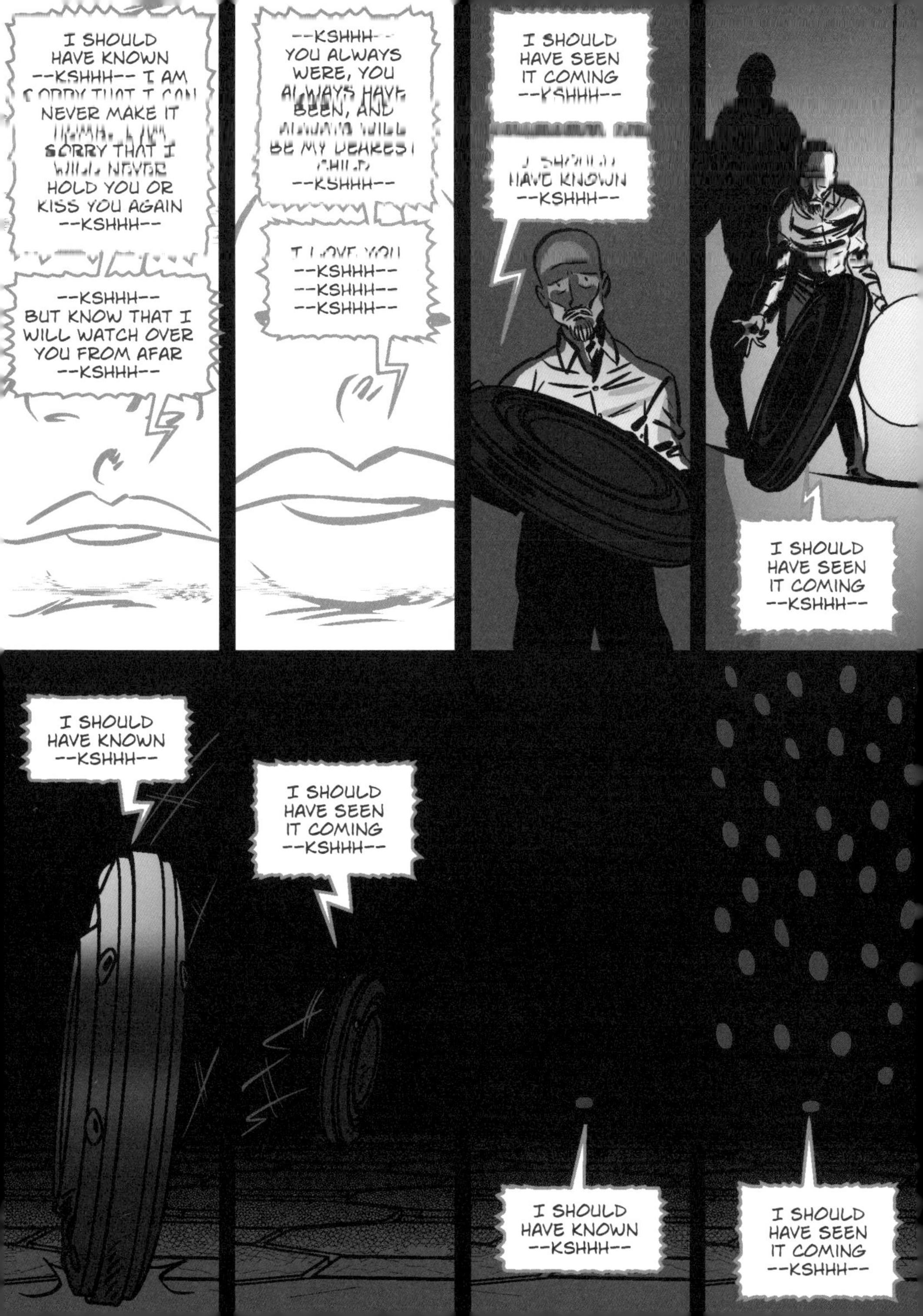
I SHOULD HAVE KNOWN --KSHHH-- I AM SORRY THAT I CAN NEVER MAKE IT SORRY THAT I WILL NEVER HOLD YOU OR KISS YOU AGAIN --KSHHH--
--KSHHH-- BUT KNOW THAT I WILL WATCH OVER YOU FROM AFAR --KSHHH--
--KSHHH-- YOU ALWAYS WERE, YOU ALWAYS HAVE BEEN, AND ALWAYS WILL BE MY DEAREST CHILD --KSHHH--
I LOVE YOU --KSHHH-- --KSHHH-- --KSHHH--
I SHOULD HAVE SEEN IT COMING --KSHHH--
I SHOULD HAVE KNOWN --KSHHH--
I SHOULD HAVE SEEN IT COMING --KSHHH--
I SHOULD HAVE KNOWN --KSHHH--
I SHOULD HAVE SEEN IT COMING --KSHHH--
I SHOULD HAVE KNOWN --KSHHH--
I SHOULD HAVE SEEN IT COMING --KSHHH--

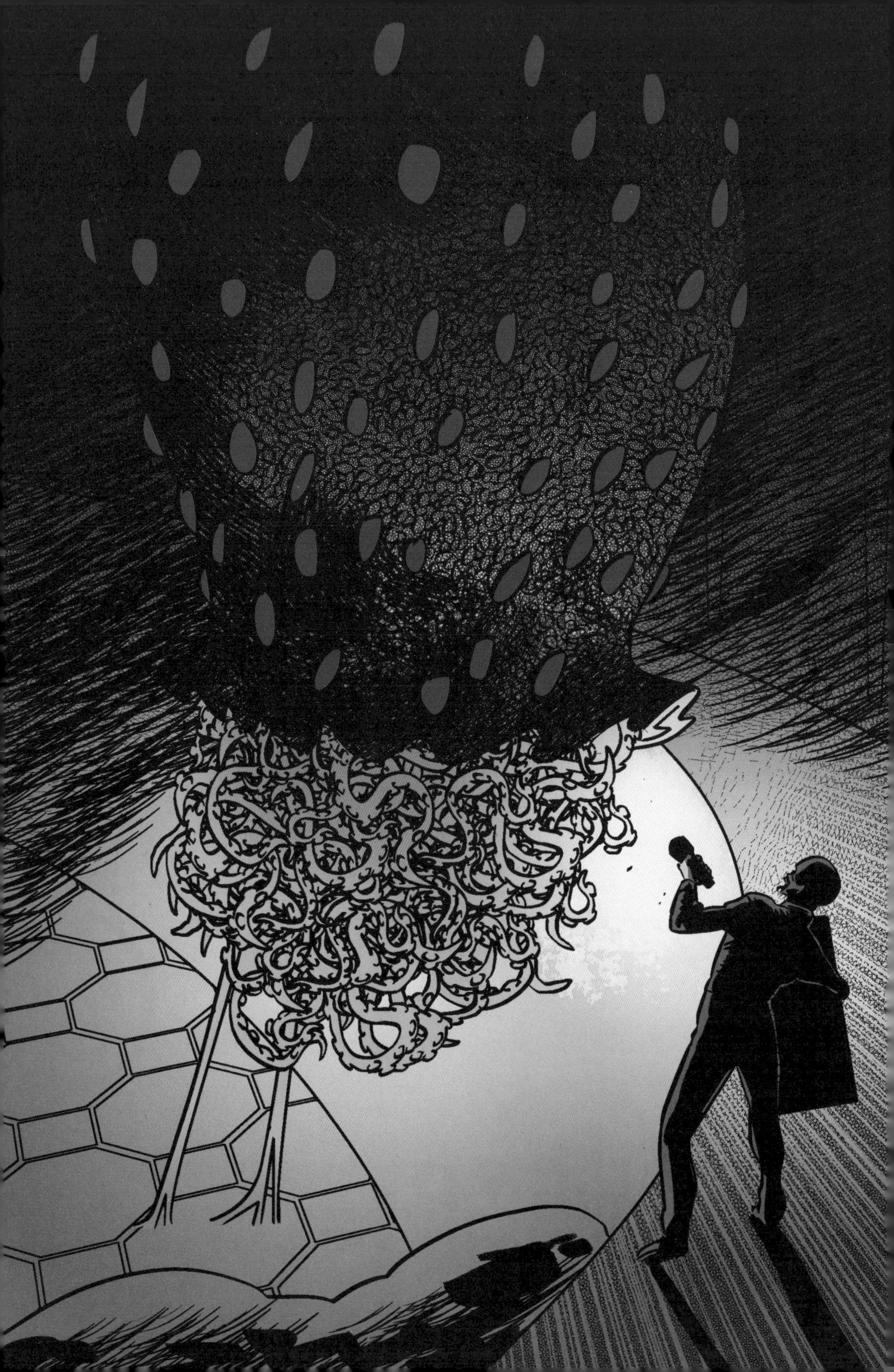

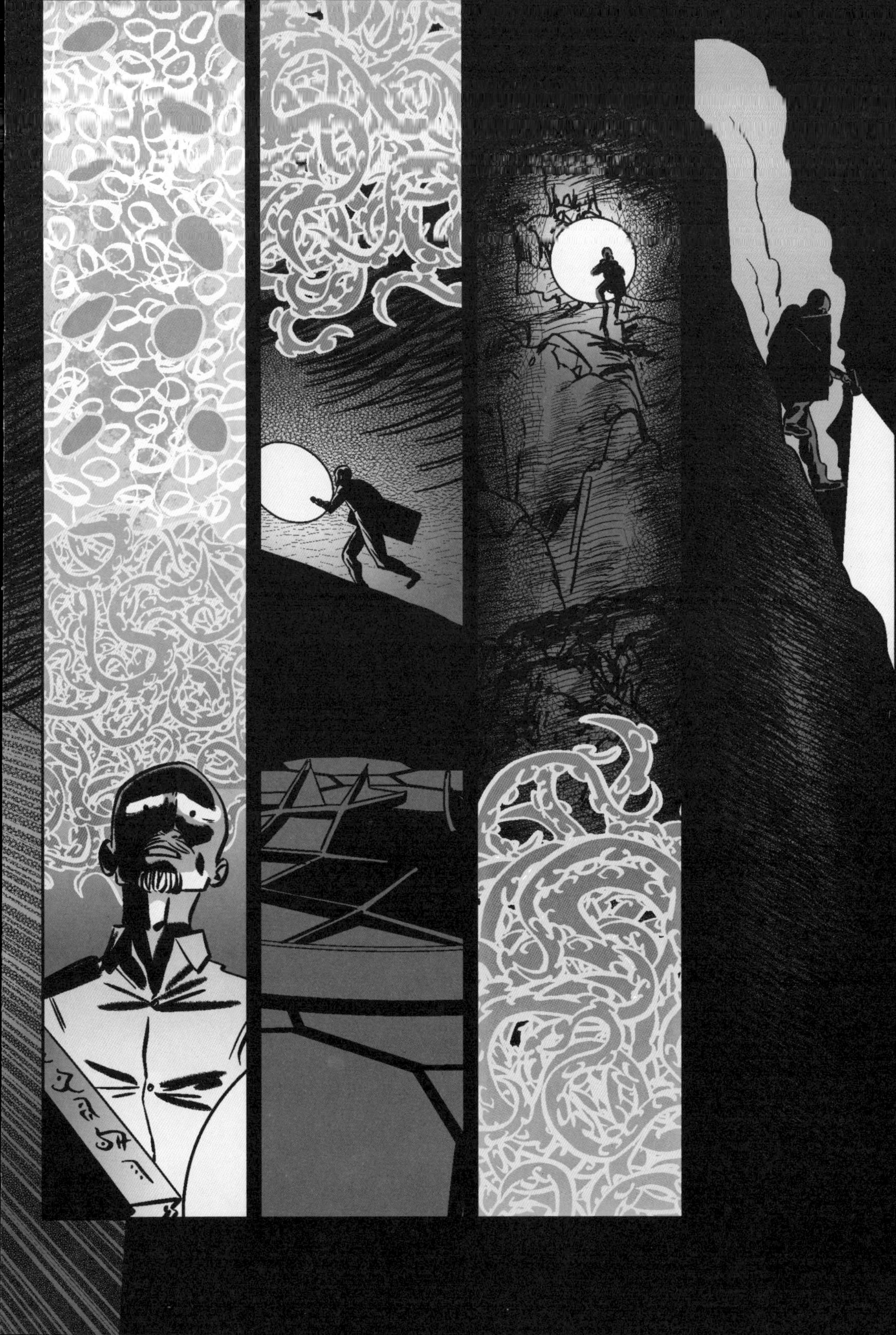

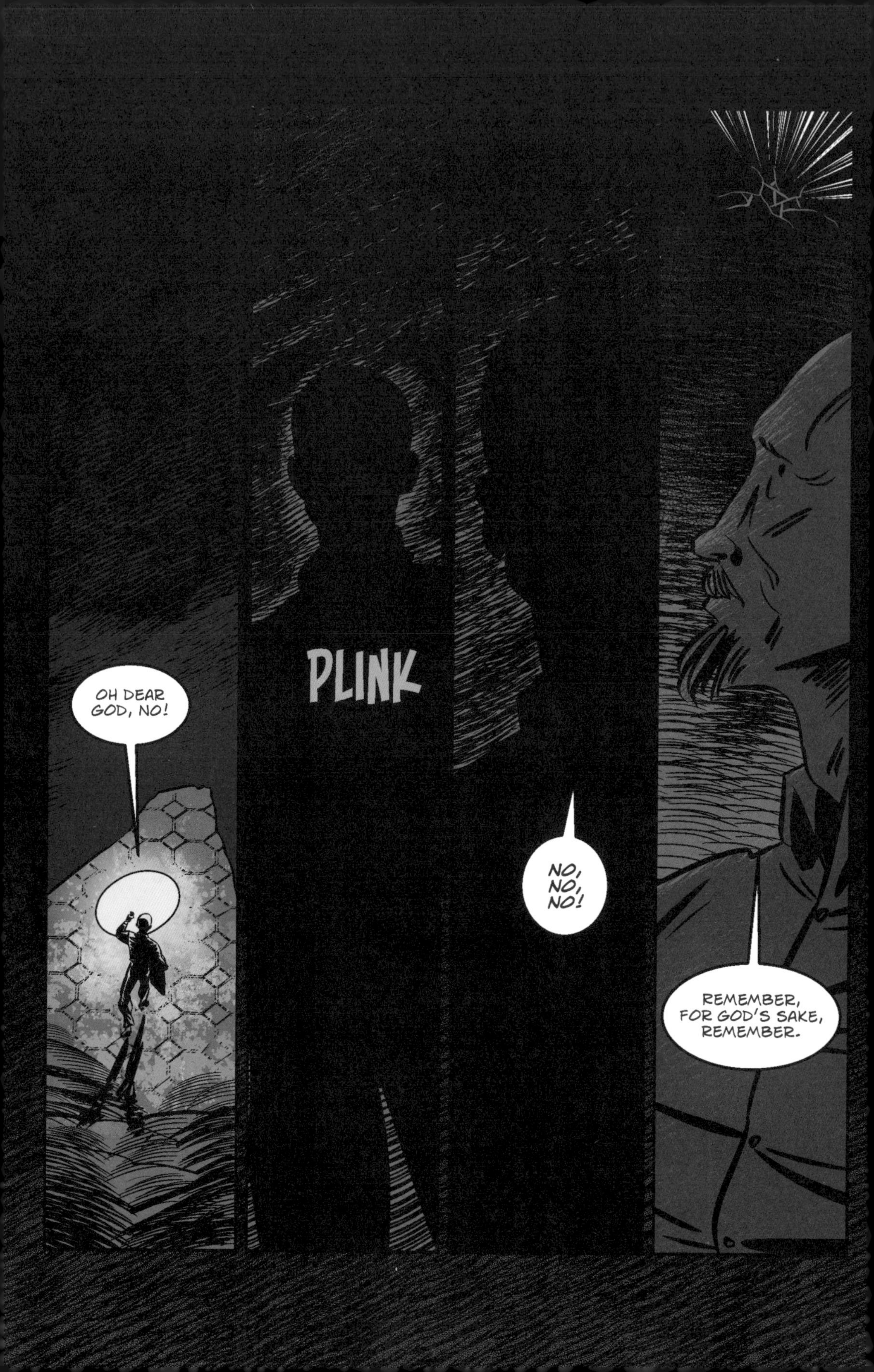
OH DEAR GOD, NO!
PLINK
NO, NO, NO!
REMEMBER, FOR GOD'S SAKE, REMEMBER.

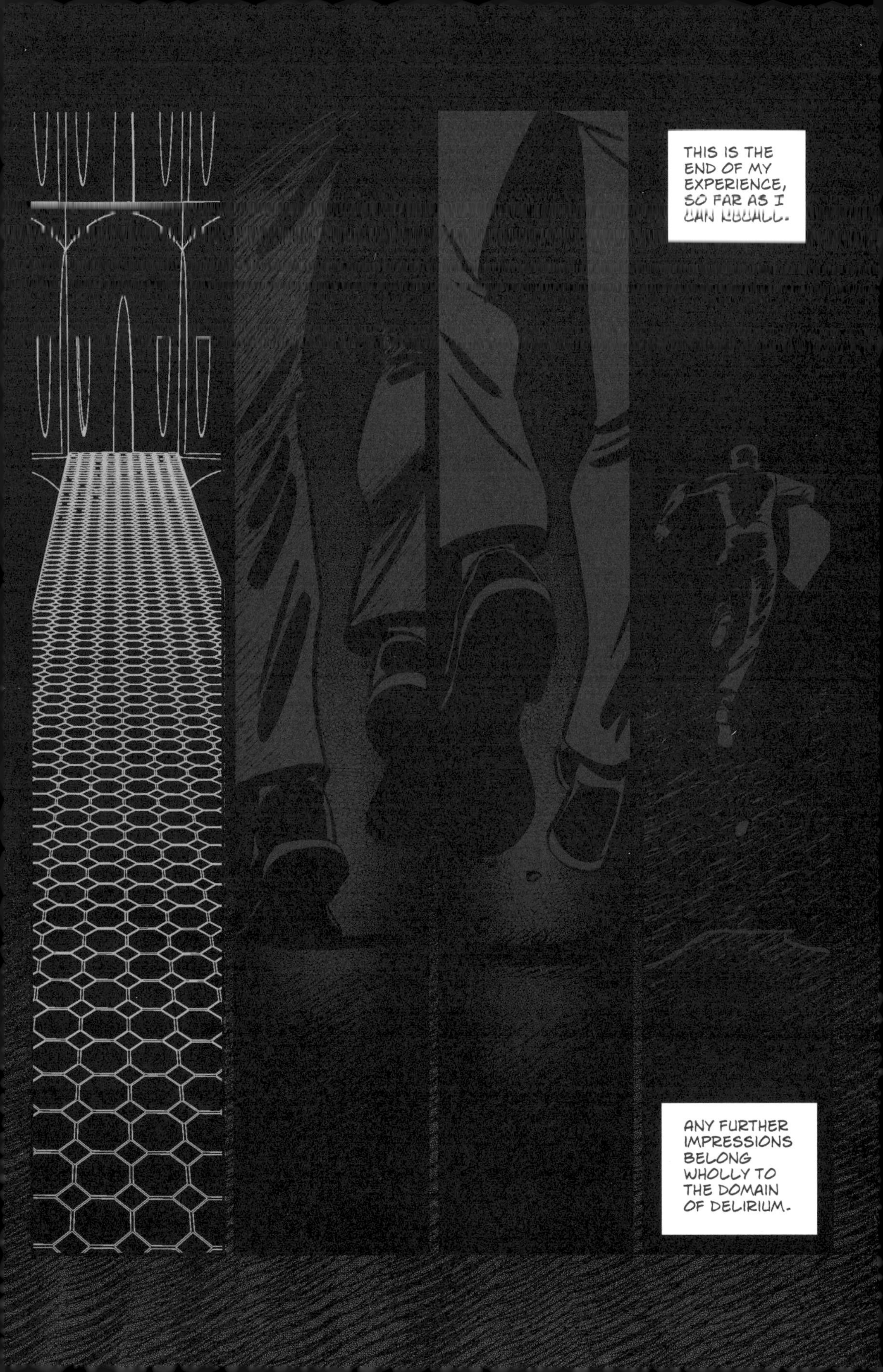
THIS IS THE END OF MY EXPERIENCE, SO FAR AS I CAN RECALL.
ANY FURTHER IMPRESSIONS BELONG WHOLLY TO THE DOMAIN OF DELIRIUM.

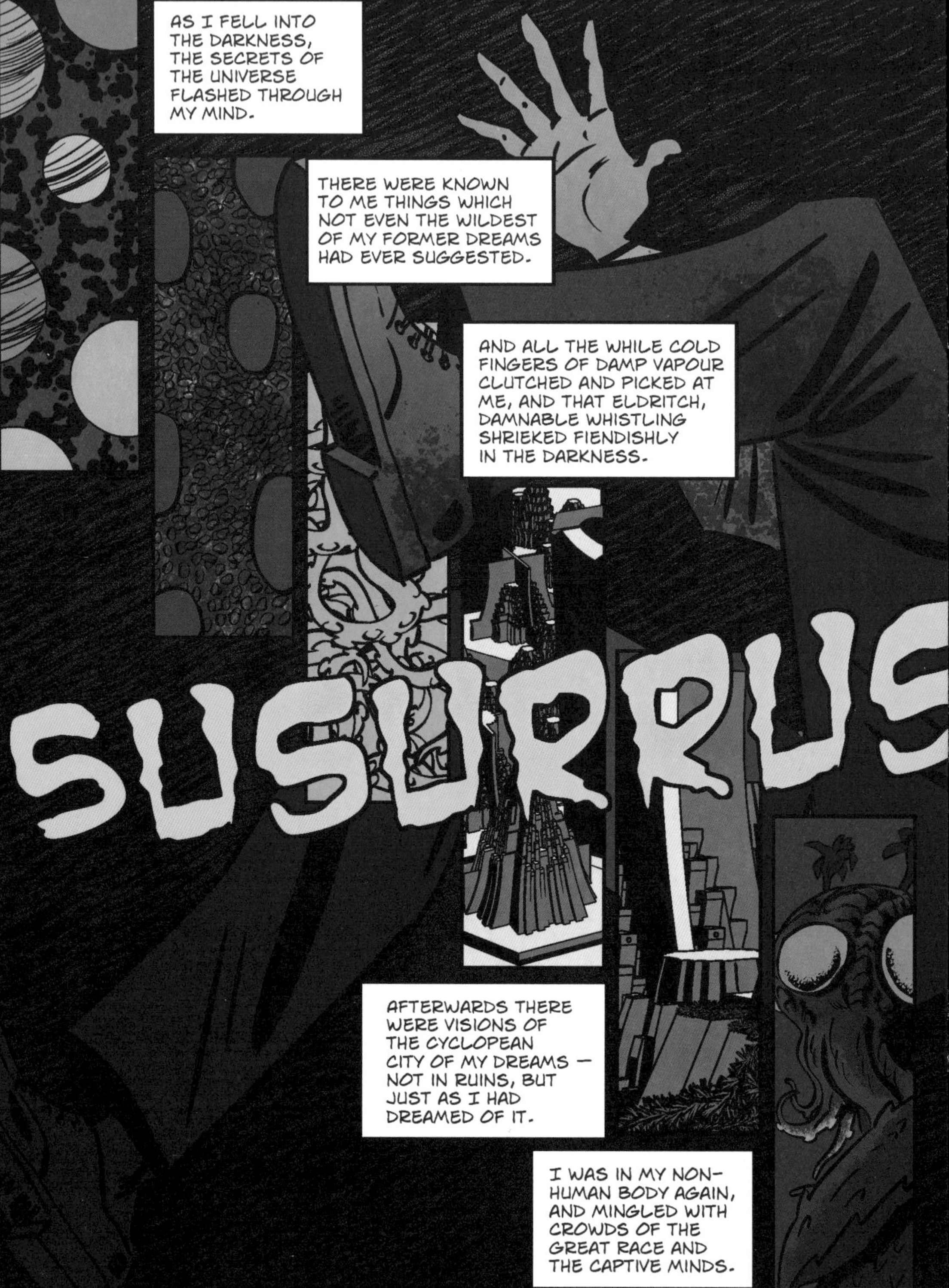
AS I FELL INTO THE DARKNESS, THE SECRETS OF THE UNIVERSE FLASHED THROUGH MY MIND.
THERE WERE KNOWN TO ME THINGS WHICH NOT EVEN THE WILDEST OF MY FORMER DREAMS HAD EVER SUGGESTED.
AND ALL THE WHILE COLD FINGERS OF DAMP VAPOUR CLUTCHED AND PICKED AT ME, AND THAT ELDRITCH, DAMNABLE WHISTLING SHRIEKED FIENDISHLY IN THE DARKNESS.
SUSURRUS
AFTERWARDS THERE WERE VISIONS OF THE CYCLOPEAN CITY OF MY DREAMS — NOT IN RUINS, BUT JUST AS I HAD DREAMED OF IT.
I WAS IN MY NON-HUMAN BODY AGAIN, AND MINGLED WITH CROWDS OF THE GREAT RACE AND THE CAPTIVE MINDS.

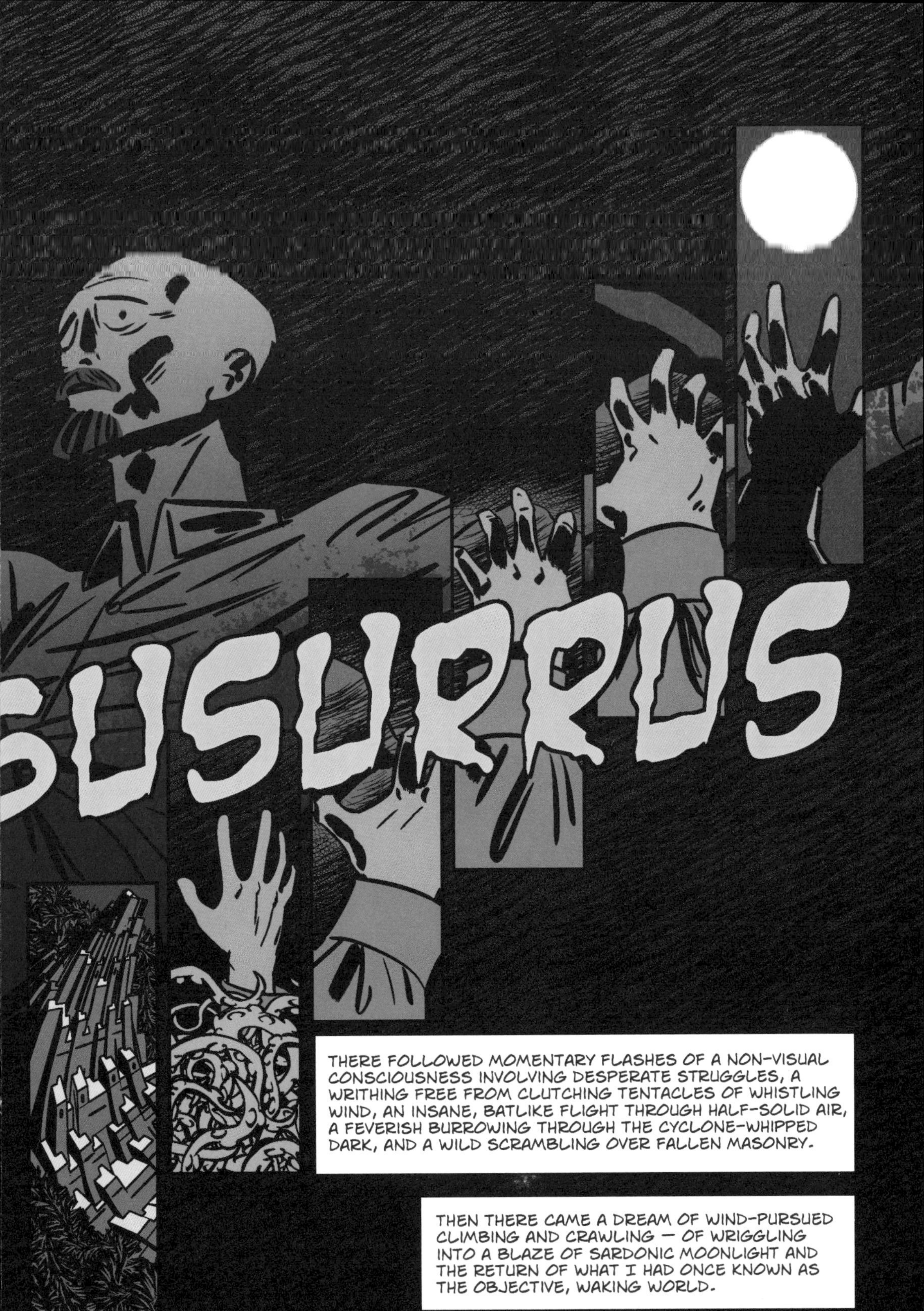
SUSURRUS
THERE FOLLOWED MOMENTARY FLASHES OF A NON-VISUAL CONSCIOUSNESS INVOLVING DESPERATE STRUGGLES, A WRITHING FREE FROM CLUTCHING TENTACLES OF WHISTLING WIND, AN INSANE, BATLIKE FLIGHT THROUGH HALF-SOLID AIR, A FEVERISH BURROWING THROUGH THE CYCLONE-WHIPPED DARK, AND A WILD SCRAMBLING OVER FALLEN MASONRY.
THEN THERE CAME A DREAM OF WIND-PURSUED CLIMBING AND CRAWLING — OF WRIGGLING INTO A BLAZE OF SARDONIC MOONLIGHT AND THE RETURN OF WHAT I HAD ONCE KNOWN AS THE OBJECTIVE, WAKING WORLD.

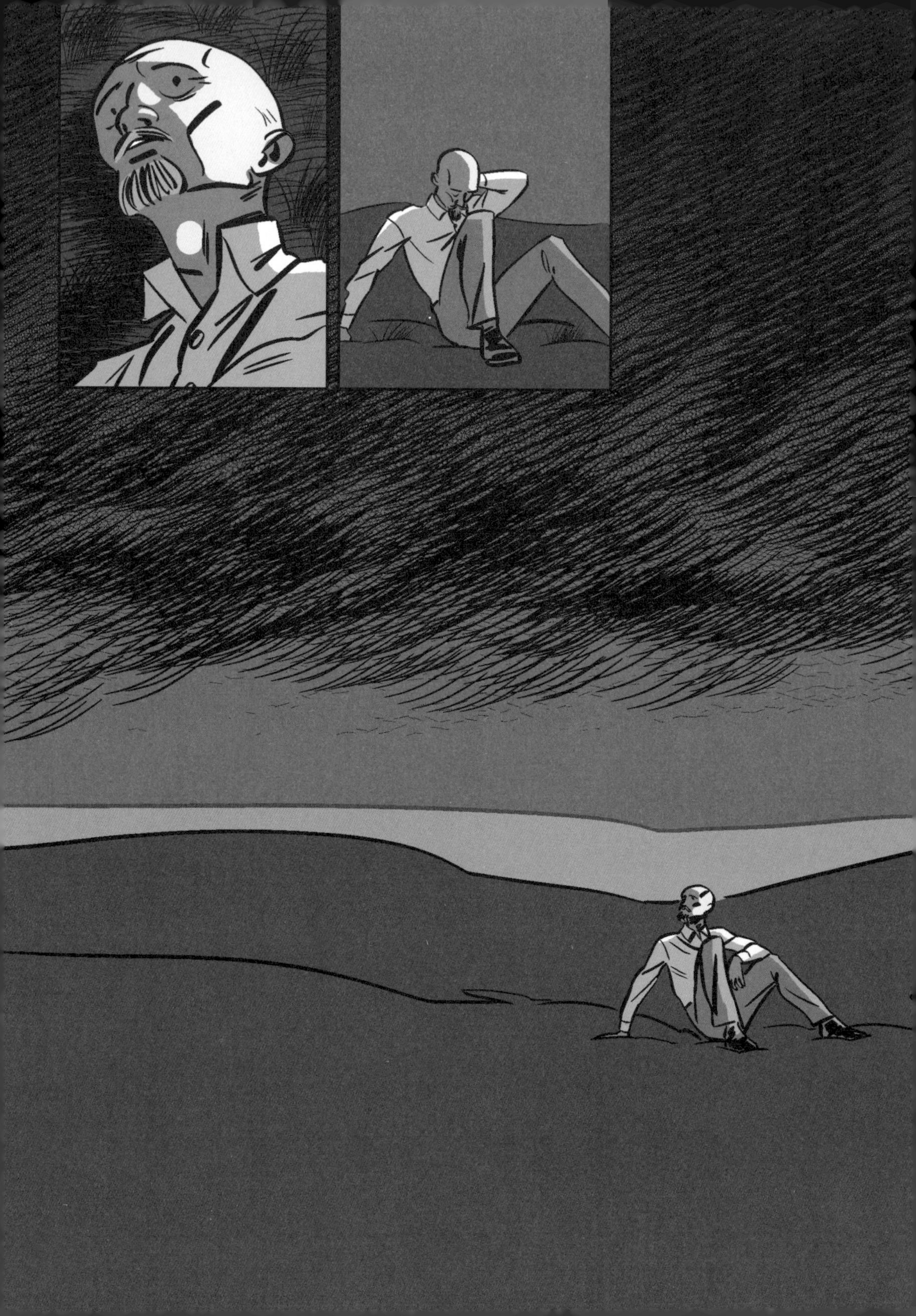

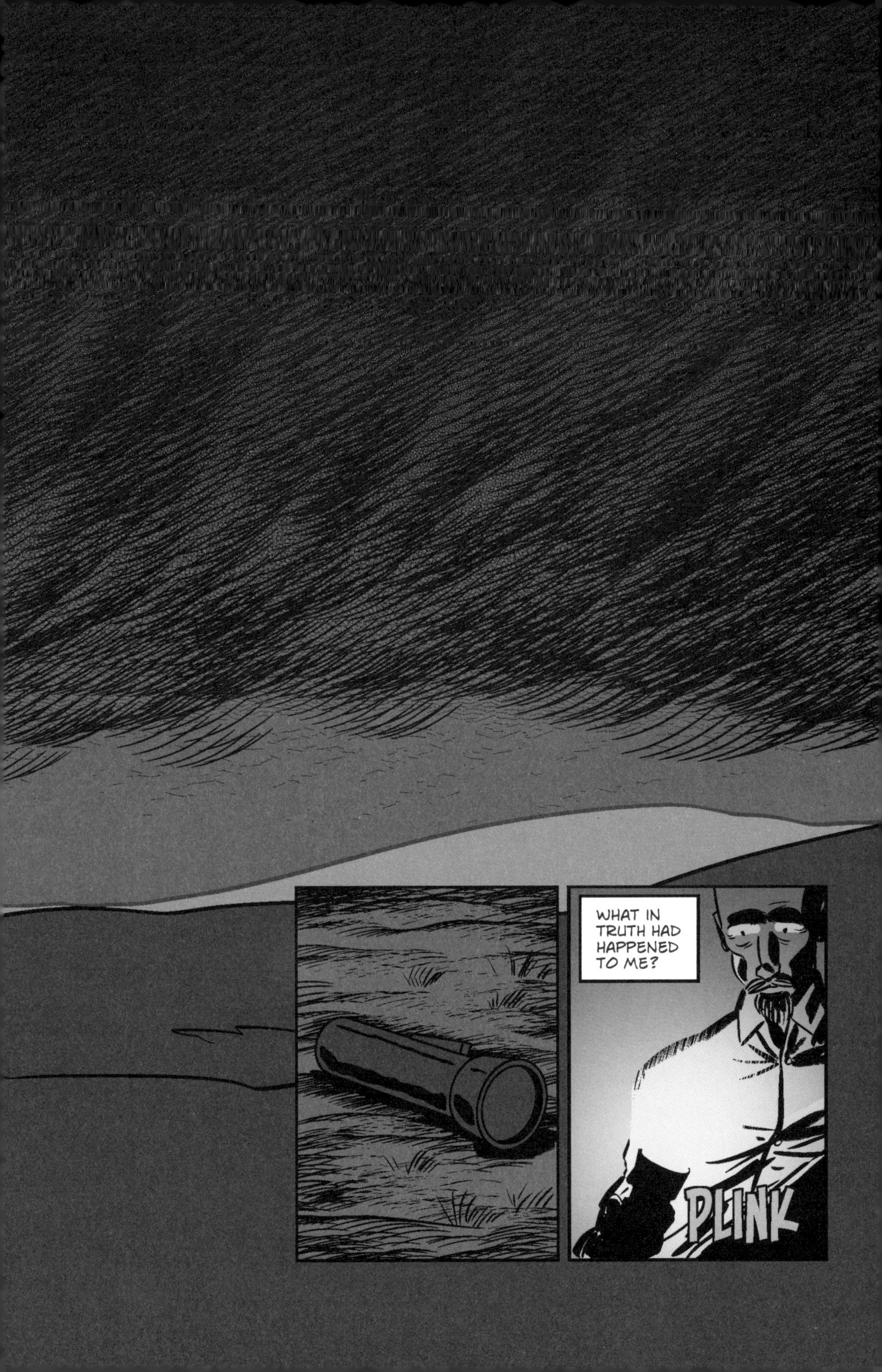
WHAT IN TRUTH HAD HAPPENED TO ME?
PLINK

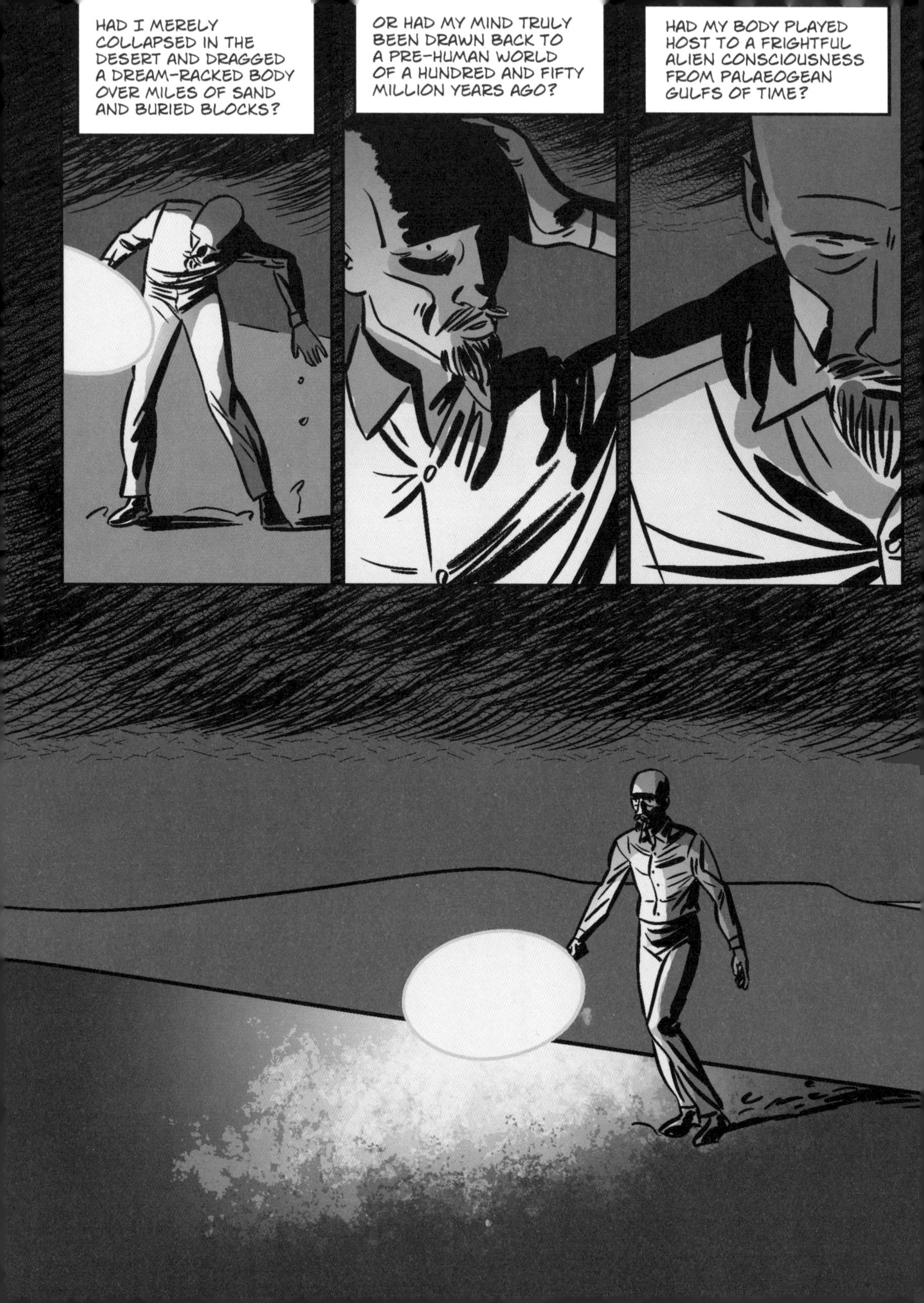
HAD I MERELY COLLAPSED IN THE DESERT AND DRAGGED A DREAM-RACKED BODY OVER MILES OF SAND AND BURIED BLOCKS?
OR HAD MY MIND TRULY BEEN DRAWN BACK TO A PRE-HUMAN WORLD OF A HUNDRED AND FIFTY MILLION YEARS AGO?
HAD MY BODY PLAYED HOST TO A FRIGHTFUL ALIEN CONSCIOUSNESS FROM PALAEOGEAN GULFS OF TIME?

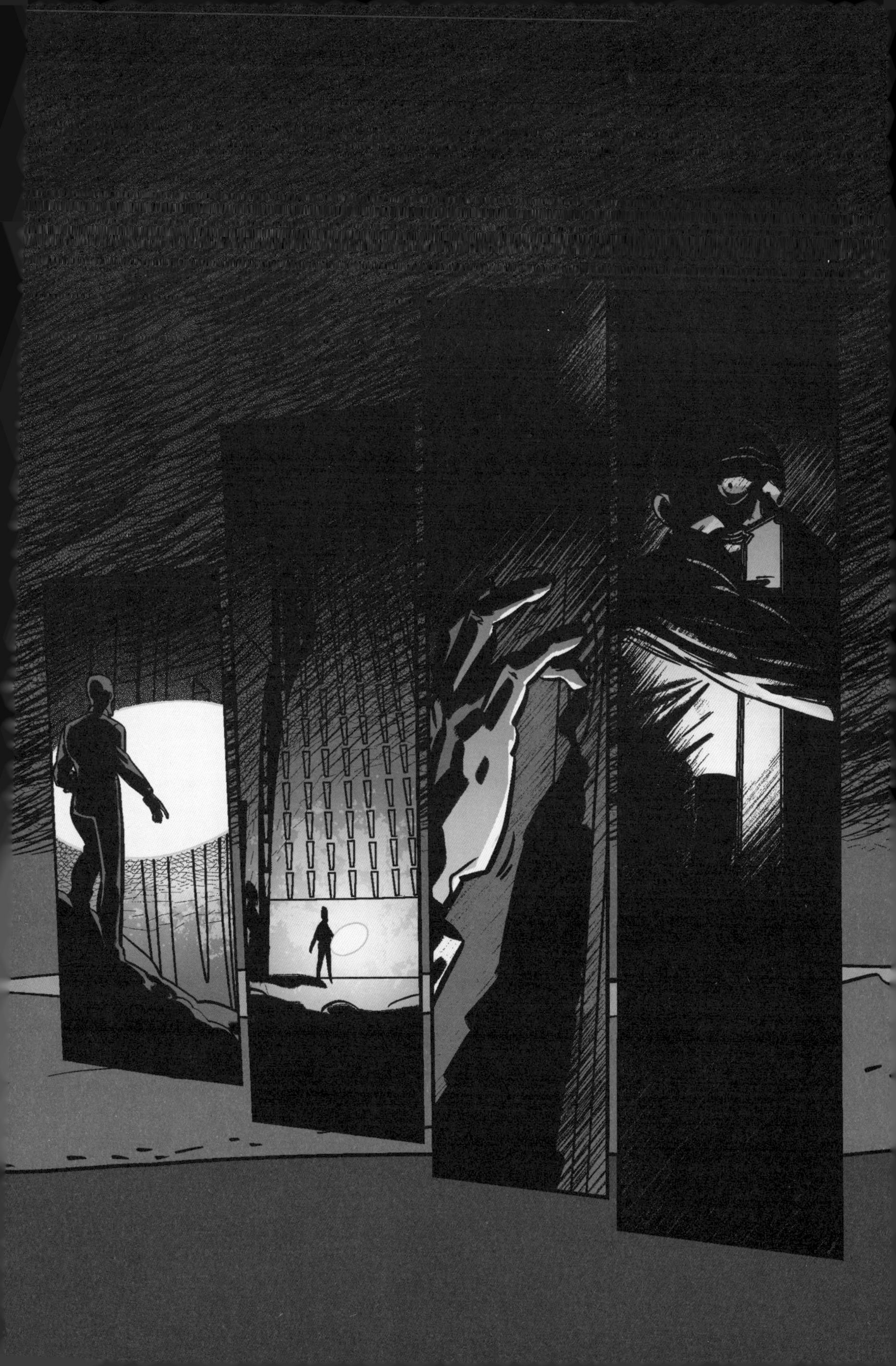

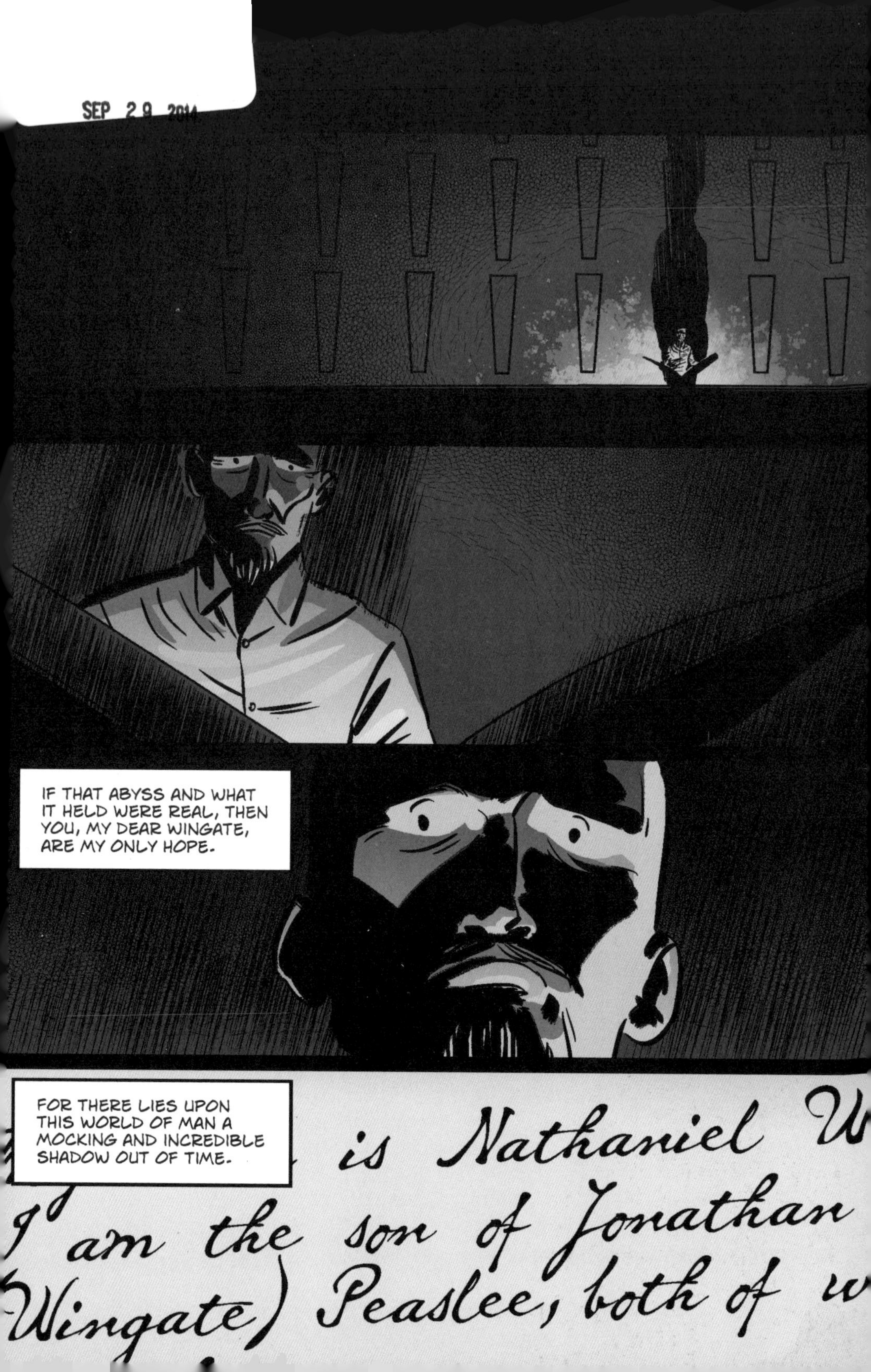
IF THAT ABYSS AND WHAT IT HELD WERE REAL, THEN YOU, MY DEAR WINGATE, ARE MY ONLY HOPE.
FOR THERE LIES UPON THIS WORLD OF MAN A MOCKING AND INCREDIBLE SHADOW OUT OF TIME.
is Nathaniel
I am the son of Jonathan
Wingate) Peaslee, both of